five golden friends

THE KALEIDOSCOPE GIRLS

ALSO BY KIMBERLY DIEDE

THE KALEIDOSCOPE GIRLS SERIES
BETTER WITH FRIENDS (BOOK 1)
SUNSHINE AND FRIENDS (BOOK 2)
FIVE GOLDEN FRIENDS (BOOK 3)
GIFT OF FRIENDS (BOOK 4)
with additional books to come...

CELIA'S GIFTS SERIES
WHISPERING PINES (BOOK 1)
TANGLED BEGINNINGS (BOOK 2)
REBUILDING HOME (BOOK 3)
CHOOSING AGAIN (BOOK 4)
CELIA'S GIFTS (BOOK 5)
CELIA'S LEGACY (BOOK 6)

WHISPERING PINES CHRISTMAS NOVEL
CAPTURING WISHES (BOOK 3.5 OF CELIA'S GIFTS)

FIRST SUMMERS NOVELLA
FIRST SUMMERS AT WHISPERING PINES 1980

five golden friends

THE KALEIDOSCOPE GIRLS

BOOK THREE

Kimberly Diede

ENDLESS RIPPLE PRESS

Cover by Carpe Librum Book Design – www.carpelibrumbookdesign.com.

Ebook ISBN: 978-1-7351343-9-0

Print ISBN: 978-1-961305-00-7

Large Pring ISBN: 978-1-961305-05-2

To my amazing dad . . .

You taught me the power of gratitude
and to just say *thank you.*
My life is better because of you.

Chapter One

ANNIE PULLED INTO HER assigned parking spot in the front row, ignoring the dust from the gravel lot that floated through her open window as she eyed the building across the street. Her home away from home. She felt that familiar mixture of both dread and anticipation. She should be used to these first-day butterflies by now. After all, this would be her twentieth "first day of school" at this place—and that didn't include her student years at Ruby Shores High School.

Her work anniversary wasn't the only milestone she'd face during the upcoming school year. Her nest was finally empty, her first grandchild was due in early March, and she would turn the big five-oh next summer.

Earlier that morning, as she'd brushed her teeth, she'd studied her face in the mirror for any new wrinkles, and it had hit her: today also could have been her twenty-fifth wedding anniversary. But since she and Michael didn't even make it to their third anniversary, it didn't count.

The realization may have caused her to tap her toothbrush against the side of her sink a little harder than necessary, because Henry gave her an odd look as he stepped out of the shower and reached for his towel. But she knew better than to share her thoughts with him. Her husband never appreciated her mentioning Michael's name.

Henry usually left the house before Annie, but she'd wanted to get to the school well before the first bell. As the high school's principal, she had plenty of last-minute tasks to attend to, and she needed to be done in time to greet the students.

The surprising crunch of wheels on gravel announced another early bird and shook her from her thoughts. When the vehicle pulled into the spot right next to Annie's, she sighed. The spot was reserved for the Student of the Month; school employees were never supposed to use it. The student to be honored in September was selected by the faculty during last week's back-to-school days, and she would reveal the winner during today's morning announcements.

Reprimanding an entitled staff member wouldn't be the most pleasant way to kick off a new school year, but her job duties included disciplinarian.

She opened her door with caution, not wanting to complicate things further by denting the passenger door on the massive SUV that had parked a hair too close, making it difficult for Annie to climb out of her own vehicle.

"Before you say anything, you're going to want to hear me out," a woman's voice said from the far side of the improperly parked black SUV.

Annie's shoulders relaxed. "You know you aren't supposed to park there, Wendy."

Her friend's grunt was followed by the dull *thwack* of a vehicle door that didn't quite latch. The early morning sun glinted off Wendy's pale wash of shoulder-length hair as the older woman met up with Annie on the sidewalk in front of their vehicles. "I hate driving that beast. I even have to jump down out of the driver's seat."

Grinning, Annie glanced from Wendy back to the SUV. "Wisconsin plates? That isn't yours, is it?"

Wendy shook her head as she adjusted the strap of the battered portfolio that went back and forth from school with the art teacher every day. It was probably empty now, but Wendy's students would start producing new art projects right away. "Not mine. My son-in-law's. School doesn't start for their kids until next week, so they dropped in for a late-summer visit. I love them all dearly, but cooking and cleaning for that crew wasn't the relaxing end to summer that I'd hoped for. My daughter offered to take my car in this morning for an oil change and tire rotation. Ever since her dad died, she's tried to help me out with some of the tasks he used to handle. She'll swing it by here when it's done, park it in my spot, and take this. The Student of the Month spot will be open by noon, so don't worry."

Annie nodded, relieved. She walked around to the passenger side of her car to remove her purse, computer bag, and canvas tote of books before locking it, then joined Wendy on the sidewalk again.

"Say, how was your trip to Maui?" Wendy asked. "I love that you girls are spending part of your summers together. I bet it's almost like summer camp all over again! I'd love to hear what everyone's been up to."

Annie really should get to her office and prepare for the day, but catching Wendy up on the lives of their mutual friends would be more fun. She'd make it quick. "Maui was amazing, partly because Hawaii is hard to beat, but also because uninterrupted time with my girlfriends is always priceless. I'm so glad we recommitted to our annual trips. It's my turn to plan the next one."

Wendy nodded. "What was it you girls called yourselves?"

Annie laughed. "The Kaleidoscope Girls, thanks to you and that craft project you had us make the first summer that Kit came to camp."

"I was so lucky to be the counselor assigned to your cabin. Doesn't it feel like our summer camp days were a lifetime ago?"

"Sometimes. But when the five of us get together again, the years fall away and we pick right back up where we left off."

Wendy nodded as she checked her watch. "I know you have to get inside. But take two minutes and update me on what my old campers are up to these days."

"Two minutes," Annie agreed. "Let's see. Kit probably has the most going on. She's marrying Dean in a small ceremony next month. Actually, they're holding it out by the lake on the old summer camp land."

Wendy shook her head in surprise. "Doesn't Owen Jamison own that land now?"

"He does. Do you know Owen?"

"I knew his folks." She tucked a strand of hair behind her ear that kept flicking across her face in the early morning breeze.

Annie grinned. "Such is life in a small town. Owen was friends with Jackie when they were kids. And speaking of Jackie, she's working hard on her new business, the one I told you about last spring. Lynette hasn't changed much. She's still in New York City, working with her mom in their business and raking in the dough. Remind me to tell you about our room upgrades she paid for in Maui when we have more time. Unbelievable. And I feel like I got to know Renee a little better this summer. Do you remember Renee? We never had as much time with her when we were kids since she didn't grow up in Ruby Shores and only came to camp that one summer. She was part of our prom group, too, during our senior year."

"Sure, I remember her," Wendy said. "I'm glad you've stayed close with all your old friends. There's just something special about friendships formed in those early days."

"They *are* special." Annie wondered if Wendy was also lucky enough to have a group of old friends, but that was going to have to be a discussion for another day. She really needed to get to work. "But I'm sorry, I better get inside."

Wendy nodded. "Duty calls."

As the two women stepped off the curb, Wendy grabbed Annie's arm and pulled her back—just as a jacked-up pickup truck barreled around the corner.

Annie's heart leapt. "That man will never learn," she muttered, eyeing the box of the speeding truck. "It doesn't matter how many times I report him, the cops don't do a damn thing. One of these days, Bud Carbo is going to kill someone in front of this school on his way to work. Thank you, by the way. You saved me again."

Wendy chuckled as she crossed the street. "Been doing that for so long that it's second nature."

Annie followed close behind. She was going to miss Wendy. "I still can't believe this is your last year teaching. Are you sure I can't talk you out of it? Don't you think you should tough it out for, say, six or seven more years? Sixty-two seems like the perfect age to retire."

"I keep telling you, Annie, I can't imagine staying here for that many more years. I need a change, and I'm sick of trying to serve students in an environment where the dollars dedicated to the arts are drying up." Wendy stopped when she reached the front of the school and took a second to gaze up at it. She'd worked here for even longer than Annie had.

Annie paused, too. She'd meant to have this discussion with Wendy over the summer months, but here they were, poised to jump into the chaos of yet another school year. "But, Wendy . . . you *know* what's going to happen once you leave. The school district will never allow me to replace you. Then what are the kids going to do? They *need* you."

Wendy narrowed her eyes. "Annie, we already talked about this. My answer is the same today as it was last spring. There are things I've always wanted to do with my art, other kinds of work I can't possibly pursue while employed here. You know I've thought about this for a few years. The students will be fine. Hopefully, other resources will pop up in the community to support their talents. But I can't do it anymore. It isn't my responsibility to keep every generation in Ruby Falls educated in the arts."

Annie knew she stood little chance of changing Wendy's mind. It was only when she had her administrative hat on that she stewed about what would happen with the arts program at the high school. She'd miss her friend. "I'm not going to change your mind, am I?"

Wendy shrugged. Her portfolio strap must have been hanging on by a thread, because the tiny movement snapped it in half, sending the large, square portfolio tumbling to the ground. When a corner of it hit the pavement, the aged container split open and three thin canvases tumbled onto the sidewalk.

Not empty, Annie thought.

Both women dropped to their knees. Annie set her own bags down, then reached for the closest white rectangle, now face down on the ground. She picked it up and carefully flipped it over. Stunned speechless by the image she held, she sat on the concrete walk, abandoning her earlier quest to get a few more things done inside before students arrived.

Wendy froze when she noticed Annie's reaction. "I just started that." Her voice was little more than a squeak. She shoved the other two canvases, both of a similar size to the one Annie held, back into their less-than-effective container, then reached for the third sketch.

Annie twisted to keep the artwork out of Wendy's reach, her eyes still trained on the faint image of the male nude in her hand. An extremely well-built male. "Just a minute. Wendy, this is stunning. *He* is stunning. Why does he look vaguely familiar?"

When she finally looked up at Wendy, still hovering on her knees next to her, she noticed an uncharacteristic crimson wash across her friend's cheeks. "Are you *blushing*?" Annie grinned as Wendy struggled to her feet and grabbed the canvas away. "And since when do you sketch nudes? I'm not sure you want the kids to see that. I'm all for supporting the arts, but I prefer to limit the naked men they see around here to centuries-old statues in their textbooks. Easier to explain to concerned parents."

Wendy shook her head, a disgusted look stealing over her still-flushed face. "You don't have to tell me that. I'm painfully aware of how narrow-minded parents can be these days. My plan was to work on that piece during my noon hour, with my classroom door *locked* so my *private* work is safely away from prying eyes."

Annie realized she'd sat on the ground in her pale-yellow slacks. She'd be lucky if there wasn't a smear of dirt across her backside. Careful not to get any dirtier, she got back to her feet, brushing herself off as best she could. "I'm just teasing you, Wendy. I trust your discretion. But don't you dodge my question. That hunky specimen of a man in your drawing looks familiar. Who modeled for you? And, more importantly, why didn't you invite me over for a drawing lesson that day? I think even *I* could pretend to know how to hold a stub of charcoal if it meant looking at him for hours on end."

The heat in Wendy's cheeks wasn't cooling. "I wasn't looking at a live model when I sketched that. And I used graphite pencils, not charcoal. I'll add paint later."

"Hmm." Annie hoped the woman would explain herself, but just then the doors to the school swung open and her most trusted janitor appeared, a frantic expression on her face. Annie suppressed a sigh and said, "What is it, Daphne?"

"It's a big ol' mess in the girls' bathroom. Second floor, science wing. No one else is here yet. Can you get a plumber in here right away?"

If the "big ol' mess" Daphne mentioned involved water in a second-floor bathroom, which Annie feared it must at the woman's suggestion that she call a plumber, she needed to see to it right away. The mystery of Wendy's model would have to wait.

Daphne disappeared back inside, and Annie groaned as she picked up her computer bag and heavy tote. "We aren't done talking about that drawing yet," she warned her friend. "*Or* your quitting."

Wendy shrugged again, but this time she kept a tight grip on her portfolio. "I can't stay," she repeated. "And we *are* done talking about it. About both. At least for now. You better get inside, boss. It sounds like they need your property management skills so our first day doesn't turn into a soggy catastrophe."

Annie held the door for Wendy, then followed her through.

Once inside, the two women went their separate ways—much as they would at the end of the school year. Wendy would walk out those same doors to start some kind of mystery second career that she'd been anxious to pursue, leaving Annie behind. She hated to think about how it would feel to work here without Wendy. As the principal, she'd never felt comfortable developing friendships with her staff. But it was different with Wendy. They'd been friends since her preteen years at summer camp.

Annie juggled her bags as she dug her phone out on the way to her office. Their usual plumber didn't pick up. Great. She'd need to hurry and find contact information for a different one.

This was not how she'd envisioned the start of the first day of the new school year. She'd hoped all of her planning would have equated to a smooth start. She could already feel the shadow of a tension headache behind her eyes.

She stowed her phone as she crossed through the shadowed receptionist area, then pulled up short at the doorway to her office. She spied a massive bouquet of red, yellow, and white roses on the middle of her desktop a split second after she detected their scent. The air was heavy with it.

The arrangement must have arrived late yesterday, after she'd left for the day. Sarah, her assistant, had still been entering schedule adjustments but promised she wouldn't stay late. She must have been the one to accept the flower delivery.

She dropped her bags and purse onto the desk next to the flowers and sighed for what felt like the hundredth time that morning.

What the heck?

She'd celebrated her July birthday in Maui with her girlfriends, and her wedding anniversary wasn't for another five months. Besides, Henry wasn't a rose kind of guy. She knew who *did* like to send roses, but he had no business sending her flowers, even if September 10th was once a special day for them both.

The twinge behind her eyes exploded into a full-blown migraine. She needed to find a plumber, get rid of the flowers before anyone else saw them, and cross her fingers that Sarah would keep her mouth shut about the roses.

Despite the eventful first hour of her workday, Annie made it back to the sidewalk in front of the school by eight a.m. to welcome students. The ache behind her eyes was subsiding thanks to the painkiller she'd tossed back after finding a plumber. Now she stood right where Wendy's portrait of that exquisite male nude had tumbled earlier. The plumbing emergency had prevented her from getting a straight answer out of her old camp counselor, but she couldn't shake the feeling that Wendy was drawing a man Annie knew from somewhere. She'd press her for more information at lunch.

Unless Wendy stays back in her classroom, she thought, *working on her secret masterpiece.*

Her brain conjured up an image of Wendy, her fingers smudged, surrounded by a group of stunningly naked male models in some mystery studio, natural light streaming in through floor-to-ceiling windows. As Annie greeted a trio of seniors walking past her into the school, she had to bite her lip to keep from laughing.

Whenever Wendy hinted at her desire to pursue a second career, she remained frustratingly vague, so Annie had no idea what the woman intended to do after her final school year ended. How significant of a change was Wendy after? Would she move away? Was there a man in the picture? Maybe after four years, she felt more acclimated to widowhood.

What do you have up your sleeve, Wendy?

Unable to hold back a giggle, Annie shook her head, earning herself strange looks from four freshmen who, arms laden with books, were crossing the sidewalk toward the school building. The kids probably had no idea she was their principal, and if she started cackling, they'd really wonder about her.

Their wary looks reminded her of the one Henry had shot her in the bathroom that morning.

She needed to work on her poker face. She was too easy to read.

A school bus pulled up, and even more kids approached from different directions. She did her best to maintain a smile and offer an occasional "good morning" to the least enthusiastic appearing students. The school day was underway.

The slam of a van door pulled Annie's attention across the street to the plumber. He was packing away a large wet vac. She'd appreciated how fast the stand-in plumber had gotten to the school, as well as his speed at solving the problem in the bathroom. Crisis averted.

From there, Annie's gaze shifted to her own car, parked next to Wendy's son-in-law's black SUV. She wondered if her interior already smelled like roses. She'd stashed the unwelcome bouquet in the trunk. She'd drop them off at the funeral home after work. It might be a morbid solution, but what the heck else was she going to do with them? She'd considered the hospital, but too many people knew her there and would ask questions. It wasn't every day that a woman tried to pass off a gorgeous bouquet of two dozen roses.

Or twenty-five roses, to be exact.

Michael always went big. She didn't have to open the tiny envelope to know he'd sent them.

As a large group of kids flowed around her, someone got knocked into her.

"Sorry, Ms. Pierce," a young man murmured.

Annie was glad to see the teen. "Not a problem, Ferguson. I'm in the way here. Welcome back."

The student glanced back over his shoulder. "Thrilled to be here," he said, but the smirk on his face said otherwise.

"Liar," Annie replied. She wished he really was thrilled, but she knew better. She was just glad Ferguson had bothered to show up for the first day at all. Maybe he'd fared better over the summer months than she'd worried he would.

The first bell rang, and Annie grabbed for one of the heavy front doors, holding it open for the stream of students. They hurried now, before the second bell, to avoid detention. The flow of kids slowed to a trickle, then ended, and Annie locked the door behind her before heading back to her office.

Anyone else arriving late would have to knock. The school resource officer would monitor the door.

Life in America's schools certainly looked different from when she was a student here.

Chapter Two

Annie was relieved to find her son's pickup parked in the lot behind the funeral home. Colton worked odd hours, so she hadn't been sure she'd catch him. If he hadn't been working, her next stop might have been the cemetery, or, as a last resort, a nearby dumpster.

She caught the irony of how she was choosing to dispose of flowers from her ex for a silver anniversary that never was. At least the envelope, nestled in the blooms, was still sealed. No prying eyes. As she tore it open before going inside, she could imagine the sparkle in Michael's eyes as he'd written out the card. He'd have laughed at his own joke about a "could-have-been" anniversary, but the line about his excitement over the two of them being grandparents for the first time was sincere.

Michael and Annie's daughter, Ava, had started telling people a few days ago that she and her husband, Daniel, were expecting a baby in March. Michael loved babies, so Annie's prediction that he'd be thrilled at the news was spot on.

While the prospect of becoming a grandfather excited Michael, it didn't have the same effect on Henry, her current husband. Annie had hoped both Michael and Henry would consider themselves to be grandfathers to the baby. Especially because the relationship between Henry and Ava, as well as Henry and Colton, was once strong. But things had changed when their dad, Michael, moved to Ruby Shores.

Annie cracked open all four windows in the car to air out the interior while she would be inside the funeral home with Colton. She hid her laptop bag under a light sweater. She'd brought the sweater to work, in case she got cold, but she should have known she wouldn't need it. The sun's rays were still strong, and the school's air-conditioning unit could never keep ahead of the high temperatures in Minnesota during the fall and spring months. The cooling unit was old, just like the rest of the school building.

Just like me, Annie thought as she climbed out of her car, twisting at her waist to loosen the knot in her lower back. Turning forty hadn't bothered her, but she couldn't say the same about her upcoming birthday. She had a feeling that fifty would be a whole new ballgame.

She retrieved the roses and realized it would be safer to move her computer to the trunk, but she decided not to bother. The roses were heavy, and besides, it wasn't like petty criminals were hanging around the funeral home.

Not enough action, she thought, smiling at her tasteless joke.

She entered Colton's place of work through the back door, imagining the people who used to call this place home before it was converted into a funeral parlor. Now the front entrance was designated for friends and family visiting the recently deceased, and Annie steered clear. The day had already provided enough drama. The last thing she needed was to run into a grieving acquaintance.

Colton started working at the funeral home the summer following his sophomore year at college. Mortuary science wouldn't have been Annie's first choice for her son, but she tried to keep her nose out of her children's career choices. It was *so* hard to keep her opinions to herself. But she'd hated the pressure her own parents, especially her mother, exerted on her back in the day and didn't want to do the same to her kids.

She averted her eyes from the stairs just inside the back door that led down to the left. Colton had given her a tour of the lower level once, and despite his professional approach and his matter-of-fact responses to her questions, she still had nightmares about what was down there.

There were certain life-and-death realities that she preferred not to think about.

Instead, she climbed the three stairs and swung to her right, hoping Colton would be in his tiny office and not working with a family.

She got lucky.

Her son was already on his feet by the time she reached his door, alerted to someone's arrival by the jangle of a small bell on the home's back door. "Mom! I'm surprised to see you today. Though I can't really see you behind that massive bouquet. How was your first day back at school?"

She almost corrected him, but she let it slide. As principal, she spent much of her summer in the office, so to call it her first day back wasn't exactly right, but she knew what he meant. "Other than a potential plumbing disaster, which was blessedly averted, it was fine. It always takes a week or so for everyone to settle in, including me."

Colton grinned, then nodded at the large vase in her arms. "You shouldn't have."

"I didn't. Your father did."

A confused look crossed his face. "Henry? Or Michael? And why would one of them get *me* flowers?"

She shoved the vase at him, grunting with relief when he took it from her. "Michael sent them to *me*. You aren't going to believe this, but today would have been our twenty-fifth wedding anniversary."

Her son snorted as he set the flowers on his desk. "Mom, you guys got divorced when I was a baby. I can't believe he sent you flowers. And you wonder why I think he's such an ass. He likes to mess with you, and he knows Henry doesn't like it."

Colton was right. Despite his innate charm, Michael could be difficult. So why did it sting to hear him say it out loud?

"I'm sure he meant it as a joke. The main reason he sent them was to say congrats over the news that we'll be grandparents. Your sister told him about the pregnancy over the weekend. By the way, please don't tell anyone about the roses, not even Ava."

He motioned toward a small round table in the corner of his crowded office. She pulled out the closest chair and sat.

"I won't mention the flowers," he said as he settled in across from her. "Michael took the baby news better than Henry, then?"

She watched as her son crossed one ankle over a knee. It always struck Annie how mature he looked at work. He was only twenty-three years old, but she'd heard from others that he did a masterful job with grieving family members.

When she was his age, she was flying off on mission trips, sure she could right some of the wrongs of the world. Maybe this was Colton's way of trying to do the same thing.

And maybe if she'd gotten a *responsible* job right out of college, like her son, the whole mess with Michael and Henry would never have happened. But then this amazing young man, dressed in his conservative suit, wouldn't be here either.

She pulled her attention back to Colton's question. "Yes, he took the news better than Henry did."

"What is Henry's deal, anyhow?" he asked.

Annie saw Colton quickly glance over to the one framed photo he had on his desk. Even the fact that Colton kept a family picture in his work office had surprised her. In her mind, Colton was still the lanky kid with a basketball in his hand and a mischievous grin—so like Michael's—on his face instead of a young man with an office of his own. Only Relic bore any physical resemblance to Henry's grin in the aged photo.

"Henry's deal?" Annie hedged, considering how best to respond. The truth was she was still trying to figure out the same thing. "He thinks Ava and Daniel are too young to start a family, and he worries about their financial situation."

While that much was true, Annie was concerned that there was more to it. Something was bothering Henry, and she suspected it had every-thing to do with her ex. Michael was her former husband, but he was also Henry's former best friend.

Which brought her back to the reason for her visit. "Given Henry's initial reaction to the baby news, I thought it might be best to not bring those flowers home. He'd be mad, even if I didn't mention the whole 'fake anniversary' angle. He'd never remember the date when Michael and I married, but I don't want to feed into the hang-ups he already has about the baby."

Colton nodded. "Good idea. Remind me, Mom, to take lessons from *you*—if I ever stay in a relationship that lasts longer than a month—on how to handle a prickly partner. You are a master at it."

Annie wondered if he would still think she was good at handling a prickly partner if he'd witnessed the screaming match she'd had with

Henry three days earlier. It was after they'd moved their son, Colton's little brother, Relic, into his freshman dorm room. They'd fought over how much spending money to give him each month. Annie wanted Relic to get a part-time job, like both Ava and Colton had done, but Henry was dead set against the idea.

Colton was correct in that she could usually smooth things over with Henry when he was upset. But lately it felt like too much work to even try.

She hated to admit it, but sometimes she thought her empty nest would be so peaceful if no one but her lived there. Those times were fleeting, but it did cross her mind.

She shook away these thoughts. Colton probably had work to do.

"Anyway," she said, "the flowers are much too pretty to toss, so I hoped you could put them to good use here."

Colton dropped his foot and leaned forward, forearms on a table that must have witnessed countless discussions of last wishes and heartbreak. It reminded her that she shouldn't be so flippant about living alone. Henry was a good man, and she was lucky to have him in her life.

"We've got an old guy in here now," Colton was saying. "His only visitor has been his wife. No one has sent flowers, but I think these could bring a little beauty into her life right now. She told me she doesn't have much money. His service is tomorrow morning, and these will brighten up the chapel nicely. Would you mind if I sent this arrangement home with her, after everything is over?"

"Not at all. That is exactly the type of thing I hoped you'd be able to do with them."

She got to her feet, and Colton followed her lead.

"Say, how did the move-in go for Relic? Is his dorm room as tiny as mine was? You know, I bet that's why Henry is so moody. He's going to miss Relic. That kid can do no wrong in his eyes."

Annie picked up on the wistful tone tinged with jealousy. "Relic is far from perfect, Colton. You know that. And you know Henry loves you. Ava, too. Things are just a little . . . *complicated*."

The tiny bell on the back door jingled, catching Colton's attention. "It wasn't all that complicated *before*," he said. "I'm sorry, Mom, but I've gotta get back to work. Was there anything else?"

Annie paused at the corner of Colton's desk to take one last deep whiff of the beautiful roses Michael had sent. She recognized the truth in her son's words, and it gave her a pang of sadness. Michael had every right to live near his two children, but before he moved here—eight years ago now—Annie and Henry and the three kids had been one big, happy family.

Well, *relatively* happy.

But Michael's arrival had complicated things. She supposed that was what she got for the wrench she had thrown into his and Henry's friendship. A girl couldn't volley her heart back and forth between two best friends without expecting to do some serious damage to all involved.

She straightened with a sigh and caught Colton in a quick hug—something she'd never dream of doing at his place of employment if anyone else was nearby. He wriggled out of her embrace, but his grin told her he didn't really mind.

"You'll want to use the front door this time," he said.

She appreciated his heads-up, as now she could hear a shuffling sound coming from the back. A delivery through the back door wasn't something she had any desire to witness on this beautiful, early fall afternoon.

The world needed people doing the work Colton had signed up to do, but Annie couldn't imagine working around death every day.

With a nod, she hurried toward the front, keeping her eyes straight ahead. At least her reason for stopping by was a happy one. That wasn't the case for most of the people who came and went through the heavily carved door in front of her.

It was the perfect reminder to appreciate the many blessings in her life, and to take the time to smell the roses.

Her stomach rumbled as she backed her car out of the parking lot, carefully maneuvering around both her son's pickup and the white ambulance emblazoned with blue lettering. There was something unnerving about the still ambulance, its lack of flashing lights and sound.

Despite cracking the windows, Annie could still detect a hint of roses inside her car. Her stomach growled again, and she realized she'd eaten very little all day. She'd left the house early, without breakfast, and the first near-scuffle of the year in the hallway outside the teacher's lounge had interrupted her lunch.

Henry would be livid if he knew how often she had to place herself between two students intent on knocking each other silly over a perceived insult. Boys or girls, they were often bigger than her. But seldom as tough. She may be short, but she was still in reasonably good shape.

"At least for someone turning fifty," she murmured.

She automatically flicked on her blinker toward home, but then she remembered Henry wouldn't be there. It was Tuesday, and as long as the weather allowed for an evening of golf, he'd be at the club for men's night every week until it got too cold or snowy. After her visit with Colton inside the hushed atmosphere of the funeral home, today wasn't one of those days when a completely empty nest sounded welcoming. Besides, she didn't feel like cooking.

"I should pick something up," she said as she turned off her blinker and grinned. "And this is why I should never live alone. I'd talk to myself constantly and end up in the looney bin."

The weather was perfect, and she felt pulled toward the lake on the edge of Ruby Shores. She grabbed takeout from her favorite burger joint—the one Henry didn't like—and drove toward the beach. She always kept a collapsible chair in her trunk for the countless sporting events she'd work throughout the upcoming school year. It was doubtful that anyone would be at the beach at this hour on an early September evening.

It would be her first quiet moments of the day.

She pulled into the dirt parking lot above the public beach area. The stretch of sand where she'd spent so much of her youth was deserted. Only the seagulls would keep her company.

She set up her chair, propped her tall fountain pop in the sand, and pulled a burger out of the sack at her feet. Before she could even take her first bite, an ambitious bird hopped over to her side to look for a handout. She admired its tenacity. She tore off a chunk of bun and tossed it to the seagull.

"I don't need the carbs," she said.

The bird just pecked at the bread, ignoring her as he ate.

Closing her eyes, Annie allowed her mind to wander back in time to what would have been a typical summer afternoon on this very beach with her besties. The bikinis and tans they sported pegged the memory as one from their high school days.

Kit's yellow two-piece glowed against her burnished skin, its bright color rivaling her orange hair. That girl never wanted to go home from their days at the lake. Everyone knew she was afraid her absentee mother might show up out of the blue one day, as was her style. In the memory, Jackie wore a red suit, showing off her sleek and strong muscles, hard-earned from countless hours of track practice. Lynette wore black, making it look stylish despite the lack of color, thanks to the silver bangles that circled one ankle and the stacks of rings on every finger.

"Ah, yes," Annie sighed. "The Kaleidoscope Girls, enjoying the carefree days of youth."

Well, everyone except Renee, of course. Renee, the fifth official member of their self-proclaimed group, had never visited this beach with them, since she lived over two hours away.

Annie's mind bounced forward, and she wondered what each of them was doing right now.

Jackie was probably working. According to Kit, that was all the woman did these days. Their mutual friend was working to get her new business on a firm footing. The idea to match up senior rescue dogs with the elderly was a good one, and Annie knew it was passion that fueled Jackie's career pivot, not profit. But she still needed to earn an income.

Kit and her fiancé, Dean, were probably at one of Isaac's football games. The couple had recently started fostering the teen, and they were working to get him integrated into his new school in a suburb of Minneapolis. Annie was excited about the couple's upcoming wedding, planned for October, but she couldn't imagine how busy they must be.

If she remembered right, Lynette was on a buying trip overseas right now, but she'd promised to be back in the States before Kit's wedding.

Renee was probably busy getting her lake resort ready for winter. It was only early September, but winter would inevitably arrive in Minnesota, and usually before most people were ready for it.

Annie took one final bite of her burger, then tossed what remained to the growing gaggle of gulls. She laughed as the scavengers wrestled over the tidbits. Her phone vibrated in her pocket. She pulled it out and glanced at the screen, noticing sand clinging to the hem of her yellow slacks. That was what she got for not wearing proper lake attire.

The Caller ID pulled a sigh out of her. She considered letting the call go to voicemail, but the memory of the roses tickled her nose.

"Hello, Michael. What's up?"

"Were they too much?"

She could sense the smile behind his words. Henry never smiled as much as Michael did. But history had taught Annie that the charming smile could mask trouble, too.

"Of course they were too much. Michael, what were you thinking?"

He chuckled. "I was thinking we have lots to celebrate."

"I can only think of one thing to be celebrated." She caught her bottom lip between her teeth. She wasn't going to get pulled into his banter and discuss their checkered past, even if today would have once been a special date. "The baby news is exciting, though, isn't it?"

She heard and could almost feel the deep breath he took. "Our baby is having a baby. Annie, how is that even possible?"

She kicked off the old pair of flip-flops that she'd found on the floor of her backseat and dug her bare toes into the cooling sand. The sun was already dipping. Sunset came earlier now that autumn was upon them.

"Michael, she isn't a baby anymore. She's a grown woman. Married, even."

"She'll always be our baby."

Annie didn't like the automatic response her body had to his words: the warmth that flushed through her. It was so hard to share Ava and Colton with the only two men she'd ever loved. It had always been *so* damn hard. She'd have been glad that her two oldest kids had the benefit of *two* father figures if the whole situation hadn't resulted in so much pain and chaos.

"Are you still there, or did I lose you?" Michael asked. "There's static on the line."

The bravest of a trio of seagulls approached her discarded sandals, pulling a grin out of her. The bird was about to be disappointed if he thought the red shoes were something tasty to eat. "I'm here. I'm actually on the beach. At the lake. The reception is never great."

"What are you doing at the lake? Did you and Henry take the pontoon out?"

"No. He already winterized that. It's Tuesday, so I'm on my own for dinner. He's golfing. It was so nice outside, and no one was home. I grabbed food and came out here to enjoy some fresh air. I needed quiet time after my hectic first day, but I knew the house might feel *too* quiet. I figured this might be a good way to celebrate the start of a new school year."

"You didn't seem all that excited about school starting up when I ran into you at the grocery store a couple weeks ago," he said. "Are you sure you didn't feel inclined to celebrate something else tonight? Like an *anniversary*?"

She recognized that hint of teasing in his voice. "Michael. I'm warning you."

He laughed, undeterred. "Sit tight. I'll be there in ten minutes. There's something I've been wanting to talk to you about. Alone."

Meaning: he didn't want Henry to be part of the discussion, whatever it was.

She eyed the setting sun, feeling torn. "I don't know, Michael. It'll be dark soon."

It wasn't really the reason she didn't want to be alone with him on a deserted beach, but he'd laugh at her if she admitted the truth. He'd always been the least cautious of the three of them. There was a time when his spontaneity appealed to her, but those days were well back in their past.

Most of the time.

"Promise you'll sit tight," he urged. "Be right there."

Click.

Annie let her head drop back in frustration. Why did she continue to let this man push her buttons?

And why did a tiny part of her worry that she was playing with fire?

Chapter Three

B Y THE TIME MICHAEL settled onto the sand to the left of Annie's chair, a family had arrived with a blanket and two large bags emblazoned with the same fast-food logo as the chain she'd stopped at an hour earlier. The adults set up on the opposite side of the beach, to Annie's right, while the two kids ran into the lake, ignoring their dinner. Annie guessed them to be around seven and nine or ten, and clearly full of pent-up energy after their first day back in a classroom.

Their arrival reminded her of the times her parents used to bring her and Millie here, during those first weeks of the school year. Back then, she'd been close with Millie. They'd grown apart over the years, and Annie missed her big sister. But she also hated the drama that was part of nearly every one of their interactions these days. There was a time when Millie liked to have *lots* of fun, back in her high school and college years. Since then, the pendulum had swung in the opposite direction and stuck there, held in place by a marriage to a zealous preacher and their move to Des Moines, where he oversaw a large congregation.

Annie sighed. She missed the old Millie. New Millie was a judgmental snob.

"They look like they're having fun," Michael said, his deep voice jolting Annie back to present time. "Where were you just now? You looked like you were a million miles away."

She glanced back at him, liking that her chair put her eye to eye with Michael instead of having to look up at him. "I was thinking back to the times Mom and Dad brought Millie and me out here after those hot, first days of school."

Michael watched the boy and girl splash each other. Neither waded in deeper than their waists, but they were clearly having fun. The woman called them up to eat, and the kids didn't have to be told twice. It only took a minute before they were tearing open burger bags she'd handed them.

"Millie would have made you stop and say grace before you could take a bite," Michael said. His tone, more than the actual words, conveyed how little he cared for Annie's sister.

"She wasn't always like that, you know."

His gaze shifted to Annie's face; one eye squinted shut against the descending yet still-bright sun. "So you say. But I've never known her any other way."

Annie wriggled her feet, digging her toes deeper into the sand. "You would have liked Millie when she was those kids' age," she said, nodding in the young family's direction.

Just then, the father glanced their way. He raised a hand in greeting, and with a start, she realized she knew him. He worked with Henry. She'd paid him little attention when they'd arrived, watching the kids instead. She waved back, and then a squabble between the children quickly diverted the man's attention.

"Do you know that guy?" Michael asked.

"Not really. His last name is Norris. I don't know if I've ever heard his first name. He works with Henry."

"Ah . . ." was all Michael said as he drew his long legs up to sit cross-legged.

"You're going to get all sandy."

He grunted. A little sand never bothered Michael. "And you're worried Norris will run to your husband and tell him you were out here with me. Alone. Because that would royally tick off Henry."

She kicked a little plume of sand. "I'm not worried."

"Yeah. You are."

He was right, and they both knew it. They sat in silence, the only voices those of the family down the beach, and the occasional squawk of a seagull.

Two more vehicles arrived, and a rambunctious group of teenagers spilled across the sand toward the water. Even from a distance, Annie recognized one or two of them. If they spied her, they wouldn't be pleased. They'd surely come here as an escape after their structured school day, not to hang out with their principal. She was glad they continued farther down the beach along the water, and she quickly lost sight of them.

"What happened to my peaceful alone time to decompress?"

Michael grinned, brushing sand from the legs of his jeans. She eyed his bare feet. The man had the strangest-looking toes. They were long, and the tips bent at odd angles. She used to tease him that his parents must have forced him to wear his shoes too small as a toddler. Her ex-father-in-law would laugh at the accusation, insisting he couldn't get Michael to wear shoes at all.

Colton had toes like his father's.

"You said you wanted to talk to me about something, Michael. What is it?"

He straightened his legs and relaxed back onto the palms of his hands, eyes on the horizon. "I'm worried about Henry."

She snorted. "Since when?"

His eyes cut to hers. "That isn't fair."

She paused, reconsidering. Truth be told, she was worried about her husband, too. But she wanted to hear what Michael was thinking before she shared her own concerns. "I'm sorry. Why are you worried about him?"

He crossed his ankles. His eyes were back on the orange-red glow of the setting sun before them. "I'm hearing things."

She laughed. She couldn't help herself. "Now you sound like a typical small-town old-timer, gossiping like everyone else around here." When she was younger, one reason she was initially so enamored with this man was because he seemed like the exact opposite of all that. Worldly, young, and never caring what anyone thought of him.

"I'm serious, Annie."

She took a deep breath. "Sorry. What are you hearing?"

He sat up and rubbed a finger along the side his nose, a sure sign he was searching for the right words. "How's work going for Henry?"

Annie suddenly wondered if this was about Henry's demotion that had caught them both off guard earlier in the year. Henry still hadn't gotten over the embarrassment, and wanted to keep it all as quiet as possible. "Come on, Michael, get to the point. If you're fishing to find out if I know anything about Henry and his work, I'll take the bait to hurry this conversation along. As far as I know, Henry's work is fine. He hasn't said anything, and I haven't heard any scuttlebutt, either. Though, to be honest, he's been on edge lately, but I haven't been able to pinpoint why."

Michael laughed. "I feel like he's been uptight for twenty years. He wasn't like that when we were kids."

"You two are so different. I've never really understood how you got to be such good friends in the first place."

"That was a long time ago." Michael began chucking rocks toward the water's edge. The first one fell short, but the second made it, splashing into the water and sending ripples spanning out over the lake's surface. "We aren't really friends anymore. But I wish we were. It would be better for everyone."

She picked up on the melancholy behind his words. They caused a stab of guilt. She thought constantly about the dynamics between Henry and Michael and the way they impacted Ava, Colton, and Relic. But she seldom stopped to think about how decisions she'd made, so long ago, ruined the friendship between the two men, back when they were all barely more than kids.

"You regret it then?" she asked, her voice low and soft.

"What? That Henry can barely stand being in the same room with me? I'd be lying if I said no. Sure. I have regrets. We all do. Fifty years is more than enough time to make plenty of monumental mistakes."

How right Michael was about that. They'd all screwed up. More times than any of them would care to admit. "I'm sorry I ruined your friendship. I never meant to hurt either of you."

Michael shook his head at this. "All that went down a long time ago. We could have handled things better, sure, but I wouldn't change much of what happened. One different move back then, and Ava and Colton might not even exist. Or this new grandchild."

It was true. The kids were the one good thing—or three good things, as Michael pointed out—that had remained despite her inability to make her first marriage work. No price was too high when it came to her children and future grandchild.

"Do you ever wonder whether we might have actually stayed together if I wouldn't have screwed up so bad?" Michael asked, catching her hand where it rested on the chair's arm. She tried to pull away, but he held tight. "I'm serious."

She pulled harder. "I'll only listen to this if you let go of my hand. For God's sake, Michael, do you *want* to give that Norris guy something of substance to tell Henry?"

He gave her fingers two quick squeezes before releasing her. "You need to chill, Annie."

She hated it when he said things like that, and she had to fight the urge to bolt. She'd bolted once before—they both had—and she still wasn't sure whether that was the best thing she'd ever done, or the worst decision of her life.

She glanced down the beach toward the young family. They'd started gathering their things. As the kids toweled off, Annie was sure she caught Norris and his wife sneaking peeks in their direction.

She took a deep breath, telling herself she was being paranoid, then tried to turn her full attention back to her ex-husband. "No. We wouldn't have made it, Michael. We were too different. *Are* too different. You wanted to travel the world and save more people, even after we had Ava and Colton. Our kids needed you. *I* needed you. But we weren't ever going to be enough for you."

"That's one reason I love you, Annie. You never pull any punches. Always direct, no matter what. And I'm sorry I ruined us."

"Please keep your voice down. You're right. Henry is going to hate that we were out here like this."

Michael shrugged. "Don't tell him."

"Maybe I wouldn't have," she said, even though she knew that wasn't true. Secrets were poison. "But now I have no choice. That guy will blab. I just know it."

Michael studied the man and woman as they made their way to the only minivan in the parking lot. "I could go warn him to keep his mouth shut."

A bark of laughter escaped before she could stifle it. "Yeah, right. You're such a tough guy. You'd be more likely to go introduce yourself and invite him out for a beer, then maybe play a round of darts. Warn him off? You'd never get around to it."

"I'm wounded," he said, grabbing at his chest.

Annie's phone vibrated inside the pocket of her slacks, and she had to straighten her leg to pull it out. Was it Henry, checking on her? She hated how guilty she felt, sitting next to Michael. But no, it was Ava, texting her a reminder about their plans for the craft show that coming weekend. She considered telling Michael it was their daughter when he glanced at the phone in her hand but decided against it. He didn't need to know more of her business than he already did.

When she stashed the phone without comment, he continued. "About Henry. I heard rumors that someone who used to work at his plant was part of a group bringing drugs into Ruby Shores."

"At the plant?" Annie said, trying to pick back up on the reason for Michael's concern after Ava's text distracted her. At least his interest didn't seem to be related to the management restructures. "The plant *is* one of the larger employers in town. I'm sure what you're saying is possible, but Henry doesn't know everyone that works there. Besides, if they aren't there anymore, why does it even matter?"

She paused, but he didn't look her way.

"Wait. You aren't implying Henry has some kind of tie-in with a drug ring, are you?"

"Of course not," he said, sounding sincere. "But Henry knew the guy."

She blew out an exasperated breath and gathered her shoulder-length hair onto the top of her head with both hands. The cool evening breeze felt refreshing on her neck. "Fine. I'll play along, if it means you'll eventually get to the point. Who was the guy?"

"Byron Oaks."

She froze in surprise, then released her hair and shook her head. "Whoever is feeding you that bullshit is wrong." She shuddered at the memory of Henry's midday call last month, telling her of Byron's sudden death. A wave of compassion for his widow passed through her. "I feel terrible for Byron's wife. Three teenagers to raise, and now she'll have to do it alone. I know how scary it feels to be a single mother. Such a tragedy. But what does Byron's heart attack have to do with Henry or a drug ring?"

If Michael caught her jab, he ignored it. "Sounds like it might not have been a heart attack that killed him."

Annie couldn't believe this. She'd heard nothing of the sort. "It *was* a heart attack. Colton even said so, when I talked to him the day after it happened. He's usually pretty tight-lipped about that kind of thing, for obvious reasons, but it really shook him up after helping Byron's wife make the arrangements. The guy was younger than us."

She noticed Michael had continued to gather small rocks, but he was piling them up instead of throwing them. He added one to the top of his tiny heap before responding.

"Fine. Maybe it was a heart attack that got him. Even so, the guy was doing some pretty heavy street drugs before he died."

"Michael, you can't go around spreading rumors like that! There is no way Byron Oaks used drugs. Henry and I . . . we went out for dinner with Byron and Sue just a few weeks before he died. I know what signs to watch for around drug use. It's so prevalent in schools these days, and it's scary as hell. I'm telling you, there was nothing suspicious about his behavior."

Michael hesitated, then shrugged. "Annie, a forty-five-year-old is going to be much better at hiding something like that than a sixteen-year-old kid would be."

"Or a twenty-nine-year-old kid?"

He winced. "This isn't about us. Not directly, at least. Stay with me on this, Annie. I have reason to believe the rumors about Byron's drug use are true. Hell, he even cornered me once, not too long ago, and point-blank asked if I had any interest in getting in on a new distribution chain in town. He said they could use a better connection between Minneapolis and New York City. Even though I don't work as a commercial pilot anymore, he'd heard I fly that route once in a while. And, believe me, he wasn't inviting me to join some pyramid scheme."

Annie paused at this. If Michael had first-hand knowledge that Byron was selling drugs, that changed things. He'd never lie about something like that. "If all that is true, I still don't see what that has to do with Henry or the plant."

"Maybe nothing. But Byron worked for Henry, right?"

She squirmed. This was the part of the discussion she'd hoped to avoid. "At one time he did, but not recently."

"Really?" He looked surprised. "I thought half that place reported up through Henry."

Not anymore.

Before Annie could figure out a way to protect Henry's pride, one of the teenagers she'd recognized earlier came running toward them. She'd forgotten the kids were even around after they'd headed farther down the beach. The panic on the girl's face had Annie on her feet before the teen even reached them.

"What's wrong, Gabi?" she asked, capturing one of the girl's hands in her own.

Annie's touch seemed to ground the girl. Gabi's other hand stopped flailing, going to her hip as she gulped for air. "Something's really wrong, Ms. Pierce. It's Ferguson! I don't know if he took something or what, but he's on the ground. I'm not sure he's even breathing."

Chapter Four

ANNIE TOOK TWO RUNNING steps in the direction Gabi had come from when Michael's muscular arms grabbed around her waist and stopped her in her tracks.

"What?!" she yelled, fighting to get loose. "Let me go! It's Ferguson!"

"Take a breath, Annie," Michael whispered in her ear as he held her spine tight against his chest. "I'll go. You need to call 911. If the kid overdosed, there's no time to waste. It'll take too long for help to find us if no one stays here to flag them down."

She nodded, battling down her own panic. He was right.

Michael released her and motioned for the high schooler to lead the way. Annie was already punching in the numbers by the time the two reached the water's edge, hurrying off to their right. She held her breath when static on the line made it difficult to hear, but the call eventually went through, and the emergency operator got straight to business. Once Annie relayed what little she knew, the woman insisted she stay on the line until help arrived.

Annie paced, ears straining to pick up the sound of sirens in the distance. The young family had already left in their minivan, and she felt utterly alone. "Where are they?! He could be dying. What is taking so long?"

"Ma'am, they'll be there just as soon as they can. You need to stay calm, and I need you to stay on the line with me until they arrive." The dispatcher's voice was impossibly calm but also reassuring.

Annie thought back to her chance encounter with Ferguson Carbo that very morning. She'd been so relieved to see him at school. Each year, there always seemed to be a kid or two who got to her, who she was willing to go the distance for if it meant keeping them out of harm's way. Of course, she did her best to treat everyone equally. That was her job. But she was also human, and Ferguson was the type of kid who could worm his way into your heart, even when his irresponsible actions made you want to pull your hair out. Or his.

The boy's homelife was an abomination, and addiction ran rampant throughout his family. The Carbos were a rough bunch. Annie remembered Kit's admission that her own mother, Mia, got into trouble with one of them way back when she was in high school. Ferguson's own father might have run her down that very morning if Wendy hadn't stopped her from stepping in front of his speeding truck.

Ferguson was following a similar path, but he'd also shown potential in his classes, and Annie had done her best last spring to get him the help that *might* save him from a lifetime of misery.

He'd made progress, too, and she'd felt a mixture of both hope and apprehension on his behalf as they'd headed into the summer months. Most everyone, students and teachers alike, reveled in the freedom that summer can bring. But Annie knew the risks when kids were no longer operating within a structured school day under the watchful eyes of staff who cared.

Annie hadn't run into Ferguson again after their initial encounter that morning. She hadn't even picked him out of the crowd of kids that had arrived at the beach while she and Michael were talking. She should have made it a point to call him into her office earlier today. She should have checked to make sure the sobriety he'd worked so hard to find last spring was strong enough to see him through any temptations summer might have brought.

But she hadn't. Instead, she'd focused on things like a flooded bathroom, an angry biology teacher upset over the size of his first class of the day, and even the obnoxious flowers Michael had sent. She should have made the time to check on Ferguson.

What if her neglect resulted in the kid's untimely death?

She knew her fears for his safety were legitimate. Even here, in the relatively small town of Ruby Shores, there were deadly drugs floating around the streets with the potential to kill kids and adults alike. The image of Byron's smiling face flitted through her mind. She hated that Michael had raised doubts about the man.

"Ms. Pierce? Are you still on the line?"

Annie shook herself, doing her best to dispel the image that kept clawing at her: Ferguson's body. "Of course. And I can hear the sirens now."

"Good. Don't hang up. They're almost there. If you have a car nearby, go turn the flashers on. It's nearly dusk, and it might help them pinpoint your location faster. But don't hang up. Not until help arrives."

She did as she was told, abandoning her chair, empty food bag, and purse to run back up to her car. When both a police car and an ambulance turned into the lot, tires spitting up loose gravel, she shoved her phone back into her pocket and waved her arms.

The next fifteen minutes passed in a blur of activity. Annie knew the police officer, John Sullivan, and the driver of the ambulance. Their calming presence helped her find and maintain a professional veneer, though her insides twisted with worry.

When Annie, Officer Sullivan, and the paramedics finally reached the knot of kids, Michael was performing CPR on a supine body. Her heart skipped.

Ferguson.

A small bonfire still burned in the sheltered cove where the kids had kicked back after their first day of school. Now the crowd of young people watched, wide-eyed and quiet, as grown men and their principal fought to save their friend's life.

If Ferguson didn't survive, would this fateful evening scar each one of them? If there were drugs here, would any of these kids be scared straight?

The paramedic's initial assessment was that Ferguson had indeed overdosed, probably on some kind of opioid. They administered Naloxone. He began breathing on his own so they loaded him on a gurney to haul him out to the public beach and the waiting ambulance. Michael helped the paramedics carry the stretcher. Ferguson was thin but as tall as the full-grown men on the rescue team. Transporting him across the uneven ground and sand wasn't easy. Annie and Sullivan remained behind with the rest of the kids.

"Gabi, do you know what Ferguson took? Where he got it?" Annie asked, trying her best to put Ferguson's too-still form out of her mind. She may have failed him, but maybe she could help prevent this from happening to any other students.

Gabi shifted from foot to foot, anxiety pulsing out of the girl.

Officer Sullivan moved a young man out of earshot, to speak with him where his voice would be indiscernible. Annie saw Gabi glance their way, and she sensed the girl might know something but was afraid to talk.

"If you know anything at all, please, tell me," Annie whispered, gently placing a reassuring hand on the girl's shoulder. "Look, Gabi, I know you, and you don't normally condone this kind of thing."

"I'm not condoning anything, Ms. Pierce. I swear. And I don't know anything for sure."

Annie felt a shiver pass through the girl. Annie lowered her voice even further so no one but Gabi could hear her words. "Even if you *think* you might know something, you can tell me. I'll do my best to keep your name out of it." She could sense Gabi's internal struggle. No one wanted to rat out their friends.

Gabi lowered her head. "Can I come see you tomorrow? I don't want to talk about it here, in front of everyone."

Annie wasn't sure waiting was a good idea, but when she surveyed the other kids—six or seven of them, most of whom she was surprised she didn't recognize—she noticed that a couple seemed to be trying to eavesdrop on their conversation. She'd hate to put Gabi in danger.

She gave the girl a quick nod and squeezed her shoulder. "That would be fine," she said, her words nothing more than a whisper.

Stepping away from the girl, Annie clapped her hands.

"Does anyone have anything you can tell us to help figure out what happened to Ferguson?"

A boy in the group nodded. It was one of the kids Annie didn't recognize, and he looked older than the others. "I think we all know what that idiot did. He took something, probably didn't even have the sense to ask what it was, and it almost killed him."

Annie hated the smugness in the young man's expression and the tone in which he delivered the words. "What we *know* is that Ferguson almost died tonight. That doesn't make him an idiot. He's young. I suspect younger than you are," she said, looking directly at him. "It makes him a victim. And when we find out how he got his hands on whatever it was he took, we'll find the individuals responsible. The last thing Ruby Shores needs is someone selling drugs to our kids."

"Yeah, good luck with that," he murmured, earning him a snicker or two, but doing nothing to endear himself to Annie.

"I'm sorry," she said, stepping closer. "I didn't catch your name."

Sullivan returned to the larger group, positioning himself between Annie and the rest of them. "It's getting late, and it'll be too dark to see before long. I'm going to jot down all of your names, and then we better head back to the parking lot. Get your identification out to make this go faster."

Annie turned to the horizon, realizing he was right. Only the upper curve of the sun was still visible over the water. "And for those of you who are my students, I'll be calling you in to my office tomorrow morning. I plan to sort this out."

The cop shot her a doubtful look but didn't say anything. He just turned to the nearest kid and pulled out a pad and pen.

It wasn't until she was alone behind the wheel of her car that she thought back to the conversation she'd been having with Michael when Gabi ran up to them. He was gone now. He'd followed the ambulance to the hospital, promising to call Ferguson's worthless father to let him know what was happening. Michael said he didn't know the man well, but he could get his phone number from a mutual acquaintance.

Before Gabi came running, he had been talking about the rumors that the death of Henry's coworker was possibly drug-related. Did he think that Henry was somehow involved?

And now Ferguson.

Annie inhaled deeply, but the hint of roses had faded from her car's interior. She watched the taillights of Sullivan's patrol car as he pulled onto the road that skirted the lake and headed toward town, leaving her utterly alone. She lowered her head to her steering wheel in frustration.

Thirty years ago, when she'd selected education as her career, it was because she wanted to help kids thrive, not just survive, and not to convince them that life was too precious to gamble away on drugs. The reality wasn't what she'd expected. Between the ever-present threat of drugs, her limited resources, and the always hovering helicopter parents, Annie wasn't sure how much more of this she could take.

And now she had to go home and tell Henry she'd hung out with Michael at the beach.

It was only day one, but Annie worried this would shape up to be another tough year. Maybe if she could just survive this first semester and get to her mid-winter vacation with her friends, tentatively planned for February, she'd feel reinvigorated enough to push through until the end of May.

She remembered the way she used to head into the start of a new school year with hope and optimism, as if the flip of a calendar could signify a fresh start. But last year was rough. Wouldn't 2020 have to be better than 2019?

Her first grandchild would be born in 2020.

Annie wanted to help make Ruby Shores a better place for her grand-daughter to grow up in. The thought gave her a little charge, and she straightened in her seat, started the car, and flipped on her headlights. It was fully dark now. The limited reach of the headlights revealed just enough roadway for her to move forward safely.

Gabi had run to her for help, and together with others from the Ruby Shores community, Annie might have helped save Ferguson. Tonight had served as a reminder that she could still make a difference, but it wouldn't be easy.

Chapter Five

Annie flinched. Something wet flicked at her outstretched hand. She cracked open one eye, then squeezed it shut again. The flick grew to a hand bath.

"Eww, Lemon, knock it off," she moaned. She pulled her hand in and tucked it under her pillow, out of the yorkie's reach. "Go find Henry. He'll take you out."

But Lemon seldom followed orders, and with Relic off at college, the small dog was sticking close to Annie these days. Lemon sidled up next to her, nuzzling her small body under Annie's armpit and licking her chin.

Irritated with the persistent dog—she'd become needier than any toddler without her big brother to hang out with, which was how the pet obviously saw Relic—Annie rolled onto her back to escape the incessant licking. But it was hard to stay mad at such a cute face, and who didn't want to wake up to a little love on a Wednesday morning?

She pulled her arm out from under her pillow, bumping a bouncing Lemon out of the way, to feel Henry's usual spot next to her on the bed. The rumpled sheets felt cool to the touch. He'd left her side a while ago, then.

She couldn't even remember him coming to bed. It must have been a late night at the golf course. The guys often played a hand or two of poker after a round of golf and late dinner. It wasn't surprising that she'd slept through his return home. Even though she'd felt a bone-deep exhaustion the night before, following her action-packed day, it had taken her a long time to fall asleep.

She sat up with a start, remembering Ferguson's too-still form on that beach. She caught Lemon and held the wriggling dog against her chest. Poor Ferguson. The strikes kept piling up against him. When she'd gotten home, she called the hospital to check on him. They assured her he was out of the woods. The floor nurse only divulged that much because she knew Annie was the principal at the boy's high school and understood her concern. But she couldn't divulge any additional details.

At least I know he survived.

Lemon struggled against her smothering embrace, so she set the dog on the floor. "Henry! Let Lemon out, will you?"

Lemon ran to their bedroom door, stopped with one ear cocked, then ran back to Annie's side of the bed, yipping.

"Henry? Can you take care of Lemon, please?"

But her only answer was another yip from Lemon.

If she didn't take the dog out, there would be an accident to clean up. A quick glance at her watch told her she didn't have time for that.

Where had Henry disappeared to?

She tossed off the light sheet tangled around her legs and left the bed, grabbing the robe she always kept over the back of her favorite chair. She normally liked to spend a few minutes reading in it before bed each night. Not that she'd used the chair the previous evening. She'd had too much on her mind.

She didn't need the robe—the room felt warm—but the family next door had two kids in middle school, and she couldn't go traipsing around the backyard in her nightgown where her future students might see her.

The house was abnormally quiet as she shuffled down the hallway. Or was this their new normal? Relic's alarm used to buzz about now, often after a third or fourth time of hitting the snooze button. Her youngest was not an early riser.

As she passed his room, a surge of loneliness hit her and she averted her eyes. His empty bedroom was too depressing. Both her child and his alarm clock were an hour away, and since he didn't have class until eleven on Wednesdays, he was likely sound asleep in his lofted bed in his tiny dorm room. Would she ever get used to the fact that none of her three kids officially lived under her roof anymore? Or would at least Relic be back at some point?

Except for a prancing Lemon by the back door, the kitchen was as quiet as the deserted upstairs. The coffee pot was clean and unused.

Where the heck was her husband? He never left for work before seven.

Just then, the back door swung inward, and she had her answer. He'd gone for a run. It was a habit he'd gotten out of in the past few years. Was he trying to get back into it? They'd both need some hobbies, she supposed, now that their days of running kids had ended.

"Morning," she said, more relieved to see him than she would have expected, sweaty hair and all. "I wondered where you disappeared to."

He gave her a quick grin, but then dropped to pet the little dog jumping against his shins. "Hey, girl," he said, trying but failing to scoop her up. It was hard to catch a frantic Lemon.

"Take her out, will you?"

"Sure," he said. He held the screen open for the small dog, then let it slam as he followed her into the backyard.

She got the coffee started before filling Lemon's dish with half of her daily allotment of food. She considered making a pot of oatmeal, but she wasn't much of a breakfast girl. Lunch was a long way off, so she settled for an apple out of the basket on the island.

She bit into her apple and considered what she'd say to Henry about the night before. Her gut told her that his coworker would be quick to tell him he'd spied her at the beach, and she hadn't been alone. Why couldn't people mind their own business?

But she'd kept secrets from Henry before where Michael was concerned, and that never ended well. She didn't feel like there were many benefits to turning fifty, but one was the knowledge that it's best to bring things out into the open in a relationship as soon as possible. When you don't, things fester and cause even more damage.

Lemon bolted back into the kitchen with Henry close behind. The little animal made a mad dash for her food bowl and Henry flung open the fridge door. He stood there so long, looking in, that Annie wasn't sure if he was deciding what to eat or cooling off from his run. A line of sweat ran down the back of his gray T-shirt, and he'd already pulled it out of the waistband of his running shorts.

How would he react if she stepped up behind him and ran her hands up under that shirt? Would he turn to her like he used to, maybe even lift her up and set her on the island in front of him? They had the house to themselves, after all. That used to be a rare occurrence, back when the house was full of kids. Or would he shrug her off, insisting they both needed to get to work? Or worse, would he wrench his back? The thought prompted a smile. She wasn't a slim 115 anymore.

But before she could discover if she could still tempt him, her phone vibrated. She grabbed it from the countertop. "Relic? Why would he be texting us so early? I figured he'd still be in bed."

At the sound of his son's name, Henry shut the fridge and gave her his full attention for the first time that morning. "Do you suppose something's wrong?"

She snorted. "You are worse than an old mother hen." She opened the text to read the whole thing. "Huh. Looks like he sent this to both of us. He's wondering what he's supposed to do about the textbook for his English 101 course. The bookstore is out, and he needs it for class at eleven."

"He should have figured that out yesterday if he needs a specific book this morning."

"Do you want to text him that back, or should I?"

When Henry only shrugged, Annie set her phone back on the island. "Maybe we should let him figure this one out for himself."

As the baby of the family, Relic had yet to master the art of fending for himself. But he'd learn. He wouldn't have a choice. That was one of the many benefits of heading off to college. Kids eventually become independent when they don't have a choice.

"You should answer him," Henry said, clearly conflicted.

"I don't think I will."

He considered this. "All right, then. Tough love. I better go shower."

She almost let him leave the kitchen, but she needed to tell him about Michael before he heard a different version of her evening from his coworker. The discussion wasn't going to be fun, but it was necessary.

"Wait, hon. Do you have a few minutes? There's something I need to talk to you about. A couple of things, actually."

She noticed him check the time on the oven's control panel. "Can it wait? You know we have our eight a.m. meeting on Wednesdays. I can't be late."

Which was precisely why she needed to talk to him before he left the house.

"No, it can't wait. I'll make it quick. Remember what the counselor said? We need to be more open with each other?"

He pulled his T-shirt over his head with a sigh. He wiped his brow with it, then pulled out a stool at the island. She caught a whiff of sweat.

"Not something either of us is very good at." The left corner of his mouth twitched up. "All right. I just need to be out of the shower by 7:30."

She took a deep breath. Where to start?

Henry snagged the last apple from the dish and chomped a big bite out of it. She set hers to the side. It was doing little to quell the butterflies in her stomach. She might as well dive right into the deep end.

"I saw Michael last night."

She noticed the usual hardening in her husband's features at Michael's name, but he took another bite of his breakfast without a word, so she kept going.

"He called. Said there was something he needed to talk to me about. I'd picked up a burger and took it out to the beach by myself to decompress. You know how first days always stress me out. You were at the club, and I needed some fresh air. Time at the lake always revives me."

"What did he want this time?" he asked, ignoring everything else she'd mentioned. He'd asked no questions about how her first day went. Anytime Michael's name came up in conversation, Henry always honed in on that. His insecurities around her ex-husband were the main fuel behind their new foray into couples therapy.

"Actually, he's worried about you."

Henry laughed, his mouth still full of apple. "Michael's worried about *me*? Yeah, right. That would be a first."

If the conversation continued down this vein, they'd accomplish nothing.

Again.

"Henry, can we please have a civil discussion? I don't want to fight."

He took one last bite of the apple, then tossed the core into the trash. "Fine. I'm listening. But I'm not happy about you meeting Michael, all alone, out at the lake."

"Thank you." She tossed her half-eaten apple, but it bounced off the rim of the garbage can and onto the floor. She raised one finger at his grin. "Not one word about that."

She scooped the apple core off the floor before Lemon could get at it, tried it again—successfully this time—and took a seat on a stool next to Henry.

"He brought up your work. And Byron Oaks. He said there are rumors floating around that Byron might not have died from a heart attack. That he'd gotten into some pretty heavy street drugs, and that's what killed him. I'm shocked. Do you know anything about that?"

"Since when do you listen to town gossip, Annie?"

She noticed he didn't answer the question but thought he looked surprised. "Henry, I can't just ignore things people are saying. It's my job to know what's going on in this town if it could impact the safety of my kids at school. And I always consider the source. Regardless of what you think of Michael, you know he'd never idly spread rumors if he didn't think there might be some truth to them."

"Wait, I thought you said Michael was worried about *me*," he said. "But now you're back to talking about you and your work. I'm not following, and I really need to take that shower."

He got off the stool and grabbed his shirt from the island, but she reached out and held his arm.

"Sit down. Please." She was careful to keep her tone neutral. Anytime Henry sensed she was treating him like one of her students, she lost his attention completely. "What do you know about Byron's death? And is there something going on at work that you aren't telling me about?"

Henry threw his shirt over his shoulder but stayed put. "What, specifically, did Michael hear?"

She sighed. "That's the problem. We got interrupted before we got further into our conversation."

"Who interrupted you? I thought you said you were alone out there with him."

She hadn't said that, but Henry had a tendency to assume the worst where Michael was concerned. "We weren't alone. There was a young family out there, letting their kids cool off in the lake. They'd picked up burgers, too. In fact, it was a guy you work with. Norris? I don't remember his first name. You introduced me to him at the picnic last year."

Henry looked like he wanted to say something, but he nodded for her to continue.

"There was also a bunch of high school kids who showed up just after Michael got there. They kept their distance. I recognized a couple of them from school."

"Sounds like the lake is still a happening place in September. Maybe even more fun than the golf course. Maybe *I* should have been the one out there with you."

She wasn't going to let him draw her into an argument. "Believe me, I went out there in search of some quiet, but that wasn't how things turned out. Michael was just getting into why he's worried when one of the kids from school came running up, screaming that another kid was unresponsive and maybe not breathing. They'd headed farther down the beach when they arrived, so we didn't know what was happening."

She could tell she finally had Henry's full attention. "Don't tell me a kid drowned."

Annie thought back to the previous night, shaking her head. "Gabi, the girl who came running, was freaking out, and I know her well enough from school that I took her panic seriously. Michael ran back with her to the group of kids and I stayed on the beach to call for help."

"Was the other family still out there?"

"They'd just left. Oh, Henry, it was awful. Gabi told me a kid named Ferguson was the one in trouble."

Her phone, still between them on the island, vibrated again. It was another text from their son. He was waiting for ideas from them. She gave it only a passing glance. Relic would have to figure it out for himself.

Henry ignored the text, too. "I remember you talking about a boy named Ferguson last year. What happened? Is he all right?"

This surprised her. She always thought he only listened to her work stories with half an ear. An irritating habit, to be sure. "That's right. I helped get him into treatment last spring before the summer break. I even saw him walking into school yesterday morning and took it as a good sign that he might still be doing all right."

Henry picked up her phone, read Relic's second text, then turned the phone face down on the island with a shake of his head. "Your tone tells me this Ferguson kid wasn't actually doing as well as you'd hoped."

Annie closed her eyes and her mind conjured the image of Ferguson that she feared she'd never forget. The boy was lying motionless on the sand, one sandaled foot in an inch or two of water, as Michael performed chest compressions.

"Ferguson took something. When the paramedics arrived, they recognized the signs of an overdose and acted fast to save him."

"Did he survive?"

Annie opened her eyes. The heavy words sounded out of place in the sunny kitchen.

She nodded. "Thanks to Michael. He performed CPR until the ambulance got there."

She braced for some caustic comeback, but he looked relieved. "That's not the first kid Michael has saved."

It was true. Way back, before the complications that clouded the relationships between the three of them, they were just three young people on a mission to help make the world a better place. They'd done some good, too, in those early days.

Annie's gaze traveled to the window above the sink. "Michael followed the ambulance and promised to reach out to Ferguson's dad. I called the hospital when I got home last night. They couldn't tell me much, of course, but I was able to find out that he survived the trip to the emergency room, and the doctor felt hopeful that he'd make a full recovery."

Henry threaded his fingers through hers. "That's a good thing. Annie, you helped save a life last night. Why don't you look happier about it?"

She squeezed his fingers, pulling her gaze back to meet his. "Maybe I could have prevented it. Like I said, I saw Ferguson yesterday morning. I remember feeling a little surprised he showed up for school. That was my gut telling me something still wasn't right with him, and I should have listened. I should have checked in with him during the day. Maybe if I'd talked to him, he wouldn't have been stupid enough to take something."

"Annie, this isn't about you," Henry said as he pulled gently at her hand. "You can't save them all. You are an educator. You work hard to provide an environment where as many kids as possible can benefit from a decent education. Stop thinking your role extends beyond that."

She gently extricated her fingers from his and got to her feet. His advice revealed the vastly different ways each of them approached their work. Henry worked hard at his job but had no problem leaving it all at the office at the end of every day. The kids at her school were human beings, with complicated family and friend dynamics that *impacted* their ability to learn. So, in her mind, helping them in every way she could was part of her job. Not that she had the energy to convince Henry of this. She'd already tried too many times.

"Look, Annie, I appreciate you telling me you saw Michael last night, and I'm sorry that happened to one of your students. But it's getting late. Was there anything else?"

Annie should have felt better about getting her meeting with Michael off her chest. But there was still something worrying her. "Michael just seems to think there might be something happening at your work tied to Byron's death. Maybe even with the way some drugs are finding their way into Ruby Shores. I need you to be honest with me, Henry. Do you know anything at all about that?"

He got to his feet, balled up his dirty shirt in his hands, and met her eye. "I swear, Annie, I do not. But now that you've told me, I'll keep my eyes open. If there is something going on, I'll figure it out."

His answer didn't give her the comfort she'd hoped for. Now her nerves were ramped up with concern over Henry's safety, too. She believed him, but that didn't mean the rumors were wrong.

"Maybe you should talk to Michael," she suggested. "Like I said, we got interrupted, so I don't know if there was more to the rumors."

"Tell you what. Let me handle whatever this is as it relates to work, which I can't believe it would. If I feel the need to call our old *friend*, I will. You need to get ready for work, too. If you almost lost a kid last night, you're going to be busy with damage control today. We can talk more tonight."

With that, he turned on his heel and left the kitchen, tossing his shirt onto the washing machine as he walked past the mudroom. She'd caught the inflection he'd placed on "friend" when he mentioned Michael, and she knew how hesitant he'd be to make that phone call.

Old habits die hard, and avoiding his former best friend at all costs was a deeply ingrained one for Henry.

Chapter Six

Annie stood under the warm stream of her morning shower, her mind flip-flopping between the earliest years of her friendship with Henry and Michael and the modern-day version of their tangled relationship.

She knew Henry was extremely skeptical of a tie between the plant where he worked and a nefarious crime ring, but he'd left the house twenty short minutes after walking out of the kitchen. Maybe his early morning meeting wasn't the only reason he was in a hurry to get to the office. He wasn't the type of person who would ignore a claim like that. He'd do his best to get to the truth.

Annie didn't want to believe it either, but she couldn't just dismiss it.

She closed her eyes as she lathered the shampoo into her hair. Twenty-seven years hadn't dimmed her vivid memories of the time she'd spent abroad—including the shock she'd experienced over the lack of hot, indoor showers. But that trip had given her so much more than an appreciation for indoor plumbing. If she'd never made that trip, she would never have met Michael and Henry.

She smiled, remembering the excitement on her father's face when she'd surprised her family, minutes after her college graduation ceremony, with the news that her summer plans had changed. She was going to Peru.

Her smile grew as she thought further back, to how it all started. A colorful poster, pinned to the billboard inside the front vestibule in the Student Union, changed everything. Her life would look so different today if she'd never spied it there.

With less than a week to go before her last round of college finals, she'd arrived at the Union early on that long-ago spring morning to nab one of the comfortable couches where she'd planned to spend the day cramming. For some reason, she could still remember the scent of a flowering tree she'd passed on her walk from their nearby apartment. Her roommates preferred the library for studying, but Annie focused better with the buzz of activity around her.

Vibrant colors in the flyer had captured her attention. The cobalt sky, punctuated with swirls of thin white clouds, hung above a dusty, rust-hued dirt road on which children walked barefoot, wearing thread-bare clothes that captured her imagination. But it was the soulful eyes of the young girls in the photograph that had grabbed ahold of her heart. The poster issued a powerful personal challenge to Annie. Could she be the one to offer those girls hope?

She had no idea what that might look like, but the flyer invited anyone interested to an informational session, to be held that very afternoon on campus. She remembered glancing down the quiet Union hallway. It was sure to be teaming with students soon. Two people stood a short distance away, locked in an animated conversation. They hadn't even noticed her.

The temperature of her shower fluctuated, and Annie flicked a trail of shampoo away from her eye, remembering how her thumbnail split as she'd hurried to pry the staples out of the corners of that poster. Feeling like a thief but unable to stop herself, she'd folded the glossy paper into quarters and tucked it into her backpack. She couldn't have said why she was so sure she couldn't afford to miss that meeting, nor why she didn't bother to jot down the time and place on notebook paper and leave the poster up for others to see.

She'd already had her first teaching job lined up for September, a position she'd originally considered perfect for her first "adult" job, but a sense of melancholy had settled over her in the final weeks of school. Hadn't she been waiting her whole life to help ease the unfairness in the world? Would she be doing that, teaching science to seventh graders in the small town where she'd grown up?

Or is now the perfect time to go out and explore the world, to really make a difference?

That thought had played through her head time and time again in the days leading up to that morning when she happened across the poster about mission trips to Peru.

When she'd arrived at the informational session, the organizer expressed surprise at the turnout: just two people. Annie still felt the familiar flash of guilt, hot water sluicing over her nearly fifty-year-old body, as she thought back to the way she'd pulled the poster off the wall. Had she robbed others of the same opportunity she'd been looking for? Surely that couldn't have been the only poster on campus. Right?

She'd never know for sure. All she knew was that her spontaneous decision to travel to Peru to help girls like the ones on that poster had a lasting impact on her own life.

The informational session felt like a mere formality, really. The prospect of helping to build a school in a rural area where children weren't receiving a formal education because of where they lived was simply too enticing to pass up. Packing for that three-month trip felt like the realization of one of her oldest dreams.

She would have been willing to give up her new teaching gig to go for a more extended time, but that would have gotten complicated with visas. It also wouldn't have been fair to the administration that was counting on her to start in September. So Peru would only be for three months, and then she'd planned to come back and get started in that *proper* job her mother had been so excited about.

She couldn't have guessed, as she'd boarded that plane for South America, that she wouldn't start teaching in Ruby Shores that following September. It ended up taking her an extra seven years to get started on her career at her high school alma mater. And by then, her entire life had changed.

As Annie squeezed the excess water out of her hair, then worked a thick layer of conditioner into her ends, she remembered how her mother's initial reaction on that long ago graduation day had been the opposite of her father's. But her mother eventually warmed to the idea, too.

Back then, Annie couldn't believe her mother thought of her as too inexperienced to go off on a mission trip to a foreign country. Annie had felt invincible and ecstatic to help others battle things like hunger, oppression, and lack of access to proper education in other parts of the world. But it occurred to her that she'd been younger than Ava was now when she'd broken the news to her mother.

If Ava came to her today to say she was leaving on a mission trip to South America with a bunch of strangers, Annie would do everything she could to change her daughter's mind. Even if Ava—married, pregnant Ava—was still childless and single like Annie had been, her daughter was too unworldly for a trip like that.

"It's funny how our perspectives change," she said, her words echoing through the swirling steam inside the shower stall. She felt the tickle of Lemon's tongue on her toe and gave the waving shower curtain a light kick to discourage the dog from stepping into the stall. Relic didn't mind showering with the dog, but Annie did.

It was indeed funny how perspectives changed. In hindsight, Annie could understand the validity of her mother's concerns. She'd returned from that trip in one piece, but the experience had opened her eyes, and her goals had shifted.

As the conditioner worked its magic, Annie shaved her legs and thought back to those earliest days in the small village in Peru. Her first assigned task had been to help clear construction debris from inside and outside the shell of a building. Originally designed as a canning factory, the construction on it had stalled because of some labor dispute. They'd abandoned the project months before Annie and the other volunteers arrived to help repurpose the building.

Initially, she'd worked beside a quiet young man who'd flown in from Tennessee. His name was Henry. She remembered thinking that Henry must be homesick. He was so quiet. Maybe he'd even left a girlfriend behind. But, on their third day together while hauling out piles of scrap lumber from what would be the school's cafeteria, he finally opened up to her.

The evening before he left for Peru, Henry was out for a walk with his beloved collie. A car sped around a blind corner, barely missing Henry but clipping and killing the dog instantly. The collie had already been battling an aggressive cancer, and likely wouldn't have lived much longer, but the sudden and violent nature of the dog's death devastated Henry.

After the truth behind Henry's mood came out, their friendship blossomed. But the death of his collie had left a deep scar.

Even after all these years, Annie still couldn't believe Henry finally let Relic, their youngest, two years before he would leave for college, talk them into getting Lemon. No matter how hard Ava and Colton had begged through the years, he'd never let them get a dog.

Once Annie's legs were smooth and the conditioner rinsed out, she turned off the shower and pulled a towel from the rack. She would have loved to have had a dog around when she was growing up. Millie, her sister, was allergic to pet dander, so the only pet Annie ever had before Lemon was the beagle Michael adopted six months before Ava was born.

When their marriage fell apart, Annie kept Ava and Colton. Michael kept the beagle.

By the time Michael came back into their lives, Barney was long gone.

Annie hadn't realized how much she'd missed Barney the Beagle. She should try to find an old picture of him. She'd stashed everything she'd kept from that time in her life, aside from the kids' photographs, in her old cedar chest in the basement. She probably should have tossed it all years ago, but doing so felt wrong. Her first marriage may have ended before she'd even had a chance to learn how much work it took to stay married, but that didn't mean she should pretend it never happened.

God knew she'd tried to block the details of her first disastrous marriage from her memories.

She put her watch on and checked the time, realizing she'd need to leave the house soon. She toweled her hair and pulled out the blow dryer. She already missed the more carefree days of summer. As the school's principal, she still went into the office throughout the summer months, but few people were around then, so she'd often skip her hair-and-make-up routine altogether. She didn't feel like she had that luxury during the school year.

As the hot air blasted against her drying hair, thoughts of her old pet, Barney, brought Jackie to mind. Jackie was working her tail off on the new business she was creating from scratch. Annie smiled at the unintended pun. Her old friend's mission was to pair senior dogs with new owners. Jackie's twist was to cater to elderly wannabe pet owners. Too many older people were lonesome, and too many senior rescue dogs went unloved.

Annie still wasn't sure how her friend could earn a decent living in her new venture, but maybe she had more savings tucked away than Annie had personally been able to amass.

She hadn't talked to Jackie since July, when they'd returned from their girls' trip to Maui.

Each of the five women in their group would plan one of those annual trips. As she'd mentioned to Wendy the day before, Annie was next up to play travel agent. They'd already agreed to do something less extravagant in 2020. Hawaii was amazing, but they couldn't all afford to spend so much on a trip that excluded their families every year.

Her hair still felt damp, but it would suffice. She stowed the blow dryer under her vanity and started with her makeup, her actions habit-driven, allowing her mind to continue wandering.

Two weeks earlier, Annie and Henry had met up with her parents for dinner one evening, and the older couple had brought up their winter plans. They owned a second home in Arizona, now that they were retired and officially snowbirds. But they had plans to celebrate their fifty-fifth wedding anniversary in February, leaving their Arizona home empty while they sailed around the southern hemisphere. Her father's expression glowed with excitement when he spoke about the many planned stops on their Caribbean cruise.

A spark of an idea had occurred to Annie during their drive home that evening. Her parents' Arizona house wasn't large, but there were three small bedrooms plus a bonus room. Best of all, there was a saltwater pool in the backyard. She knew that if she asked, her parents would gladly let her use it in their absence.

That was, as long as they hadn't already agreed to let Millie and her husband vacation there.

Annie tossed her mascara into the top drawer and left the bathroom, flicking off the light, hoping Millie hadn't already asked to use the house.

Would a trip to Arizona in February be enough of a getaway for her girlfriends? After all, the only stipulation they'd laid out for the trips was sunshine and water. They'd thrown around the idea of a trip while Annie was on spring break, but her parents would be back by then.

She could use some vacation time if it wasn't during a school break.

She'd check with her folks soon to see if staying in their Arizona house this winter was even possible, then she'd reach out to her friends. Would the girls be interested in a week in the desert? With all five of them having their fiftieth birthdays in the coming months, there was plenty to celebrate.

Her phone buzzed with a text from one of her senior high physics teachers, asking if the rumor he'd heard about Ferguson was true and if the boy was going to be okay. Annie pulled on her ivory linen shirtdress, running her hands over the fabric. Already wrinkled, but it would have to do. She didn't have time to pull out the iron they seldom used anymore.

Day two of the school year promised to be more challenging than day one, and she had to get going.

But she really needed to start planning their girls' trip before too long. If Arizona didn't work out, she didn't know what she'd do. She opened her notes app on her phone and made a note to call Jackie, Kit, Lynette, and Renee, after she talked to her folks.

Maybe she'd even ask Jackie what dogs she was currently trying to place in her business. Annie might be a little younger than her friend's target market, but she was tired of letting Henry keep her from getting the pet she'd wanted for years. Lemon would always be Relic's dog, even when he was away at school, and their son would probably take the yorkie to live with him when he got an off-campus apartment in a year or two. In the meantime, Lemon was lonesome and might benefit from having another dog around.

Annie was lonesome, too, now that Relic was gone.

Last night, when she'd been unable to fall asleep because of the guilt she'd felt over what happened to Ferguson, Lemon had curled up next to her in bed. It was as if the dog could sense that Annie needed companionship. A pet of her own wouldn't make up for her kids being gone, or Henry's regular absences since he traveled overnight for work at least a few times a month, but she'd welcome more noise in the house.

Maybe Jackie could even find her an old beagle to adopt. If she brought home a beagle of her own, she'd have to invest in a set of those doggy steps. Otherwise, she'd still be falling asleep alone after Relic took Lemon.

guy friends

MINNEAPOLIS, MN

1993

Chapter Seven

ANNIE STRUGGLED WITH THE wonky lock on the door to their apartment. The palm of her left hand stung where she'd scraped it on the chipped handrail after tripping over the shell of a frozen pumpkin on the front stairs. If their landlord didn't start handling the pile of maintenance issues that were stacking up, the three of them might have to find a different place to live.

She took a shaky breath and tried the lock again. No luck. Maybe the problem was exhaustion and not the lock. After picking up another extra shift at work, she was practically asleep on her feet. She'd almost missed her bus stop after dozing off in her seat.

She gave the door a frustrated kick, then fell forward when it swung inward. Henry caught her under her arms, effectively halting her forward motion before she could top off her ridiculously long day with a graceless face plant onto the ugly, green shag at their feet.

"Whoa, careful!" His arms remained around her for a beat longer than necessary before he stepped back and shoved his right foot into his battered snow boot. "Good thing for you that I was on my way out. By the way, I swear, I called the super *again,* like I promised, and asked him to fix that door," he said. "But I wouldn't hold your breath."

"If I'd tried to hold my breath waiting on that guy, I'd be dead already." Annie unlaced her own boots. She had to rearrange Michael's worn Converses to make room for all the shoes and boots on the rubber mat. When all three roommates were home, which was rare, someone's footwear would inevitably end up on the shag carpet, adding to the years of grime. "I wish we could afford a better place than this."

Henry zipped his parka and pulled a stocking hat on over his dark curls. "That isn't likely if we want to stay this close to downtown."

Annie knew it was the truth. Most of the time, she enjoyed living so close to the shelter where they all work and to the city's nightlife. An old friend of Michael's had nine months left on his lease for this place when he'd enlisted in the Navy. Rentals were scarce, so when Michael said he knew of a great place they could sublease when they'd returned from Peru, Henry and Annie were quick to agree. When the original nine months were up, the trio signed a new lease after realizing moving would be too expensive.

But now she was starting to question whether she'd made the right decision to commit to another year here. Following Henry and Michael to Minneapolis after their three short months together in Peru was a blast at first, but things were starting to feel a little off between the three of them.

When she'd first told her mother she was moving in with the two boys she'd met in Peru, she'd done her best to calm the woman's fears over the arrangement by promising to never become romantically involved with either. Her mother was so disappointed when she'd given up her teaching job in Ruby Shores.

Maybe her mother had been right.

Had she been foolish to give up her job at the high school in Ruby Shores for this?

Their time in Peru had opened her eyes to the plight of those who suffered extreme poverty. Even though she couldn't stay in that country beyond their mission trip, she'd returned to the States with a burning desire to make a difference closer to home. She'd decided that teaching mostly middle-class kids, back in her hometown, wouldn't allow her to make the impact she craved.

But at least she wouldn't have had to work so many hours just to pay her own bills. Even a teacher's salary sounded like a fortune right now.

"Are you all right?" Henry asked. "You aren't usually down like this. Is it the holiday blues? Maybe you should go home and see your folks, too."

She shrugged. "I'm fine. Just tired. I had to pick up an extra shift today. I was a little short on cash after buying Christmas gifts for my family, and I had to make sure I'd have enough for my share of the rent for January. I'd maybe go home for a day or two, but Mom and Dad and Millie are going to North Dakota for Christmas this year. I can't take that much time off work."

"I'm sorry. I don't like leaving you and Michael here alone while I go traipsing off to Tennessee for our big family Christmas. You guys will probably get bored."

She hung her apartment keys on her designated hook next to the door, biting back a sigh at the barely concealed longing behind his words. She was starting to suspect it wasn't Michael that Henry hated to leave.

When she'd first met Henry and Michael in Peru, the three of them clicked. The guys were already friends, and she fit right in. There were never any romantic undertones in their friendship. At least not any that

Annie had picked up on. She'd finally ended her confusing relationship with Elliott, the boy she'd started dating in high school after allowing him to take her to prom. They'd continue to see each other periodically throughout her college years, but Annie never felt like he was *the one*.

When she'd boarded that jet for Peru, she'd sworn off men.

So, when it was time to return home and Michael and Henry had sat her down to convince her to come work with them in Minneapolis, she agreed to both the detour in her career path and the slightly unconventional living arrangement. They were all just friends. It was the only way any of them could afford to continue to work in the non-profit sector in an expensive city like Minneapolis.

Living with two men was turning out to be more of a challenge than she'd expected. Growing up with one sister and no brothers meant she had little experience in the mannerisms of men. Her father didn't count.

While Henry wasn't as messy as Michael, neither of her male roommates thought anything of leaving the toilet seat up, parking a ten-speed in the living room of their apartment, or walking around in their boxers at any time of day.

By their first Halloween, the three had settled into a routine. All three had realized they needed to supplement their paltry paychecks they earned at the combination food pantry and shelter where they worked with second jobs. The variety of part time gigs meant it wasn't unusual to go days at a time without all three of them being in the apartment at the same time. But they did their best to keep their Friday nights open to go out together.

The threesome eventually expanded their circle to include other young people they met at their various jobs. Even Annie's old friend, Kit, met up with them once in a while to spend a Friday night out on the town.

In fact, it was Kit who brought up the notion that Henry might be starting to see Annie as more than a friend. Annie had told Kit she was being ridiculous. Henry reminded Annie of her old boyfriend, Elliott. Both Henry and Elliott were cute, boy-next-door types. The kind she'd always envisioned marrying someday.

But once Kit planted that seed, Annie started to notice things, too—and not just where Henry was concerned. She would sneak glances at Michael's well-toned abs when he stood in front of their cupboards, scrounging for food in his underwear. Michael seemed like someone her old friend Lynette might date. Not her type at all.

Which was why she'd been feeling so confused lately.

"Don't worry about us. I doubt I'll even see much of Michael. I'm working double shifts, and it seems like he's hanging out with Claudia whenever he has free time."

Michael was casually seeing a girl he'd met at his bartending job. Annie liked Claudia well enough, although she didn't like that she'd walked into the apartment after work one evening in mid-November to the undeniable smell of marijuana. Only Michael and the girl were there, snacking on bags of chips and Ding Dongs in front of the television.

Henry still looked skeptical. "If you're sure," he said, hoisting his knapsack onto his shoulder.

"I'm sure," she said, as much to convince herself as to persuade Henry that she'd survive her lonely holidays. Maybe spending this holiday alone and putting in lots of hours at her waitressing job was the price she had to pay for delaying her return to the world of adulting. "What time is your flight?"

"Midnight. It was my cheapest option." He checked his wrist-watch. "I better hustle, just in case security is busy this close to Christmas."

"I thought Michael was going to give you a ride." She glanced around the small living room. "Where is he?"

"Not sure. He apologized this morning, said something had come up, and hoped it wouldn't be a problem for me to take a cab."

Annie thought of her Toyota, parked at her parents' house, back in Ruby Shores. Parking around here was an expensive hassle, and since she could take the bus anywhere she needed to go, it had seemed like the best solution. "Sorry I don't have a way to give you a lift."

"No worries," he said. "Oh, wait, I forgot to give you something."

He dropped his knapsack and hurried back to the room he shared with Michael, reappearing a minute later with a small wrapped package in hand. "Don't worry, my boots are dry."

Her heart fell when she spied the gift. "Henry, I thought we agreed none of us could afford presents for each other this year."

He thrust the small wrapped package into her hands. "It's just a little something. I'd already bought it for you before we talked about gifts. And it wasn't expensive. I promise. But I don't want you to open it yet. Wait and open it on Christmas Day. That way, I know you'll have at least one thing to open."

She laughed. "Don't worry. Mom and Dad already sent a box of presents over. I stashed them in my room. Michael mentioned getting a package from his father, too. Kit said she'd try to swing by on Christmas Day, since she isn't going back to Ruby Shores this year either. We'll find a few minutes to open gifts together. Don't worry about us."

Still looking uncertain, Henry picked up his bag again. "Fine. But I'm sorry you won't be with your family this year. I guess Christmas will be different for both of us. My taxi is probably down there waiting for me."

She knew part of Henry's unease was because this would be his family's first Christmas without his beloved grandmother, who'd died unexpectedly the previous summer. Impulsively, she hurried to the door and gave him a quick hug. "Have a merry Christmas, Henry. I'll miss you."

She could have kicked herself when she saw a spark of hope ignite in his eyes. He dropped a quick peck on the top of her head, but she stepped away quickly. She didn't want to lead him on.

If Kit was right about his feelings, Annie hated the thought that she might screw up the friendship that she'd come to cherish with Henry.

"I'll miss you, too, Annie." He gave her shoulder one last squeeze before he hurried out, the door banging shut behind him.

CHAPTER EIGHT

"ARE YOU ABOUT READY? We're going to be late!"

"God, Annie, quit yelling!" Michael stepped into the living room with wet hair and his dress shirt half-buttoned. "We aren't even clocking in today. I don't think they'll fault us for being five minutes late to our volunteer shift."

Annie tapped her foot, impatient to get going. "But you know how many people will line up for their Christmas Eve dinner. It isn't fair to keep them waiting."

Once he'd buttoned his shirt, Michael dropped onto the couch to pull on a pair of socks he'd tucked into his pocket. "I thought Kit was coming with us. Don't we have to wait for her?"

"Change of plans for her," Annie said, shrugging into her winter jacket. "Her Aunt Marge called and invited her home for Christmas. I guess neither of her brothers are going to be in Ruby Shores, and her Grandma Hazel was feeling bad about that. Marge and her husband are going to host Hazel and Kit."

He grinned. "That sounds like a rocking good time for Kit."

She hated the way her heart hitched when he smiled like that. "It'll be nice for her, Michael. Christmas is supposed to be about family."

"Tell my dad that," he said, grabbing his coat off the back of a nearby kitchen chair.

She knew Michael hadn't grown up in what anyone would consider a traditional family environment, so it was hard for him to understand the appeal of things like the holidays. As his friend, maybe her gift to him this year could be to show him how much fun Christmas could really be when you put in a little effort.

Annie hummed the melody to "Silent Night" as she pulled the last tray of freshly washed cups out of the industrial-size dishwasher, careful to avoid the hot steam. She smiled at the ruby color of the murky plastic cups.

"All locked up," Michael said as he strolled back into the kitchen with a dishrag draped over his shoulder. "Hey, you did fast work in here. Where's Tim? And why are you smiling like that? You look like you have a secret."

She laughed. "I was smiling at the red cups. Today is the only day these old things look remotely festive."

He stared at her with a confused look on his face.

"I sent Tim home," she continued, choosing to ignore his lack of imagination. "His three-year-old goes to bed at seven, and apparently it's a family tradition to open their gifts tonight instead of tomorrow morning."

Michael nodded. "Good idea. He should be with his kid." He took the dishwashing rack full of red cups and placed it on the top of the stack of dishes. "This was fun tonight. I checked the tally board. Believe it or not, we served over five hundred and fifty people. We made a differ-ence tonight, Annie."

"We did, didn't we?"

Then she remembered her idea. Michael had his issues, just like they all did, but his mission in life was to help the less fortunate, and he made time to do that. If not for him, she knew she'd already be back in Ruby Shores, living a safe and predictable life. There was nothing wrong with that, of course, but she'd also dreamed of help-ing those in need for as long as she could remember. Together, along with other volunteers at the shelter, she and Michael had helped many people experience a moment of holiday generosity tonight.

Michael deserved to experience a touch of Christmas magic, too.

"I can't believe that guy just *gave* us this little tree!"

Annie laughed in response as she hurried a few steps ahead to make sure Michael didn't trip on the frozen pumpkin. It would take either a chisel or a thaw to remove that tripping hazard.

She *could* believe it. Christmas often brought out people's gener-ous sides. The scrawny pine reminded her of the notorious tree in the *Charlie Brown* Christmas special. It wasn't likely anyone would have bought the poor thing on Christmas Eve anyway, and this saved the guy the trouble of disposing of it himself. But Annie thought it was perfect.

After leaving the shelter, Michael had suggested stopping in for a burger and nightcap at one of the bars they frequented, but Annie had other ideas. Instead, they'd feasted on soft pretzels dipped in melted butter and sprinkled with cinnamon and sugar, which they'd washed down with peppermint hot chocolate.

When Michael complained about the lack of substance, Annie was quick to remind him that sugar overload was all part of the perfect holiday celebration. She'd dragged him around the downtown city blocks, dodging frantic shoppers in their quests to pick up adequate, last-minute gifts. As a light snow fell, beautiful decorations, mounted high atop light poles and gracing window displays, appeared even more magical.

They even rented skates and took a few spins around an open-air rink while tinny holiday tunes spilled out of old box speakers set up next to the ice. He'd been impressed with her graceful technique, and she'd told him about the years of extra dance classes she'd taken as part of her demanding gymnastics training.

Michael surprised her with his good-natured acceptance of each clichéd activity she suggested, joking that he felt like a star in their own personal classic holiday movie. It wasn't until she pointed to a nearly empty Christmas tree lot, a block off one of the main streets, that he put up any resistance.

"Annie, don't be ridiculous. There's nothing decent left and we don't even have any decorations at the apartment. We'll just have to throw the dumb thing out in a couple of days anyhow."

But she'd always felt a pang of sadness for the less-than-perfect trees; the leftovers that didn't get picked to go home with someone for Christmas. Maybe they reminded her of the heartbreak she'd felt when she wasn't selected to attend the regional gymnastic meet at the end of her sophomore season in high school. An injury had sidelined her for months, and while the coach could have taken her as an alternate, he picked one of the younger girls instead. She'd decided that was her last season. After the fanfare she'd enjoyed earlier in her gymnastics career, the fizzle she ended on left her feeling defeated.

She'd spied the sparse tree Michael was now wrestling up their apartment stairs in a back corner of the lot. The beam from a nearby security light highlighted its soft needles while throwing the imperfections into shadow.

"Michael, you're always looking out for the underdog. Think of this sweet tree as the lot's underdog. It needs a loving home."

Her excitement wore not only Michael down, but the shop owner, too, when they'd discovered neither of them had any cash remaining in their pockets after their treats and skating.

After guiding her roommate safely up their apartment stairs, Annie struggled again with their door.

"I don't understand why you have so much trouble with that lock," Michael said from behind the tree he held upright in the dingy hallway.

"My key doesn't work," Annie said, giving it another try. Then, as if a magical elf had touched a finger to the mechanism, her key turned like it was in butter.

Together, they rearranged their tiny living room to make room for their tree in a corner where it wouldn't block the path to their equally small kitchen.

Michael stepped back, bumped Henry's ten-speed with his foot, and had to scramble to keep the bike from tipping over and causing more chaos. "Well . . . there," he said, once he'd righted the bike again. "There's your Christmas tree. Now what do we do with the damn thing? We don't even have any lights or decorations."

But he was wrong. They just needed to get creative.

Thirty minutes later, they sat side by side on the shag carpet, their backs propped against the hand-me-down couch and their stockinged feet on the old white sheet Annie had wrapped around the tree's trunk as an impromptu skirt. White lights twinkled in the semidarkness and the scent of pine danced around them.

"We should leave the lamps off in here until New Year's," she said as she inhaled deeply.

"I can't believe you had those lights in your room."

She smiled. "Michael, they've hung around the bulletin board above my desk since we moved in here."

He casually dropped his arm across the threadbare cushion behind her head. "You've never invited me into your bedroom. *Yet.*"

She almost missed the whispered word. "Yet?" she repeated.

If she'd given it even one second of thought, she would have ignored his comment. Instead, the relaxed atmosphere that followed them home from their downtown Christmas activities evaporated. The air took on a charge that wasn't there when they'd first settled onto the floor in front of their tree.

Annie had no idea if Michael sensed the shift, but she did, and she stared intently at one of her handmade ornaments. She'd created it by cutting an angel out of a Christmas card—the one from her parents, apologizing again for leaving home over the holidays. She reminded herself of her promise to her mother to never allow any romantic entanglements with either of her male roommates. The look in her mom's eyes still haunted her, as if the woman knew it was a promise her daughter could never be able to keep, even if she had meant the words she uttered in the moment.

She hated it when she proved her mother right.

Had Michael's thigh been pressing against hers ever since they'd sat down, or did he move it there on purpose?

She sat perfectly still, frozen as solid as the ice they'd skated on earlier.

Then he was up and the contact disappeared, giving her a chance to catch her breath.

"Where are you going?"

Even she could hear the breathless quality in her voice.

"I forgot—I have something for you."

She groaned. *Not him, too.* Why didn't they take their promises to not exchange gifts seriously? Now she'd look cheap. Again.

Michael returned. He held something in his left hand, wrapped in a towel.

"If that's a present, Michael, I can't accept it. We said no gifts." She didn't point out the stark contrast between the wrapping he'd chosen in the spur of the moment versus the elegantly wrapped gift Henry had left for her. But it was a quintessential example of how different the two of them were.

He shrugged as he took his seat beside her again. This time, his thigh definitely pressed against hers, and it was no accident. "You're the one playing up Christmas tonight. I know what you're doing, too. Don't think you can fool me. I know you feel sorry for me because I didn't get to have the Christmases you grew up with when I was a kid, so you tried to make it up to me tonight."

She hated the heat she could feel crawling up her neck and onto her cheeks.

He set his towel-wrapped offering in her lap, and his hand brushed against the underside of her breasts. She couldn't tell if it was an accident or not.

"Shouldn't I wait and open this in the morning? I have gifts from my parents I was going to open, and you said you have one from your dad." She wasn't sure why she didn't mention Henry's gift.

She stole a glance at his expression. His smile made him look so young and innocent, like a little kid excited to give someone a present they'd picked out all by themselves.

"No," he said. "I picked this up for you a while ago. I'm tired of waiting to see if you like it."

Was his stomach turning in slow circles just like hers?

"Come on, Annie," he said, giving her shoulder a little shake.

She hadn't noticed that he'd put his arm back behind her head again.

"Oh, fine," she said, allowing his boyish charm to win her over.

She unrolled the towel and gasped at the wooden tube that remained in her lap. She didn't have to hold it up to her eye to know what he'd given her.

"A kaleidoscope? But how did you know I like these?"

He laughed. "I know more about you than you give me credit for, Annie. I pay attention. Hold it up to the light. I bet the lights on the tree will make the colors pop."

They did. It was like viewing priceless royal jewels, displayed on black velvet, behind the glass.

"It's gorgeous . . ." She sighed, mesmerized, as she spun the wooden tube and watched as the patterns inside shifted into another glorious arrangement.

"Just like you."

His whisper didn't penetrate her happy surprise right away. When the words reached her consciousness, she slowly lowered his gift to her, choosing instead to stare at the angel ornament. But it wasn't enough.

She finally looked at him, knowing she was about to break her promise.

"This is the prettiest kaleidoscope I've ever seen. You can't afford something like this. Where did you get it?" she asked, trying to maintain her wits while knowing it was a battle she didn't really want to win.

He shifted to face her, and she almost sighed with disappointment when his thigh pulled away from hers. "Don't you remember when you told us all about your days at summer camp and the way you and your friends called yourselves the Kaleidoscope Girls? You and Kit and the others? And you told us how, someday, you wanted to have a whole wall in your house filled with a big collection of these. I thought this one would be a nice addition."

She turned the smooth wooden tube, about as long as her forearm, around and around in her hands. Two thin gold lines ran through the dark grain, forming decorative circles near both ends. It was an amazing piece of art.

"It's perfect. But, Michael, it's too much. I can't accept this. And I can't afford to pay your third of the rent because you spent all of your money on this thing." She tried to press it back into his hand—a hand that had somehow found its way to her knee without her noticing.

"Don't worry. I picked it up in Peru. There was a guy who wanted to trade me something for two pairs of Levi's that I'd packed. I knew it would be too hot for me to wear them down there, but my dad told me before I left that people will sometimes pay lots of money for things we take for granted in America. I was waiting for the right time to give it to you."

Some of her anxiety over his generous gift evaporated, and she giggled. "This cost you two pairs of jeans?"

"Sure did. And you're worth it." He looked into her eyes, and as his grin slipped away, his gaze traveled down to her lips.

"Michael . . . we shouldn't."

He looked up at the tree, at the narrow space between the couch and her makeshift tree skirt, his grin coming back even wider. His eyes sparkled with a dare in the glow of twinkling white lights.

"Why not?"

"Because it'll complicate things."

She held the kaleidoscope between them, as if that would ever be enough to stop what now felt inevitable.

"Life *is* complicated. We can never avoid that," he said, his voice deep with a wanting she'd never heard from him before. "Here, let me set that someplace safe."

She felt as if his words were casting some kind of magical spell over her, and so she allowed him to drag the kaleidoscope out of her hands. He got to his knees, gently set her gift beneath the tree, and pulled her up onto her knees, facing him. He inched forward until they touched from their chests to their thighs, bending his head toward hers as if he was about to kiss her. She closed her eyes in anticipation, but the kiss didn't come.

"Merry Christmas, Annie," he whispered. "I've thought about this moment for so long. Almost since the first day I met you. Are you going to invite me into your bedroom now?"

Her eyes flashed open. Things were moving too fast.

His arm slipped behind her waist, and he pulled her tighter against him. "Because that would be the most precious gift you could ever give me."

She felt like she was caught up inside one of her beloved kaleidoscopes, and the hands of fate had just rotated enough to shift everything. With a single nod, she got to her feet and reached for his hand, frightened that she was about to give this man so much more than a simple Christmas gift.

She was about to hand over a piece of her heart.

CHAPTER NINE

ANNIE SHOULD HAVE FELT guilty when she woke on Christmas morning in Michael's arms. She'd broken an important promise to her mother. Instead, despite the blustery weather beyond the apartment windows, she woke feeling warm and happy. She'd had sex before, but she'd never spent an entire night with someone. When Michael's stirring woke her before the sun was even up, she lay motionless, waiting for the first wave of regret to hit. But it didn't.

Until three weeks later, when she realized her period was late.

She sat on the edge of the bathtub in her childhood home, blinking fast to clear the tears that were making it hard to read the results on the test window.

Banging on the bathroom door knocked her out of her fog.

"Annie! Are you about done in there? Dad needs to check in by eight and I still need to get ready! If you aren't out of there in five minutes, I'm going to find that old nail and unlock the door myself."

She heard her sister shuffle back toward her old bedroom. Her gaze found the trusty alarm clock that still sat on the back of the stool. Millie was right. They needed to get moving.

That clock had pushed them to hurry in the bathroom ever since Annie was in grade school. A wisp of a memory surfaced, clouded in a haze of hairspray and perfume. She'd gotten ready for her senior prom in here alongside her closest friends. The Kaleidoscope Girls. They'd been so young. So full of hope. Their escorts that night were a hodgepodge of friends, coworkers, and even one blind date.

Prom—that had been her first official date with Elliott. He was a year younger, and though her friends didn't tease her, she knew they thought she was too quick to say yes when he'd asked. Their tumultuous relationship would continue in different forms throughout Annie's college years—until they ended just before Peru—but she remembered most of their times together with fondness. Still, Annie had always felt like something was missing from their relationship. It was the reason she ultimately ended things with Elliott.

She liked to secretly blame Lynette for her conviction that she needed something more from a man than Elliott had to offer, though she'd never admitted that to anyone.

Lynette's prom date had been a guy named Storm. His ridiculous name still made Annie smile, almost six years after the fact. Storm was older than the rest of them. Lynette met him through work. He was the kind of guy Annie's own parents would have never let her date in high school. He wore black from head to toe, drove a big pickup truck, and liked to party.

Annie thought he was sexy as hell, but she wouldn't have had the nerve to actually date him, even if Lynette hadn't already asked Storm to be her date.

Elliott, on the other hand, was an easy conquest. He was a nice boy from an equally nice family, and he was cute. Plus, she always knew he was a little in awe of her and her willingness to go out with him. He'd admitted to feeling like she was out of his league.

It occurred to her that the differences between safe Elliott and sexy Storm were strikingly similar to the contrast between Henry and Michael.

Was Michael her Storm? Her "bad boy"?

She sure as hell hoped not, given what she held in her hand.

She was carrying his baby.

Storm had disappeared from Lynette's life after some end-of-senior-year drama. What if Michael vanished, too?

A lighter tap sounded on the door. "Honey, are you about done? Your father is getting nervous about being late, and your sister is complaining over her coffee about still needing to put on her makeup."

She jumped at the sound of her mother's voice. She looked from end to end across the cluttered vanity countertop, then back to the pregnancy test in her hand. Would her mom ever forgive her for breaking her promise in such a monumental way?

"Don't worry, Mom. We won't make him late," she cried.

Quickly, she scooped the box and instruction sheet for the home pregnancy test back into the bag. She'd have to be careful. She couldn't let her mom or Millie see any of this. She needed time to process things before she told anyone else.

Michael deserved to be the first one she talked to, even though she'd much rather run to Kit and bawl in her friend's arms the minute she got back to Minneapolis.

What was she going to do?

All she knew for sure was that today needed to be about her dad. The mess she'd managed to make of her own life would have to wait.

They'd been able to repair her father's heart issues, at least for the time being, through an outpatient procedure. That very same evening, Millie had said her goodbyes. She had her new husband to get home to.

Good riddance, Annie had thought. She desperately needed quiet time.

She wasn't as anxious to leave as her sister, deciding instead to stay at home for at least one more week. She didn't want to go back to the apartment; that meant confronting her mistakes, and she wasn't ready to do that yet. It wasn't like they'd fire her from either of her two jobs, anyway. The shelter was always woefully short-staffed. Few people would work in downtown Minneapolis for the low wages the organization could afford to pay. And while she was still relatively new waiting tables, the restaurant's repeat customers loved her.

No, she wasn't worried about losing her job if she stayed in Ruby Shores for an extra week or two.

But she was worried about losing the friendship of two great guys. Henry's interest in her was more apparent than ever, and Michael had started acting like nothing had changed between the two of them the minute their third roommate walked back through their apartment door on New Year's Day.

She reached up to touch the cardboard tube of her very first kaleidoscope, the one she'd made at camp. It had sat on the shelf above her childhood desk ever since that long ago summer, and was the same one Michael had referenced on Christmas Eve. Then her hand moved down to her old desktop to finger the enamel globe she'd attached to her keychain—Henry's gift to her—remembering the kind message he'd included on the small card. He'd been honored to work beside her in Peru building that school, he'd written, and he hoped to work beside her spreading more light around the world. It would have been corny coming from anyone other than Henry. But he was sincere: he wanted to impact the world positively, just as much as Michael did.

How could she travel the world doing important work to improve humanity with a little kid in tow?

"I can't," she whispered, collapsing onto her old, lumpy mattress, eyeing her small collection of kaleidoscopes and thinking back to the beautiful scope Michael had given her. She'd decided, then and there, that she would have this baby and raise it herself—alone even, if that ended up being her only option.

At least she had eight months to figure things out.

Why had she been so excited to reach adulthood? She no longer felt as sure of herself as she had that spring day a year and a half ago when she'd announced to her family that she was leaving for Peru. Suddenly she didn't want to be an adult at all. She wanted to go back to her carefree college days, where the biggest thing she had to worry about was whether she passed an exam or made Elliott angry again.

But that, of course, wasn't possible.

When her father had offered to drive her back to Minneapolis, she'd told him she'd decided she needed the flexibility of having her car. He incorrectly assumed this must mean she was doing better financially, and she hadn't corrected him.

She sighed as she sat back up on her bed, knowing she'd break his heart with her news later. But there were other people to tell first. Decisions to be made.

It was time to head back to Minneapolis.

She was surprised when the lock on their apartment door didn't give her any trouble. Maybe she was finally getting the hang of living here.

Michael and Henry hadn't known when to expect her back. Both looked surprised to see her when she let herself in. She'd walked in on her roommates playing a video game. Henry pushed off the couch and offered to take the heavy bag from her shoulder. She gladly allowed him to take it. When he disappeared into her room, Michael gave her nothing more than a quick glance and a "Hey" before turning his attention back to the television screen.

Before she could think too much about his less-than-welcoming behavior, the stench of old garbage wafted up her nose. She dropped everything else she'd carried up, kicked off her boots, and rushed for the bathroom, not caring that their outer door was still wide open behind her.

She'd barely closed the bathroom door before she retched, the suddenness of it leaving her weak and shook.

The doorknob rattled and Henry's concerned voice reached her where she lay, curled up on the cold tile in front of the toilet, mortified. She'd puked in the apartment before when the boys were there, but that was after a night of too much blackberry brandy, compliments of a new signature drink Michael had attempted to perfect for his bartending gig.

This was different, obviously. But they might believe she had the flu or food poisoning.

When she didn't reply, Henry let himself in. He dropped beside her and touched her forehead. "Hey. Are you all right? Did you get sick?"

She sighed. If the sound hadn't given her away, the smell of vomit would have by now. She forced herself to get to her knees so she could reach up and flush the toilet, then sank down with her back against the wall.

"You shouldn't be in here," she said, embarrassment making her face burn.

"I was worried about you," he said. He got back to his feet, grabbed a clean washcloth from the narrow linen closet beside the door, and soaked it in cold water. "Here. This always helps me when I get sick."

She snatched the cloth from him, then dropped her head to hide her face against her bent knees. "Please. Can I have some privacy? I'll come out in a few minutes. I'm fine. I promise."

He hesitated, as if unsure what to do, then left the room without another word, closing the door gently behind him.

Naturally, it would be good old, empathetic Henry rushing in to check on me, and not Michael, she thought. *What was I thinking, allowing this to happen? This is all Michael's fault.*

She laid the washcloth across her knees, not caring that her jeans were getting wet, and let her head fall back down. The cool moisture felt nice.

She heard voices beyond the bathroom door but couldn't make out what the two of them were talking about. After giving herself a few minutes to make sure the nausea had passed, she brushed her teeth and went back out into the living room. Henry was on the couch, playing the game, but Michael was nowhere to be seen.

"Where did Michael go?"

Henry nodded toward the kitchen. "He took the garbage out, then he headed down to the shelter to help serve dinner. After that, he's headed to the club to work. He closes tonight. I'm sorry neither of us remembered to take out the trash. Can I run down to the store and pick you up some crackers? Or 7 Up?"

During the final half hour of her drive, she'd decided she'd tell Michael right away. She couldn't stand the fear of how he'd react. She'd learned years ago, as a competitive gymnast, that it was best to face your fears, right up front. Otherwise they could paralyze you. But he'd taken off while she writhed on the bathroom floor, and now she'd have to wait.

Maybe she should go see Kit. Kit was a scientist and never one to shy away from things related to the body. Annie remembered how she'd calmed the nerves of their friend Jackie when she got her first period at summer camp.

Kit wouldn't judge her. Though she would be disappointed when Annie admitted that the first time she'd had sex with Michael, they hadn't even thought to use a condom. They'd used protection on subsequent days, but now she knew that was too little, too late.

A wave of dizziness hit, and she gripped the back of the closest chair. Even if Kit was available, Annie wasn't in any shape to drive twenty minutes to see her. But if she could get Henry out of the apartment, she could at least call her friend.

"Actually, that would be great, Henry. Millie was sick at Mom and Dad's. I must have caught the flu from her. I'm sorry if I brought the crud back here to you and Michael."

"No problem." He tossed the game controller to the side and headed for the door.

"Take my car," she said. "I've got some work things coming up, so I thought I better drive it back. It's too cold for you to walk down to the store."

Henry shot her a surprised look, but he grabbed the keys and headed out, promising to be right back.

A deep breath helped her feel steadier on her feet. She headed for her bedroom, peeked out the window to make sure Henry wasn't running back inside for something, then picked up the extension next to her bed.

It took five rings, but Kit finally picked up.

By the time Henry got back with the crackers, Kit knew everything and was on her way over.

Chapter Ten

ANNIE HOPED TODAY WOULD finally be the day when she'd catch Michael alone in the apartment. She'd been trying for three weeks. Kit had assured her there was still time before her pregnancy started to show, but that did little to settle her nerves. A stop at the free clinic near the shelter where she worked provided confirmation that the home pregnancy test was accurate.

When Michael saw her come in, he abandoned a half-eaten bowl of cereal on the counter and disappeared into his bedroom, shutting the door in her face with nothing but a curt hello.

He was avoiding her, and she was tired of it. It was as if their magical time together over Christmas was nothing more than a dream she'd conjured up. But her right hand flitted to her stomach, where proof to the contrary lay deep inside her.

She followed him into the boys' bedroom without bothering to knock.

He was flat on his back, eyes trained on the ceiling. She kicked a hoodie out of the way as she strode to the foot of his unmade bed. She noticed Henry's half of the room was noticeably neater, though he'd left his bed mussed, too.

"What do you want, Annie?"

She wasn't sure what stung more: the fact that he didn't even bother to look at her or the monotone of his voice.

"How long are you going to keep ignoring me, Michael? I don't understand why you are acting this way."

"I don't know what you're talking about."

She was done with the games. She slapped his foot out of the way so she could sit on the end of his bed. "Michael, we have to talk."

He sighed, then rolled onto his side and propped his head up on one hand, squinting at her with a look that felt accusatory. "Why? What's there to talk about? You made your decision, and I can accept that. I admit, it surprised me after . . . you know . . . what happened between us. But it's a free world. It's not like I would ever force you or anything."

The tickle of nausea, now all too familiar, burned the back of her throat. She couldn't be sure if his confusing comment was the culprit or if the musty odor of unwashed laundry was to blame. Two deep breaths helped the sensation subside enough for her to speak.

"Force me to do what? If you're referring to what happened between us at Christmas, I never thought you forced me to do anything."

He flopped onto his back again and resumed his infuriating upward gaze, as if he were enjoying stargazing on a warm summer night, without a care in the world, rather than annoying the hell out of her. "Oh, I know. You were more than willing to have sex with me when Henry was out of town. But, hey, who am I to judge? It was fun."

For a moment, she had the disconcerting sensation she sometimes felt when she tried to hold a conversation with one of the less lucid residents at the shelter. This was an important discussion, though. It might be better to start over, because she and Michael were clearly on different pages. He was acting like he was mad at her about something. Did he regret their time together that much? If that was the case, the news she had to share with him was going to be even harder for him to hear than she'd thought.

She stood, arms clasped around her midsection. "Michael, please . . . would you at least sit up? I have something to tell you, and it's important."

He slapped his mattress with both hands and sat up with a heavy sigh. "If you're here to tell me you're pregnant with Henry's baby, then let me save you some time. Fine. Congratulations. I'm happy for both of you. You just better make damn sure that kid is his and not mine."

This time deep breathing didn't work. The chicken noodle soup and saltines she'd eaten for lunch came back up, and she barely made it to the garbage can beside Michael's bed before she vomited.

She sank toward the floor with a moan, eyes squeezed tight in mortification, and then tipped onto her side to avoid the duffle bag under her. At least her head landed on something soft.

"Shit, Annie," Michael cried, the bed creaking behind her. He hopped down beside her and gently lifted her head into his lap, stroking her hair. "I'm sorry. That came out all wrong. I've just waited so long for you to say something about this, and I admit I was hurt and angry at first. But now I'm resigned to the fact that you picked Henry over me. I've already started looking for a new place and I'll be out by the end of the month. You two will need room."

Could pregnancy make a woman delusional? Because she wasn't able to follow a word of what Michael was saying.

"I'm sorry I threw up in your garbage can."

His hand paused for a moment, then went back to stroking her hair, almost like he was trying to calm a nervous puppy. He let out a short laugh. "That's okay, that one's Henry's. Those were his underwear your head landed on, too."

Suddenly, his touch was too much. It was all too much. She sat up and scooted as far away from him as the crowded bedroom would allow.

"You know I'm pregnant?"

He nodded. "Henry told me."

"*Henry* knows I'm pregnant?"

The change in Michael's expression made him look as confused as Annie felt.

"Ugh," she moaned as she used the bed to pull herself back up to standing. "Look, I don't know what Henry told you, but whatever it was, it couldn't have been the truth. I've never even talked to him about what happened between the two of us when he was in Tennessee. And I sure as hell never slept with him. Why would I tell him I was pregnant? I'd never tell him before I told you."

"You aren't pregnant, then?" he said, looking up at her from the floor. "God, you have no idea what a relief that is. When he first told me, I worried maybe I was the one who got you pregnant. I never said anything to Henry about what happened between us, either."

She held up her hands in a time-out signal. "Michael, stop talking. You've got things all wrong. Come on. Let's go out to the kitchen table and have an adult conversation about what's really going on."

She turned to go, remembering to grab the trash basket on the way out. Footsteps outside their apartment door stopped her in her tracks. She held her breath, praying Henry wasn't home early. They faded away as someone headed elsewhere in the building.

Michael came up behind her and took the smelly can from her hand. He crossed through their kitchen, and it took him a few tugs before the frozen door to their tiny balcony slid open. He stashed the can outside.

"We'll throw the whole thing after it freezes," he said. "I think I'll leave this open for a few minutes."

"Good idea," she said. Henry might not appreciate them throwing away his trash can, but if he'd lied to Michael without even knowing the truth, she didn't care what he thought.

"Can I get you something to drink? I suppose a beer is out of the question, if you're sick, but I'm not sure we have much else in here," Michael said as he pulled open the refrigerator door.

He always was the best host of the three of them anytime they had friends over. She supposed it was why he was so good at his bartending job.

"No, thanks." He really wasn't getting it. She did need a glass of water, though.

Once seated with their drinks of choice, Annie got straight to the point. "Michael, I *am* pregnant, and you are, without a doubt, the father. There has never *ever* been anything more than friendship between me and Henry, regardless of what he might have told you."

Michael was seldom speechless, but her blunt delivery seemed to have whisked any quick retort clean out of his mind. He'd been about to take a sip of his beer, but the bottle never made it to his lips.

She gave him time to process the news. It was only fair. She'd been gnawing on the situation for much longer.

He stared at his bottle, stealing an occasional glance at her, as if weighing for himself the legitimacy of her words.

When he shivered, his tank and shorts offering little protection from the cold air wafting through the patio door, she left him to shut it herself. "Henry might want his garbage can back."

"I'm pretty sure I don't give a damn what Henry wants," he said before chugging half the bottle of beer in a few healthy swallows. "He *lied* to me?"

She shrugged. "Sure sounds that way. Which surprises me. I've always considered Henry to be trustworthy."

"You say that like *I'm* not. Which might be a problem for you if you *are* having my baby. Unless you aren't going to keep it?"

She reminded herself to stay calm. Now she suspected Michael's apparent indifference toward her ever since she'd learned she was pregnant was because Henry had lied to him. In the time that she'd known Michael, he'd always been decent to her. To Henry, too. This would be upsetting news to anyone.

"I'm keeping it," she said. She wasn't sure of much right now, but that was the one thing she knew for sure.

"And you are positive it's mine?"

She sipped her water and nodded. She'd spent the better part of three days in this very apartment, having a very merry Christmas with this man, but they'd only ever been friends leading up to that stolen weekend and they made no promises after. He had a right to ask that question.

"There's been no one else in almost a year."

"But Henry said you two—"

She slapped the table. Water inside her glass dribbled over the edge, but she ignored it. "Henry has only ever been my friend. There is nothing going on between us, Michael. There never has been. I admit that in the month leading up to his trip back home, I was picking up some signals that he might be interested in more. But I never really considered it, mostly because of what I promised Mom."

"Your mom?"

She hadn't meant to bring that up. It made her feel like a child, making promises to her mommy. "Never mind."

"No, I want to hear what you promised your mom."

His grin was infectious.

"Fine," she said, unable to keep her expression neutral. "Mom was worried about me living with two very hot guys—her words, not mine—and I had to promise her I'd never get romantically involved with either of you. Never mind. It's stupid."

"Your mom thinks I'm *hot*?" The flirtatious wiggle of his eyebrows couldn't quite mask the blush on his cheeks.

"Oh, stop!" He had her laughing now. "Come on. We have lots we need to talk about. To decide."

"Fine. You're right. We do. But I have to know why a woman your age has to make your mom any kind of promise when it comes to who you choose to live with. You're an adult. Why would she even care?"

Annie pinched the bridge of her nose—something she found herself doing often, as it helped calm her unsettled stomach. That one question encapsulated so many of the differences between how she and Michael had been raised. How could she even consider raising a child with him? Would that even be something he'd want to do?

"My parents paid my share of both my deposit and my first month's rent here. They had a legitimate say in things."

He looked skeptical, but he let it go. "I suppose I should have caught on when you puked after getting home from your dad's procedure. But we *used* a condom?"

She suppressed another sigh. Telling Kit that she'd accidentally gotten pregnant from a one-night stand with one of her roommates—or, technically, a three-night stand—was so much easier than discussing this with Michael.

"Michael, girls get sick and throw up just like anyone else. We don't only throw up when we're pregnant, so I wouldn't have expected you to guess. And, yes, we used a condom, *except* for the first time."

He slid his beer bottle out of the way and laid his head down on the table.

Annie wished she could read his mind.

He gave two quick raps on the table, then sat up, his eyes finding and holding hers. "If you want to keep our baby, then I want to help you raise it. And I want to marry you. Before the baby is born."

She shoved her chair back from the table, shocked at his words. "I don't expect you to do that, Michael. We aren't even dating. Look, I'll never regret what we did, and I'll never call this child a mistake, but he or she is all I can handle right now. The only type of relationship I want to have with you, at least for now, is to learn how to be parents together."

He got to his feet and rounded the table, sinking onto his knees in front of her. He grabbed her hands and kissed her knuckles. "Come on, Annie. For once in your life, be spontaneous. I've told you before that I hate that my parents were never really together, never married, and that my birth mother took off a month after I was born. She left me to be raised by my inept father. I swore that if I ever became a father, I'd do it differently. Better. Let's do this together, Annie. We'll have the adventure of our lives."

She could feel her resolve swaying under the onslaught of his words, his dancing eyes, and those deep dimples.

He was wrong about one thing. She could be spontaneous. Spontaneity had sent her to Peru, then to say yes to rooming with two guys she'd only known for three months, and finally into his arms in front of the mesmerizing lights of their sparse little Christmas tree.

Would saying yes to his spontaneous proposal really be the adventure of a lifetime, or would it turn out to be one of the biggest mistakes of her life?

Sometimes you have to take the leap to find out.

Chapter Eleven

Before she was mother to two miniature humans, Annie enjoyed stormy summer nights. Rain on the rooftop soothed her, put her to sleep even.

She remembered the relief a storm would bring to their one-room cabin on a miserably hot night at summer camp. Wendy, her favorite counselor, used to let them pull their blankets and pillows off the bunk beds and gather in a circle on the floor. The only light inside the cabin would come from her flashlight as she held it under her chin and told them stories of ghosts and goblins and things that went bump in the night. Thunder made the glass panes in the windows vibrate. All these years later, the screeches of her best friends still echoed through her mind.

The baby at her breast threw his tiny head back and wailed. She must have dozed off again. Why did Michael have to pick up an extra shift tonight of all nights?

He'd been doing that a lot lately.

Three and a half years ago, she'd thought marrying Michael might be the start of a fun new adventure. As she looked around the shadowed, cluttered room in their rental house that sat less than twenty minutes from their first apartment, disappointment washed through her again, mimicking the rain sluicing down the dark windows. This wasn't the kind of adventure she'd envisioned.

Nursing baby Colton was so much harder than it had ever been with Ava, and neither Annie nor their newborn was getting enough sleep. Tomorrow was supposed to be her first day back at work after maternity leave; she had no idea how she was going to stay awake at her desk.

Thunder rumbled off in the distance.

"Please don't let it wake Ava up," she whispered.

Not that there was anyone there to hear her request—aside from Colton, who was making so much noise, no one would have heard her even if they were sitting on the couch across the room.

Thunder and lightning terrified her daughter, nearly three years old now. She would bolt from her room and jump into their bed anytime a storm woke her. Annie hoped her play date earlier that evening with the little girl next door had worn Ava out enough that she'd sleep through this. She was so used to her baby brother crying that by the time he was a month old, he didn't wake her anymore.

She shifted the baby to her other breast. He latched on, settling in as Annie kept the rickety wooden rocker moving. In the middle of the night, during the darkest of hours, was always the time when Annie felt the most alone. The overwhelming responsibility of keeping a tiny baby safe and fed threatened to buckle her.

If only she'd stuck with her original career path and become a teacher straight out of college. Then she wouldn't have to go to work in the morning. It was June—school wasn't even in session. But nothing had turned out the way she'd planned, and on a lonely night like tonight, she could admit, if only to herself, that her marriage to Michael was turning out to be the biggest disappointment of all.

He wasn't happy. He'd had dreams, too. Dreams of traveling to the far corners of the earth to bring food to the hungry, clean water to the thirsty, and medicine to the sick.

But a weak moment on a magical holiday evening had changed everything.

Michael still wanted to chase those dreams, and he didn't understand why Annie wasn't willing to follow him. She knew he'd visited a local recruiting office, even though she'd begged him not to. He wanted to learn to fly, to be the one to carry aid workers to remote areas. But the only way he could afford to become a pilot was to enlist.

He couldn't understand why Annie wasn't willing to at least try to make it work. If she wasn't comfortable moving the kids to wherever he was first stationed, she could stay here, he said, and he'd send for the three of them later. Or she could move back home to be with family while he put in his time. He was convinced their family could survive a separation, but she knew better.

Michael did love her. Part of her still believed that, despite the heartbreak she'd felt when she'd discovered he'd cheated on her when Ava was only seven months old. They'd been married for eight months, and he admitted to a brief fling with a bar patron. The signs were all there, so he couldn't deny it. But he swore he'd change. He swore it would never happen again.

She swore it would be the only time she would ever forgive him for straying.

To her knowledge, he'd stayed true to his word. But it felt like they were constantly bickering. Annie knew her own temper was trigger quick, thanks in large part to her sleep deprivation. But she wasn't happy, either.

Michael wasn't the only problem in their marriage.

She heard a mournful howl from below, and Annie held her breath. The dryer must have turned off. Michael, in all his initial excitement over building a family with her, had brought a puppy home to their apartment the same week Henry moved out. Pets weren't allowed in their building, and since Barney loved to howl, they were caught eventually, and their roommate wasn't the only one who had to find a new place to live.

That part of their story actually had a happy ending, because Annie loved the cozy little house they'd found to rent. The washer and dryer were down in the basement, which wasn't very handy—especially with all the soiled laundry that go hand in hand with a toddler and a newborn—but it was where Barney liked to hide when it stormed. The dog didn't like storms any more than Ava did. When the dryer was running, he couldn't hear the thunder.

The howling stopped, and Annie realized the storm seemed to have moved off. The baby, finally asleep at her breast, barely fussed when she burped him, so she forced herself to get up and oh so gently transfer him into the bassinet next to their bed. She held her breath until she was sure he'd stayed asleep.

She used to think it was ridiculous when she heard people say they were too tired to sleep. Now she understood it.

With Colton safely stowed in his bassinet and Ava having slept through a storm for once, she should probably throw in another load of laundry and check on Barney. As quietly as she could, she scooped her husband's pile of dirty clothes from the chair in the corner of their room and dumped it into the clothes basket. Once downstairs, she set the basket on the dryer and began sorting. Barney moved out of her way, stretched his long body, then started licking her bare toes, making her giggle.

She yanked the belt out of Michael's uniform pants and checked his pockets, pulling out gum wrappers, loose change, and a tissue. She dumped the handful of odds and ends on the closed washing machine lid, intent on sorting out the coins. At this rate, she'd save enough to buy herself that new curling iron she'd been wanting. Hers conked out just after Colton was born, but until it was time to start back to work she hadn't really cared.

That's when she realized it wasn't a tissue that she'd pulled out of her husband's pants pocket. It was a little paper envelope. When she opened it, she wasn't sure what she was looking at. Then it dawned on her. It was marijuana, along with those little papers to roll a joint.

Michael used to smoke pot once in a while when they would go out partying downtown, before they were a couple. She'd even caught him smoking it in the apartment that one time. When she'd agreed to marry him, drug use was one of the hard rules she'd laid down from the start.

How much more of this was she supposed to take?

This wasn't what her life was supposed to look like.

Deserting the clothes, she shooed Barney up the basement stairs. She shoved the envelope with its incriminating evidence into the pocket of her robe, then cringed when she felt the baby's pacifier in that same pocket.

Drugs and babies don't mix.

It took all the energy she had to drag herself up the basement stairs.

The dog had a sixth sense when it came to the kids. The way Barney entered a room with a sleeping baby was different than when he plodded through the house when everyone was awake. There was a softness to his waddle as he entered the bedroom ahead of Annie, almost like he was tiptoeing.

Barney loved to sleep on the bed, but his stubby legs meant he always needed a lift. Once she'd deposited him onto Michael's empty side of the bed, Annie took the envelope out of her pocket and stashed it in the top drawer of her husband's dresser. She'd confront him about it when she got home from work the next day, and Ava wouldn't be able to reach it there. The last thing they needed was for the three-year-old to get her hands on Daddy's pot. The very idea made Annie shiver with disgust.

She tried to shut the drawer, but it was too full, and another, much larger envelope was sticking up a little so she couldn't close it all the way. Curious, she pulled out the envelope, but it was too dark in the room to see what it might be. Barney was already curled up and asleep, and Colton's soft baby snores assured her he was fine, so she took the envelope into the bathroom for more light.

Her hands shook when she read the return address. The seal was already broken. She pulled out the contents and read the top sheet of paper.

Her heart skipped a beat.

He'd done more than visit that recruiting office. These were his orders.

He'd lied to her again.

And he was out of passes where she was concerned.

Pure adrenalin allowed her to stay awake all morning at her desk.

Her first day back at the insurance agency was more hectic than usual. The storm she'd worried would wake her babies the night before had caused damage north of town, so she'd spent her morning hours on the telephone, recording claim information to pass on to the agents. They always wanted to check details on all claims before submitting them to the home office for processing.

By noon, she could feel her energy sag. She called home from the breakroom to check on the kids. It surprised her when their elderly neighbor answered instead of Michael. He was still asleep. They'd arranged to have the woman sit with the children until eleven, so Michael could get a few hours of sleep before taking over as caregiver until Annie could get home. Then he'd head back to work another evening shift.

They couldn't afford the cost of a sitter for more than those few hours each morning. She'd remind him of that later, when she got home and he got ready to leave for work. The arrangement meant Annie and Michael would seldom see much of each other on weekdays, but it couldn't be helped. Michael had even used that point in his argument as to *why* he should enlist. He said she might not have to work at all under that scenario.

What he didn't understand was that she didn't want to stay home fulltime. She wanted to get back to her original dream of teaching. Traveling the world was no longer a practical option with two kids under four, but teaching was still a noble profession. The military career Michael envisioned would mean lots of moving, which wouldn't be conducive to the long-term teaching career she wanted. She admired men and women who sacrificed to serve their country. She'd just never thought of herself as one of them.

But now Michael seemed to have taken the choice right out of her hands.

Alone in the breakroom, she pulled from her purse the small notebook of things she needed to remember to do now that she was back at work while still maintaining a household. She sighed when she read the names at the top of her list—their old friend Henry and his fiancée. Annie owed them a thank-you card for the baby gift they'd sent when Colton was born. Maybe she could catch Henry on the telephone instead. There wasn't much she liked about her job at the insurance agency, but management allowed employees to make unlimited personal long-distance calls, just as long as they did so during breaktime. And since Henry was now running the small manufacturing plant his father had founded back home, he could take personal calls.

She still marveled over how close they'd come to losing their friendship with Henry three years ago when they'd all stumbled over their complicated feelings for each other. She knew they could never go back to the carefree days of their fledgling friendship in Peru, but all three had moved on from the toughest of days following Henry's betrayal. Annie had worried she would be the one to put their friendship at risk, but it was ultimately Henry's lies that almost tore the three of them apart.

The unplanned pregnancy linked Annie and Michael. The only way Henry could remain their friend was to beg for their forgiveness. In his ill-fated, desperate attempt to win Annie over, he'd made up the lies to scare Michael away. But Michael could be tenacious, too.

Henry swore he accepted Annie's decision to raise her baby with, and ultimately marry, Michael. She'd almost come to believe him, especially since he was now planning his own wedding to a girl back home.

She dug through her purse for the small address book containing Henry's contact information. A professional-sounding receptionist answered her call. Mr. Pierce had stepped out of his office for a moment, but he should be back shortly, if she cared to wait. With fifteen minutes remaining of her lunch hour, she decided she could. A walk outside might have helped boost her energy, but since both the temperature and the humidity hovered above ninety, she'd already scratched that idea.

Annie used the remote to turn up the soap opera playing on low in the breakroom's corner while she waited. A young woman on the screen was screaming about not being able to forgive her husband for his many transgressions. With a start, Annie realized her own life was starting to mirror that too-common soap opera storyline. She flipped off the set and endured the quiet while she waited, doing her best to block her latest findings of Michael's drugs and enlistment papers from her mind. Henry was the last person in the world she should complain to about her marriage. He'd have every right to say he told her so, though she doubted he'd be that harsh.

Finally, the receptionist put her through, and she grinned at the smile she could hear in her friend's voice.

"Tell me your little Colton didn't already outgrow the outfit we sent," Henry said, skipping any formalities.

Annie laughed. "No, he hasn't outgrown it yet. In fact, he's only up a couple pounds from his birthweight. But the doctor assures me he's back on the right track now. I was calling to apologize for not getting a thank-you note sent off to you yet. I can't seem to find time to shower or go to the bathroom, let alone take care of mail correspondence these days. Well, at least until today. This is my first day back at work."

She hated the way her voice caught on those last words.

"Oh, I'm sorry, Annie. I'm sure that must be hard. But just think. It won't be long now and you can be home with those two beautiful babies of yours all the time."

It felt like déjà vu all over again. Somehow, Henry must already know that Michael enlisted. Obviously, based on the lighthearted tone of his voice, he had no idea that it wasn't what Annie wanted. It seemed the tables had turned and now Michael was the one lying to Henry.

"You've talked to Michael, then," she said, trying to keep her voice neutral.

"Yeah. It'd been a while, but I actually called him to see if he'd be willing to be a groomsman in my wedding. We wanted you and the kids to come, too, of course."

What else wasn't Michael telling her? He hadn't uttered a word to her about Henry's wedding.

"I see. When did you call him?"

"Sorry, can you hold on a minute, Annie?"

He must have covered the mouthpiece on his phone, as there came a rustling and muted voices in the background. Maybe she shouldn't have called him at work.

"I'm back. Sorry. There's always something distracting around here. What was that you asked, Annie?"

She hated the tears welling in her eyes. There was something endearing about the way Henry always said her name. She sniffed, hoping he wouldn't notice the defeat she doubted she could keep out of her voice.

"Michael didn't mention your call. When did the two of you talk?"

There was the slightest pause on the other end of the line. "Annie, are you all right? You sound down. I'm sure Michael didn't mention my call because, well, unfortunately, he said that while it honored him to be asked to be part of our wedding, it overlapped with his basic training. No way he can get out of it."

"Damn him," she whispered, then squirmed when she realized she'd uttered those words aloud.

"Hold on a minute, Annie. I need to shut my door."

She knew this would happen. Henry was the last person she should be talking to right now. She should have called Kit or Jackie or Lynette. But if she didn't get some of this off her chest, she might explode.

He came back on. "Annie, what's going on? You don't sound okay, and something tells me this is more than the first-day-back-at-work blues."

"Oh, Henry, you have no idea. I should have listened to you. You were right." She tried and failed to keep the bitterness out of her words.

He gave a nervous laugh. "While I normally love to hear that I'm right about something, I don't like the way you sound. Do you want to tell me what's going on? Is it Michael? Did you two have a fight? I know the guy can be irritating as hell, but he loves you and the kids. It took me a couple years to realize the truth of that, but he does."

She snorted. "He *loves* me? Henry, that man doesn't know the meaning of love. First he cheated on me before Ava was even a year old, and now I'm finding pot in the pocket of his work pants. And he never even told me he was going to enlist! In fact, I told him *not* to!"

Her raised voice attracted a coworker's attention.

"Is everything all right, Annie?" It was the secretary to the owner of the agency, popping her head in. "I was on my way to the bathroom. You sound upset."

It was Annie's turn to hold her hand over her phone's speaker. "Thank you for checking on me, Justine. I'm just a little upset that I had to leave my baby this morning. You understand."

"I certainly do," the woman said, granting Annie a warm smile. "Hang in there, dear. Each day will get a little easier. I'll come check on you this afternoon."

Annie knew she would, too, and that she didn't have to worry about Justine gossiping about her behind her back. Justine was the glue that held the agency together.

"Annie, are you still there?" Henry's concerned voice brought her back to the phone call. "You honestly didn't know that Michael signed up?"

"I didn't know until I found the papers last night. He knew exactly how I felt about the idea. I haven't told him that I know what he did yet."

"But that's ridiculous. That isn't how a marriage is supposed to work." His voice, much as hers had done, was rising in anger.

"Go ahead, Henry, say 'I told you so.' " She collapsed against the back of the sofa in defeat. "I deserve it."

"I'd never say that to you, Annie, you know that. But if I was still in Minneapolis, I'd choke that man. What the hell is the matter with him? I can't believe I was actually stupid enough to ask him to be a groomsman."

He was getting so riled up on her behalf that she almost had to laugh. "Take a breath, Henry. I know you mean well, but you don't have to be my knight in shining armor, trying to ride in and defend me all the time. Remember, the last time you did that, our friendship barely survived."

His deep breath was static in her ear. "Don't remind me. I'm still embarrassed about how I handled that."

"Don't worry, that's water under the bridge. We all made our choices. Choices that have brought us to where we are today. But I'm going to be honest with you. I'm scared. I don't know if I can keep doing this with Michael. I didn't want him to enlist. It'll mean time apart, and I'm pretty sure our marriage couldn't survive that."

Henry took a moment to absorb that news before responding. "I can see if I can catch a flight to Minneapolis tomorrow. Stephanie will understand."

His fiancée would probably *not* understand, at least if he'd ever told her about their past. Besides, the friendship between Michael, Henry, and herself was complicated enough.

"I can't let you do that, Henry. It's sweet of you to offer, but this is between me and Michael. We have to figure this out. No one can do it for us."

He sighed again. "Fine. I tried to push my nose in where it didn't belong once before, and that was disastrous. I still have trouble with my sinuses from that punch Michael gave me. And I know I deserved it."

"No one deserves to be physically assaulted."

She thought back to the nasty scene in their apartment, hours after Henry's deception came to light, and again her anger at Michael flared.

"Actually, I did. I was an ass. I'll do as you ask this time. But at least let me call Kit for you, if you haven't already. You need friends around you right now, Annie, even if that can't be me. Have you talked to her? Or any of your other girlfriends about this yet?"

She paused at this. She'd told no one of Michael's earlier betrayal, and the rest of it was still too fresh. There'd been no time. But maybe he was right.

Two women came into the breakroom, her privacy gone. Annie needed to get back to her desk. Getting into trouble at work would tip her over the edge.

"Henry, I have to go. My lunch hour is up. But I promise I'll give Kit a call soon. Oh, and thanks again for the baby gift you sent for Colton. It's darling."

She could imagine Henry's worried expression as he sat, frustrated, at his desk halfway across the country. His concern for her was genuine. But there was nothing he could do to help this time.

Chapter Twelve

Henry respected Annie's request and didn't jump on a jet to come to her rescue. But he did help. He reached out to Kit, knowing Annie might put off asking for help from her friends. It wasn't like she'd called him to spill the ugly truth about the way her impulsive marriage to Michael was crumbling. She'd called to say thank you for the baby gift. But the truth usually comes out between the best of friends. At first, she'd been irritated that he'd called Kit. That didn't exactly equate to keeping his nose out of her business. But not only had Kit swept in to help save Annie, she'd called in reinforcements.

So much had transpired in the three months since her first day back at work.

In fact, yesterday had been her last day of work at the insurance agency.

And today? Today, they were leaving.

She had to take a step back to catch her breath as she watched Kit try to convince Ava to let her buckle the girl into her car seat in the back of Annie's old Toyota. The girl's behavior had taken a turn last week when Michael left for California. Even the birthday party Annie's friends helped her throw for Ava the night before hadn't helped with the three-year-old's surly attitude.

Jackie and Lynette were still inside with Colton, attempting to change his diaper. As the only one of the Kaleidoscope Girls with children, it was comical to watch her three besties navigate the world of bottles, pacifiers, temper tantrums, and dirty diapers. Last she heard, Renee didn't have kids either, although she wasn't part of her moving party today.

But the rest of them were here for her. They'd swooped in and helped her realize there was no real reason for her to move to California with a husband who'd been unfaithful and who'd lied repeatedly.

She looked around her at the tiny front lawn that could have used a cut. The cozy little house she'd been so excited to move into with her young family was empty now. All their things were stashed in the back of the packed U-Haul, and they'd leave for Ruby Shores as soon as they'd safely tucked the kids into her vehicle.

Michael had taken little when he'd left them. Heartbreak shadowed his eyes, but even he seemed to realize his mistakes were unforgiveable. The only thing he'd asked of her was that she allow him to still play a part in their children's lives.

Standing on the leaf-strewn, straggly front yard of the little house where they'd made such big plans, Annie harbored doubts over how much effort he would actually make to maintain a loving relationship with Colton and Ava. Little more than a sense of duty held together the fragile relationship with his own father. If the two men loved each other, they hid it well. Annie had foolishly believed she could teach her husband what it could mean to be a family. She'd failed. But perhaps the deep love she'd always sensed between Michael and their two kids would prevail in the end.

Time would tell.

Jackie and Lynette exited the front door with their hands full. One carried baby Colton in his car seat and the other a stuffed diaper bag. They spied her on the lawn.

"Do you still have keys to lock this door?" Lynette asked from the top step.

She didn't. She'd turned them in with the leasing agency earlier that morning while her best friends finished packing their things into the truck and getting the kids fed.

"No. If we're sure we don't need to get back inside for anything, just push the button on the doorknob. Don't worry about the deadbolt. The landlord is coming by in an hour or two to let the cleaning company in and clean up this yard. The new renters move in tomorrow."

Jackie gave her a nod as she walked by with Colton. "The only thing I saw was a bag of Barney's dog food."

Annie blew a frustrated raspberry, despite her commitment to herself to not bash Michael anymore over the implosion of their marriage. They'd both been caught up in a fantasy of what a life together could look like when they'd discovered she was pregnant. Neither had wanted to believe that they weren't prepared for the commitment of marriage.

But why couldn't he even remember to take the damn dog food?

Poor Barney. She hoped he'd survive under Michael's care. The man didn't have the capacity to take care of her and the kids the way a husband should. She'd just have to pray that he could at least keep their sweet beagle alive.

"I can't thank the three of you enough for all of your help. And I can't quite believe I'm back home in Ruby Shores with *two* children and no husband," Annie said as she closed the empty pizza box and walked it over to the garbage can, which was chained to the structure that was above their picnic table providing limited protection from the elements. Her muscles groaned in protest when she lifted the can's heavy lid. Three full days of moving was almost as hard on the body as divorce was on her heart. "This reminds me of when we came out here the night before our wedding festivities started. Can you believe that was three years ago already?"

"What I can't believe is that you and Michael made it to your third anniversary," Kit said. Her tone was joking, but Annie sensed she wasn't really kidding, and it stung.

"Technically, he was already gone by the time this anniversary rolled around. But I know what you mean," she said. "In hindsight, I can see what a big mistake it all was."

Lynette shook her head as she dug another round of wine coolers out of the small, insulated bag they'd brought along. "Annie, don't think of it as a mistake. No relationship that produced those two amazing kids of yours should be considered a mistake."

Annie declined Lynette's offer of a second bottle. She'd driven the four of them out to the lookout over the lake. After everything these women had done for her, coming all the way to Minneapolis and taking responsibility for getting them moved into her new apartment in Ruby Shores, the least she could do was act as the designated driver.

"You're right, Lynette. I vowed a long time ago to never refer to either Ava or Colton as mistakes. Were Michael and I ever destined to be one cohesive family? Probably not. I still have a lot of growing up to do, and it wasn't like I was always easy to live with, either."

"If anyone can raise those kids on their own, it's you, Annie," Kit chimed in as she twisted the top off her second drink. "Trust me. I know the kind of woman who can't handle being a single mom. For example, my own Mommy Dearest. And you are the complete opposite of her."

Annie appreciated their votes of confidence. She was afraid they gave her too much credit, but at least she felt better prepared to face her uncertain future now that she was back home in Ruby Shores. Her parents wanted to help. Even tonight, she knew her mom was helping Ava figure out costumes for Halloween. Colton wasn't quite six months old yet, but her three-year-old had plenty of costume ideas. Most included tiaras and gowns.

"I just wish I'd found a teaching job for this year, but there wasn't time," Annie said. "Plus, there were the kids to consider."

"Actually, your job at that new daycare in town seems like the perfect fit for you right now," Jackie said. "You were lucky to find a place where you can bring your kids along to your work and not have to pay extra. Maybe you could propose teaching lessons to the oldest kids. Oh, that reminds me. I put a good word in for you with my dad at the high school. He said they might have an opening or two for next fall and that he'd keep you in mind. I know you ultimately want to teach, so why not at our old school?"

Lynette placed her empty wine cooler in the nearby trash, then wandered over to the edge of the concrete slab the picnic tables sat on. "Like I was saying, there are no mistakes in life, Annie. Life has brought you full circle and it won't be long before you are right back at the school we all graduated from, but as a teacher instead of a student."

It surprised Annie that their friend had downed her second beverage so quickly, but she didn't mention it. She'd gotten into the habit of judging Michael's every move. She needed to let that go. These women were her friends, not her spouse, and how they chose to relax was none of her business. Unless they ever reached a point where they needed her help, too, of course. She'd always be there for them, just like they'd stepped forward to help her when her world was falling apart.

But Lynette's words grated a little.

"You make it sound like I'm all washed up, Lynette. Coming back here for the same old thing. We can't all move to New York City and live a life of glamor like you."

As soon as she'd said the words, she realized with a twinge of regret just how ungrateful she sounded.

Lynette shot a look back at her, but her expression was hard to read. "Trust me, city life isn't all it's cracked up to be. And I didn't mean that as a putdown, Annie. Believe me, if I had any kind of life to come back to here in Ruby Shores, I'd move back here in a heartbeat. But Mom is in New York, too, and she's always been the only true family I've ever had. She loves the city and has some big ideas about a business we can do together, so that's what we're doing."

Annie could hear the sincerity in her friend's voice. "I'm sorry, Lynette. That was bitchy of me. I love all three of you more than you can imagine. You three literally saved me. *The Kaleidoscope Girls forever!*"

"Hey, Lynette, did you ever keep in touch with Renee?" Kit asked. "Have any of you seen or heard from her since we all went to prom together? God, that was almost ten years ago already."

"I was wondering about Renee the other day, too. Which means, by the way, that we'll have our ten-year class reunion next year," Annie added. Her observation earned her plenty of groans.

Lynette returned to the picnic table, but not before grabbing a third wine cooler on her way back.

Stop counting, Annie scolded herself.

"I try to stay in touch," Lynette was saying. "It's funny you should ask, because I just received a baby announcement from her about a month ago. It's a girl!"

Annie laughed. "Really? And here I was mistakenly thinking I was the only Kaleidoscope Girl who was a mother now. I really like Renee. I wish we hadn't lost touch. What else do you know? Is she married?"

Lynette nodded. "She married a guy she met in college, but I can't remember his name."

"Huh," Annie said. "It would be fun if we could get our kids together some day. Maybe they could become friends, too. When are the rest of you going to get on the ball and have some kids of your own?"

Kit and Lynette exchanged a look, then burst out laughing.

"Right," Lynette said. "Because you make marriage and motherhood sound like so much fun?"

"True," Annie conceded. "But despite the chaos of my current situation, being a mom *is* amazing. And marriage had its moments, too. Right, Jackie? How are you and Todd doing? You haven't talked about him much."

She shrugged. "He's fine. We're fine. He works a lot. We're actually thinking about trying to get pregnant one of these days. But he wanted to just have fun as a married couple first."

Personally, Annie had never really liked Jackie's husband. But it wasn't like she was in any position to critique anyone else's spouse.

Kit nodded. "You'll make a great mom, Jackie. And Annie, Michael may be an ass, but he's sexy as hell. I bet there were some enjoyable moments. Or at least good sex. And Henry is amazing, too. I always said you could have had your pick between those two. Not all of us are that lucky to have two cute guys chasing after us."

Annie wondered if maybe this was Kit's third wine cooler, too. She was getting loud, a sure sign she was well on her way to tipsy.

"Me and Henry were never anything more than friends."

Kit tipped her bottle in Annie's direction. "Much to Henry's chagrin. And don't you mean 'Henry and I'? I thought you wanted to be a teacher. You might need to brush up on your grammar skills."

"Wait." Talk of Henry reminded her of his impending wedding. "Aren't we getting close to Henry's wedding date with Stephanie? Michael blew our chances of getting an invite, but I know you were friendly with him, Kit. Did you get an invite?"

Kit froze, setting her bottle back onto the picnic table with a *thud*. "What?"

"You don't know, do you?" she said, squinting an eye in Annie's direction.

"Know what?"

"Annie, when was the last time you talked to Henry?"

She thought back through the blur of the past few months. "Gosh, it might have been a day or two after Michael and I decided to split. I thought Henry deserved to know. Why? He's all right, isn't he?" Kit was making her nervous.

"I think so. But he isn't getting married," Kit said, glancing between the other three women around the picnic table. The sun was setting, so it was getting hard to see expressions. "I guess I didn't think too much of it, since I never met his fiancée, and he didn't sound particularly upset when he called me to check in on how you were doing."

Annie hadn't known Henry was using her friends to keep tabs on her, but it shouldn't have surprised her. After all, he was the one who called Kit when she was so upset about Michael enlisting.

"You've been giving Henry updates on me behind my back?"

Kit rolled her eyes. "Chill, girl. It's not like that. We've had one quick conversation since he called me that day to let me know you were in trouble. He just wanted to make sure you were doing all right. He sounded relieved to hear you weren't going to follow Michael out to California. Then he made some joke about how both he and Michael might end up being old, lonely bachelors at this rate. When I asked what he meant, that was when he said he'd called off his wedding."

"And you didn't think that was important information you should pass on to me?" Annie asked, stunned. She'd met Stephanie once and thought she and Henry made a cute pair.

Lynette shivered, pulling her light jacket tighter around her. "Ladies, it's getting cold. I suggest we take this party somewhere warmer."

The suggestion spurred them all to gather their last few things.

"I feel bad for Henry," Annie admitted as they picked their way back to her Toyota through the dusk.

Lynette pulled open the passenger door on the driver's side. "I wouldn't worry too much about him, Annie. Remember, the Universe has plans for all of us. We just can't always understand what those plans are until we get further down this road."

"You're drunk, Lynette," Kit said, laughing from the other side of the car.

"Not yet. But mark my words. Our friend Annie's little love triangle hasn't totally played itself out yet."

Annie sighed at the weight of Lynette's prediction. Something told her that her tipsy friend wasn't wrong when it came to her and Michael and Henry.

plans with friends

RUBY SHORES, MN

2019

Chapter Thirteen

The first thing Annie did when she arrived at her office for the second day of the new school year was to call and check on Ferguson again. She was told he was awake and showing no significant ill effects from his overdose, so the doctor planned to release him to a parent later that morning.

Unfortunately, Annie knew, Ferguson wasn't likely to get much support at home. What the boy really needed was a more stable homelife. As soon as he was back in school, she'd call him in and see if she couldn't encourage him to look at colleges. The boy was bright, but she knew that if he'd ever consider college or trade school after he graduated in the spring, she'd have to have their guidance counselor work with him to apply for aid and scholarships. It could be done, but only if Ferguson wanted it badly enough. Last May, Annie had felt more confident in the kid's future than she did at this moment. But she couldn't give up on him. She wouldn't. Certain kids—and Ferguson fell into that bucket—made her feel like they were worth pushing for.

At ten o'clock, she met with the task force they'd built the previous year knowing something like what had happened with Ferguson was a possibility. The team included two teachers, a representative from their local law enforcement, the school's social worker, the resource officer, and Annie. She appreciated being able to pull together the hive mind to help decide how best to handle these sticky situations.

They discussed how much to share with the student body at large, as well as the kids that were with Ferguson when he overdosed. Since the teen was already on the mend, they decided against any kind of formal notification of the student body. Annie would speak one on one with each of the kids who were at the lake the previous evening and report back to the crisis management team.

By the time the bell rang at the end of the school day, Annie had visited with five of the kids, including Gabi. Most thought the episode with Ferguson was a fluke, insisting he'd been clean all summer. If Gabi was hiding something about last night, she gave no sign now. Annie hoped no one had gotten to the girl, scaring her into keeping quiet.

The staff parking lot was empty except for her car when she stepped outside at 5:30. Henry was working late again, and her daughter's husband had coaching duties until seven, so she and Ava were meeting for dinner at the Crystal Café.

With Relic off at college, Annie wondered if she'd ever cook again.

She stowed her things in the trunk of her car. The scent of roses was decidedly gone. It was a beautiful evening, and they'd likely see snow in a couple months, so she walked. A few leaves, hints of gold and orange, fluttered at her as she strolled.

Would this turn into another typical school year, where the first half would pass quickly but the second half would inevitably drag?

Ava pulled into a parking spot just as Annie reached the front doors of the restaurant. There were open spots up front, since the café did most of their business earlier in the day.

"Hey, Mom! I'm glad you called. I need to go to the grocery store before I can cook anything decent at home again."

Annie caught her daughter up in a quick hug as the pregnant woman reached her. When she released Ava, she let her hand rest on the little baby bump that was finally protruding from her midsection.

"You know you are the only person besides Daniel who I let touch my belly like that, right, Mom?" Ava said with a shake of her head.

"Just wait. As it grows, so will the number of people who'll be patting your tummy. Some people have no respect for a woman's personal space," Annie warned.

"Like you?" Her smile told Annie she wasn't really irritated.

The two women entered the café and settled into their favorite booth under the window that looked out onto Main.

"Daniel is coaching tonight, right?" Annie asked while they perused the menu.

Ava nodded. "He is. I swear, he's like a little kid this time of year when football starts up. I'm just glad it keeps him busy. He has a tendency to hover when we're both at home."

"Is he worried about the baby?"

She watched her daughter's hand go to her belly. It was an automatic reflex. Annie remembered doing it herself, even though her youngest baby had just turned nineteen and was off at college. There are things a mother never forgets.

"He is. After losing our first pregnancy, he's very protective of us both."

Ava hadn't been very far along when she'd started having complications the first time, so other than Annie, no one else even knew the couple had suffered the miscarriage. Ava had needed comfort from her mother, but she refused to tell either Henry or Michael. Annie's heart still ached over the grandbaby she'd never hold, never watch grow up.

It took months before the couple started interacting with the world again. No one else in the family understood why they acted as they did, but Ava had sworn Annie to secrecy. She respected their desire for privacy, even though that left Henry convinced the young couple was having marital problems.

"I told you it would never last," he'd said to her one night after Ava and her husband refused to come over for Sunday dinner.

It wasn't easy to keep the kids' secret to herself, but she did. If she'd betrayed their confidence, it might be the last important thing Ava ever shared with her, and that wasn't a price she would pay.

They placed their orders with a waiter Annie didn't recognize. She ordered her usual out of habit.

"But you aren't having any issues now, are you, hon?" Annie said.

Ava shook her head as she took a sip of water. "No. And maybe the four-month mark is my magic number, because I haven't even had any morning sickness for the past two weeks. I can't imagine how awful my week of training in Minneapolis would have been if I'd had to keep running to the bathroom every time I caught a whiff of food."

Annie laughed. "No kidding. Was the training any good?"

"It was all right. Most of the topics were as dull as dirt. Lots of background on banking regulations and credit policies. If I could have snuck back to my hotel room every afternoon for a nap, it would have been better."

This wasn't the first time Annie noticed the old hint of excitement was missing from Ava's voice when she talked about work lately. "Are you rethinking your commitment to the training program? I know how hard you worked on those interviews to get in."

Their discussion continued around Ava's job until their food arrived. Once they were alone again, her daughter sighed. "I worked hard to get into the program. I know I need to complete it if I ever want to move up at the bank. But I hate the thought of having to fly to California for that two-week stint in October. Then there's another one in late February, but since that will be so close to my due date, I'll have to catch it later. After I'm back from leave. *If* I go back."

"What do you mean, *if*?" Annie asked, putting down her fork. She pushed her dinner salad away and leaned forward, concerned. "Ava, I know what math teachers at the middle school make, and you guys could never pay that mortgage of yours on Daniel's salary alone."

Ava wriggled on the booth bench. "Mother, my financial situation with my husband is really none of your business."

Annie snorted and picked up her fork again. "Believe it or not, I remember saying those exact words to my parents when I was pregnant with you. I thought they were being overprotective. Now I know they were far wiser with money, and relationships, than I could have possibly been back then."

"Mom, I work in a bank," Ava reminded her, as if that meant she already knew all there was to know about finances. "With my employee discount, we qualified for a reduced interest rate on the house."

On too large of a mortgage for the combined salaries of a teacher and a new banker, Annie thought, but she didn't want to repeat *that* discussion. She and Henry had tried to talk Ava and Daniel out of the large house the young couple had fallen in love with. They had worried the monthly expenses would leave the kids too strapped, but the newlyweds had gone ahead with the purchase against their advice. Annie hoped she wouldn't end up saying—or at least thinking—the dreaded, *I told you so.*

Henry might. Which would do nothing to repair the cracks in the already strained relationship between Ava and her stepfather.

Or maybe he wouldn't say that. There was a time when he could have said it to Annie where Michael was concerned, after their short marriage fell apart, but he never did.

Annie sat back and took a breath. She'd looked forward to this time with her daughter, and she didn't want to spoil it. They'd have time to discuss Ava's career aspirations later, now that motherhood would be part of the equation. Her daughter wasn't in a receptive mood at the moment, so it would be pointless to keep talking about it.

Instead, she knew the best way to draw a smile out of her daughter. As she sliced her chicken sandwich in half, she said, "I went and saw Colton at work yesterday."

Sure enough, Ava grinned. "At the funeral home? Mom, you hate that place. Wait. Don't tell me someone we know died."

"Of course not. I would have called. Besides, who *wouldn't* hate going to a funeral home?"

"Other than our dear Colton," Ava interjected.

"Right. Other than him," Annie said, shaking her head.

"If no one died, why'd you go? I know how busy your first days with kids are. And you didn't get Colton in trouble, did you, showing up out of the blue?"

Annie sighed. Her two eldest had always been extremely close. As the older sister, Ava grew up mothering Colton. He had her back, too. While their close sibling relationship was endearing, it often left little brother Relic feeling left out. Even Annie sometimes felt like she was on the outside looking in. "No, I didn't get him in trouble. I made sure things looked quiet before I went in, and I only stayed for a few minutes."

"Mom, it's a *funeral* home. It's *always* quiet," Ava shot back with a giggle.

Colton's chosen field was an endless source of humor for the rest of the family. *Poor kid.* But at least Ava's mood was improving.

"Why did you go see Colton at work then?"

Annie opened her mouth to tell Ava about the flowers, then snapped it shut, realizing the mention of her biological father might wipe the smile off her daughter's face. She could never be sure how Ava would react when Michael's name came up.

"Don't tell me you miss Relic so much that you're going to be popping up unannounced to see Colton and me at random times at work. Because you know what a stickler my boss can be."

She watched as Ava dug into her plate of stir-fry—an unexpected specialty for a hometown diner like the Crystal Café known for their baked goods. She took a bite, then whirled her fork in Annie's direction, as if encouraging her to explain herself.

Colton must have kept his word and not mentioned the bouquet of flowers Michael had sent, but she might as well tell her the truth now. Ava was a smart girl, and math came easily to her. "When I got to work yesterday morning, there were two dozen roses on my desk. Well . . . technically twenty-*five* roses."

Ava paused with another forkful halfway between her plate and her mouth. "Why would Henry send you that many roses on your first day back at school? He hates roses."

"Henry didn't send them. Michael did," Annie said, using a french fry to draw circles in her ketchup. Suddenly she was regretting telling Ava about her visit to Colton.

"Michael did," Ava echoed. She didn't look mad, but she set down her fork, and Annie watched the young woman's eyes swing to the window and the road beyond. Then they snapped back to Annie's face. "Oh, wow. Yesterday would have been your twenty-fifth wedding anniversary, wouldn't it?"

Annie nodded. She'd married Ava's father a month before the girl was born, and Ava would turn twenty-five in four weeks. "But he's also excited about your baby news. I'm glad you finally told him. I didn't want him to hear it from anyone else, and now that you're showing, you can't keep it quiet."

Ava picked her fork back up and stabbed at a chunk of carrot. "We didn't want to keep it a secret forever. Just until we . . . you know . . ."

"I know, honey." She reached across the table and patted the back of Ava's hand. "Michael is super excited about the baby."

Ava rolled her eyes. "Unlike Henry."

Annie was still mad at Henry for his lackluster response to the baby announcement. She knew he worried Daniel didn't make enough money to support a family, and that the baby would make things even more difficult for them financially, but Annie had always thought there was more to the man's dislike of Ava's chosen life partner. She just had never figured out what the real reason was. But it was creating another division in their already complicated family dynamics. She almost assured Ava, yet again, that Henry would come around, but she couldn't be sure about that, so she let the comment go.

"Honestly, Henry wouldn't like Michael sending me flowers, so I thought it best not to take them home. And if I left them on my desk, people would ask questions. The arrangement was *big*. I figured Colton could put them to good use."

"That's downright sneaky of you, Mom—and, dare I say, brilliant." Ava wiped at the corner of her mouth with her napkin. "Let me ask you something. Don't you ever get tired of walking around on eggshells, trying to keep both your current husband and your ex happy?"

The fry caught in Annie's throat. "That's not what I do," she insisted between coughs. She drank more water, doing her best not to choke.

Ava gave her a moment but never broke eye contact. Once Annie could breathe again, her daughter made a surrendering motion with her hands. "You just keep telling yourself that, Mom."

She hated it when Ava could verbalize something that she'd been stewing over. Why did her daughter have to know her so damn well?

It was time to change the subject.

She picked up a half of her chicken sandwich, hoping to spur Ava to keep eating as well. The girl hadn't put on any weight yet, given how sick she'd been during her first trimester.

"Are you still able to go with me and Mom to the craft show tomorrow? I'm picking her up at nine. That way, we can grab a late breakfast at that cute restaurant right where we turn off the highway. The weather is supposed to be nice."

Ava took a bite of garlic toast and nodded.

"Great! Your grandmother will be so happy to see you. And maybe we can grab pizza afterward."

Ava grinned, swallowing. "Mom, it's almost as if you are trying to fatten me up or something. As long as I bring a bag of kettle corn home for Daniel, I'm sure he won't mind. He has a game at eleven, so he'll be gone most of the day, too. Hey, what the heck are we going to do when we want to go to the craft show next year? You know how people with strollers always drive me crazy at those things. Maybe Grandpa will watch her for us so we can still go."

Annie bit her lip. She doubted her father would be up for a full day with an active six-month-old on his own, but they'd deal with that next year. "Maybe becoming a mother will give you a little more empathy for parents of young kids. I remember thinking *my* kid would never throw a tantrum in a grocery store. Ha! Relic was a master tantrum-thrower. Never say never!"

"I have *plenty* of empathy!"

You don't, she thought. But babies have a way of bringing even the most self-assured people to their knees.

Ava shrugged. "We'll have to see. But, for now, let's make tomorrow the perfect girls' day."

Chapter Fourteen

T HE OUTDOOR CRAFT SHOW Annie had attended with her mother nearly every year since she was a little girl did not disappoint. The early September day no longer held the heat of summer, leaving the air cool and fresh. They'd parked in a designated field and boarded the horse-drawn trailer that would take them to the booths. The quaint transportation was one of her favorite parts of the day.

"Welcome back, Patsy," the crusty old driver greeted Annie's mother. "I see you've brought your girls again this year."

"And would you believe my granddaughter is expecting?!" Patsy said to the man, pulling Ava closer and laying her open palm on Ava's pregnant belly. "I'm going to be a great-grandmother!"

Annie winked at Ava when she caught the girl's eye, remembering their conversation from the evening before about personal space.

The three of them got settled in the wagon. It was normally used to transport hay during non-showtimes. The craft show was held in a small rural town that had been slowly losing its population until a few years earlier, when outsiders had discovered its charm and the appeal of nearby skiing. They started buying up many of the rundown little houses and refurbishing them for weekend use.

"I told your father we should have purchased his sister's house here when she moved to Florida five years ago," Annie's mother was saying as the horses clip-clopped at a measured pace down the road to the show. She noticed Ava smiling, likely over her grandmother's repeated telling of this same story. "The man could have fixed her old porch, slapped a coat of paint on the siding, and doubled our money."

Annie snorted. "Mom, you say this every year. I thought you were the one who said it was a bad idea. You thought this town would die off."

"Or you worried Grandpa would like it here too much if he fixed up your sister-in-law's old house, and he'd make you move here," Ava chimed in from the bench across from her mother and grandmother. "I remember you mentioning that fear, too, Grandma Patsy. Besides, Grandpa Lyle hates painting."

"*I* don't recall those conversations, dear," Patsy shot back, adjusting the light jacket she wore, despite the mild temperature. "Now, what are we on the lookout for today? Have you fixed up a nursery for that little one yet, Ava?"

Ava nodded and dug her phone out of the cross-body purse she wore. "We started to. Daniel painted one of the spare rooms a pretty sage green last week. Look."

Annie watched as her daughter and her mother flipped through pictures of the actual nursery and screenshots Ava had saved of decorating ideas. After the heartbreak her daughter had suffered over the miscarriage, the sight warmed her heart. She was so excited to become a grandmother, but she hadn't really considered that the baby's birth would make her own mother a *great*-grandmother.

They climbed down from the hay wagon when they reached the edge of the show, both Patsy and Ava taking extra care. The trio wandered up and down the aisles of white tented craft and vendor booths, finding numerous treasures along the way. It didn't take long before Annie was wishing they had a stroller along this year—not for a baby just yet, but for somewhere to stash all their purchases. The bags were getting heavy, and their car was a long way away.

"Mom, stop buying things for the baby," Ava insisted, stifling a yawn. "You are going to spoil her rotten, and she isn't even here yet!"

Annie checked her watch, surprised to see the three of them had already spent two hours amongst the artistry vendors and the crowd. One glance at Patsy told her that the older woman was also tiring.

"I don't know about you two, but I could use a break," she said, shifting the multitude of shopping bags between her hands. "How would you like some of that pie we always try to get down in the church basement when we're here?"

Ava's eyes swung to the steeple of the old church that sat nestled in the center of the craft booths. "I bet we're early enough to still get a piece of banana cream. We waited too long and missed out on it last year, remember? I could use a bathroom, too. How about you, Grandma? Ready to take a break?"

Patsy nodded. "I am. Aren't you chilly? I could use a hot cup of coffee."

Annie wasn't cold. It had to be seventy degrees outside, and there was no wind. She hoped her mother wasn't getting sick. "Let's go find you one then, Mom," she said, keeping her reply noncommittal.

They settled at a long folding table in the crowded church basement with pie, coffee, and lemonade. Ava excused herself to use the restroom. Annie thought she noticed Patsy shiver.

"You feeling all right, Mom?" she asked.

Patsy nodded, then took a sip of black coffee out of her Styrofoam cup. "I'm fine. I've just been battling a bit of a cold for a couple weeks. Nothing to worry about."

"Did you go to the doctor?"

Patsy grimaced at her daughter. "No. It's a cold, Annie. For heaven's sake, I'm fine. I'm glad to see Ava is looking so good. She has that glow. It was a relief to hear they got pregnant again so quickly."

Annie froze. "What do you mean, *again*?"

Patsy leveled her with that no-nonsense glare she'd been on the receiving end of her entire life. "I didn't stutter. I know perfectly well that Ava was pregnant a year ago. None of you bothered to tell me, of course, but I could tell. When they disappeared for a while like they did, stopped coming to family functions, my heart ached for them. Why didn't you ever tell me, Annie?"

Annie took a deep breath. She never had hidden much from her mother. "Ava and Daniel didn't want anyone to know. They swore me to secrecy. I'm sorry, I couldn't go against their wishes."

"Ah," her mother said, considering Annie's words. The two sat in silence for a minute or two, nibbling at their pie. "I understand. I never wanted anyone to know either."

Annie nodded before her mother's words sank in. "Wait. What do you mean? Mom, did you lose a baby, too?"

The older woman nodded. "More than one. Three, in fact. The pain was indescribable."

The ache Annie felt over her lost grandchild returned and magnified at her mother's confession. "But you never told me."

Patsy reached over and patted her hand where it sat limply beside her paper plate and a half-eaten piece of pumpkin pie. "I would have, if you'd had any trouble. But you didn't. Did you?"

"No. To the best of my knowledge, I was only ever pregnant three times."

There was a shuffling behind her, and Ava dropped back into her metal folding chair. "Whew. That was close. This baby isn't even big yet. How can she already be wreaking so much havoc on my bladder?"

Patsy laughed. "Oh, honey, your bladder will never be the same. Get used to it. Now, how is that banana cream? It looks yummy. I even considered getting a piece, along with the cherry, but then I remembered I'll be putting a swimming suit on when we take that cruise this winter, and decided I better just stick to one piece."

Ava scooped another big bite of pie into her mouth. Once she'd swallowed, she smiled at her grandmother. "It tastes amazing, and since I'm eating for two and have no intention of getting into a swimming suit until at least next summer, I think I'll go grab another piece." She got to her feet. "Do either of you want anything else?"

They both declined, and Ava made her way back to the coffee and pie line.

"I truly am sorry, Mom," Annie said.

Patsy nodded. "I am, too. For me. For Ava. And for you. Life comes with loss. But enough of that talk. We are here to have fun, and I'm confident Ava's little bundle is going to stay safely tucked away, right where she is, until the due date. And talk of our cruise reminded me—I wanted to see if I could find a cute caftan here today. Maybe a fanny pack, too. I may wear a swimming suit on our trip, but I'll definitely need a few cute coverups."

"I love that you and Dad are taking such a nice vacation to celebrate your anniversary," Annie said. Then she remembered her idea. "And speaking of your trip, there is something I've been meaning to talk to you about."

"No, dear, as much as I love you, you can't come with," Patsy shot back with a grin.

Annie was relieved that her mother seemed to be feeling better now. "Don't worry, I wouldn't want to intrude. But I wanted to ask whether your Arizona place will be empty when you are on your cruise."

Ava came back with an even bigger slice of banana cream pie. "Look at this. All I had to do was touch my belly when I ordered, and that nice old granny up there cut me an extra big piece."

"Hey, careful with the 'old granny' line," Annie warned her daughter with a grin as she settled back into her chair. Then she turned her attention back to Patsy. "Mom?"

"The house?" Patsy repeated. "In Arizona?"

"Yes, when you take your cruise," she said again. Her mother seemed to hesitate with her answer. "Mom, is Millie using your house when you're gone?"

Patsy sighed. "I don't know for sure, dear. She mentioned a few months ago that they might like to when I said your father was looking into booking an anniversary cruise."

It took all of Annie's willpower not to roll her eyes. "But she hasn't finalized anything with you yet?"

"No, she hasn't." Patsy picked her purse up off the floor and pulled out her lipstick. "So, I guess if you want to finalize something with me first, then Millie and that husband of hers might have to find a new winter getaway this year. Are you and Henry wanting to go somewhere warm? It's always a good idea to make time for your spouse, Annie."

Sometimes a discussion with her mother felt oddly like a seesaw. Up and down, around and around.

"Actually . . . remember how I went to Maui with my girlfriends a couple months ago? We plan to take a trip together every year. Like you used to do with your friends, back when I was in high school. It's my turn to plan our trip for next year. I wanted to go early, before Ava has her baby, instead of next summer, because I'm going to help watch my new granddaughter, one day a week. I already worked it out in my contract."

Disapproval was written all over her mother's face as she waved her lipstick tube at Annie. "That's all fine and good, dear, but you really should make a bit more effort where your husband is concerned. How do you think your father and I have made it to fifty-five years?"

"How long has it been since you've taken a trip with your girlfriends, Grandma?" Ava interjected.

Annie appreciated Ava's help in steering the conversation back to her girls' trip.

The question seemed to surprise Patsy. "Well . . . it's been a long time, dear. Life got too busy. It would have been fun to keep doing them, but I'm afraid it's too late now."

"Why?" Ava countered. "You still do lots of travel. I remember you talking about a group of friends you've known for a long time. You asked me to invite a few of them to my wedding. Didn't you all get married and have babies at the same time?"

Patsy didn't reply immediately. She finally rolled up her lipstick, applied the orangish-hued color she always brought out this time of year, then dropped the tube back into her purse with a sigh. "I suppose a trip with Betsy would still be a hoot. She's fun, and we traveled well together. But she lost her husband a few months back. I doubt she'd be up for it. As to the other two I had you invite, sadly one passed a year ago, and the other is in the nursing home. She suffered a stroke."

"God, Mom, that's depressing," Annie said. How had she not known about those things? Her mother kept too much from her. "That does it. When we get home today, you are going to call Betsy up and insist the two of you take a trip somewhere."

Her mother scoffed. "I can't do that. I'm already taking that big trip with your father."

Annie waved her excuse away. "You can and you will. If Betsy is trying to adjust to widowhood, she needs you more than ever."

The small smile that stole onto Patsy's face meant she was reconsidering. "Well . . . I suppose I could at least call her."

Annie picked up her cup of watered down lemonade and raised it in a toast to her mother. All the ice had melted during their lengthy visit in the stuffy church basement. "That's the spirit."

The smile blossomed into a giggle. "And getting back to your original question about the house, Annie. Yes, you can use it while we're gone. I can't promise your father will get any of those little honey-do items on our list done before you get there, but I can promise that there will be beds, a pool, and a functioning blender for the five of you to use. What was it you girls used to call yourselves?"

It was Annie's turn to laugh. "The Kaleidoscope Girls. Thank you, Mom. I'll make sure the dates you are gone will work for everyone and let you know definitively. But promise me you won't let Millie slide in ahead of me this time."

"Oh, I won't. It's about time that husband of hers pays for something for a change."

Annie gave her a thumbs-up. Maybe she felt warmer at her mother's dig aimed at Millie's spouse than a mature woman should, but it was nice to come out ahead of her big sister where her parents were concerned. It didn't happen often enough.

And learning how her mother's friend group had fallen apart left her more convinced than ever that time at her parents' Arizona house could provide the perfect backdrop for the Kaleidoscope Girls' annual trip. They'd alternate between longer, maybe more expensive trips, and shorter, cheaper options like Arizona.

Annie had no intention of letting her annual trips with her friends peter out, the way they had for her mom. Kaleidoscope Girls stuck together.

Chapter Fifteen

The midmorning bell rang, prompting Annie to get out of her chair and join kids out in the school's hallways. Experience had taught her that spontaneous discussions with students could lead to important revelations. The remaining days of September and the entire month of October had passed with little drama following Ferguson's near-fatal overdose on the first day of school, but Annie couldn't afford to let her guard down. Maybe she should have appreciated the reprieve. Instead, she felt like she was holding her breath, worried about what was barreling toward them.

As she passed her assistant's desk, Sarah motioned toward a small package atop the morning mail. "This came for you."

A glance at the wall clock warned Annie that she'd miss the students if she didn't get out there. Time scheduled between classes was short. "Set it on my desk, would you? I'll open it after the bell rings again."

Even if there wasn't time to talk to any students, it was still important for her to be out amongst the kids. Too many school administrators lost that critical connection while sitting behind computers, their time consumed by work far removed from the people they were there to serve. An image of the imposing Glen Turner sprang to mind. Glen was their long-retired school principal and father to her friend, Jackie.

When they were all students here, Mr. Turner—as they'd been required to call him—was a regular fixture in these hallways. His booming voice and broad shoulders kept most mischief at bay. When his mere presence wasn't enough, he was quick to slap the head of a wayward boy or verbally berate a girl, usually resulting in tears. Strict disciplinary tactics like that were a thing of the past, which was good, but it made open lines of communication even more important in her quest to earn the kids' respect.

As Annie stepped into the hallway outside the administrative offices, the student council's Halloween decorations served as a reminder that she needed to pick up candy for the trick-or-treaters on her way home from work. If she forgot, they'd have to leave their front light off tonight. She'd always hated dark houses on Halloween. Where was their spooky holiday spirit?

But she needed to be diligent, too, and keep a keen ear open for trouble brewing. What kid didn't want to go out and party on Halloween? The students in her school were too old to go door to door, which left far less desirable options for celebrating.

Sarah had let her know she overheard three girls in the bathroom that very morning gossiping about a big house party, but they must have noticed an occupied stall because they'd clammed up before spilling any helpful details like names or locations. Her assistant thought she'd recognized one girl's voice: a senior with a near genius IQ level who excelled in all her science classes. This same student though, was also prone to bizarre behavior and skipping class.

She made her way toward the upstairs section of classrooms that housed most of the senior-level courses, nodding at scurrying teens and voicing the occasional hello to students who couldn't avoid making eye contact with her. She hurried up the stairs, one hand gliding atop the handrail in case she caught a heel. Decades spent running up and down this set of stairs had resulted in more than one stumble. She wouldn't heal as quickly as she used to if she suffered a fall.

As she rounded the corner at the top of the stairs, she came face to face with none other than Ferguson. Or, more accurately, face to chest. Her heels still didn't bring the top of her head any higher than the teen's shoulder. Her hand shot out automatically to keep from plowing into him, her fingers clutching his upper arm.

She knew Ferguson had been avoiding her lately, and their unexpected encounter took him by surprise. He stopped mid-step, giving her a wary nod. "Ms. Pierce," he said, his gaze quickly sliding away from hers.

"Hey there, Ferguson," she said, working to keep her tone light. "Happy Halloween. Where's your costume?"

They allowed mask-free costumes at the high school, as long as they didn't cross any lines. The practice made Annie's nerves jump every year with worry that someone would show up in something outrageously inappropriate. It happened a time or two during previous Halloween seasons, but she hadn't had to send anyone home today.

Ferguson gave a one-shouldered shrug. "At least I'm *alive* for Halloween. Given the shitty way school started for me this year, I thought I'd skip the whole costume thing. Since I damn near ended up as a *legit* ghost, I thought I better not tempt fate."

Annie let the cussing slide, given the kid's background and recent brush with death. His comment reminded her of the way Lynette twisted her ankle one day after flipping the bird to the heavens above Maui while on their girls' trip. They'd all laughed and said she shouldn't have tempted fate. She might have even laughed at Ferguson's tasteless attempt at humor, but she noticed his self-deprecating smile didn't quite reach his eyes. Realizing she still had a grip on his arm, she gave it a reassuring squeeze before dropping her hand just as the bell rang again.

"I sent you a note to come see me last week. You didn't show up. Care to explain why?"

"Umm, I didn't get a note. Must have gotten lost," he said, fidgeting.

Annie knew he was lying. She'd specifically asked Wendy to give the note to the boy during his fifth period drawing class. Wendy would have followed through on her request. But she let the likely fib slide, too.

"Hmm, maybe. But we need to talk again. I'd like you to stop and see me this afternoon when you finish up with your last class. Will that work?"

He groaned. "I might have to work."

"Ferguson, I'm sure you'd know by now if they expected you to clock in this afternoon. I'll clear my calendar and see you at a quarter after three."

He reluctantly agreed before skirting around her. "But now I'm late, and you know how Smith hates that!"

She watched the boy hustle down the stairs. He was right. Smith would probably swing by her office to complain about the boy's tardiness again. Not everyone saw Ferguson's potential the way she did. Hopefully her faith wasn't misplaced.

Later, once she was back in her office following a meeting, Annie fished through her desk drawer for the handy old letter opener. One of her predecessors had left it behind. Maybe it had even belonged to Jackie's father back in the day.

Finding it, she pulled the package out of the stack of mail that Sarah had left on her desk, planning to use the opener to slice the tape. A shiver ran down her spine when she spied the return address. What the heck could Lynette have sent her, and wasn't it a little creepy that she'd *just* been thinking about the woman while speaking with Ferguson in the hallway?

At least I'm not short on creepy Halloween spirit, she thought, shaking off the coincidence and smiling at Lynette's name.

Maybe it was another gift for Annie's first grandbaby. March was getting closer. When she'd told her friends in confidence about Ava's pregnancy in July, the other four women got busy. None of the Kaleidoscope Girls were grandmothers yet, so Annie's exciting announcement had felt like a rite of passage for them all.

She removed the box's lid and discovered plenty of packing materials inside.

"Ms. Pierce, you have a student here to see you," Sarah announced from her doorway. The younger woman spied the small, open box on the blotter in front of her boss. "Oh! Is it too pushy to ask what you got? I know you didn't want to talk about the roses a while back."

The question *felt* pushy, but Annie considered Sarah a friend. Besides, this gift wasn't likely something that would upset her husband. Not like the roses. "An old high school friend sent me something. She wrapped it with extra care, so it must be fragile."

Annie kept pulling back the cushioning layers of tissue until her fingers brushed against something substantive. "I'm guessing it might be something for Ava's baby."

News that Principal Pierce would soon be a grandmother had spread quickly through the administrative offices, so she wasn't giving anything away by voicing her guess as to what Lynette's package might contain.

She removed a small brass stand and set it on her desk. It was only a couple inches tall. Under a layer of foam, she discovered an egg-shaped item, ensconced in more tissue paper. Once she finally freed the piece, she set it atop the stand with a wide grin.

"Your friend sent you a wooden egg?" Sarah asked, clearly not overly concerned about keeping a student waiting.

Annie snorted. "Not exactly," she said, picking up the oval-shaped item and holding it to her eye. "It's a kaleidoscope."

Sarah moved through the office doorway to stand closer. "A kaleidoscope? Really?"

"Really," Annie confirmed, lowering it to meet Sarah's surprised gaze. "And based on this mark, I'd say it's about as old as you are."

Annie held the gift toward the other woman, pointing to the engraved brass ring on one end of the piece. "See? It says 'Van Gort, USA.'"

Sarah accepted the kaleidoscope from Annie with care. "And that name means something to you?"

"It does, actually. The two kaleidoscopes on these bookshelves behind me are only a small sample of my bigger collection at home. I've collected them for years. Ever since I was twelve years old, as a matter of fact. Believe me, I've done my research. Henry doesn't understand the appeal and hates it when I bring another one home."

Sarah brought it up to her eye, mimicking Annie's earlier action to gaze through one end of the instrument. She turned slowly toward one of the two windows in the office. "Henry needs to lighten up. This is beautiful."

He should lighten up about my collecting hobby and so many other things, Annie silently agreed. Not that she'd admit something like that about her husband out loud.

She checked the package for a note and found a small, sealed envelope. Instead of opening it in front of Sarah and keeping the student—who she hoped was Ferguson, given the time—from having to wait any longer, she returned the note to the box and held out her hand to Sarah.

"I haven't seen one of these since I was a kid, and never one shaped like an egg. Neat." Sarah handed the collectible back to Annie before turning to go. "I'll send the student in if you're ready to see him."

Annie rewrapped the kaleidoscope in the white tissue. She'd take the gift home and be sure to call Lynette to thank her. Then she remembered she wanted to call Kit, too, to see how the newlyweds were faring after their beautiful lakeside ceremony earlier in the month. Would either Kit or Lynette be home tonight? It was Halloween, after all. Maybe, unlike her, they still had a social life.

She heard footsteps just as she was locking Lynette's thoughtful gift in the bottom drawer of her desk, where she also stored her purse. A prick of relief coursed through her at the sight of Ferguson standing in her doorway. At least he hadn't blown her off this time.

She waved the teen in. "Take a seat."

He sauntered in and dropped into one of the two chairs facing Annie's desk. The old chair groaned at the sudden weight.

"This thing gonna hold me?" He wriggled his butt to test it.

"Normally I'd say yes. But plop into it like that again and you might find yourself on the floor."

Ferguson threw his head back, presumably to get the long curtain of bangs, in dire need of a trim, out of his eyes. At least for the moment. "Sorry 'bout that."

She could tell he wasn't really, but as long as he hadn't broken her chair, she'd let it go.

He was grinning at her.

"I'm not sure I like that look," she admitted.

The grin widened. "What look? I'm just waiting for you to ask me where the big party is tonight. You know, since it's Halloween and all. Plus you seem to think I know all about the crap happening in town these days. Well, I hate to break it to you, but I don't have a clue. I'm not much of a partier anymore. Not since . . . you know . . . the last time. Learned my lesson that night."

Annie pushed her own chair back far enough from her desk that she could cross her legs. "You learned your lesson?"

"Sure did." The nod he gave her caused his hair to flip forward again.

She felt her smile slip away, cracked open her pencil drawer, and retrieved an elastic hair tie. She tossed the black circle across the desktop to him. He caught it.

"Use that."

He shrugged, then leaned forward and scooped his shoulder-length hair, bangs and all, into a knot at the top of his head.

Annie could only imagine what Principal Turner would have thought of Ferguson's impromptu man-bun. He wouldn't have liked it. He wouldn't have liked, or tolerated, much of what Annie now had to deal with these days. Lucky for him, he'd retired years ago. Then she remembered his more recent diagnosis with Alzheimer's and decided there was nothing lucky about his situation.

Two additional men had served as principal during the years between Turner's retirement and Annie's promotion, but neither of them occupied her thoughts the way Jackie's dad still did. She supposed that was partly because she used to fear the way the man ruled this place with an iron fist when she was a student. She wouldn't want to be feared like that, even if societal expectations would have still allowed the methods Turner used, but she would have appreciated a little more respect.

With his hair secured, Ferguson relaxed against the back of his chair again and crossed an ankle over a knee. "Did you call me in here to shoot the shit, or was there a specific reason you wanted to see me?"

"Language, Ferguson," she warned, tired of his attitude. There was an edge to him he hadn't had the previous spring. Or at least one she hadn't picked up on. She didn't like it. She suspected it was an armor of sorts. "Is there something bothering you that you want to discuss with me?"

This time, when he gave a hard shake of his head, his hair stayed put. "*You* called me in here, remember? Not the other way around."

She was going to have to take another tactic to get him to be honest with her about how he was really doing after his brush with death. She knew he'd never followed up with the counselor like she'd asked. She'd checked. Maybe he'd be more open to talking about his future than his past.

"Have you thought any more about what you might do after graduation? You know, now is the time if you want to look at any schools."

The teen scoffed. "As in *college*? Yeah. Right. My old man can't even flip me a twenty for gas. And don't get me started on my mom. She took off in July, by the way. Bet you didn't know that. Doubt we'll see her around here again."

This was news to Annie, and it was disheartening. His mother had represented the only real chance of support at home for Ferguson. The boy's father was a convicted felon, spending most of his son's younger years in jail. The few times Annie had interacted with the man while working to find Ferguson help at the tail end of his junior year, she recognized him for what he was—a worthless piece of garbage who had no interest in making sure his youngest son got a fair shake at life.

Again, not that she'd have admitted as much out loud.

Good thing the outside world couldn't read her thoughts.

"I'm sorry to hear that about your mother," she said. "Do you want to talk about how you feel about her leaving?"

Ferguson let his boot-clad foot drop from its perch on his knee. It clunked heavily against the hardwood beneath his chair. "Don't act like you give two shits about my homelife, Pierce. I know you just want to keep pumping me for information about who gave me the drugs that night. Isn't that the main thing you want to ask me? Because that's where this conversation has ended up every time you've called me in here since. So fine. Yes, I admit I ignored your note about coming to see you last week. I'm sick of this shit."

Annie was trying to remember why she'd ever thought there was a spark of something special in this kid.

And why had she ever thought running a school could be *fun*?

If anything, work felt more like a dangerous game of Russian roulette these days. The dangers kids faced were real, and so many of the students were still too immature to realize it.

Ferguson might have expected a reprimand for his swearing, but when she crossed her arms and stayed silent, eyeing him thoughtfully, he squirmed.

Eventually, he threw his arms up with a sigh. "I'm mad, all right?"

Were they finally going to get somewhere? She relaxed her arms, realizing her stance might come across as combative. "What, specifically, are you mad *about*?"

The boy snorted. "It's hard to know where to start."

"Start anywhere," she prodded.

The teen got to his feet in a rush, surprising Annie enough that she slid her own chair back involuntarily. It was reflex. She wasn't actually scared of Ferguson.

But the boy's expression hardened. "I'm mad about *that*! That *you* gave up on me, too. Last spring, I actually believed you had my back. You stood up to my dad. You got my mom to see that I had potential. But that's all changed now."

Annie fought the urge to get to her feet. Maybe if she stayed in her chair, she could better defuse the situation. "What's all changed, Ferguson?"

He shoved his thumbs in his back pockets and let his head fall forward. "Mom took off. Dad took my truck when his old piece of crap conked out. Told me I can walk to work. I use my bike, but I've been late so many times my boss is threatening to fire me. I had to give up on the group meetings you lined me up with last spring because I can't physically get there. Then, when I can barely stay awake during the first day of school and some dude I barely know slips me something that's just supposed to help me stay awake, I damn near die. I basically threw it all away again, and no one will give me a second chance."

She considered his words. She was relieved he was finally opening up, but sorry that he sounded so dejected. He was teetering on the edge, and his terrible homelife just might push him over. She wanted to trust him, to trust that he wanted to get his life back in order again, but should she?

She watched as he sauntered over to her office window that looked over the street in front of the school. He left his thumbs in his back pockets. She wished she could tell what he was thinking. The bad-boy attitude he'd entered the room with seemed to have evaporated.

"Ferguson, if you're serious about getting back on track again, I'll help you. But I need to know you mean it. I understand you've hit some roadblocks that weren't of your making, but you can't afford any more screwups."

Instead of responding directly, the teen let out a low whistle. "Hope they aren't here for me."

"Who?" she asked.

She was curious about yet another change in the boy's posture. He looked ready to bolt. Pushing out of her chair, she joined him at the window. Two police cars had pulled up to the curb in front of the school. Annie checked her watch. At least the buses were gone for the day.

"I don't suppose they're here to trick-or-treat?" Ferguson joked, though she picked up on a thread of concern in his tone.

"I doubt it. I better go see what they want." She turned from the window. "Look, Ferguson, think about what we talked about. If you're serious about cleaning up your act, you need to get back to your group meetings. We can find a way to get you there. And be careful who you hang out with. Let's see what I have open in my calendar tomorrow. We need to keep talking. But Fridays are busy around here."

She tapped the keyboard to wake her computer and check her schedule, but Ferguson shook his head. "Can't tomorrow. I work at four, so I need to hit the road at last bell," he said. "It'll have to be next week."

Heavy footsteps echoed through the nearly empty halls, announcing the approach of the three officers she'd spied exiting their patrol cars. Ferguson must have heard them, too, because he was quick to grab his jacket from the back of his rickety chair. After a mumbled promise to set up an appointment with her, he bolted.

Annie followed him to her door and watched him go. All she could do was cross her fingers and hope that he wouldn't find any dangerous ways to celebrate Halloween.

Chapter Sixteen

S ARAH USHERED THE OFFICERS to Annie's office. She recognized all three of them, and their grim expressions didn't bode well.

"Annie, sorry to barge in on you like this."

"We have to stop meeting like this, John," she said. She stepped aside to allow the officers access to her office. "And I see you brought Ivory and Beth, too. Never a good sign. The last time I saw you, John, was when Ferguson Carbo overdosed out at the lake in early September. I've enjoyed *not* seeing you since then. I'm guessing it's something serious to warrant all three of you stopping in like this? Should I see if our school resource officer is still in the building?"

"That won't be necessary," Officer Sullivan said, pulling a third chair closer to the desk so they could each take a seat as Annie closed her door.

She held her breath when he lowered his beefy frame into the same chair Ferguson had occupied minutes before. There was an ominous creak, but the chair held. She sat and faced the trio with her hands joined on her desktop, bracing for whatever bad news was behind their somber demeanors.

She noticed Sergeant Ivory Gilbert's eyes snag on the framed photograph of Annie and the rest of the Kaleidoscope Girls. It was a snapshot from their fun-filled evening at the luau in Hawaii in July. While Ivory had met all of them when they were kids at summer camp and attended high school with everyone but Renee, she didn't comment on the recent photo.

If Annie wasn't so concerned about the reason behind their visit, she might have clued Ivory in on the details of the photograph, but now wasn't the time. Her friends didn't like Ivory, though Annie had grown to respect the woman, at least professionally. She'd never completely forgiven Ivory either, but she didn't hate her like her old friends Kit and Lynette still claimed to.

The third officer, Beth Talley, was a friend of Ava's. It was difficult for Annie to think of the younger woman in her professional capacity as a police officer.

John cleared his throat, glancing toward his superior.

Ivory nodded, then met and held Annie's gaze. "We received an anonymous tip about some suspicious activity at a house down on Second Avenue. When we first arrived, we didn't think anyone was around. But the back door looked like someone had forced it open, and we found a pile of old mail just inside the front door, under a mail slot. The house belongs to an old couple that always heads south in mid-October. You might know them. The Fosters? Calvin and Irene? Maybe they forgot to turn off their mail. But the busted door was a concern."

Annie recognized the names. "Don't tell me something's happened to the Fosters? They are such a nice old couple."

"We are still trying to reach them," Ivory said. "As far as we know, they left town two weeks ago. That's why someone called in. They knew the Fosters were out of town, but they noticed strange comings and goings from the house. The caller found it odd."

None of this told Annie why three police officers were sitting in her office on a Thursday afternoon. She was going to run out of time to pick up Halloween candy on her way home. "What does this have to do with me? Or the school?"

Ivory's lips pursed in disapproval at the interruption. "The house wasn't empty."

An image of a group of kids throwing an impromptu party popped into her mind. Lots of people likely knew the house sat empty for several months each year. "Don't tell me you had to break up a party already. I know it's Halloween, but it isn't even five o'clock yet."

"I wish that's all it was," Ivory said. "Initially, we didn't think anyone was in the house. But when we checked the basement, we found something. Or, should I say, some*one*. Two people, as a matter of fact. And, unfortunately, both individuals were deceased."

"Oh, no!" Annie gasped, her fingers fisting tighter. "What happened?"

"We suspect they both overdosed. There was drug paraphernalia found with the bodies."

She forced her hands to unclasp, rubbing the back of her neck as she waited impatiently for the specific reason the police were sitting in *her* office.

"They weren't any of your students," John broke in, as if able to read her mind.

The air rushed out of her lungs in a sigh of relief. Not that she wanted anyone to be dead. "Yet here you are. Why?"

John nodded. "Do you remember the group of kids at the lake with Ferguson the night he collapsed?"

"I do. A few *are* students here. There were others I didn't recognize. I thought they looked a little older. One was quite the smartass. He rubbed me the wrong way. But I didn't catch his name."

Ivory sat forward in her chair, as if to take back control of the conversation. "We aren't officially releasing the names of the two deceased individuals yet, so this has to stay between us. Families need to be notified first."

"Wait." Annie's blood ran cold. "You aren't here because I'm next of kin, are you?"

"Of course not," John jumped back in, shaking his head vigorously and earning himself a sharp look from Ivory. "I recognized one of the deceased. I remembered checking his identification at the lake that night in September when we were there for the call on Ferguson Carbo. I'm sure it was the same kid you mentioned. I didn't get a good vibe from him either."

He was pushing to get the story told faster. Maybe he had kids waiting at home for him to take trick-or-treating.

Beth, quiet until now, sighed. "Annie, one of the deceased individuals was Zeke Carbo. I believe he has a younger sibling or two who are your students."

Annie's immediate thought was of the boy who had just left her office. "But Ferguson Carbo doesn't have any brothers. Just an older sister, and she doesn't live around here anymore."

Beth nodded but didn't respond, as if giving Annie time to connect the dots.

It only took another second. "Zeke Carbo . . . Is he *Jason* Carbo's older brother? I had Ferguson in my head because I just talked to him today. Jason is one of Ferguson's younger cousins. It's a big family."

"A big, *troublesome* family," Ivory said. "The other deceased man doesn't appear to be from around here. The identification on his body listed a California address."

Annie felt a twinge of pity for both Jason and Ferguson. The deck was stacked against both of them, deep in their genes. "I appreciate you letting me know. I'll be sure to check in on Jason. That poor family. I've talked with his parents before, on more than one occasion."

"I bet you have," Ivory said. They all understood that the extended Carbo family was notorious for making trouble.

"We appreciate that," John said. "We wanted you to hear about this directly from us. But that isn't the only reason we're here. Look, Annie, we're concerned. There seems to be an increase in the amount of fentanyl on the streets of Ruby Shores. Did any of your students who were with Ferguson out at the lake that night give you any information as to where he might have gotten his hands on it?"

"Do you know for sure that Ferguson took fentanyl?"

Beth nodded. "That's what his tox screen showed from that night."

Annie sat back in her office chair and let her head fall back to stare at the ceiling. The tile above her head held an ominous brown stain, as if pipes had leaked at one point. If these walls around them could talk, they'd have decades' worth of teenage angst to share. But had kids ever faced the magnitude of dangers that lurked in the shadows these days? She closed her eyes and went back through the conversations she'd had with the kids after the incident at the lake. Nothing stood out.

She straightened. "I'm sorry. Do you want me to call them in again? If people are dying, they might be more willing to talk. Or more terrified than ever."

Ivory slapped her hand twice on Annie's desktop, then got to her feet. All three officers were in full uniform, and her old classmate had caught her long blond hair in a high, tight bun. The woman in front of her now bore little resemblance to the girl who was once the nemesis of Annie's friend group. "Talk to the kids. You may even want to pull together an assembly tomorrow. We could send over our special education liaison to talk to them, if you think it might help. These kids need to understand how dangerous it is to take *anything* these days."

"Scare them straight, you mean?" Annie asked, thinking the idea had merit.

"Hey, whatever it takes," Ivory said, her expression grim. "We swung in here first, on our way out to Zeke's parents' place, because we figured they'd both be getting off their shift about now. I hate that we have to go tell them that their twenty-three-year-old son is dead. That's news a parent should never ever have to hear, and if we can prevent even one more kid from dying, it would be worth it."

Annie rose, as did the other two officers. "I'll set something up for ten tomorrow morning, if that will work for your liaison. Now we just have to pray nothing else goes wrong tonight. Halloween isn't usually a quiet night. I heard rumors about a big house party, but I don't know where."

John swung the extra chair he'd pulled in at their arrival back to where he'd found it. "We already shut that one down," he informed her with a satisfied smile.

"How the heck did you manage that?" Annie asked, surprised but relieved.

He winked. "Trust me, we've got eyes and ears where you'd least expect it."

Chapter Seventeen

B Y THE TIME ANNIE got to the grocery store, there wasn't a bag of chocolate bars to be found. All that remained on the picked-over shelves were the brands of candy her own kids used to throw away, months after the fun of trick-or-treating became a distant memory. But since it was too late to check elsewhere, she grabbed three bags. As she endured small talk with the cashier, her mind was still caught up in the horror of the news Ivory and her people had delivered. She hurried home through the semidarkness. Small knots of people were already out and about, parents ushering tiny costumed children from house to house before full night fell.

Henry must be home, as a few lights glowed inside, but the front of the house remained dark. She was getting home later than she'd wanted to with the candy. Hopefully her husband remembered to pick up their order for Chinese that she'd scrawled on a scrap of paper and shoved into his hand on his way out the door that morning.

But as the garage door opened, she was in for a shock. Henry's stall was still empty, and it was Relic's old Toyota in the garage, tucked into the third stall and surrounded by boxes he must have had to move out of the way. It was a Thursday night. Was he already falling into the dangerous trap of skipping his Friday class?

As she pulled into her spot in the garage, she felt an odd mix of confusion and relief. Why was he home? But now she wouldn't have to hand out candy by herself. For the past few years, Relic always helped monitor the door and hand out candy. She'd expected to have to do it alone tonight, and it wouldn't have felt the same without her youngest.

The terrible news she'd received at the end of her day had also left her in dire need of hugs from all three of her kids, but especially Relic, since she hadn't seen him since he'd come home to catch a high school football game weeks earlier.

Maybe they'd canceled his Friday class.

Deciding that his surprise visit was good news, Annie gathered her things—including the adequate but less-than-stellar candy—and headed inside.

Unlike other Halloweens, she'd only put out a few decorations this year, since she hadn't expected any of her own kids to be home. But the candy bowl they always used sat on the kitchen island, ready and waiting. As she filled it with candy, she caught the telltale ticking of Lemon's little feet on the hardwood upstairs.

The little dog was no doubt thrilled over Relic's arrival.

She could hear her son's voice, too. It sounded like he was on the phone with someone. Her stomach rumbled as she took the full candy bowl out to the entry table and flicked on the light. Maybe their food wasn't quite ready and Henry was waiting at the restaurant for the take-out. Good thing she'd ordered extra, thinking they'd both take leftovers for lunch tomorrow. There should be enough for Relic, too.

The doorbell rang, and Annie wished she'd changed out of her business suit and into her go-to Halloween sweatshirt sporting a massive smiling pumpkin that helped put little kids at ease. As she headed for the door, she wondered what cute costumes the first group would be wearing. Too bad Relic wasn't down here to see them. He and Annie always picked a favorite for the evening.

She swung the door open. It wasn't a group of cute little kids on her front step.

"Ferguson? What are you doing here? How do you even know where I live?"

He opened his mouth, but no words formed, and she could read the agony behind his eyes. Childish voices and giggles floated around the teen, and Annie pulled him inside and out of the way of a trio of miniature pirates. After she dropped a few pieces of candy into each of their outstretched treat bags and waved hello to their chaperone standing back on the front lawn, the three skipped off with muttered thanks, bound for the next house on the block.

She couldn't see anyone else approaching at the moment, so she closed the door and turned to face her student.

Just then, Relic came jogging down the stairs, barefoot, wearing ripped jeans and a slouchy sweatshirt bearing his college's mascot. Lemon was sticking so close to him, they were both lucky he didn't trip over her.

"I'm home!" Henry yelled from the back of the house. "Let's eat!"

Annie felt like she was getting bombarded from every angle. Where should she even start?

Eyeing Ferguson up and down, Relic said "Hey, Carbo, you're a little old for trick-or-treating, aren't you? Or did Mom catch you nabbing some poor little kid's candy?"

Annie could have kicked her son, though he couldn't know what Annie suspected was the real reason Ferguson was at their door. Still,

Ferguson was clearly upset. Sometimes she worried Relic, who'd played school sports with the boy years earlier, didn't have an empathetic bone in his body. Maybe that's what can happen when you're the baby of the family and a tad bit spoiled.

Ferguson spun away and rubbed at his face. He was likely embarrassed to have Relic see him like this. She needed to find out exactly why the boy had shown up on her doorstep, though she was sure it had something to do with his cousin Zeke.

The reason behind her son's impromptu visit would have to wait. And if Henry walked in and saw one of her students standing in their house, he wouldn't like it.

She turned to Relic. "Hey, kiddo. I'm surprised to see you. But I need a minute, all right? Go make sure your dad remembered to pick up dinner. I'll be back shortly."

Relic looked between his mother and Ferguson, clearly curious, but food usually served as a deciding factor for him. "Nice to see you, man," he said, giving the other kid a quick nod before heading back toward the kitchen. Lemon wasn't leaving his side.

"I'm sorry. I probably shouldn't have showed up here like this, but I didn't know what else to do," Ferguson said, spinning back to face Annie. Evidence of tears still marred his cheeks. "Did you hear? Zeke is dead. My cousin. I bet that's why the cops came by, wasn't it? Do they think I had something to do with it? I swear, Ms. P, I didn't. But I have to find out who did this to him."

Despite Annie's hope that Relic could keep his father in the kitchen, a hand settled on her shoulder.

"Is everything all right out here?" her husband asked. He hated when she brought work home with her, and even though Ferguson's arrival was unexpected, even Annie realized this was unusual. She wasn't sure how much Henry had overheard.

"Yes, Henry. Ferguson is dealing with an awful family emergency tonight, and he just stopped by for a moment." The last thing she needed was for Henry to make Ferguson feel any worse. She patted his hand where it rested on her shoulder. "Why don't you and Relic go eat? I'll be back in a few minutes."

The squeeze he gave her before dropping his hand suggested that he didn't appreciate being sent out of the room. But he did as she asked. "Don't be long. It's getting cold."

When it was just the two of them remaining by the front door, Annie thought to flick off the front light to avoid any further interruptions and ushered Ferguson into the living room.

"Sit. Tell me what happened. Why would the police think you were involved in whatever happened to your cousin?"

He did as she instructed, plopping into one of the side chairs with even less grace than he'd displayed in her office a few hours earlier. He bowed forward, elbows on knees and head in hands. What he probably needed more than anything right now was a hug, but Annie always felt like she had to walk a fine line where her students were concerned. Instead, she gave him what she hoped was a reassuring pat on his shoulder before taking a seat across from him on the couch. She waited for him to collect his thoughts.

Finally, he dropped his hands with a heavy sigh and raised his eyes to hers. "Zeke is dead."

She nodded. He seemed to still be trying to process the terrible news. "Were the two of you close?"

He shrugged. "Close? Yeah. Kind of, I guess. He was the only one who stood up to Dad when Cissy got knocked up. He helped her get out and move to Wisconsin. You know . . . to get away."

Annie knew Cissy was a few years older than Ferguson and his only sibling. She hadn't known the girl left town because of an unplanned pregnancy. "How did you hear the news today? *What* did you hear?"

The teen rubbed both of his knees hard, as if he had too much pent-up emotion. He was suffering, but the tears had stopped. "After I left the school, I stopped at a buddy's place, but no one was home. So I rode by work, checked my schedule for this weekend, then headed home. I thought I'd grab something to eat quick, if there was any food in the house, and then head out, before my old man got home from work. But my truck was out front, which meant he was there. I bet he never gives me my keys back, even though I bought that hunk of junk from Zeke last year fair and square."

She bet it was the same truck she'd spied Ferguson's father speeding past the school in on the first day of classes.

Annie's mind flashed to Relic's vehicle in their garage. *How can some kids have so much, while others have so little?* Life wasn't fair. "Did your father tell you about your cousin?"

"Nah. He didn't know yet when I went inside. I tried to avoid him, but he saw me. Before he could yell at me for whatever he's pissed about today, the cops showed up looking for Uncle Jack and his wife. They told us about Zeke. And you know what my piece-of-shit dad had to say about it?"

She was pretty sure she didn't want to hear, but Ferguson needed to talk.

"He said he figured Zeke would wind up dead, given he was such an idiot." The teen hiccupped on the last word. "What a dick thing to say. Zeke wasn't perfect, but he wasn't an idiot. He was like a mentor to me. You know?"

Annie's first thought was that Ferguson might be lucky not to have someone who ultimately died of a drug overdose as a mentor, but she shouldn't judge a man she'd only met once, and under unusual circumstances. She didn't remember him ever attending Ruby Shores High School. "What did the police say happened?"

Ferguson's left eye squinted at her, suspicion flooding his features. "I'm sure you already know what they said. They think he overdosed. But that can't be true. Zeke didn't do drugs."

It was Annie's turn to be suspicious. "Ferguson, wasn't Zeke at the lake when you collapsed in September?"

The question seemed to surprise him. "Umm, yeah, he was, but that doesn't mean anything."

"How old was Zeke?"

Another shrug. "Twenty-three. Why?"

She'd forgotten the police had already mentioned his age. "Ferguson, why would a twenty-three-year-old be hanging out with a bunch of high school kids? I need you to be honest with me. Did Zeke give you whatever you took that night that almost killed you?"

The flash of what looked like legitimate horror on Ferguson's face was more telling than the denial he gave.

"I'm sorry," she said. "I had to ask. I think I talked to him that night. He wasn't . . . I don't know . . . *pleasant.*"

This earned her a brief grin.

"No, Zeke wasn't exactly a *pleasant* guy. But he always had my back. That was the same day Dad took my truck, so Zeke gave me a ride over to my buddies. I convinced him to hang with us. It wasn't a big deal."

Annie shook her head. "I'd say you practically dying that night was a big deal."

"Shit, Ms. P, that wasn't what I meant. Look, Zeke doesn't do drugs. *Didn't* do drugs. At least anymore. When he was a kid, he spent time in juvie. He told me it scared him. I don't know what really happened today. How could they say he overdosed when the Zeke I knew didn't do drugs? But I want to help figure it out. That's why I'm here. I want to talk to the cops. See if we can't figure out who did this, who is putting this dangerous shit on the streets. Is there a cop you'd trust, if you were me?"

A bundle of fur flew into the room and slammed into first Annie's legs then Ferguson's. Someone cleared their throat, pulling the attention of everyone else toward the doorway to the living room. Henry stood there, his expression neutral. "Relic stepped out back to take a phone call. I thought I'd come check on you."

Annie did her best to hide the way her teeth gritted in frustration. She didn't need checking up on. Ferguson was harmless.

Wasn't he?

The teen fumbled for Lemon, scooping the squirming dog into his arms. She licked his face and calmed down enough for Ferguson to stand while holding her. It was as if the dog was giving him her stamp of approval as she eyed Henry, as if to say, *Not to worry.*

A phone rang. Ferguson set Lemon down and pulled his cell out of his jeans pocket, checking the screen.

"I gotta bounce. The family is all getting together at Uncle Jack's. But will you think about what I said?"

Annie thought he looked more relieved after reading the message. "Are you sure you'll be all right tonight? Do you need a ride home?"

"Annie," Henry said from the doorway. In that one word, his warning to watch herself was clear.

Ferguson spared him a quick glance, bent over to give Lemon one last back rub, then faced Annie again. "That was Mom. She's back. Zeke's mom probably called her. And Cissy is almost here, too. I'll be fine, Ms. P. Remember, I have to work after school tomorrow, but I'll come see you next week and we'll figure this shit out together. 'Kay?"

With that, he headed for the door, nabbing a piece of candy from the bowl. He let himself out, but just before the door closed, he reached back in and turned the front light on again.

"Happy Halloween!"

Annie smiled at his parting words. The resiliency of kids always amazed her. They seemed to have a special knack for bouncing back from tragedy.

Unless it killed them first.

Chapter Eighteen

"WHAT HAPPENED? WHY DID that Ferguson kid come to the house, Annie?" Henry asked, his eyes on the front door, moments after Ferguson had slammed it shut. "You know I hate it when you bring work home with you. But this is extreme, even for you."

Annie didn't hear any bite in her husband's tone. He seemed genuinely concerned. She let out a heavy breath and said, "The police came by my office this afternoon."

Henry joined her in the living room, taking the chair Ferguson had recently vacated. "That's never a good thing. Wait. Wasn't Ferguson the kid you said overdosed a while back? Did the cops come to talk to you about him?"

"No. I mean, yes, he *is* the kid who ended up in the emergency room back in September, but the police weren't in my office to talk about him. Ferguson's last name is Carbo. He comes from a long line of troublemakers, but I'm still convinced that he's different. He's special. The poor kid has been through a lot in his short life, and today was another blow to the family."

Henry shrugged. "Kid looked fine tonight. Maybe a little distraught."

"He's not fine. The police came by to inform me they'd just come from a house where they found two deceased young men. They suspect drugs.

One was Ferguson's cousin. That's why the boy came here. He heard after I did, and he's upset. Scared. He's not dumb. He knows that could have been him. Besides, he said Zeke was a mentor to him. Most of the men in Ferguson's life are worthless."

Henry sat back in his chair and extended his legs, crossing them at the ankles. "Damn. I knew Zeke. I mean, I didn't *know* him, but he was one of our delivery guys. If the guy died from an overdose, he couldn't have been a great mentor."

Although those were Annie's initial thoughts, too, she couldn't help but defend Ferguson. He didn't have enough people in his corner. And after today, he had one fewer. "Henry, that isn't nice. The poor guy is *dead*."

"Fine. Look, I'm sorry your student is going through so much. That's heavy stuff. But, hey, aren't you even a little curious about why your own son came home tonight?"

The abrupt shift in the conversation took her by surprise. "I haven't talked to him much yet. I assumed that maybe his Friday class got canceled, and he wanted to run home so he could help me hand out candy."

As if on cue, the doorbell rang.

"I've got it!" their son yelled from the back of the house. Relic appeared, sliding the last two feet in his socks to reach the front door. He picked up the big bowl of candy, grimacing as he glanced at its contents. "Ick. Mom, this candy is crap."

For the first time in what felt like hours, Annie laughed. It was good to see her son again. "Don't tell the little kids that," she said as he swung open the door.

Once he'd delivered handfuls of candy to the ghosts and goblins on the front stoop, Relic joined his parents in the living room. "No Reese's?"

"Sorry, bud. They were out. No chocolate left of any kind."

He shook his head. "You waited too long to buy it again, didn't you?"

"What can I say? I'm a busy girl. Just like you're supposed to be a busy boy. At school. So, Relic, what brings you home in the middle of the week? Is everything all right with your classes?"

Their son took a seat on the armrest, right next to her. "Jeez, can't a guy come home for Halloween?"

She snorted. "Relic, you're a college freshman. I'd assumed there'd be plenty of fun for you to find at school tonight. I was prepared to lie in bed and worry about you for half the night. And now, here you are. What's the real reason you're home on a Thursday night? I didn't think we'd see you again until Thanksgiving."

The bell rang again. The trick-or-treaters were out in force.

She stopped her son from getting the door with a hand on his knee. "Henry, can you get that?" As Henry rose, she pulled at Relic's hand. "You know I hate it when you sit on the armrest. It's already wobbly. Sit here next to me."

He did as she asked, but not without the mandatory roll of his eyes.

"Now. The truth," she said.

"Mom, when are you going to stop interrogating me like I'm one of your students?"

She took a deep breath. "Relic. Come on. It's been a long day. I have some phone calls to make, and I'm worried about you. Give me a break here."

"You don't need to worry about me. I promise. I just ran home to see Kaylee. Something is up with her. Plus, you know I like to hand out candy with you."

"Kaylee? Is she not dealing with your breakup as well as you'd hoped?"

A large group of kids must be approaching, because they could hear their laughter outside on the walk. Relic bolted for the door.

Annie exchanged a worried look with Henry, who had sat back down after the last batch of kids. She'd been secretly relieved when Relic called things off with his on-again-off-again girlfriend—for good this time, she'd thought—before packing up for college. He'd wanted her to enjoy her senior year in high school, but he'd also admitted he thought college would be more fun if he wasn't still tied to someone back home. A troubling thought surfaced. The girl wasn't pregnant, was she?

All Relic's plans for his future could disappear in a flash.

She was excited about the arrival of their first grandchild in a matter of months, but Ava was already through college and married.

"You're doing it again," Henry said.

"Doing what?"

"Overreacting." He got to his feet when Lemon whined at him, spinning in circles. "I'll take her out back."

"What do you mean, 'overreacting'? You're the one who just asked me why I wasn't worried about our own son. You don't think she's pregnant, do you?"

Henry shook his head. "I didn't say 'worried.' I said 'curious.' "

"*Mom*. For God's sake, stop it." Relic shut the door a little too hard and set the candy bowl back down. He helped himself to a Jolly Rancher, popping it into his mouth as he rejoined his parents. "Kaylee isn't pregnant. She's just been hanging out with some new people her friend Gabi works with at the grocery store, and they've been partying pretty hard. I don't want Kaylee to screw things up for herself. Now, if you two can handle the door, I'll take Lemon out. I want to try Kaylee again. She was supposed to call me right back, but she hasn't."

Henry watched Relic leave the room, then he turned back to Annie. "Look. I know you work with a lot of kids with colossal problems. But you have to quit assuming the worst with our own kids. Go. Eat. I saved a plate for you back in the kitchen. I'll hand out candy."

"But you hate handing out candy."

He held out a hand to her and pulled her up off the couch. "Not as much as I hate it when you plant your seeds of worry into *my* brain, too. I'm already up to my eyeballs in trying to figure out what's really going on at work. And now I'm going to have to find a new delivery guy. Zeke was part of Byron's group, which they've temporarily folded into my team. Don't give me something to worry about with Relic, too."

With that, he turned her toward the kitchen and gave her a playful swat on the butt.

"Fine, but only three pieces per kid," she said, earning herself another eye roll. Like father like son.

"Annie, you really need to stop trying to control everyone and everything around you. The more I give to each kid, the quicker we'll run out of candy and be able to turn off the front light. I want to watch our show."

"But that's not fair to the kids who haven't gotten here yet," she protested over the rumble of her empty stomach. She really was hungry.

"Annie, when are you ever going to figure out that life isn't fair?"

Twenty minutes later, Annie cracked open the one remaining fortune cookie and pulled the paper tab out.

Before preparing to improve the world,

first look around your own home three times.

Her phone vibrated with an incoming call. She dropped the slip of paper onto her empty plate and scooped the phone off the island, smiling at the picture on her screen of her dear friend in a wedding dress, the sunset as a backdrop.

"I was just thinking about you earlier today, Kit. I wanted to call you and see how things are going with Isaac. Is he settled in at school? Oh, and of course, how are you enjoying married life? We had so much fun at your wedding. Henry really hit it off with Renee's husband."

A giggle cut her off. "Hello to you, too, Annie. I was the one who called you, remember? And you're hitting me with twenty questions. Slow down. What are you up to? Oh! And happy Halloween!"

She got off the stool and walked to the fridge. Chinese food always made her thirsty. "Actually, right when you called, I felt like I was getting gobsmacked by the Universe."

"The *Universe*, huh? Now you sound like Lynette. What happened? Is everything all right?"

She popped the top on a can of fruity mineral water and sat back down as tiny bubbles that smelled like cherries rained down on her hand. "Everything is fine. Work is crazy as usual. Relic surprised us by coming home tonight. And since I spend most of my time helping kids with serious issues, one tiny whiff of trouble with my son and my mind assumes the worst. You know?"

A sigh came through the phone. "If you'd asked me that question six months ago, I might have said no. I didn't understand what a mother goes through. But now I sure do. In fact, that's why I called."

Annie put her can down. "Did something happen to Isaac?"

Kit laughed. "Jeez, Annie. Relax. I see what you mean about your tendency to jump to conclusions. Isaac is doing fine. At least, I think he is. He asked to go out with friends to a movie tonight, but all I can think about is whether that is really what they're doing. What if he went to some wild party instead? I called for advice. I have no idea what I'm doing. I've never been a mother before."

Annie disagreed with that last statement. Kit had practically raised her two younger brothers, along with help from their grandparents, because neither of their parents were around during their teen years. She had more experience than she gave herself credit for. But Annie understood Kit's anxiety. Kit and her brand-new husband were also the new foster parents for a fifteen-year-old boy they'd only known for a few months.

It had to feel overwhelming.

"I think it's a good sign that Isaac has already made friends to do things with, so you must be doing some things right," Annie said. "Can't you just check his location on your phone?"

Kit was quiet.

"He has a phone, doesn't he? All kids do these days."

"Sure. I even asked him to allow me to access his location. He said no."

Annie smiled, despite the hesitancy in her friend's voice. "Of course he wasn't thrilled with the idea. But I suggest you insist on this one."

"Really? I can't imagine what I would have done if my grandmother snooped into my privacy like that growing up . . ."

"I know. But the world is a different place than it was when we were kids. Just the notion that almost every kid has what basically amounts to a powerful computer in the palm of their hands means that we, as their parents, have to change how we parent. These kids have access to virtually anything and everything through those things. If there is a party within driving distance, it only takes a second for word to spread. Unfortunately, some very bad people also pollute the internet. I don't say that to scare you. Just like anything else, there is good and bad that comes with most technology. Believe me, you'll feel better if you can see that he is where he says he's going to be."

Annie heard a shuffling through the phone. Or maybe it was sniffling.

"Kit? Are you all right?"

It sounded like her friend was blowing her nose. She waited.

"I don't think I'm cut out for this, Annie. What if I can't keep him safe?"

This was territory Annie knew well. "Remember before you and Dean stepped up and offered to take Isaac in? He and his grandfather were muddling through things, and Isaac was hanging out with a tough group of kids back here in Ruby Shores. Now look at him. You're doing your best."

Even as she said those words, she realized just how blessed Kit's Isaac was to be away from here. The boy he'd spent time with during the summer months was Jason Carbo, and Jason's big brother had just died, probably from drug-related activities. Annie updated Kit on the situation. The police had wanted her to keep things to herself until families were notified, but it seemed they were getting through that process.

"Oh wow, Annie. I'm so sorry. That is heavy stuff. And you're right. I think Isaac is better off here. Poor Floyd . . . Isaac's grandfather is a dear man, but someone who is almost ninety isn't in any position to raise a teenager. Not if there are better options."

"Exactly. And you are a much better option. You two have so much to offer a boy like Isaac. I remember Dean said he even has an interest in some things Isaac wants to do after college."

Kit sighed. "I'm so glad I called you. You always give my ego a boost."

"Isn't that what friends are for?" Annie said, smiling as she took a sip of her sparkling water. "I'd planned to call you to check on Isaac, and to tell you what happened with the Carbos. Set up the tracking on his phone. Trust me, you'll feel marginally better with that. But there was something else I meant to talk to you about, too."

"I hope it's something fun. Because between worrying about Isaac, and this big reception-type party Dean's mother is planning back in Iowa at Thanksgiving to celebrate our wedding, my nerves are about shot."

Annie had forgotten all about the party Dean's mom had insisted on. The couple's wedding came together quickly earlier in the month, once Kit finally agreed to set a date, and not everyone could make it. It was no surprise the party was making Kit nervous. She didn't like a fuss.

"If the progress I'm making on planning our next girls' trip sounds like a fun discussion topic, then yes."

"Perfect," Kit said, and Annie could hear the smile in her voice. "I already miss the warm weather, and it's only the end of October! What have you figured out so far? And don't worry, I won't disagree with anything you're planning. I know how stressed I got over planning our trip to Hawaii, and I'm glad I could pass the planning baton on to you. Just tell me your idea includes warmth and water. And maybe a little wine. We have to go early this year, right? That's what we all agreed to?"

"Right. With Ava's new baby due in early March, I don't know what life will look like after that. I plan to help her out with some babysitting next summer, when I can get away from work. As the principal, I don't get summers off, but I do have some flexibility, and daycare is so expensive. This will be the one summer I arrange things so I can help. Then they'll have to figure things out."

Henry came in, looking for another bag of candy.

"Give me a second, Kit."

When she had him restocked, she turned her attention back to her friend. "You still think you can get away in February, even though you have Isaac now?"

"Absolutely. Dean can handle Isaac for a week. He knows how important these annual girls' trips are to all of us. He'd never interfere with the Kaleidoscope Girls' fun!"

That reminded Annie of the surprise present Lynette had sent. She told Kit about it.

"Lynette has always seemed like the most sentimental one of us all," Kit said. "Who would have guessed that? When we were kids, Lynette was so wild."

Annie considered this. "I think she just felt pretty lost when we were teenagers. Her mom tried hard, but I know it was tough. I work with so many kids who have it rough. Whenever I'm tempted to give up on one of them, I remember what a success Lynette has made of her life, despite everything. Every kid deserves a chance."

"That's exactly what I was thinking when I came up with the crazy notion of fostering Isaac. I hope I don't come to regret it. But he's a great kid, and you've made me feel better. Now, what have you figured out about the trip?"

Annie gave her a quick rundown of the discussion she'd had with her mother about their home in Arizona. Kit said she thought that all sounded fabulous. She was about to ask Kit about work when Relic yelled down to her from his room.

"I suppose I better go see what he wants," she said. "Besides, we need to save things to talk about in February. That'll be here before we know it. I need to call Lynette tonight, too, to thank her for the kaleidoscope. And I'll call Jackie and Renee, too, to make sure these travel plans I'm pulling together will work for them."

Kit assured her it all sounded wonderful and signed off, promising to call her after Dean's family's party at Thanksgiving to give her a full rundown of the event.

After she'd helped Relic find some spare underwear—since, of course, he'd forgotten to pack any—he showered and left. She tried Lynette and ended up leaving a message when her friend didn't pick up.

She was searching for Jackie's number in her phone when Henry came back with an empty candy bowl.

"The candy is gone, and I turned off the front light. Relic took off and said he'd be back in a couple hours. Why don't we go watch another episode of *Yellowstone*? Or better yet, we could go play a little trick-or-treating of our own upstairs, in our bedroom."

Annie clicked off her phone, giving her husband her full attention for the first time that day. "A little 'trick-or-treating' of our own, huh? Is that code for you wanting to fool around a little?"

"Maybe," he said, wriggling his eyebrows at her.

His grin looked more relaxed than it had in a long time, and she saw a flash of the man she'd fallen in love with so long ago. It occurred to her that maybe he was struggling with the whole "empty nest" thing as much as she was, but he usually kept it hidden. Relic was back in town but out of the house for the time being, and Henry finally looked happy.

She considered pointing out the fact that he'd shown very little interest in sex in the two months that their youngest had been off at college, and it was ironic that he finally wanted to fool around when there was a chance of discovery instead of when they were completely alone. But she didn't want to squelch his good mood.

"Give me a second to put away my dishes and I'll be up. Maybe I'll bring my witch's broom."

He laughed and left her alone in the kitchen with a quick salute. He was already reaching for the bottom of his shirt as he headed for the stairs.

Men, she thought, as she stashed her dishes in the dishwasher and wiped off the island.

She noticed a slip of paper on the floor. Picking it up, she reread the message she'd pulled out of her fortune cookie earlier. Was the Universe reminding her to do a better job of keeping things at home a priority?

The floor creaked above her. Henry was waiting.

Too bad she didn't really have an old wooden broom in the pantry. It might have made for a fun prop. It never hurt to change things up a little after so many years of marriage.

Out of an abundance of caution, she locked the door from the garage into the kitchen. She remembered the way she'd laughed with her girl-friends while in Maui over the struggles of maintaining any kind of sex life with teens around. The last thing she needed was to have Relic show up and surprise them again.

On her way to the stairs, she pulled up his location just to double check. It looked like he was indeed at his ex-girlfriend's house, giving her and Henry at least a little window of privacy.

It feels good to feel wanted, she thought, unbuttoning the blazer she still hadn't had time to change out of.

That feeling didn't happen often enough anymore.

Chapter Nineteen

The month of November always felt too short to Annie, hectic even, and this year wasn't any different. There was so much going on. After Halloween, Annie and Henry had sat Relic down before he headed back to college and talked to him about what was going on with the drug situation in town. His old girlfriend, Kaylee, was best friends with Gabi, and Annie worried Gabi knew more than she'd admit. They wanted Relic to appreciate how serious the problem had become in case the two girls were pieces of the puzzle.

They also wanted to make sure Relic was settling in at college. His running home on Halloween had come as a surprise. Had he made up or exaggerated his worry over Kaylee as an excuse to hide homesickness? Feeling homesick wasn't serious, but regardless, open communication with their youngest was key.

It bothered Annie that Relic didn't attempt to see either Colton or Ava while he was home. They used to be so close. But there was only so much she could do to repair any relationship strife the three of them were suffering. They were all growing up, and she couldn't force anything where her kids were concerned, even though she hated the idea that they might never feel like a cohesive unit again.

There had been little progress, as far as Annie knew, in the situation with the drugs in town. Maybe if Zeke Carbo had come from a more upstanding family in the community, or if the other young man who died had also been local, people would be pushing harder for answers.

She had put Ferguson in touch with Ivory down at the precinct, and while the police seemed to appreciate his offer to help, Annie wasn't aware of any breaks in the case. Henry was still insisting that nothing unusual was going on at work, and any rumors seemed to have died off.

Maybe one bad batch of illegal drugs *had* made it to the streets of Ruby Shores, but now things were settling back into a more normal routine. Annie wasn't naïve; she knew there were likely things still going on that could keep a parent sleepless with worry.

But at least no one else had died.

Relic was back at school. Ava's baby bump seemed to grow each time Annie was lucky enough to spend time with her daughter. Colton was busy at work—which wasn't necessarily a good thing for the town, given he worked at the funeral home, but such was life.

Her looming question for today was whether she should invite Michael to spend Thanksgiving with them. She didn't talk to him often because of the way it upset Henry, but Ava had reported back to her that Michael had no Thanksgiving plans. She was the one who'd suggested they invite him. It was Annie's turn to host Thanksgiving for her extended family. Her parents planned to be there. Millie was noncommittal, as usual, adding to Annie's angst over the upcoming holiday.

The one thing she was no longer too concerned about was their February girls' trip. She'd reached Lynette, Jackie, and Renee after she'd talked to Kit, and everyone was game for a winter escape to the desert. They'd booked flights right away. She would worry about planning their daily schedules after the holidays. Staying at her parents' house in Arizona simplified things.

She needed a little *simple* right now.

In the meantime, she'd prepare for Thanksgiving.

After parking in the grocery store lot, she double-checked the list she'd typed up on her phone. She couldn't *wing* this holiday dinner. The most important thing on the list was to find the largest frozen turkey available. This was always her kids' favorite meal of the year, and regardless of the exact number of guests, everyone would want leftovers.

Once inside, she grabbed a cart and headed for the meat department, fingers crossed that she'd find a big enough bird. The store was busy, and even though Thanksgiving was still twelve days away, shoppers were snatching up the most common holiday fixings.

Instead of trying to check the black and green olives off her grocery list on the way to the back of the store, she should have watched where she was going.

Smack.

In her distracted state, she'd rammed right into another shopping cart, parked off to the side in the bread aisle. Luckily, she didn't hit the *person* pushing the cart.

"I am so sorry," she said, mentally kicking herself for being so distracted.

A man swung to face her, and recognition dawned. "Hey, Annie. Fancy running into you here."

She laughed. "Oh God, *Owen*. I wasn't watching where I was going. Dumb, I know, given how busy it is in here. Let me guess. You're shopping for Thanksgiving, too?" She nodded first to the package of Brown 'N Serve rolls in his hand and then to his half-filled cart.

"I am. My boys and I decided to have Thanksgiving in Ruby Shores this year. Usually they spend it with their mother, but she had something else going on this year. So, we are just going to hang out here. Actually, that reminds me. I was going to call you."

This came as a surprise. Owen was an acquaintance, but not someone she talked to often. He was more of a friend to Jackie. "Really? What about?"

"About Jackie. She turns fifty the weekend of Thanksgiving, right? She'd mentioned having so much fun celebrating last Thanksgiving at her folks' house that they hoped to get back in the habit of coming to Ruby Shores every year."

Annie nodded. "That's right. She did. You have an excellent memory."

The man shrugged, and she could have sworn his cheeks looked pink. *Is he blushing?*

Annie and the rest of the Kaleidoscope Girls—aside from Jackie, of course—had talked more than once about how nice it would be to see Owen and Jackie give dating a try. Why couldn't they acknowledge the attraction that seemed so obvious to everyone else?

"Anyway . . ." he said, dropping the rolls into his cart. "I thought it might be fun if a bunch of us went out to celebrate her birthday. Do you know if anyone else is planning something while she's in town? Will Lynette or Kit be around? I suppose Renee wouldn't be, since this isn't home for her."

Clearly Owen had put some thought into Jackie's upcoming milestone birthday. Annie thought it was cute.

"Actually, the five of us are planning to celebrate all of our birthdays in February. We're taking a little trip to Arizona together. We thought it might be too hard to plan individual parties, given everyone's busy schedules, and we didn't want to leave anyone out."

He didn't hide his disappointment.

"Shoot . . . I was hoping to see her."

"Owen, why don't you just call her? Ask her out? I'm sure celebrating her birthday over dinner with you would be enough for Jackie."

He looked skeptical. "Ask her out? Like, on a date? She'd never go out with me."

"I think you're wrong about that."

"No." He shook his head emphatically. "I don't date. But I was hoping to celebrate with her. With all of you, actually. It would be fun. What if we planned something less formal? Maybe a little get-together for the Friday after Thanksgiving? I bet she won't leave town right away."

"Oh man, I don't know . . ." Annie paused. A party *was* tempting. "She made me promise not to do that. I don't think she enjoys being the first of our group to turn fifty. She didn't want any special attention before our trip."

He grinned. "That sounds like Jackie. But it would be foolish not to at least do a little something for her if several of us are in town. Come on. There's that fun little pub downtown, right next to the Crystal Café. I know the owner. Let's keep it informal, and maybe not even tell her. I promise I'll tell her it was my idea, so she can't get mad at you. And, you know, most of our kids are at least twenty-one, too. They could join us. None of the rest of us will get to celebrate with you on your girls' trip."

Annie appreciated his tenacity. And it would be fun, as long as Jackie wasn't too upset. "I suppose I could mention it to Lynette and Renee, just in case they could make it work. Kit has plans with Dean's family in

Iowa. We *have* been meaning to get our kids together, too. My two oldest are just a little older than Jackie's twins. Would you invite your boys?"

"Sure!" He looked excited. "It would give us something to do."

Annie realized his excitement was contagious. It would be fun to have a little pre-party now, and they could still celebrate all of them turning fifty come February. Besides, she had only promised Jackie that *she* wouldn't plan anything on her actual birthday. She never said she wouldn't *attend* a party someone else pulled together.

"Fine. You've convinced me. But remember, that day is Black Friday. I know people often celebrate turning fifty with black sashes and black balloons, but she may already be in a black mood if we do this behind her back. Take it easy with any decorations."

He nodded, a bright smile on his face. "Jackie is always a good sport once you get her past her stubborn streak. I'll take care of everything—other than looping in your kids, plus Lynette and Renee. If you could talk with them, that would be great. I'll even call Jackie's mom and ask her to help me figure out a way to get her to the party. And whoever else in her family that Charlotte thinks would like to join in on the fun. Let's aim for, say . . . seven, to start? We aren't twenty-one anymore, so we probably shouldn't get started too late. We don't want our guest of honor to be too tired!"

After saying their goodbyes, she turned away with a new pep in her step. Making Jackie wait to celebrate her fiftieth when they would all be together again hadn't felt fair to Annie, but Owen offered the perfect solution, and this way Jackie couldn't be mad at her for breaking a promise.

Chapter Twenty

Annie loaded her groceries into her car. Regret was already settling in over agreeing to Owen's secretive birthday plans for Jackie. She'd promised not to plan anything. Was she obligated to warn her friend if someone else was doing the planning?

Maybe the Universe was already paying her back for her disloyalty to Jackie. By the time she'd reached the meat department after speaking with Owen, the largest turkey she could find was eighteen pounds. Given the number of guests she might host for Thanksgiving, she'd need something bigger. Two smaller birds might have been another option, but her oven was on the small side. Two would never fit at once.

The store was also out of frozen corn. *Unbelievable.* Canned corn would never do.

She'd have to drive over to the larger grocer, one town over.

Then she remembered Henry's idea that they go out for dinner later. The suggestion had come as a surprise. Back when the kids were all home, they'd made a habit of taking them out for dinner on a Saturday night, once or twice a month, but she couldn't remember the last time just the two of them had made the effort.

There was a popular steak place in the town with the grocery store where she might find frozen corn and a larger turkey. Maybe they could do both, though there was snow in the forecast. One section of the road between Ruby Shores and Angel Falls was notoriously tricky in blustery weather. But Henry had new tires on his SUV. They'd be fine. She'd wait to mention the need to swing by the store until they were on the road. As long as she made reservations, Henry might agree to drive the extra forty minutes for an excellent dinner. She looked up the phone number and called before leaving the parking lot.

Her husband must have heard the weather forecast, too, because by the time she arrived back home with the groceries, he was up on a ladder, hanging Christmas lights. She parked next to his vehicle in the driveway and walked over to stand at the base of the ladder.

"Look at you, getting in on the holiday spirit early. Are all the strands working?"

"Almost. Half of the strand I usually wrap around the garage doors didn't light up, but I'd picked up a few extra sets on sale after Christmas last year."

Like everyone else, Henry had his share of faults, but Annie had found his love of Christmas charming. It was yet another difference between Henry and Michael. Despite the fun she and Michael had had during that long-ago Christmas holiday that ended up dramatically altering the course of all three of their lives, her first husband had never embraced the holiday the way Henry always did.

"Need any help?"

He glanced down at her. "Don't you have a carload of groceries to put away?"

"I do."

"I'll tell you what. Hold the ladder so I can come down, and we'll move it over a few more feet. Then I'll be good for a while. I may need your help when I get to the top peak, but I'll let you know."

She nodded and, wedging her boot against one leg for a little extra stability, held tight to the ladder. "Sounds good. And I'll warm up the soup we still have left over from Thursday night for lunch."

He groaned as he reached the bottom rung. "I hate leftovers."

"Too bad, bud," she said as she stepped out of the way. "Neither of us like to cook, and without Relic home to eat with us, leftovers are part of our lives going forward. You like to eat, right?"

He grinned at her logic. "I like to eat."

Annie unloaded the groceries while Henry got back to the lights. The afternoon passed quickly as they both went about their weekend tasks. There was comfort in the routine. By four, Henry had all the outside lights strung, the lawnmower winterized and put away, and the snow-blower pulled out with fresh gas and oil. While he worked outside, Annie turned her attention to the neglected interior of their home. There was plenty to do before they'd host Thanksgiving, and she regretted not following through on her friend Wendy's suggestion to hire a cleaning lady.

Not that she felt they could afford to hire someone to come in and clean a house that didn't get nearly as dirty now that it was just the two of them. Annie made a decent living, but there were plenty of expenses to cover. The two largest outflows were both something Henry insisted on. He liked the idea of paying off their mortgage early, so he'd set up automatic payments twice a month instead of just one. He also wanted to cover Relic's tuition for all four years of his undergraduate studies, plus room and board for his first year. It was what they'd done for both

Ava and Colton, but unlike his older siblings, Relic hadn't secured any academic scholarships. He'd relied instead on the gamble that he could earn some scholarships based on his talent on the baseball field. Competition was fierce, and no scholarships surfaced. That disappointment hit around the same time as Henry's demotion at work. But Henry wanted to maintain their plan, even with a lower income coming in, and Annie worried she'd upset him if she pushed too hard.

So, she scrubbed her own toilets on weekends. It was a sacrifice she made to keep the peace. Maybe in her next lifetime she'd have a live-in chef and maid.

By the time dusk fell, they were on the road to the restaurant.

"The soup didn't stick with me. I'm starving," Henry said. "Thanks for making reservations. We shouldn't have to wait for a table."

Annie fiddled with the radio and complimented him again on the Christmas lights. He'd done a nice job with them, and she needed him to be in a good mood given the things she'd have to discuss with him later over his T-bone and baked potato.

She noticed as he set the cruise and bit back a sigh as she glanced over at the heavy cloud bank, off to the west. Maybe the setting sun was making them look more threatening and the snow would hold off. Annie's father had taught her to never use cruise control while driving in the winter, but Henry was stubborn and used it when he thought the roads were clear enough.

She preferred the years when they didn't get any measurable snow until closer to Christmas, but the snow that already lined the ditches meant they might be in for a long winter.

"You seem quiet tonight," Henry said. He turned the radio down a click. "Everything all right?"

She'd been rehearsing in her head how she would broach the subject of inviting Michael to their Thanksgiving celebration, and let her husband know that Millie finally got back to her an hour ago to say they would be coming. He wouldn't be pleased about the expanding guest list. Dislike of Millie was one thing both Henry and Michael agreed on.

But talking about it while seated in a decent restaurant, surrounded by other patrons, would be best. There'd be no yelling.

"Everything's fine," she said instead. "I didn't sleep well last night, and I'm hungry, too."

He seemed to accept that, driving on in silence. The snow began before they reached their turnoff. At least he clicked the cruise control off without her having to ask.

He wasn't going to be happy about an extra stop at the grocery store after they finished eating, especially if this snow kept up, but she needed that turkey.

This wasn't feeling like a fun-filled Saturday night date. Sometimes she missed the thrill of a relationship that hadn't settled into the comfortable zone. But, on the other hand, she didn't have the energy to break someone new in.

Besides, he hung a mean strand of Christmas lights.

She'd keep him around.

Henry let out a low whistle as the crowded parking lot surrounding the steak joint came into view. They'd be lucky to find a spot.

Fifteen minutes later, the two sat at a table on the outer edge of the main room, next to a window that would have a view of a snowy golf course if it wasn't dark outside. Henry was nursing the one beer he'd allow himself while Annie sipped a chardonnay and they waited for their meals to arrive.

"Say, Henry . . . I wanted to visit with you about Thanksgiving."

Her comment pulled his attention from the darkened window where he'd been gazing for the past few minutes, lost in thought.

"I wish it wasn't our year to host," he said. "It's so much easier when your parents cook."

He was correct. It was easier for the two of them, but their kids all preferred to celebrate in the house they'd grown up in, now that they no longer lived at home.

If he was already unhappy about hosting, he'd resist what was coming.

"I think the kids want to develop holiday traditions more focused around our house. Besides, Mom and Dad are talking about heading to Arizona even earlier next year. Who knows, this may be their last Thanksgiving in Minnesota."

Henry helped himself to a piece of warm bread from the basket on the table between them. He looked like he was considering her words. "I don't like change."

She laughed. "I know. But you've done it before. Remember how you hated it when your parents moved from Tennessee to Florida, and then we couldn't afford to keep flying south every year with three kids? We had to create new traditions here. Well, at my parents', I mean. And now they are probably going to pass the baton to us."

Her in-laws were both in the nursing home now. Henry was ten years younger than his three siblings. His parents were older and had always felt more like grandparents to Annie.

"Fine." He sighed. "I understand why your folks want to escape this."

She followed his hand as he motioned toward the darkened window to his left. Flakes of snow were sticking to and melting down the glass. It would be a tricky drive home.

"At least, by this time next year, our first grandchild will be in a highchair at the Thanksgiving table," she said, hoping to kick him out of the funk he seemed to be stuck in. He still hadn't shown much outward excitement about the baby, but Henry loved kids. She hoped he'd come around.

Her words earned her nothing more than a small smile that faded so fast she might have imagined it. Her frustration inched upward.

"Henry, nothing is more important to me than maintaining the relationship the five of us have. We are getting older, and there will come a day when we aren't around to help maintain a strong relationship between Relic, Ava, and Colton. I hate the idea of them growing apart. And now, with Ava and Daniel's new daughter on the way, it's more important than ever that we maintain a strong family unit. Don't you agree?"

He shrugged. "I'm not close with my brothers and sister, and I do fine."

"I want things to be different for our kids. I don't want them to settle for *fine*. Blending families is difficult, I know that . . . but, to be honest with you, Henry, you used to be better at this."

Annie wished she'd kept the hint of accusation out of her tone, but she couldn't help it. Her husband needed to adjust his attitude.

She thought he'd deny it.

He didn't.

Instead, he watched her over the rim of his water glass as he took a sip. "It wasn't easy, Annie."

"What wasn't easy?"

"Raising his kids. I'm not sure I can do it anymore."

His blunt response knocked the wind out of Annie's lungs. She thought the setting for this conversation would prevent Henry from yelling, but *she* was the one biting her tongue now.

How dare he say that.

"Henry. I've always thought of all three of them as your kids. You used to, too. I know you did. What changed that?"

He switched from the water back to his beer, his eyes taking on a wary look. "Are we really going to do this here?"

She opened her mouth to respond, but found she was at a loss for words. Her heart literally ached. She felt betrayed. Again. Instead of admitting as much out loud, she busied her hands with her own piece of bread.

When their food arrived, the uncomfortable silence expanded. They both pretended to eat.

Eventually, their waiter returned, his expression concerned. "Was there something wrong with your entrées?"

The question snapped Annie out of her thoughts. "Oh, no. I'm sorry. We had a late lunch. Would you mind bringing us a couple of boxes? We'll take this home with us. It looks like the snow isn't letting up, so we better be on our way."

He looked only slightly relieved as he scurried off for the boxes.

This discussion had gone even worse than she'd feared. No sense trying to salvage it. "Fine. If that's the way you really feel about it, we will need to talk about this later. But you should know that I've decided I'm inviting Michael over to celebrate Thanksgiving with us. Ava asked me to, so he won't be alone, and it isn't fair to her and Colton to have to celebrate without their father. Relic gets you, after all."

She could see the rigidity in Henry's body, but he held her eye without a word.

"Oh. And Millie and her husband are coming, too. I know she can be rather difficult, but she is my sister, and that means something to me."

He slowly set his napkin over his half-eaten meal. He ignored the box the waiter placed next to his plate.

Annie went through the motions to transfer her steak, green beans, and sweet potato into her box. She had a feeling she wouldn't be in the mood to cook tomorrow.

"Is there anything else you wanted to throw at me tonight?" he asked.

She knew he was furious because his lips barely moved, but it was unlikely anyone else would sense his animosity. Unless they could feel it rippling off him in waves like she could.

"Yes. We need to stop at the grocery store on the corner. They were out of the big turkeys at home. And I need corn. They didn't have corn either."

He looked at her like she'd lost her mind, then wordlessly picked up the tab and headed for the hostess station up front.

"That went well," Annie muttered, pulling on her own jacket and grimacing when she caught a sympathetic glance from the woman one table over.

CHAPTER TWENTY-ONE

ENRY WAITED IN THE vehicle while Annie ran inside to grab a turkey . . . if they had one. The snow was falling harder, promising a difficult drive home.

She clomped the snow from the boots she'd donned at the last minute when they'd left the house. The mat in the entryway of the glaringly bright store was already sodden from the coming and going of customers.

"How many weeks until I can escape this misery for Arizona?"

"Can I come, too?"

Annie hadn't meant to say those words out loud. She grinned at the boy bagging groceries who'd invited himself along. "Sorry. Girls' trip."

He shrugged. The smile remained on his youthful face. "It was worth a try. Be careful. These floors get slick in here when the snow and muck get dragged in."

Appreciating the advice, Annie took two steps, then stopped, turning back to the helpful clerk. "Would you mind pointing me toward your turkeys? I've only shopped here once or twice."

He hoisted a full bag of groceries into an elderly man's cart. "I can do one better. I'll walk you back and help you pick out the best bird. But give me just one minute," he said to Annie before turning back to the man. "It's pretty nasty out there, Sam. I'd be happy to take this to your car for you."

Annie was eager to grab a turkey and get back outside, but the helpful kid's guidance would save her time in the long run. She waited as the other customer pulled battered yellow gloves on and shook his head.

"Thanks for the offer, but I got this. Help her. She looks like she's in a hurry."

She felt a rush of both gratitude and shame over the man's comment. If he fell and broke a hip outside, it would be her fault.

"I'll be fine," he assured the young man, who appeared unsure which customer needed him the most.

But the elderly man turned and left the store with his cart, so the clerk turned his attention back to Annie. "Here. I'll show you. What brings you in on a night like this, if you don't normally shop here?"

She hurried to keep up with the boy. He'd warned her to be careful, but he was moving fast. Maybe he'd decided she wasn't as old as he initially thought.

"I live in Ruby Shores but came over here for dinner, and I thought you might have a bigger turkey than I could find at the grocery store back home."

He nodded, veering right at the end of the aisle. "You're in luck. We got a shipment in two hours ago. If it wasn't snowing outside, we'd probably be out of them already. Everyone seems to want big birds this year."

Annie wondered if the clerk was still in high school. Looks could be deceiving, and he had a mature air to him. She supposed her profession was the reason she was always trying to guess ages.

"Will this work?" he asked, hoisting a frozen turkey in the air with a grunt.

"How many pounds is it?"

He referenced the tag that was helping to secure the plastic netting encasing the bird. "Almost twenty-six pounds."

"That'll be plenty," she said, a sigh of relief rushing out. "I was worried I wouldn't find one large enough."

She reached for the bird and his expression turned doubtful.

"It's pretty heavy. Are you sure you can carry it? I probably should have grabbed you a cart."

While she appreciated how helpful he was, her ego had suffered enough bruising for one night. "I can handle it. Here. Thank you for your help."

"Hey, can I get a little help over here?" A woman who looked twice Annie's age struggled with a similar-size turkey on the other side of the waist-high cooler.

"Go," Annie said, taking the turkey with both hands.

The words *dead weight* skittered through her brain, but she'd be damned if she'd admit how heavy it felt. She took the most direct route back to the front registers, paid for the turkey, and grinned her appreciation at the cashier, an older woman, who took her money and then pulled a cart over for her to use to get her prized bird outside.

Frozen snow and ice were already causing ruts in the parking lot, so it took all her might to push the cart to the running SUV. Henry couldn't have noticed her struggle, or he'd have helped, regardless of how mad he was at her.

She tapped on the back hatch, and it popped open. After hoisting the bird up and inside, she shoved the cart into the closest corral and tapped the button to close the back of Henry's vehicle.

Henry ended a phone call as she climbed into the passenger seat. She knocked her feet together outside before swinging them around and in.

"It's really getting bad out there."

He nodded. "You found one then?"

"Yep. A nice kid helped me out. He kind of reminded me of Relic. We have what we need now for Thanksgiving."

Then she remembered she still needed corn.

Apparently, however, that was the extent of Henry's willingness to talk, because he eased out of the parking lot and onto the deserted street without another word. She'd have to pick up corn next week. The wiper on his side was doing a poor job of clearing the front windshield. He put his window down, reached outside, and snapped the wiper when he could catch it.

"I hope it doesn't take too long to get home," she said. "Lemon will need to go out pretty soon."

Flashing lights ahead brought them to a crawl, then a full stop. The crossing arms were down on the tracks, but Annie couldn't see a train. Three vehicles stood between them and the rails. They listened to a full song on the radio, but there was still no train or movement ahead.

Another car was approaching from behind.

"Screw this," Henry bit out, throwing the vehicle into reverse and turning around to leave the growing row of cars while he still had room. "There has to be another way out of town. Pull it up on your GPS."

Annie didn't like the idea of attempting unknown backroads in this weather, but Lemon couldn't wait forever. "Fine. You're going to have to give me a minute."

It took more like two minutes, but eventually a new route popped up on her phone and they turned left, driving through a residential neighborhood where lights burned brightly in homes. It looked like the two of them were among the few dumb enough to be out on a night like this. She pointed and Henry turned onto what the map said was a county highway. The shrill whistle of a train cut through the cold night air.

She hoped their impatience didn't turn out to be a terrible call. It was getting hard to see the road, and the snow was starting to obscure the white line marking the shoulder.

"I need you to help me watch," Henry said, his voice tense.

She let the comment slide. Obviously she *was* watching. She didn't need to be told what to do.

"And this is why we should have just stayed home," he ground out.

"Hey, dinner out was your idea," she said, the words slipping out before she could stop them.

Pillow drifts were forming across the road.

"How much farther before we can get back on the main road?"

Annie checked her phone, moaning when a warning popped up: her battery was down to ten percent power.

"What?"

"Nothing," she said quickly. Henry was always on her to keep her phone charged. "It looks like there's another road about five miles ahead that will take us back to the highway we came in on earlier."

He angled his body forward, as if putting his face five inches closer to the windshield would help with the poor visibility beyond the glass.

Everything that followed happened in a blur.

Henry swore and hit the brakes.

Brakes and icy highways are never a safe combination, and the SUV fishtailed.

Annie heard two thumping noises and felt the car bounce, as if they'd hit a speed bump too fast.

A spinning sensation came next, like riding a Tilt-a-Whirl at the county fair but in the middle of a snowstorm instead of on a hot summer evening.

Finally, a wall of powdery snow burst against the windshield and the SUV banged to an abrupt stop.

"Shit," Henry moaned, sitting back against the driver's seat, one hand on his forehead. His glasses were gone.

Annie froze, her senses on overload.

"Annie, honey, are you all right?" Henry asked, his right hand fumbling weakly in her direction, groping across her face.

A faint white glow shone in front of her, punctuated by pinpoints of orange and red.

"Are we dead?" she whispered, blinking hard, then she slapped his hand away when he poked her in the eye. "I see the light."

He laughed, then groaned. "No. I don't think we're dead. Those are the headlights in the snow. We're in the ditch."

She rubbed at her eyes and the scene in front of her cleared. "What happened? Why'd you hit the brakes?"

"Deer."

"Deer? On the road? On a night like this?" She glanced behind her, remembering the thud and bump. "I thought that was a weird place for a speed bump. I don't think the deer made it."

All she saw behind her was a red glow.

"Henry, put the car in park. We need to get out and see what we're dealing with."

He grunted, then did as she had instructed. The red glow from the brake lights subsided.

"I hope we're off the road far enough that another car won't hit us," she said.

Her words snapped Henry into motion. This time, when he reached over for her, his hand gripped her left thigh. "You stay put. I'll get out and see if I can back out of here."

Warnings her father had drilled into her head as a teen, when she was an inexperienced driver, echoed through Annie's brain.

Never leave your vehicle in a snowstorm. Stay with your vehicle. It's the safest place.

"Be careful, Henry. Keep one hand on the vehicle at all times in case the snow makes it hard to see."

The overhead light popped on as he opened his door.

She screeched at the blood running down the side of his face.

He hesitated, then angled the rearview mirror so he could see what she was seeing. "I'm fine. Really. Head wounds always bleed like a mother. See if you can find my glasses. They got knocked off."

He got out and closed his door behind him, leaving her alone in the dark interior once the dome light clicked off again.

What would he find out there?

What would happen if they couldn't drive out?

She unhooked her seatbelt and turned the dome light back on manually to look for his glasses. It didn't take long, and they were still in one piece. She turned the light back off. If they were stuck out here for any length of time, they couldn't afford to wear down the SUV's battery.

How much gas did they have? Was Henry's phone fully charged? She listened to the low moan of the wind outside. She imagined it snaking inside through the vents and wrapping its icy tendrils around her, sucking the life out of her.

This time, when Henry's door opened again, the dome light didn't turn on.

"What happened to the light?" he gasped out as he angled his body back in, under the steering wheel.

"Sorry," she said, reaching up and moving the lever on the side of the light by one notch. But by then the door was closed.

"Leave it," he said.

She could see him let his head drop back while he caught his breath. Wet, sticky snow coated his salt-and-pepper hair. This wasn't the soft, fluffy snow of Hallmark movies.

"What does it look like?"

He sighed. "It looks like we might be here for a while."

"Shit."

"Yeah, shit. The good news is we *are* off the road by about six feet. So hopefully no one will come by and wipe us out."

"That's reassuring."

It wasn't.

She snapped her seatbelt back on, just in case. "Do you think there's any chance we can drive out?"

Henry raised both hands as if to say he didn't have a clue what they should do. "I don't. It might just get us stuck closer to the road and in harm's way. I think I need to call for help."

Annie thought that sounded wise. She pulled the map back up on her phone and took a quick screen shot of their location.

Henry was searching for something.

"What are you doing?"

He reached up and turned the dome light back on. "I can't find my goddamn phone. Help me look."

Five minutes later, they'd concluded his phone wasn't inside the SUV.

"It must have fallen from my pocket outside."

It was Annie's turn to swear again. This could get really serious, real fast, if they couldn't get help.

"Good thing we still have yours. Here. Give it to me."

She handed it to him and braced for another barrage of frustration. She didn't have to wait long.

"Annie," he said, his voice low and slow. "Why is your phone at less than ten percent?"

"Don't you have a charging cord in here?" she countered.

"The cord split and it looked like a fire hazard, so I threw it out. How many times do I have to tell you—"

"Stop," she insisted. "We don't have time for lectures. We need to call someone *right now*. Before my phone dies. Who is our best bet? Colton? He has a truck."

"Fine. Yes." He thrust her phone back at her. "Call him."

She took it and called her son, hoping he'd pick up. He wasn't good at answering his phone.

The call eventually went to voicemail. She left him a harried message, but when she hung up, she wasn't hopeful that he'd be their hero on this snowy evening.

Silence hung in the air for a beat.

"I'm calling Michael. His truck is bigger than Colton's, and he has more experience driving in this type of weather."

She braced herself for Henry's pushback, but none came.

She placed the call and put the phone on speaker, praying he'd pick up. He almost always answered for her.

"Hey, Annie, what's up?"

His voice was like that of the angels.

"Oh God, I'm so glad you picked up."

Her ex must have heard the panic in her words. "What happened? Are you all right? Is it Ava and the baby?"

"Listen," she said, cutting him off. "I'm with Henry. We were driving back from Angel Falls. Visibility got low, and we hit a deer. Maybe two. We are in a ditch in the middle of nowhere. I think we are off the road far enough, but we're in trouble. Please, can you come get us with your truck? It's cold and we're stuck in deep snow. My phone is almost dead. Henry lost his outside. I can send our location. Can you do that for me? For us?"

"You idiots," he said, but she detected a smile in his tone.

"Michael, I'm serious! We need help. I need to know you are on your way before my phone dies!"

"Honey, take a breath. I've got you. Send the location. I'm leaving right now. I'll also call the highway patrol. They may get to you faster. Stay in the vehicle. I'll see you guys soon."

Michael ended the call, and Annie immediately sent him the screen shot of their location. She wished she could remember how to drop a pin on the map app, but there was no time. The tiny bar across the top of her phone screen inched slowly forward. It was taking too long to send.

"What if it doesn't go through?" she said, her panic rising.

Henry took the phone from her and held it closer to the windshield. Maybe the change in position didn't really help, but the word *Delivered* flashed below the picture in her text message a second before her screen went black.

"Why did it die so fast? It was just at ten percent."

Her husband sighed. "Who knows? I think it might have gone through, though. I'm going to go back outside again and see if I can find my phone. Just in case it didn't."

This time Henry was gone a full ten minutes. She could tell by his expression when he got back inside that he hadn't found it.

She fished a spare napkin out of the pocket in her door and reached over to dab at the blood on his face. It seemed to have stopped bleeding, but the red smear made the whole situation that much more terrifying for her.

"Don't worry. Michael will save us," she said.

Henry angled his body so she couldn't reach him, instead taking the napkin from her and using the mirror to clean himself up.

She knew it was killing Henry to rely on Michael for anything, but this time, they didn't have a choice.

Chapter Twenty-Two

Annie opened her oven and peeked under the tinfoil to check on the turkey. The plan was to have her Thanksgiving feast on the dining room table at two o'clock. Her day had kicked off at 6:30. A twenty-six-pound turkey can take six hours to roast, so she'd baked the pie shells first, then slid the bird into the hot oven promptly at 7:30 that morning. She'd been on her feet preparing other various holiday dishes ever since. She doubted she'd sit until everyone gathered around the table.

Would her family even appreciate the amount of work it takes to get all their favorite dishes prepared and on the table at precisely the right time? No. They would not. Aside from her mother, of course. Patsy would appreciate it because she'd handled Thanksgiving for all of them, many times. She could still prepare the perfect holiday meal, surely, but this was Annie's year.

"Ava needs to learn how to do this, too," Annie muttered as she poured steaming chocolate pudding into the two cooled pie shells.

"What do I need to learn how to do?" her daughter asked, pulling the door from the garage closed behind her. "Make pie?"

Annie hadn't heard the garage door open. "When did you get here?"

"Just now. We parked in the driveway and the garage door was open, so I took a shortcut," Ava said. She scanned the kitchen as she shrugged out of her winter parka. "I don't know how you do it, Mom. Grandma, too. What can I help with?"

Annie considered repeating herself about Ava learning how to prepare their holiday meal, but she stopped herself. Singling out her daughter was a sexist move. Any of her three kids could learn, though Colton and Relic were notorious for avoiding the kitchen anytime something other than actual eating was happening. If she dropped over dead tomorrow, they'd have to figure it out if they wanted their holiday traditions to continue.

She supposed she wouldn't be around to worry about it, so she let it go.

Instead, she turned her full attention to her daughter, catching her in a warm hug and loving the taut feel of Ava's pregnant belly against her own.

What would the new baby mean to their holidays in future years? A pigtailed toddler baking cookies next to her in this very room was so much more fun to consider than what would happen to this family after her own demise.

"You can set the table for me, if you'd like," Annie said, once she released Ava. "I want to use the good set of stoneware. I think I have the perfect number of place settings."

Ava nodded, moving to the tall cabinet at the end of the kitchen where they stored the items that weren't used regularly. "How many of us will there be?"

Annie moved the kettle she'd emptied to the sink, but before filling it to soak, she treated herself to a finger full of chocolate pudding. "Mmm . . . now *this* is what Thanksgiving is supposed to taste like."

She flipped on the faucet and got back to Ava's question. "I counted eleven, but let's double check. You and Daniel, Colton, Relic, my folks, Millie and Ed, me, and your dads. Yep, eleven."

"Both Henry and Michael?" Ava asked, one hand remaining on the open cupboard door and the other at the top of the swell of her belly. "They both agreed?"

Reluctantly, Annie thought, but she kept that to herself; she'd vowed to avoid any drama by remaining neutral on all potential pain points throughout this day, no matter how much her tongue bled by biting it.

"Of course," she said aloud. "What kind of holiday would it be if both your fathers weren't here to celebrate with you?"

"The kind of holiday we usually have," Ava said. A flip of her long blond hair added a punch to the sarcasm as she turned to pull a stack of plates out of the cupboard.

"My poor tongue," Annie muttered to herself.

Ava threw a questioning look over her shoulder but got right back to counting out plates.

"They're heavy," Annie advised. "Don't carry the entire stack at once."

The door from the garage opened again and Ava's husband, Daniel, grunted under the weight of a case of bottled water. Annie hurried over to help, pointing to the island as she got the door.

"Hey, Annie," he said, backpedaling to the rug in front of the back entry once he'd set the waters down. "It smells amazing in here. Nothing smells as good as a roasting turkey! Sorry . . . I tracked a little snow in here."

Once he'd removed his wet boots, he placed them in the garage, out of the way, and grabbed a paper towel to clean up the mess he'd made of her floor.

"Whoa, let me do that," he said when he noticed his wife pulling plates. "You aren't supposed to lift anything heavy."

Ava let him help. She counted out a few more, then followed her husband into the dining room.

Annie always appreciated how conscientious this young man was about the little things. It was yet another reason she couldn't understand why Henry wasn't a fan of Daniel.

The buzzer on the stove top went off. Her daughter returned to the kitchen just as Annie snapped off the annoying alarm.

"The turkey isn't done yet, is it? It's only noon. I thought we weren't eating until two."

"No. That was a reminder that I need to throw together the green bean casserole and the sweet potatoes. You know how your Grandpa Lyle loves plenty of butter and brown sugar with his sweet potatoes." Annie pulled out a myriad of canned vegetables and soups from the pantry.

Ava nodded. She took a seat on the stool beside the island. "Hey, Mom, do you have another leaf for the table?"

"Nope. Henry put them all in this morning. That should be enough. The table seats twelve when it's fully extended. Hey, put the gold tablecloth on first, would you? I'm sorry I forgot to tell you that."

"Can it go bigger?" Daniel asked, returning to Ava's side.

"Guess not," Ava told him. "Mom, is the folding table still in the storage room downstairs?"

Annie pulled the canister of brown sugar out and gave it a shake. "Crap. This might not be enough."

"*Mom,*" Ava said, raising her voice.

"What?!" Annie snapped back. Couldn't Ava handle a simple job like setting the table?

"I need room for thirteen, and we don't want to be squished. Can I set up the card table? Me and Daniel can sit at it. Relic, too, maybe."

Frustrated, Annie plopped the plastic canister of sugar onto the island. "Ava, what is the matter with you? We just figured out we have eleven today."

Ava made a funny face, snagging Annie's full attention.

"Who are the extra two, Ava? You know I don't like surprises."

"Oh, you'll like this surprise. I promise. But I also promised not to tell until they get here. I've said too much already. Never mind. I'll handle it. Come on, Daniel, let's go downstairs and dig up the card table. Mom is busy."

Before Annie could trail behind Ava for answers, the doorbell sounded.

"Henry? Relic?" Annie called out. "Grandma and Grandpa must be here. Can one of you get that, please?"

The only response to her question was another ringing of the bell.

She couldn't hear any signs of her husband or son. Abandoning her cans and a pathetic excuse for a can opener that she'd been meaning to replace, she headed for the front door.

"Where did they go now?" she muttered.

She swung the front door open, fully expecting to come face to face with her mother, laden down with the extra side dishes she'd volunteered to make, and hopefully the rolls Annie had asked them to swing by the store and pick up.

But it wasn't her mother.

She quickly glanced at the dark walnut door. Had it morphed into a time portal? But it still looked like their old front door.

She looked back at the person standing before her. "Donna?"

"Sweet little Annie," the woman crooned. "You haven't changed a bit. Here—it isn't much, but I'm afraid it's the best we could do."

Annie took the bottle of red wine being offered and glanced behind the woman as her brain fought to understand why her friend's mother was at her door. No one else was in view. "Is Lynette with you?"

"Yes. I mean, no, but she'll be right back."

Annie heard slamming car doors, so she looked toward the driveway. It was her parents.

She stepped back from the doorway, motioning for Donna to come in out of the cold. "But . . . I don't understand."

Donna's bright blue eyes twinkled, much as Annie remembered them doing when she and Lynette were kids. Donna's once glossy dark hair had gone pure white, and there were wrinkles now, but otherwise Lynette's mother looked much the same as she had when Annie was a girl.

"It looks like Ava is good at keeping secrets," Donna said as she clapped her hands together.

Footsteps approached from behind, and Annie glanced back, expecting to see either Henry or Relic. But it was Michael, looking handsome in a rust-colored dress shirt and dark jeans.

"I let myself in through the back. I hope you don't mind," he said to Annie.

He spotted the older woman in the open doorway.

"Well, I'll be damned. Donna Howe. How long has it been? Twenty-five years?"

With a start, Annie realized he was correct. Donna had attended their wedding. Had she really not crossed paths with Lynette's mother since then?

"Here, let me help you with that," Michael said, stepping behind Donna to remove her long wool coat. "I see your folks are here, too, Annie."

Donna allowed Michael to help her out of her wrap, a confused expression on her face. "But I thought you two split a long time ago."

Her comment made Annie realize how this must look. "Oh, we did, Donna. But Michael moved here to Ruby Shores about eight years ago. Sometimes he joins us for holidays, when he isn't out of town."

Michael snorted as he pulled a hanger out of the front hall closet and deposited Donna's coat inside. "This is the first Thanksgiving I've spent here."

"It is?" Annie said, realizing, as she asked, that indeed it was—though he'd sometimes stopped by for Christmas morning over the years.

A commotion on the front steps snapped Annie back to her hostess duties. "Donna, come in. Make yourself comfortable in the living room. It's right through there. Henry, my husband, is here somewhere, too. I'm just going to help my folks with the things they brought, and then I'll send them in to join you."

"And Lynette should be back shortly. I'm afraid I left my purse in our hotel room when we swung by and checked in. She took the rental back to see if she couldn't find it for me. All my medications are in there. It sucks to get old. Popping pills like candy."

Annie couldn't help but grin as she watched their surprise guest disappear into the living room.

Michael had already made it back outside and accepted a box of goodies from Annie's father and headed for the kitchen with it, leaving Annie alone to greet her parents.

"Hi, honey," her father said, dropping a quick peck on her forehead. "I got you those rolls, but I forgot them in the car. Be right back."

"What is *he* doing here?" Patsy asked, thrusting her chin after Michael.

Annie bit the side of her tongue and took a breath before responding. She knew Patsy had never completely forgiven Michael for what happened all those years ago. The relationship between her mother and her ex had never benefited from a stable foundation.

"Happy Thanksgiving to you, too, Mother. I don't know how you always did all of this and made it look so easy. Cooking for Thanksgiving is a lot of work!"

"Oh, come here, you minx," Patsy said, catching Annie up in a warm hug. "Quit avoiding the subject by trying to butter me up. You know you are every bit as capable of feeding this crew as I am. And speaking of crews, where's your sister? I don't see their car. And who was that woman who got here just as we drove up?"

Annie caught her mother's hand, pulled her inside, and shut the door. "Dad will go through the garage with the food. It's a more direct line to the kitchen. Millie is still thirty minutes out. She called. You know how she likes to make her entrance once everyone else has arrived."

Patsy sighed. "That isn't nice of you to say, Annie. Are you going to be snippy all day?"

Annie held out a hand, and her mother shrugged off the puffy jacket she wore.

"No. Actually, Mother, I promised myself I would engage in zero drama today, no matter how much snark was floating around me."

Patsy laughed, removing her sensible shoes before stepping into the front hallway. "I'll believe that when I see it."

But Annie was determined. This would be a Thanksgiving that everyone would remember for all the *right* reasons.

"Believe it or not, that woman is Donna Howe," she said. "Do you remember her? My friend Lynette's mother?"

"From when you were in high school?" Patsy asked, surprised. "I haven't heard Donna's name in ages. But, sure, I remember her. Is Lynette here? I didn't know they were coming today. Aren't you just full of surprises?"

Annie shrugged. "You can thank your granddaughter. Ava is the one full of surprises."

Chapter Twenty-Three

Annie added an extra splash of gravy to her meat. She worried the turkey was on the dry side, but by the way it was disappearing from the two enormous platters positioned on each end of the long table, she figured no one else found the turkey lacking.

She took another slow sip of the delightful wine Lynette and Donna had provided, as she studied the expressions of the individuals around her table. Nearly all the most important people in her life were right here. Despite the hours of work to prepare the meal and clean the house, she wouldn't want it any other way.

"And next year, we'll have to make room for a high chair around the table," Michael was saying, his wine glass held high. "Patsy and Lyle, are you excited at the prospect of being great-grandparents?"

Patsy grinned. Her upset over finding her previous son-in-law in attendance at their family holiday seemed to have diminished. Michael had a habit of charming his way into everyone's good graces, regardless of past transgressions.

"Other than the term *great-grandmother* making me sound ancient, yes, Michael, we're thrilled," she said, patting Lyle's hand on the table next to her plate.

Annie scanned people's expressions as talk of the new baby continued. The only two who didn't seem to enjoy the topic were her sister and brother-in-law. Even Henry smiled as Daniel accepted good-natured teasing about changing diapers and sleep deprivation.

"Ava, dear, would you *ever* consider allowing me to serve as an honorary great-grandmother to your little princess?" Donna said. "I promise I'd spoil her accordingly."

Lynette tapped her fork against her crystal water glass. "That's a wonderful idea, Mom. And if Donna gets to be an honorary great-grandmother, then I want to be an extra grandma to her."

Relic got up from his seat next to Ava and Daniel at the card table to refill his plate with seconds. "The kid might as well have an extra grandma. Between Daniel's dad and both Henry and Michael, she already has plenty of grandpas."

Groans met his weak attempt at a joke, and Annie held her breath, praying Henry wouldn't take offense. The subject of the baby was a touchy one with him. But his smile remained.

This was curious to Annie. What was behind his good mood? She'd expected him to try her patience today, but he seemed to be on his best behavior. She knew she should be grateful.

"So, Annie, Mother tells me you stole our week at their house in Arizona," Millie announced loudly, squashing the lighthearted banter about the baby.

A spoon Patsy had just used to drop another helping of green beans onto her plate clanked against the stoneware dish at her eldest's cutting tone. "Now, Millie, I told you no such thing. You mentioned a possible interest, but then Annie asked to use it, and since she's never wanted it before, I figured it was her turn."

Annie watched her irritated sister tear a hunk off her roll, dropping the shredded bread onto the plate that still held full helpings of turkey, dressing, and mashed potatoes. Millie never ate much. She was always too worried about keeping her *trim figure*. Annie hated the way her sister wasted so much food.

While Henry was surprising her in a good way, Millie was acting exactly how Annie suspected she would.

Hoping to divert the subject, she passed the black olives while inquiring about the state of her parents' plans around their anniversary cruise they'd take in February.

"When I agreed to this little voyage, I didn't realize your mother would insist on purchasing a whole new wardrobe," Lyle said.

Donna poured herself more wine. "An anniversary cruise? That sounds delightful! Is it a Caribbean cruise? What stops will the ship be making? And congratulations on your anniversary. Will it be your fiftieth?"

"Only if Grandma and Grandpa would have had Aunt Millie and been already pregnant with Mom before they were married," Colton said. He'd remained unusually quiet ever since his late arrival, getting to the house just as they were all sitting down. He'd been held up at work, he'd said. "Mom is turning fifty next summer. Remember?"

Lynette tapped her fork against her crystal water glass again. "She sure is! And so am I. Our entire group is, which is why we're in town this weekend. We'll celebrate Jackie first. Her birthday is this weekend. I'm so glad her friend Owen decided to plan a surprise party. And can I just say, Ava, thank you again for helping me surprise your mother. I hope you'll forgive us, Annie. My initial conflict for this weekend fell through, and I thought it would be fun to surprise both you and Jackie."

Millie snorted. "That's right. All of you are turning fifty. What was it you girls called each other again? The Cross-Eyed Girls?"

"Really? What a ridiculous name," her husband replied. After insisting on saying grace at the beginning of the meal, he hadn't bothered to contribute another word to the conversation until now.

Annie had never understood what Millie saw in Ed, her husband. He was one of the most pretentious people she'd ever met. No wonder their only daughter had moved across the country and cut all ties with both of her parents.

"No, it's the Kaleidoscope Girls," Lynette corrected Millie, staring back at Ed with an unwavering gaze.

The irritating man eventually looked away.

Annie doubted there was a man alive that Lynette couldn't put in his place.

"In fact," her friend continued, "you should check out Annie's collection of kaleidoscopes on the wall in the living room. It's quite impressive."

Annie beamed appreciatively. "Thanks again for the darling addition you sent me last month, Lynette. I didn't have any shaped like that."

Henry's sigh was loud enough to earn him curious looks.

"What?" Annie said, challenging him to speak his mind, despite her promise to avoid any drama.

His smile returned, but Annie knew him well enough to see that it didn't reach his eyes. "I just didn't realize you were still adding to your collection."

"She sure is," Lynette said. "We got her one for her birthday, too, when we were in Hawaii."

Annie caught Lynette's eye, doing her best to communicate to her old friend that it would be best if she stopped talking about kaleidoscopes now. But the grin she received told her Lynette knew exactly how she was pushing Henry's buttons.

Is the Universe conspiring against my efforts to keep the peace?

Patsy got to her feet with an offer to refill the gravy boat and anything else they were running low on. When Relic asked for more dark meat, she inch-wormed a finger at him to help her in the kitchen.

Side conversations started up again, and Annie helped herself to a bite of stuffing, grateful for her mother's impeccable timing. Her turkey might be a little dry, but she'd nailed the stuffing this year. She might just survive this meal after all.

Her father dabbed at his mouth with his napkin, then cleared his throat, capturing most people's attention.

Now what?

"I understand we owe you a great deal of gratitude, Michael," Lyle said, pointing a finger, crooked with arthritis, toward Annie's ex.

The comment interrupted a conversation between Michael and Colton.

"What was that, Lyle?" Michael asked, looking confused.

"I hear you saved my daughter from freezing to death in a ditch during a freak blizzard. That had to have been dangerous, and I wanted to thank you personally."

Relic looked surprised as he placed a refilled turkey platter in an empty spot on the extended dining table. "Blizzard? What are you talking about, Gramps?"

"He saved Henry, too," Annie blurted out before she thought better of adding that tidbit.

"Okay, I need to hear this," Relic said, picking a sizeable chunk of meat off the platter with his fingers.

"Relic! Manners!" Annie cried.

He shrugged at her and dropped the third helping onto his plate. "What happened, Dad?"

Henry's lips compressed. Annie knew he wouldn't want to relay the story.

"You want me to tell it?" she asked, trying to let her husband off the hook.

"No, don't," Michael said. He caught Annie's eye. He probably understood Henry wouldn't enjoy looking like the one who needed saving by his wife's ex. "Look, it wasn't a big deal. Glad I could help."

"No way," Relic said, grinning. "This sounds good. Come on, Dad."

"Fine," Henry said, pushing back a foot from the table. "We had some trouble a couple weeks back. We were driving in bad weather, and we probably shouldn't have been out there. They'd forecasted a little snow, but it was worse than expected. Actually, you can blame the turkey for all of it."

Annie laughed. He was being a good sport, and she appreciated it. "Darn turkey."

Relic looked between his parents like they were nuts.

Henry shrugged. "We'd driven over to Angel Falls for dinner. Annie also grabbed the turkey at the store over there because she couldn't find one here in town that was big enough. On our way home, an incoming train blocked the main road out of town, and I got impatient. I told Annie to use her phone to find a different route back to Ruby Shores. Visibility was poor. Then two deer popped up out of nowhere. I hit the brakes and we slid. Don't ever do that," he said, eyeing Ava, Relic, and

Colton, one at a time. "I know better, but it was a reflex. The road was icy. We spun out and landed in a ditch."

"Why didn't you call me? I have a truck," Colton said. "I didn't know anything about this either."

Henry nodded. "It isn't something we go around bragging about. Actually, your mother tried you first, but you didn't pick up."

"Shocking," Ava teased. She looked curious about the story, too.

"My phone was almost dead, and we knew we were in trouble. When I couldn't reach you, Colton, I thought of Michael. He drives a big truck, too. My phone battery was about to give out, so we took a chance and called him quick."

Michael nodded. "And *I* didn't ignore your mother's call. You should think about that, Colton. Don't you ever listen to your messages?"

The guilty flush on Colton's cheeks told Annie maybe he had noticed her call but ignored it. That could have been deadly. But luck had been on their side.

"Why didn't you just call 911?" Millie asked, as if that was the more obvious solution.

Annie didn't have a suitable answer. "I guess we could have."

"How did you find them in a snowstorm, Michael?" Daniel asked.

"I took a screenshot of the map app I was using and sent it to him."

Michael looked her way, curious, and shook his head. "I didn't get that."

"But you still found us," Annie said, confused.

He shrugged. "I can track you. Remember? I checked your location the second I hung up with you. Then I lost the connection, but it was enough."

She'd forgotten about that. *Damn.* Even to her own ears, allowing her ex-husband to track her location sounded inappropriate.

"Interesting," Henry said, his eyes narrowed.

Her wish for a drama-free Thanksgiving flew right out the window.

"To be fair, the highway patrol arrived five minutes after I did," Michael went on. "We wouldn't have gotten Henry's SUV out without their help. So I wasn't much of a hero. But the story had a happy ending, and everyone got home in one piece."

Relic laughed. "Wait. Dad, did something happen to your phone that night? You told me you dropped it and it broke. That was why you had to get a new one."

Henry squirmed. "I might have dropped it outside in the snow, right after we hit the ditch."

Michael pushed back from the table. "Hey. Don't give your dad a hard time. He's saved my ass plenty of times. I was at the right place at the right time to help."

Annie got to her feet and began to clear the table. "I don't want to rush anyone. Keep eating if you aren't done. I'll start cutting up the pie."

She didn't really care about dessert, but she figured they could use another change in topic. They'd all fought their way around enough landmines for the day.

What was it about celebratory family dinners that put everyone on edge?

Chapter Twenty-Four

ANNIE BENT AT THE waist and flipped her hair forward, torching it with her blow dryer set on high. She'd expected to have plenty of time to shower and get party-ready following a dinner of turkey leftovers, but it was already 6:30.

Henry stepped out of the shower. She grinned up at him from her upside-down position.

"What are you smiling at?" he asked, giving her a smirk of his own. "And what time does this shindig start? I still don't see why I have to go. She's *your* friend."

Annie straightened. Her hair still felt damp, but she needed to hurry. "Henry, you know Jackie. And you met Owen at Kit's wedding."

"Only briefly. Will Kit and Dean be there? Or Matt?" He reached for a towel and draped it around his still-slim waist.

Annie was reminded of a similar scene in their master bath during her first week back at school. She sighed. Henry wasn't able to run last winter after an ankle injury, but once he got back to it over the summer, the extra weight he'd put on melted right off. Why did guys have it so easy?

He stopped drying off and stood there, staring at her.

"What?" she said. Why was he looking at her like that?

"I asked you who was going to be there tonight."

She shook her head. "Sorry. Your naked body always distracts me."

He snorted. "I wish."

She glanced in the mirror, eyeing her wild hair. She really should have allowed herself more time. "Who will be there? Um, I'm not sure. Lynette and Donna, of course, but you already knew that. Owen is setting it up. I think he planned to convince his two boys to come. He talked to Charlotte, Jackie's mom, and she was excited. I don't think she gets out much, given Glen's struggles. She promised to have Jackie there by 7:30. She was going to try to convince Jackie's brother to come, too. He's home for Thanksgiving."

Henry lathered his face with shaving cream at his mirror. "Did you invite the kids?"

"I did. Ava promised to stop by if she wasn't too tired. Daniel will do whatever she wants to do."

"Of course he will." Henry took the first swipe down his cheek with his razor. "That kid needs a backbone."

Refusing to react, Annie reached for her argon oil to tame her hair down and said, "Colton said he's coming. He always liked Jackie."

"Relic is doing something with his old baseball buddies tonight. He's not old enough to go to the bar," Henry added. "But you didn't answer my question about Kit, Dean, or Matt."

Annie remembered Henry had spent most of his time at Kit and Dean's wedding visiting with her friend Renee's husband, Matt. "Kit and Dean are with his family in Iowa. His mom planned some type of wedding reception, since their ceremony came together so quickly that lots of their family missed it. I called Renee, but she's hosting a gratitude retreat this weekend and her husband is on duty."

Henry completed his shaving routine and pulled out his toothbrush. "Oh, that's right. Matt is a highway patrol officer or something, right?"

"Sheriff, yeah. Come on, Henry, please be a good sport. I don't ask you to do much when it comes to my old girlfriends. Can't you do this one thing for me and not complain?"

He spit into the sink, stowed his toothbrush, then dropped his towel as he walked into their bedroom, sashaying like a runway model. He was trying to be funny, but she barely managed a smile in response.

She suspected he felt bad about the fight they'd had the night before over the notion that Michael could track her location with his phone. He had a right to be angry, but he'd gotten loud enough that Relic knocked on their door to make sure everything was all right.

It wasn't like Henry to react in such an extreme way, but maybe his guilt would make him behave better tonight.

She swiped a light coat of mascara over her lashes, hoped for dim lights in the pub, and followed her husband out of the bathroom.

What the heck do you wear to a fiftieth birthday party? She considered dressing in black from head to toe but decided against it. Jackie might already be mad at her for allowing Owen to plan a surprise party for her. She wasn't likely to see any humor in Annie wearing an outfit to her birthday party that was more appropriate for a funeral.

Besides, she wanted to set a festive tone for this first of five fiftieth birthday parties, or at least the big joint one she'd plan for Arizona in February. She wanted something bright.

Then she spied the glittery gold arm of a dressy sweater she'd purchased from a local boutique during summer sidewalk days, intending to wear it for New Year's Eve, even though they seldom went out on the last night of the year anymore.

This would serve a better purpose. She'd save the golden balloons and black sashes for the joint party in Arizona. Fiftieth wedding anniversaries were golden. Couldn't they consider turning fifty to be a golden *birthday*, too?

Annie heard the party even before she picked out anyone she knew in the crowd. The pub space was on the small side, and dimmed lights made it feel more intimate. Henry bumped into her from behind as they stepped just inside the door, getting their bearings.

"Sorry. This place is crowded. Do you see anyone for Jackie's party yet?"

She reached behind for her husband's hand to pull him along behind her. "I can't see Jackie's twins, but I swear I can hear them laughing over there."

Her short stature was always a hindrance in crowded bars. This was her first time inside this pub. She thought she remembered them advertising a grand opening party last spring.

Henry slowed her down. "I feel old."

Annie understood. She did, too, in this crowd. "Looks like there are lots of college-age kids home for Thanksgiving."

"I see black balloons back by that wall."

She let him take the lead.

"I think I see Owen, too," he said, moving them across the crowded floor.

"Henry! Annie!" a male voice yelled over the hum of activity and music. "Over here!"

"Yep, that's Owen!" She had to yell, too, to be heard above the noise.

Annie could see the balloons now, a mixture of black and gold ones that nearly touched the low ceiling of the pub, swaying from the circulating air of multiple ceiling fans. The pub was cute, but with this noisy atmosphere, would they be able to have any decent conversations? Then she noticed, with relief, that the balloons were flanking another doorway.

Henry stopped to shake Owen's hand as the other man met them partway.

Annie twisted to stand in front of Henry and gave Owen an impromptu hug. "This place is insane!"

He nodded. "I know. It's too loud out here. But I rented their party room in the back. Charlotte texted me. They were just leaving the house, so Jackie will be here soon. Come on. Several of us are hiding out back there. It isn't so loud. God, that makes me sound old, doesn't it?"

"We *are* old. That's why we're here," Annie said with a smile. News of a separate room came as a relief.

They followed Owen, and Annie caught sight of Hailey and Mackenzie, Jackie's twin girls, standing next to the column of balloons. A wave of amazement washed through her. Many of their kids were already old enough to party in a bar with them. It felt surreal that the twins were there to help Jackie celebrate reaching the half-century mark.

The girls squealed as they caught sight of Annie. Owen and Henry kept walking, disappearing into the back room.

"You two are so grown up!" she exclaimed, giving each of them an extra squeeze. "All right, ladies, are we going to be in trouble for this?" She glanced back over her shoulder. She didn't yet see Jackie or Charlotte, but she spied her son, Colton, wandering through the crowd as if he was lost. She jumped and waved to catch his attention.

"In trouble over the party?" Hailey said. "She might be pissed at first, but not at us. We are innocents in this. She can blame Grandma Charlotte. And Owen."

"She won't be mad at anyone for long," Mackenzie said. "She acts like she doesn't want this birthday to be a big deal, but I don't think she means it."

Annie understood. It was a similar push-and-pull for her, too. While fifty used to sound so old, she was tired of the apprehension she felt over the approach of the big milestone. Even though she wouldn't personally hit the big fifty mark for another eight months, she was ready to move on.

Colton reached them, dropping an arm over his much shorter mother. "Hey, everyone. You ladies all look amazing! Mom, you know it isn't New Year's yet, right?" he teased.

She elbowed him in the stomach. "I decided that since we're celebrating Jackie's golden birthday, I needed to dress accordingly."

He laughed, rubbing his stomach. "I thought golden birthdays were when you turn the same age as the day of the month of your birthday. Like when Relic turned nineteen on August nineteenth."

"Fifty counts, too," Annie insisted. "Hailey and Mack, do you two remember my son Colton? He wanted to stop by to celebrate with us, too."

"Of course. Hey there, Colton," Hailey said, throwing her arms around his neck in a friendly hug. She had to stand on her tiptoes to reach.

Mack, Hailey's twin, wasn't as demonstrative, but she gave Colton a little wave.

"Who else is here?" Annie asked, checking her watch. She noticed a text from Lynette on the tiny screen, asking where the hell she was because the party was getting started. She smiled. "Lynette, I'm guessing!"

"Yep, there are already a bunch of people in the back room. Go say hello," Hailey said. "We're supposed to stand watch out here and warn everyone when we see them coming in."

Annie nodded. "Will Charlotte know where to bring her?"

Mack waved at the massive bunch of balloons behind them. "Who do you think decorated? Now, go! She has to be almost here."

Not having to be told three times, Annie looped her arm through Colton's and pulled him into the party room with her. She expelled a sigh of relief when the door closed behind them and the cacophony of noise softened.

This room was a little brighter, too, thanks to strings of golden lights that crisscrossed the ceiling. She couldn't tell if they were always there or part of Charlotte's decorations. Either way, they cast the perfect ambiance.

A long table along one wall bore a two-tiered birthday cake and other treats. They'd set one corner of the room up with a small bar, and Annie smiled when she recognized the bartender. Ron, Jackie's older brother, hadn't changed much, aside from the gray hair. She'd know that smile anywhere. He was filling a glass of wine for a woman with her back to Annie, but she, too, was impossible to miss.

At Annie's squeal of delight, the woman turned toward her with a wave.

"Mind if I go say hi to Wendy?" she asked Colton.

"Tell her hi from me, too," he said, heading for a nearby table. "I'm going to grab a chair by Ava and Daniel."

Delighted to hear her daughter and son-in-law had also made it, she gave them a finger wave before heading for Wendy.

"You made it! I didn't think you'd get back from your kids' place in time!" she said, grabbing hold of Wendy's free hand.

Wendy shook her head. "I couldn't miss this! One of my favorite little campers of all time is turning fifty."

Annie stuck her bottom lip out. "I thought *I* was your favorite camper?!"

"No, but you are my favorite *boss*. Jackie was my favorite camper. When you were a little kid, I always thought you were a bit of a suck-up. The way you always helped me and my sister with our counseling duties, I wondered if you had an ulterior motive. But I know now that you didn't."

Annie's pretend pout took on a hint of sincerity. "You thought I was a *suck-up*? I just wanted to help. Most of the girls, like Ivory and her crew, were little snots, and I didn't think it was fair for you to have to wait on them. I couldn't change them, but I could make things a little easier for you."

Wendy laughed, squeezing Annie's hand and raising her wineglass. "And that's why I love you, Annie. Always trying your best to make life as fair as possible for everyone else."

"Well, I *used* to think I could do that. But I know better now."

Wendy's smile slipped. "Don't say that. Don't let troubles at school tarnish you. You do the best you can with what you've got. I've always admired that about you."

Annie hadn't been referring to school specifically, but she wouldn't try to make Wendy understand. *She* didn't even understand why she'd been feeling so unsettled for the past year.

A squeal from behind her brought her smile back.

"Oh. My. God. Is that Wendy Long, standing in this very room?"

"Here comes the whirlwind," she warned Wendy with a wink. "Brace yourself!"

Lynette pushed right past Annie without so much as a "hello" and grabbed Wendy in a massive bear hug. Wine sloshed over the rim of Wendy's glass onto the carpeted floor.

"Good thing that's white wine," Annie said, though she doubted either of the other two women heard her as they exclaimed their delight at seeing each other again.

A shrill whistle cut through the air, and everyone turned their attention to Owen where he stood next to the door leading from the main bar. Conversations died away quickly as he raised both hands.

"She's here! Everybody stay where you're at for a minute and be quiet. I'm going to cut the lights until Charlotte gets her in here, and then we'll really get this celebration going."

Annie held a finger up to her lips, giggling, and took in the rest of the room. It felt refreshingly childish to hold her breath in anticipation of the surprise. Owen had been right to set this up. Celebrating turning fifty with only the Kaleidoscope Girls in Arizona was sure to be a blast, but this way Jackie got to celebrate with all the people she loved, including most of her family.

Darkness descended. It wasn't completely silent, but it was quiet enough to hear Jackie talking to someone on the other side of the door. It sounded like she was complaining, probably to her mother.

"I don't understand why we couldn't just stay home with Dad tonight. Next week is going to be a rough one for him. Really, for all of us. Who did you say this retirement party is for?"

Annie pressed both hands against her mouth to keep from laughing at Jackie's question. Charlotte had her completely fooled. It didn't sound like she had any idea why her mother was really dragging her out on a Friday night to a small pub in her hometown on the weekend of her birthday.

I wouldn't be that gullible, Annie thought.

The door opened, and she could see the silhouettes of the two women. Jackie's daughters must have melted into the crowd outside the door in order to keep the party a secret for a minute longer.

"Mom, this is the wrong door. No one's in here."

As if that was the planned password, the strings of golden lights flicked back on and shouts of "SURPRISE!" sprung forth from every corner of the room.

Jackie froze in the doorway, a hand over her mouth.

Lynette wrapped an arm around Annie's neck and pulled her close to whisper in her ear. "If she suspected anything, she's one hell of an actress."

Drama had never been one of Jackie's passions, so maybe Owen and Charlotte really had pulled it off. Not that it mattered. Everyone was here now, and it was time to celebrate.

A short time later, Jackie snuck up behind Annie where she was sitting with her family, plus Lynette and Donna, and squeezed her shoulders.

"Ouch, that hurts," Annie said, trying to squirm away from the pinch that didn't *really* hurt. "Just because you're the birthday girl doesn't mean you get to be mean."

"Ha-ha, hilarious," Jackie said. She pulled out the empty chair next to Annie that Henry had vacated minutes earlier to collect another round of drinks for everyone. "I'm mad at you. You, too, Lynette. We promised each other that we wouldn't do this."

"Do what?" Lynette said, her eyes wide and innocent. "Annie and I had nothing to do with this. We are just guests tonight. Like you."

"Right. And I'm supposed to believe you and Donna just happened to be back in Ruby Shores for Thanksgiving after what . . . like *thirty years*? You guys don't have any family here."

"I was home for our reunion," Lynette reminded her.

"Besides, that's not true, Jackie," Annie said. "We are all family."

Jackie sighed, and her smile told Annie and Lynette that she wasn't really upset. "I can't believe Mom did all this. She has her hands full with Dad. Next week, he's finally moving into that new memory care facility on the edge of town. The last thing she needed to worry about was some silly party."

Annie scanned the room again. It was a good turnout for a holiday weekend, especially since Jackie hadn't lived in Ruby Shores since her college days. "This isn't a silly party, Jackie. Lots of people who love you came out to celebrate tonight. And it actually wasn't your mom's idea. Owen came up with it."

Jackie snorted. "I bet. Why would Owen do something like that? This party has Mom's fingerprints all over it. I know she baked that cake. She made almost an identical one for me when I turned forty."

Lynette leaned forward. "Hey, girl, what do I always say?"

The interruption caught Jackie off guard, and the two women stared at each other for a beat. Then Jackie smiled. " 'Just say *thank you*.' "

"Correct. Say 'thank you'! This *was* Owen's idea. He talked to Annie about it first, then it snowballed from there."

Annie shrugged. "It's true. Don't be hard on your mom, either. I'm sure she needed this distraction, given all that is happening with your dad right now. And I'm sorry it's come to that for Glen. I didn't realize."

Henry returned with a tray of sloshing glasses. Jackie stood, but he insisted she stay where she was. He slipped a drink in front of her before handing out the rest and disappearing again.

"Kit and Renee were sorry they couldn't be here," Annie continued. "Renee is hosting a retreat, and Kit has that party Dean's mom wanted to throw for their family to celebrate their wedding."

"I wouldn't have expected them to be here. Not that I expected any of this. We were supposed to all celebrate together in February," Jackie said.

Annie took a sip of wine, nodding. "And we will. But Owen made a brilliant point when he talked to me about this. He said it wasn't really fair that only the Kaleidoscope Girls got to party with you. He wanted you to celebrate with your other friends and family here, too."

"Plus, he still has the hots for you," Lynette said.

Jackie pretended not to hear her, but Annie knew better. She hoped Kit was right about Jackie and Owen finally being on a path to something more than a faded grade-school friendship.

The door opened and two young men entered the party room. Owen yelled a greeting to them from the bar area where he was visiting with Jackie's brother, then hurried over to talk to them both.

Jackie grinned and pushed her chair back. "Those are Owen's boys. Do you mind if I go say hello?"

"Go," Lynette said, making a shooing motion at the birthday girl.

Once Jackie was gone, conversations resumed around the table. Henry sat back down next to Annie, but he was quiet. He always shut down an hour or two into a party. Annie glanced his way but chose to ignore the fact that he looked like he might be ready to go. She wasn't, and he'd probably understand.

"How did you two get started with your online business, then?"

Ava's question caught Annie's attention, and she realized her daughter was visiting with Lynette and Donna. The mother-and-daughter team ran a very successful online women's clothing boutique. Annie wasn't surprised that Ava was curious about it. She'd always had an entrepreneurial streak in her, dating back to her early childhood lemonade stands, followed by babysitting gigs as she got older.

Annie listened in for a while, curious what Ava was thinking as she peppered Lynette and Donna with questions. Daniel seemed to be enjoying the discussion between the three women as well. She also noticed her Colton, sitting between Jackie's twins, and the three of them seemed to have plenty to talk about.

Annie saw Mack glance toward the door where Owen still stood talking with the two latecomers. She wondered whether Jackie's twins had ever met Owen's boys. They certainly looked handsome from where she sat. Wouldn't it be something if Jackie's daughter developed a crush on one of Owen's sons?

"Hey, do you guys want to go check out the blackjack table on the far side of the pub?" Annie heard Mack ask her sister and Colton.

The three rose and moved off. Annie supposed they were lucky the party had held the kids' attention for this long. Annie watched as they reached Jackie, Owen, and his boys near the door and introductions began.

Henry laid a hand on her thigh. "You about ready? It's almost nine and I need to put in half a day at the office tomorrow. I'm beat."

This was news to Annie. "You're working tomorrow? On the Saturday after Thanksgiving?"

He shrugged. "You know how busy it gets between now and year's end."

As if that was a sufficient reason to give up part of their holiday weekend.

"I wanted to decorate inside for Christmas tomorrow," Annie said, hating the idea of lugging all the boxes of decorations out by herself.

"I'll be home by noon. We could start then. Didn't you say something about maybe grabbing coffee with Lynette and Jackie tomorrow morning, before Lynette and Donna fly out?"

Annie glanced around, hating to be one of the first to leave the party, but she noticed others were drifting off, too. Wendy seemed to have disappeared. As Owen had so eloquently reminded her when he first mentioned a party, they weren't twenty-one anymore.

Besides, this was just the warmup celebration for Arizona.

"Fine. We can go," she said. "But remember, you promised to help me tomorrow."

"I know. Finish your drink and let's get home. Lemon will need to go out."

She didn't feel like finishing her gin and tonic, so she pushed it away, made their excuses, and followed Henry out to the car after getting commitments from Lynette and Jackie for coffee in the morning. Wendy had already left, but Jackie insisted Annie call and invite her to join them in the morning, too.

They all had more catching up to do.

Fifty certainly didn't feel like twenty-one, but her girlfriends were still a big part of her life, and time with them would always bring a smile to her face.

Chapter Twenty-Five

"I AM SO TIRED of these heavy sweaters," Annie muttered as she thumbed through her stack of winter weather items reserved for the coldest of days.

Henry popped into their master closet to switch out the suit jacket he'd donned earlier for a wool sweater of his own. "They're talking about the possibility of a blizzard. Poor Lemon. Mornings are brutal for dogs this time of year. I just let her out so Relic won't have to get up with her. I'm not sure this cold snap is ever going to break. Are you sure I can't tag along with you to Arizona next week?"

She gave up on her hunt for her blue wool cardigan and settled instead on a fine-knit cashmere in a dusty neutral tone that reminded her of the Arizona desert. "Sorry, Henry, we don't allow any boys on our trips. And please don't say one more word about a potential blizzard. I *have* to get out of here on time."

"I can't remember the last time I took a trip with friends," he said, his words muffled as he pulled the sweater over his head.

She shrugged. "So plan something. You and your running club have talked about catching a marathon somewhere warm this time of year, haven't you?"

He tugged the wool garment into place. "Yeah, but no one has the time to plan it, so it never happens."

When she left the closet without responding, he must have realized he'd said the wrong thing. He followed her back into their bedroom and caught her by the wrist.

"I'm not saying that you had all this extra time to plan your Arizona trip. I know how busy you are," he said, pulling her close so he could drop a peck on her lips.

She didn't want to fight, and he sounded sincere. "I *am* busy. Especially today. And next week. Do you ever feel like the plant will implode when you take vacation?"

"Annie, I promise the school will still stand when you return from your girls' trip. You have a good team in place. Now . . . we're still on for tonight, right?"

If she were honest with him, she'd admit she had forgotten all about their anniversary dinner plans, but she didn't want to hurt his feelings. "Right. I'll be home by six and we can ride together."

He shoved his wallet into the back pocket of his dress pants. "Our reservations are for six. You said not to make them for too late. We should leave here by 5:30. And now I have to run, or I'll be late for my Friday morning meeting."

As his footsteps faded away, Annie thought ahead to her day. Spirit Week always culminated in a big pep rally on Friday. If she couldn't get all her work done before she had to leave for her anniversary dinner, she could always run into the office tomorrow morning. Henry couldn't fault her for that. He'd spent most of his Saturday mornings since Thanksgiving at his office.

She finished brushing her teeth, then headed down, hopeful that Henry had thought to brush the snow off her car. Relic's starter was giving him trouble, so the garage was a mess while father and son tried to figure out how to fix it. Personally, Annie would have skipped that step, admitted defeat, and taken it straight to the shop. It would probably end up there by tomorrow anyway, despite their best efforts.

Relic couldn't go without a car. Her son had used his vehicle trouble as an excuse to come home for the weekend, skipping his Friday class. At least he hadn't skipped since Halloween—to her knowledge, anyway—and he was in a new semester now.

Before she reached the stairs, she caught Lemon scratching at the corner of their son's bedroom door. If she didn't let the little dog in, her whining would wake Relic. She opened the door as quietly as she could, let Lemon slink inside, then closed it just as softly.

She'd just turned away from the door when Lemon barked.

"Guess that wasn't such a brilliant plan," she said, talking to herself.

She went back to Relic's room, but when she opened the door, Lemon stayed inside, barking up at the bed. That was when she noticed Relic wasn't *in* the bed. It was still made up just as she'd left it after changing the sheets in anticipation of her son's arrival for the weekend.

There was no sign of Relic.

"That little shit," Annie said, leaving the dog to bark. She didn't have time for this. Relic was in college now. He could stay out all night, any time he chose, while away at college. But rules still applied at home.

Relic knew better than to do this.

A distant memory surfaced of a drunk Millie, stumbling into the house during the wee hours of morning when she lived at home during her freshman year of college. If her son thought she'd allow him to travel down a similar path as his aunt, he'd better think again.

She hurried down the stairs, already compiling the speech she'd give him when he found his way home.

The back door swung open as she reached the kitchen and Relic stepped inside.

When she opened her mouth to begin her tirade, he held up one hand and shook his head at her. The look on his face froze her anger.

Something was wrong.

But he'd scared her, dammit.

"Where have you been? What's wrong? You know it's disrespectful to not bother to call if you aren't going to come home, right? What do you think that phone in your pocket is *for*, Relic?"

"Please, just stop, Mom." The boy sighed as he pulled off his jacket and tossed it onto the nearest chair. It reminded her of Michael's irritating habit of always doing that same thing, years ago, when entering their apartment.

Boys. Men.

"Hang your jacket on the hooks by the door, Relic. That's what they're for."

Ordinarily, Relic would bristle at her scolding. She knew he preferred his father's lax expectations. But, instead of the expected flash of irritation over the reprimand, he looked concerned.

She eyed the coffee pot, wishing she had time for a quick cup, then looked back at her son. He looked lost in thought, with maybe a hint of an apology for his inconsiderateness in his expression.

Or was that just a wish on her part?

"Well, I'm glad you're home. I need to get to work. We'll talk about this more tonight." Then she remembered their dinner plans. "Wait. It'll have to wait until tomorrow morning. Your dad and I are going out to celebrate our anniversary right after work. But you aren't to go anywhere tonight. Understood?"

Lemon must have finally heard their voices because she came bouncing down the stairs to jump against Relic's shins.

"At least Lemon is happy to see me," he said, bending down to pet the dog.

Annie threw her hands up in defeat, then searched for her keys. "Believe me, kid. I'm your mother. Nothing makes me happier than to see you walk through that door in one piece. But I have a big day at school. It's Spirit Week. There won't be enough hours to get everything done, and I can't work late."

Relic straightened. "Mom, I need to talk to you. I think you're going to want to hear this before you go to school."

"It can't wait?" she asked, snatching her keys up when she discovered them under a dishcloth on the counter by the sink.

"Probably not."

Something in Relic's voice made her pause.

What is the matter with me?

This was her son, and she'd been worried sick about whether something had happened to him not even three minutes earlier. She could afford to give him whatever time he needed. The rest could wait.

But that also meant she had time for coffee. "Want a cup?" she asked, fishing around in the basket of pods next to the coffee machine for the flavor she preferred.

"No. I just want to sleep. I'm sorry if I worried you. But I'm glad I caught you before you left."

Something really was bothering him. She was quick with the coffee, then pulled out two stools, side by side. "Tell me."

"I saw Gabi and Kaylee last night."

Annie had suspected Kaylee was the reason Relic was out all night, but she decided against interrupting him. The girl must have picked him up, since his car was torn apart in the garage. She nodded, encouraging him to continue.

"Gabi is worried about Ferguson. They work together. I think she'd even like to go out with him sometime, but either he hasn't noticed or he's scared to ask her."

She remembered the two worked at the same after-school job. The local grocer employed lots of high school kids. She ignored Relic's comments around Gabi wanting to date Ferguson, honing in instead on why she might be worried about him.

"Don't tell me he's having more trouble with drugs?" she said, holding her breath.

Relic may or may not know that Ferguson suffered an overdose earlier in the school year, but enough other people did that she didn't feel like she was betraying him to her son with her question.

He shifted on the stool. "Not exactly. Well . . . kind of."

"Tell me, Relic. I only want what's best for Ferguson."

"I know, Mom, and that's why I wanted to talk to you. Did you know that Ferguson is working with the cops to find out who brought in the extra-juiced drugs that killed his cousin?"

The coffee machine sputtered, indicating her cup was full, so she grabbed it. "He told me he was going to offer to tell them what little he knew after his cousin died," she said, rejoining her son at the island.

Relic shook his head. "It's more than that, Mom. They're using him on the inside. Like . . . an informant. I think he already had some kind of connection, beyond just his cousin, with people the police think might be involved. Gabi is scared Ferguson could end up hurt . . . or even dead, just like his cousin."

This went beyond the level of involvement she'd envisioned when she put Ferguson in touch with the police.

An informant?

He was just a kid. Well, technically Ferguson was eighteen, but still.

She needed to talk directly to Ferguson about this, and as soon as possible. Her empty stomach churned with worry for the likeable yet vulnerable kid.

"I appreciate you telling me this, Relic. I don't like what I'm hearing either. Did the girls mention anything else that you think might be helpful?"

Relic rubbed the back of his neck. "Just one thing I thought was super weird. Did you know the guy's cousin, the one who died, worked at the same place as Dad? They—the cops, I mean—they think those deliveries might be how they're moving product from Minneapolis out to smaller communities like Ruby Shore. They pulled some strings and got Ferguson a job unloading trucks early in the morning and on Saturdays. Gabi is worried he's getting in too deep."

On Saturdays . . . ?

Annie frowned. Did Henry know about this?

He knew Ferguson had come to her, distraught, over the news of his cousin's death on Halloween. If he had inside knowledge and hadn't said anything to her . . .

But she didn't want to say anything to Relic that could make him feel caught between his parents on this.

"I'm not happy to hear how involved they've got Ferguson, either. It sounds dangerous. Thank you for telling me. I'll call him in to the office today. Try to talk to him about it."

Relic grabbed her hand. "Mom, it's okay for you to talk to him, but you *can't* say where you heard this from. Promise? Gabi doesn't want to be pulled into anything shady. He told her all this in confidence."

Annie didn't want Gabi or Kaylee—or, God forbid, *Relic*—pulled into anything drug related either.

"I promise I'll leave all your names out of it. He'll probably assume Henry told me, anyhow, since he's a manager at the plant."

Relic looked relieved. "Good. Now, do you mind if I go hit the sack? I'll take Lemon with me."

Annie nodded, distracted now by these new worries. "Go sleep. But, Relic, I still insist you stay home tonight. Got it?"

He rolled his eyes, smiling. "Got it."

When she was again alone with her thoughts, she pondered how much, if any, of this her husband might be aware of. He and another coworker were now overseeing all the distribution runs in and out of the plant. They'd shuffled duties around after Byron Oaks, who used to handle all the runs, had died. And Michael had told her Byron was involved with the drugs.

Why hadn't Henry updated her on any of this?

Chapter Twenty-Six

When Annie attempted to call Ferguson into her office, she discovered he wasn't in school.

No one seemed to know where the boy might be. There'd been no calls to explain his absence. Attendance records showed he'd been in school on Thursday.

Knowing it was a long shot, she tried to reach Henry, but her call went to his voicemail. She left him a terse message, insisting he call her back as soon as possible.

Did she dare call Ivory down at the station? Was Ferguson's absence related to the police department's investigation? If Ferguson had just overslept or even ditched school, she didn't want to bother the police with something that was her job to handle. And maybe she wasn't even supposed to know they were using Ferguson, though that seemed absurd; shouldn't she, as principal, have access to this kind of information about her students?

She tried the emergency contact number for Ferguson that they had on file, but an automatic message reported that the line was disconnected. Maybe that number had been for a landline at some point. Even though she knew Ferguson's mother was no longer living at their home, she was still also listed as a primary emergency contact, along with a cell number.

Annie tried the cell but hit another wall when there was no answer.

That left Ferguson's dad. Annie had his number, too, in Ferguson's student file. The man was probably at work, and she braced herself for the tongue lashing he would surely give her—if he even took her call.

She closed her office door and took a deep breath. The few times she'd dealt with Bud Carbo in the past, the confrontational man had made the exchanges difficult.

A man's gruff voice answered. "Yeah?"

He sounded like he might have been sleeping.

"Bud Carbo, this is Annie Pierce, the principal at your son's school."

There was a heavy sigh. "Pierce. What do ya want this time? My kid's eighteen now. Any trouble he's gettin' himself into now ain't my problem."

Annie couldn't imagine ever approaching parenthood with that mentality, but her years of experience with parents had taught her that some people actually cut their kids off completely at the arbitrary age of eighteen. They were usually the same parents who were pretty much worthless in the years before their kids turned eighteen, too.

She refused to rise to the bait.

"Mr. Carbo, I'm afraid Ferguson isn't in school this morning. Do you know where he might be?"

"Hell, woman," he started, but a phlegmy cough cut off his words. "Ain't that your job to keep track of my kid during school hours?"

Annie took another deep breath. She could handle this disgusting man's verbal abuse for as long as it took if it allowed her to help Ferguson. That poor boy had dealt with this sorry excuse for a father his whole life.

"That is what I'm trying to do, Mr. Carbo. Please, if you are at home, can you take a minute to see if he's in the house?"

More coughing. "Shit, woman. I'm sick in bed and you want me to go traipsing around in my boxers trying to find Ferg? Fine, if it'll get you off my back. Hold on."

Annie hit the mute button so the man couldn't hear her gag at the vision his words conjured in her mind.

"He ain't here," the man reported back. Either his home was very small or he'd made little effort to check for his son.

"Are you sure?" she pushed, not caring if she irritated him more.

"Yeah, I'm sure. The little shit took my truck. He's not here. And trust me, if he comes back, he's going to pay for leaving me without a set of wheels. My shift starts at two."

She wasn't any closer to finding Ferguson, and his father clearly wasn't going to be of any help. Annie remembered the boy saying the man had commandeered Ferguson's pickup for his own needs.

What a terrible environment to have to fight to survive in.

"Thank you for checking. Please be sure to call me back if you hear from your son," she said before slamming her handset down. "You miserable piece of shit."

Someone knocked on her office door.

"Come in," she yelled, her vision still clouded with frustration over Carbo's lack of humanity.

"Everything all right in here?" Sarah asked. The pointed look she gave Annie meant the entire office staff probably heard that last bit about Carbo.

She collapsed back in her chair in frustration. "I'm scared for Ferguson. Where the hell is he?"

Sarah looked confused. "Scared? It's not like the kid hasn't skipped school before. He probably crashed at a buddy's and overslept or something. I'm sure he's fine."

"I'm calling the police," Annie said, sitting up straight again. "Shut the door behind you, Sarah."

She didn't need to explain herself. It wasn't like she was at liberty to tell Sarah that the boy had turned himself into an informant for the local police department. But her gut told her something wasn't right.

Sarah backed out, her expression still skeptical, but she shut the door firmly and Annie picked up her handset again. Just then, she heard her husband's ring tone coming from her cell in her pocket. She switched phones.

"Annie, hon, I need you to drive over to my office. We need to talk. Right now."

She pulled her purse out of her bottom desk drawer. "Henry, does this have anything to do with Ferguson?"

His pause meant she'd surprised him.

"Y-yes," Henry said, stuttering, "but how could you possibly know that?"

"Just tell me, is he all right?"

"Ferguson? Yeah, he's going to be fine. But we've finally got some answers on those drugs."

"I'll be right there."

Annie's mind kept chewing on Henry's words during her short drive to the plant on the outskirts of Ruby Shores. *He's going to be fine.*

What had happened?

Even from a distance, she could see pulsating blue and red lights ahead. As she pulled off the county road into the front parking area of the plant, she saw two police cars parked right in front of the building with their lights on. A few officers milled about outside.

Office shooting popped into her head.

But her husband would never have called her to come if something dangerous was still in progress. Too many active shooter drills at school were warping her brain.

She pulled into the closest open spot and hurried toward the front door. She spied John Sullivan in the driver's seat of the second squad car. When she took a step in his direction, he noticed her and gave a quick shake of his head. She kept toward the front door of the office building, but she noticed someone in his backseat. It was a man that Annie didn't recognize.

At least it wasn't Ferguson.

A uniformed woman approached, and Annie was relieved to see it was Beth, her daughter's old classmate and one of the three officers that had visited her on Halloween.

"What happened?" she asked. She didn't slow as she headed for the door to the plant's reception area. Beth fell into step beside her.

"We caught a big break in the case."

"The case?" Annie repeated. Henry had mentioned drugs, but she was seeking confirmation.

"The sergeant might want to be the one to update you. She's in your husband's office now, along with the kid."

Annie yanked the door open and walked right past the receptionist despite the way the man behind the desk jumped to his feet at their approach.

"Can I help you?"

Since she seldom visited Henry at the office, Annie didn't know the young man, but he didn't attempt to stop them. Beth's presence beside her was probably the reason.

She could have sagged with relief when she burst through Henry's office door without bothering to knock and she found, seated next to Sergeant Ivory Gilbert in front of her husband's desk, Ferguson.

"Oh, thank God. What happened? Ferguson, why aren't you in school? I've been calling all over town looking for you this morning. I don't think your dad is too happy with me. What are you doing here?"

Ivory stood. Seeing her in uniform always gave Annie pause. "Here, Annie, have a seat. I'm done in here and need to go see to things out front. Henry here can give you the rundown on things. Call me if you still have questions after you talk with him."

Annie glanced behind her to see a look pass between Beth and Ivory.

"Oh, no, you don't, Ivory," Annie said. "You can't just run out of here. It recently came to my attention that you may have been putting one of my students in grave danger."

Ferguson sat up straight in his chair. That was when Annie noticed the boy had a shiner around his right eye. "Excuse me, Ms. Pierce. I'm *right* here. And I'll have you know that, thanks to my stealthy actions, we cracked this case wide open."

Annie sighed at the teen's smug expression. "You watch too much television."

He seemed to deflate at her biting tone.

"Ferguson, do you think this is a game?"

He shrugged, trying to regain some of his swagger.

Disgusted, Annie turned back to Ivory, given she was the one in charge. "I'm sorry I snapped. Beth said you caught a break. That sounds like good news. I was just afraid something had happened to Ferguson when I couldn't find him this morning, and then Henry called me. I need to hear what happened from you. And why are we even in Henry's office right now?"

Ivory pulled a phone out of the breast pocket of her uniform and read the screen. "Fine. Beth, go tell Sullivan I'll be out in a minute."

Once the younger officer was gone, Ivory again motioned for the chair she'd recently vacated, but Annie was too wound up to sit.

"I really don't have much time," the sergeant began. "What we uncovered here at the plant is only part of a more intricate, expanded distribution network, and I have to make some calls before anyone slips through our fingers. We'd suspected for some time, even before Byron Oaks died, that this plant was involved in bringing drugs into Ruby Shores. We weren't sure how, but now we know."

"Wait," Annie said, holding up a hand. "Was it not a heart attack that killed Byron? I heard rumors."

"It was *not* a heart attack," Ivory confirmed, but she didn't appear inclined to share the cause of death. "Our first break was when Henry called us and offered to help in whatever way he could. I believe you had passed a rumor on to him some time ago?"

"Henry?" Annie shifted her gaze to her husband, but he didn't look her way. She spun back to Ivory. "I thought *Ferguson* was your snitch."

"I hate that term," Ivory said, shaking her head.

"Henry offered to help us figure out how Byron might have been involved. As you probably know, before he died, Byron was in charge of the transportation routes between Minneapolis and Ruby Shores. No surprise, but Minneapolis has long been the hub for some big narcotics organizations to get their product out to the smaller communities. We suspected Byron might have recruited drivers to use the company's delivery vehicles to move the drugs into this community."

"And we were *right*," Ferguson interrupted, looking pleased with himself.

"You need to be quiet," Annie said, though she secretly liked the satisfaction in Ferguson's expression. This might help him work through the loss of his cousin, and even his own addictions. Playing a part in cleaning up the town may be good for him after all.

"We were right," Ivory said, echoing Ferguson's words.

"But I don't understand," Annie said. "If Byron was handling the movement, and he died, why didn't this part of the distribution channel just naturally grind to a halt?"

"It might have," Ivory agreed. "But Zeke Carbo and his delivery partner decided not to even tell the higher-ups about Byron's death."

"Byron wasn't murdered then?"

"Now who's watching too much TV?"

Ivory glanced at Ferguson impatiently, then back to Annie. "No. His own drug use was his downfall. We think when the people above Byron figured out Zeke wasn't honest with them, they came after him and that other guy who died. We are still trying to figure out all the pieces, which is why I really should be out there doing my job right now."

"Sorry, but . . ." Annie paused, but she was determined to get her answers before Ivory left, so she charged on. "Something obviously happened this morning. And I still don't see why Ferguson is here, with a black eye, instead of in school."

Ivory shrugged. "The kid wanted to help after Zeke died. He'd met Zeke's delivery partner before. A guy named Dawson. Turns out Zeke handled more of the local contacts here in Ruby Shores, and Dawson took the lead in the movement of product with the trucks between Minneapolis and here. He knew Ferguson as Zeke's cousin, and even knew the boy had his own troubled history, so he approached the boy at Zeke's funeral about maybe doing a little work for him."

Annie's blood ran cold. "He recruited you? Oh my God, Ferguson. That's crazy. Why didn't you tell me?"

"I told *her*." The teen pointed at Ivory. "What were *you* going to do about it, other than freak out? I wanted whoever was part of why Zeke wasn't able to stay straight—and maybe even killed him—to pay."

"But that's so dangerous."

Henry cleared his throat. "Annie, let the woman finish. This is bigger than us, and she still has plenty of work to do out there. This is just the tip of the iceberg."

"Fine. Sorry, Ivory. I won't interrupt again."

The sergeant gave her a doubtful glance, but she nodded.

"Byron must have known that the easiest way to move the drugs out into the Ruby Shores community was to have a third person working in the plant with regular physical access to the trucks. If they could get their hooks into someone who was already responsible for unloading the trucks, he'd have his solution."

A radio squawked and Annie jumped at the sound. She hadn't noticed the younger officer had come back to stand just outside Henry's office. Ivory paused.

"Officer Sullivan is ready to head down to the station whenever you are, Sergeant," Beth said.

"Tell him I'll be right out," Ivory said.

The younger officer nodded and left for a second time. Ivory turned back to Annie.

"I need to make this quick. Byron had just hired a new guy to work here at the plant before he died. That new unloader was the same guy who died beside Ferguson's cousin on Halloween. We initially thought he wasn't from around here, because no one recognized him and his driver's license showed California. But we found a paystub from here with his name on it at Zeke's place. There was very little information in his employment file. After a few calls, we had a clearer picture of who he really was. He worked here and slept on Zeke's couch. When both Zeke and the new guy turned up dead, Dawson wanted to take over, but he needed a new gopher in the plant. Ferguson was the answer to his prayers—or so he thought. He had no idea that Ferguson's interest wasn't in dope or cash, but revenge."

"He shouldn't have underestimated me," Ferguson said.

Ivory cleared her throat. "Long story short is that we asked Henry to hire Ferguson if Dawson suggested him. Employees are always recommending friends to the managers here because help is hard to find. Things fell into place, just as we'd hoped, and Henry brought Ferguson on to work some late night and super early shifts. Dawson thought he had his gopher."

"For God's sake, you had this child moving drugs into Ruby Shores?" Annie couldn't believe what she was hearing. "And . . . Henry . . . you *helped*?"

"We only needed one instance of Dawson moving the drugs from Minneapolis to Ruby Shores," Ivory insisted, "and handing them over to Ferguson for further distribution. We have another guy on the inside who works the streets. He made sure *he* was the one Ferguson handed the drugs to. This morning, the exchange was made, and everything went off perfectly. When Dawson left the plant at the end of his shift, we were outside waiting for him. He had nowhere to run."

"But where did you get the black eye?" Annie asked, swinging on Ferguson. "Something obviously went wrong."

"Oh, this?" Ferguson asked, pointing to his face. "That was my old man. He took a swing at me two days ago when there wasn't any milk in the fridge."

Annie couldn't believe what she was hearing. She looked at both Ivory and Henry.

"It's like I keep telling you, hon," Henry said, getting to his feet. "Life is never as fair as you'd like, and Ferguson isn't lucky enough to have a peaceful homelife. There are monsters everywhere. I guess all we can do is help to keep them off the streets. He did a brave thing. Was it dangerous? Yes. But, sadly, even home is a dangerous place for him."

"Home was bad," Ferguson said. "*Was.* Not anymore. I'm done letting my dad use me as a punching bag. The sergeant here arranged for a place for me to stay. The rent is cheap and she's putting me to work to earn enough to live on my own. No more bagging groceries for me. Hell, I might even look into checking out a community college next fall. I'm thinking maybe law enforcement might be something I'm interested in."

Annie finally dropped into the chair Ivory had asked her to sit in earlier, feeling exhausted. "Ivory, tell me you've moved him out of the role of informer, now that you've made progress on this case, and you've got him doing nothing more dangerous than filing or something."

Ivory winked at her. "That's the plan. I hope that school of yours gave this kid a firm grasp of the ABCs, because he'll need it."

Ferguson groaned. "Filing? I'd rather work on actual cases."

"Let's get you through high school first, son, and then we can talk about letting you see a little more action. You've already proven you've got the stomach for it, but let's not push our luck. You're only eighteen."

The sergeant patted Ferguson on the back on her way to the door.

"Was that Dawson in the squad car out there when I came in?" Annie asked.

Ivory paused at the door. "Sure was. And with a little luck, he's just the first of many dominos to fall. Thanks again, Henry. You were a big help, too."

Watching Ivory head down the hall and back outside, Annie was again reminded how effective the woman was at her job. Ferguson wasn't the only one with courage around here. Ivory had to have plenty of it, too. She was nothing like the young girl who used to torment Annie and her friends at summer camp.

Henry was full of surprises, too. He'd told her he would get to the bottom of what was going on at the plant, and he did.

Together, they all made a great team, and today they had helped make the streets a little safer for everyone.

celebrate with friends

ARIZONA

February 2020

Chapter Twenty-Seven

Annie exited the Phoenix–Mesa Gateway baggage terminal into the bright Arizona sunshine. Her parents' winter home was a shorter distance from this small airport than the larger and more congested Sky Harbor. Travelers streamed around her in both directions, but all she wanted to do was take a moment to sit and let the sun melt the chill right out of her bones. The Minnesota winter had felt endless, and she'd been looking forward to this moment for months.

Off to her right, she noticed an empty metal table. Other tables offered umbrellas for shade, but those were all full. A few of the occupants fanned themselves as they awaited their flights, even though it didn't feel warmer than the low seventies to Annie. Most people exiting the building hurried toward vehicles that would whisk them away.

Annie had time. She'd arrived a day before her friends, so she could make sure the house was in order, they'd have the groceries they needed, and all the party preparations were complete. Since this would be a shorter girls' trip than last year—and she'd planned it—she felt responsible for making sure the Kaleidoscope Girls made the most of their time in the sunshine.

Logistics weren't fun, so her goal was to get as much of them out of the way as possible.

She wasn't worried about the house. Knowing her parents, they'd made sure everything was in tiptop shape before leaving two weeks ago for their extended cruise. Annie planned to show them the same courtesy at the end of her week, by making sure the house was exactly as they'd left it.

They'd even suggested Annie and the girls use their vehicle to get back to the airport at the end of their trip and leave it in overnight parking. That way, Patsy and Lyle wouldn't have to hire a ride home after their long vacation.

Things were lining up perfectly.

As Annie sank into one of the two metal chairs, a woman walking by shook her head at her.

"Honey, grab a chair back in the shade. This sun will positively melt you."

Annie gave her a polite nod, not bothering to say that melting was exactly what she planned to do. It didn't even feel as warm in the sun as she'd hoped, but it was a far cry from the below-zero temperatures back home.

After five minutes, she remembered she wasn't wearing any sunscreen, so she should probably get moving. She had plenty to accomplish in the next twenty-four hours, anyway.

And then the real vacation could begin.

Annie opened the front door to her parents' home, and a wave of stale, warm air hit her. "Why is it so hot in here? I'm afraid it might be hotter inside than outside."

"What's that?" Her Uber driver asked as he deposited her second, heavier bag on the lower porch step. Normally she could have packed for a five-day trip in a smaller, carry-on roller bag, but the party supplies she'd brought along meant an extra bag. When one wheel had caught between two pads of hot concrete and broke at the airport curb, her driver kindly offered to help her with it. This had earned him a high rating and an extra tip. She'd also arranged for him to pick her friends up at the airport the next day, when they were scheduled to arrive. They'd be in excellent hands.

"Don't worry," he said. "It isn't real warm out today, but we get plenty of nice days, even in February. I know you snowbirds come here hoping to lie in the sun and play in the pool. It might be too chilly to swim today, but maybe you'll get lucky. As far as the house being too hot, maybe the air went out. How can I help?"

Annie shook her head. "You've done more than enough. I've got it from here. And thanks again for agreeing to bring my friends here tomorrow." She handed him the extra bills she'd pulled out of her wallet when they'd arrived.

He accepted the money with a grateful smile and pulled out his wallet, stuffing the bills inside. "No problem. And here's my card, in case you need a ride back out to the airport at the end of your stay, or if your friends' travel plans change."

She had so much to do. Maybe he could give her a place to start with the potential air conditioning issue. "Say, there is one thing," she said as she accepted his card. "You don't have the name for a reputable heating and cooling business, do you?"

His wallet disappeared and he pulled out his phone, nodding. "It just so happens that I've got a guy."

Thankful for all his help, Annie took down the information, then waved him on his way. Alone again, she grabbed hold of her second bag and grunted as she lifted it up one step at a time and through the front door. Henry had helped her haul it through the snow and slush at the Minneapolis airport. Whatever they didn't use here this week was going to become a "welcome home" gift for her parents, because she didn't plan to lug the thing, broken wheel and all, back home.

Once inside, Annie started peeling off layers of clothes. Traveling always made her hot and sweaty, and she hadn't exaggerated when she said the temperature felt higher in the house than out on the front walk. They must have had some abnormally hot days after her parents left; this was a well-insulated house. The blue shimmer of her parents' backyard saltwater pool beckoned, but she'd cool off later. Her new top priority was to get the air working.

But what if the air-conditioner wasn't actually broken? What if the power was out? A fridge and freezer full of rotten food and meat would be a much bigger problem. She remembered her dad mentioning they'd come back to that here once before.

Skipping barefoot across the tiles, which didn't feel as cold as she remembered, she hurried to the fridge and yanked open the door, delighted when a blast of cold air hit her in the face.

"You could have just flipped on a light to check the electricity," she said, enjoying the solitude of the empty house more than she'd expected.

But she'd enjoy it more if it wasn't almost a hundred degrees inside.

She found the thermostat and realized she'd exaggerated. It was only eighty, but definitely warm and musty.

"What are you complaining about? The last eighty degrees you enjoyed was probably the first day of school."

She really should quit talking to herself.

Not that there was anyone there to hear her, so she changed her mind. She'd do whatever the hell she wanted for the next twenty-four hours and enjoy every minute. While an empty house back home had depressed her as the winter dragged on, this was different. This was the start of what promised to be a fun-filled vacation with her very best friends in the whole world.

As long as she could get the house cooled off.

Annie sighed as cold saltwater enveloped her. It was more bracing than she'd expected, but it felt refreshing after her busy day. She was beat.

The sun, now little more than a slash of gold on the western horizon, offered a vibrant base for broad strokes of orange and violet that slashed across the sky, all topped with a cap of the deepest midnight blue.

She wondered if the breathtaking display was the sun's way of celebrating the completion of another day, much as her solitary swim was her reward for checking everything off her list—including getting the air-conditioner functioning.

She'd learned that having an "in" always helped speed up the process when bringing a specialist in, and her Uber driver had come through for her again.

As expected, her mother already had fresh sheets on all the beds. Annie claimed the smallest room for herself, and would let the other four duke it out over the remaining three rooms. Two would have to share the bonus room, but there was plenty of space for everyone.

Closing her eyes, she flipped onto her back. It took very little effort to stay afloat in the salty pool water. As she relaxed, she thought back through everything she'd accomplished.

Had she forgotten anything important?

She'd filled the kitchen cupboards and refrigerator with the items she thought they'd need in the days ahead. She'd even locked her parents' liquor away and purchased a fresh supply. They were gracious enough to let them use their house; they didn't need to drink their booze, too. But they could spare a few lemons. The next morning, she'd be sure to pick some fresh ones—and limes, too—off the fruit trees lining the fence on the north side of the yard. They'd be a nice addition to cocktail hour.

After a few minutes, she swam to the side of the pool and hoisted herself onto the patio deck. In her mind, Patsy was scolding her for swimming alone.

What if something were to happen? echoed through Annie's brain.

It had to be the most common phrase she'd heard the woman say while Annie was growing up. She was still surprised her mother had allowed her to take part in gymnastics for so many years. By the time injuries had stalled out Annie's career in the gym, she was throwing some difficult skills. Nothing like the Olympic gymnasts, of course, but there were still elements of danger.

Annie was already looking forward to the excitement of the upcoming Summer Olympic Games. Maybe they should have skipped this winter trip to Arizona and held their girls' trip in Tokyo in late July instead.

But they'd agreed that not every annual trip would be as expensive as Maui had turned out to be last summer. Besides, Jackie would probably be the only other one in their group who would enjoy attending many of the Olympic events. She wasn't sure about Renee, but she knew Lynette and Kit didn't care much about sports.

She'd have to add it to her own "someday" bucket list. There was no way she'd be attending the games in July 2020, even though it was something she'd always dreamed of doing. First as an athlete—because every kid has to dream—and now as an adult. Maybe she'd find a way to make it happen by July 2036. Wouldn't she have more free time when she was sixty-six and retired?

Her stomach growled. She decided to make herself a sandwich. Then she'd shower, change into her pajamas, and read that new book Ava had given her for Christmas. The hardcover copy of *Where the Crawdads Sing* was yet another reason her spare suitcase was so heavy flying in. The book would come home with her if she didn't have time to read it.

She pulled out the loaf of bread she'd purchased, and then the deli meat and other sandwich fixings from the refrigerator, moaning in dismay when she realized the tub of butter was practically empty. Butter hadn't made her grocery list earlier because she'd spied the large container and assumed there'd be plenty. She debated whether to try the mayonnaise she'd picked up for her friends but decided against it. It wasn't her favorite. She'd have to run and get more butter at the grocery store in the morning.

Her trip there today had left her frustrated, not knowing where anything was located. Sitting down with her dry sandwich and a bottle of water, she thought back to the store's layout so she could make it a quick in-and-out next time.

Tomorrow was her first official day of vacation, and she didn't want to waste any of it.

Then she remembered the display of magazines she'd spied next to the cashier. One cover mentioned a rising death toll worldwide from some kind of virus. The headline must have stuck in her mind because of her conversation with Michael the day before. He'd called her to see if she had any updates on Ava, given her due date was quickly approaching.

"I think she's getting sick of me asking her," he'd joked.

Annie had assured him that Ava's obstetrician was keeping close tabs on their daughter, and everything seemed to track right on schedule. Then she'd updated him on what had gone down at Henry's office related to the drug situation. They were going to try to keep it out of the papers, so it was the first Michael had heard about it.

"See, I told you it wasn't just idle gossip, Annie," he'd said when she congratulated him on his role in the drug bust. The police might have reached out to Henry anyway, but both Michael and Annie agreed it was fun to think they'd helped to keep dangerous drugs off the streets of Ruby Shores in the future. "I imagine there will be some kind of fallout at work for Henry now," Michael said.

"Actually, the top brass at their headquarters in London requested that Henry and a few others make the trip over to Europe to discuss some significant restructuring. While they were upset to learn of their former employees' involvement, three of whom actually ended up dead, they appreciated the way Henry worked with the police in putting an end to the company's unwitting involvement in a drug ring. He's hopeful this could lead to a big promotion for him. He'll fly out while I'm in Arizona, and he could be gone for a few weeks. I just hope he makes it home before Ava has the baby."

"Really?"

Annie had thought she detected concern in her ex's tone. She remembered Ava's comment last fall about how she always seemed to have to walk on eggshells when it came to the relationship between her ex-husband and her current husband. Was this what her daughter had meant?

"Don't worry," she had told him. "If you are there and he isn't, there is no way he could spin that as being your fault."

But his next comment had sent a shiver down her spine.

"I don't think this is a great time for Henry to be heading overseas. Have you been paying any attention to talk of this virus that has some folks pretty concerned? I talked to an old Navy buddy of mine who moved to China with his wife after he got out. He'd met her while on tour over there and she wanted to go back to be closer to her family. He said the government has enforced some pretty strict lockdowns. Starting in January, I think he said."

"To be honest, things have been so crazy, I haven't watched the news in a while," she'd said. "But Henry will be in England, not China. I'm sure he'll be fine."

"Hmm . . . just be sure he's at least aware before you leave, all right? And Annie, watch yourself in the airport and on the plane, will you?"

Annie remembered laughing over his concern for her wellbeing. "Do you mean because of some strange virus half a world away? I'm sure it's nothing that will impact us here in the US. Michael, I'm literally flying straight from Minneapolis to Mesa. There's no way I'd be at any risk."

He'd assured her she was probably right, but by the time they'd ended the call, a tiny worm of worry had begun making its way through her brain. Michael knew more about airplanes and airports, given the years he'd worked as a commercial pilot. People traveled all over the world, passing through various airports on their journeys. But with so much to do to get ready for the trip to Arizona and hosting everyone, she'd promptly forgotten about it.

Now that she thought back, she realized she hadn't mentioned Michael's warning to Henry.

It was probably for the best. He never liked it when Annie had conversations with Michael. You'd think after twenty years, he'd be over his jealousy, but he wasn't.

And they all knew it.

As she started on the second half of her sandwich, she decided maybe she should turn on the television and see if she could catch any of the nightly news before relaxing with her new book. Even if they were safe here in America, maybe Henry and her parents should be a little careful.

She flipped on the television and started channel surfing, having no idea which stations carried the news around here. The buttons on her father's complicated remote were hard to make out without her readers. Her mother seldom watched TV, especially when she could be outside in the beautiful Arizona weather.

The loud shrill of a telephone grabbed her attention. It was coming from the kitchen.

She couldn't believe they'd maintained a landline in this house.

Giving up on the remote, she tossed it onto the sofa, grabbed her empty plate, and headed for the kitchen, picking up the ringing telephone before whoever was on the other end of the line gave up. She'd be upset if a telemarketer was interrupting her evening.

"Hello?"

"Hello, is this Patsy?" a voice Annie didn't recognize asked. The caller sounded congested, as if she might have a cold. Something about her tone didn't sound like a telemarketer.

"No, I'm afraid Patsy isn't available at the moment. But this is her daughter. Can I maybe help you with something?"

"Millie?"

"No, this is Annie."

"Oh, heavens! Hello, Annie," the woman on the other end of the line said, her voice a little stronger now. "This is Georgia, Betsy's daughter. You know, your mom's friend Betsy?"

Annie held the telephone between her ear and shoulder so she could clean up the kitchen. At least her parents' landline didn't have a cord.

"Sure, Georgia. I was just talking about Betsy with my mom not too long ago. Well, I guess it was last fall now, but I told Mom she should give Betsy a call and line up another one of those girls' trips they used to take way back when. That's actually why I'm in Arizona at their place now. For a girls' trip, I mean. My girlfriends arrive tomorrow, and we're all going to celebrate our fiftieth birthdays together. Do you know if Mom talked to Betsy about that?"

"I don't. But even if they talked about taking a trip together, it's too late now," Georgia said.

This time Annie heard a definite hitch, beyond possible congestion. "Oh, no. Don't tell me something happened to your mom?"

"Unfortunately, that *is* why I'm calling. Mom passed away this morning. It was quite unexpected—aside from some struggles with her diabetes since Dad died, that is. The doctors said it was a stroke, but my brothers and I, we're afraid she actually died from a broken heart. Can that be a real thing?"

Annie tried to imagine how her own mother would cope if something happened to her dad. She'd be in trouble. They were practically joined at the hip, as the old saying goes.

"I am so sorry to hear that, Georgia. Mom had told me that your dad had passed away recently as well. That has to be so hard."

"You can't imagine. Enjoy your parents, because when they are gone, it leaves a huge hole. And speaking of your parents, would you be willing to pass this news on to your mother? I know it is a terrible message to convey, given how long Mom and Patsy were friends, but I have so many more people to call and arrangements to make."

Annie wandered over to the large window overlooking her parents' backyard. Nighttime had snuffed out the sun's last hurrah for the day, and twinkle lights strung between trees provided the only illumination. She hadn't thought to turn on the pool lights.

"Don't give it another thought, Georgia. My folks are actually on an extended cruise to celebrate their fifty-fifth wedding anniversary. Sadly, they'll probably miss any service you might be planning. If you don't mind, I think it's best if I wait until they get home to tell Mom about Betsy. They were so looking forward to this trip, and I know Mom will be heartbroken over this news."

She could hear Georgia blow her nose.

"We completely understand. My mother would probably send a lightning bolt down to knock some sense into me if I let you ruin their trip with this news. You know how they used to travel together. And speaking of travel . . . promise me you will not only have an amazing trip now with your friends at your folks' place, but that you'll keep traveling together. I hate that my mom and Patsy and their friends gave it up. In fact, I have an old group of high school friends who I'll probably see at Mom's funeral.

I think you just inspired me to put a bug in their ears about getting our own girls' trip scheduled."

Annie couldn't help but smile. "I promise. We are just getting going on our annual trips, too, and we have no intention of letting anything get in the way of them."

Georgia sighed. "I'm really glad we had a few minutes to talk, Annie. I feel better and may even get through the rest of the calls I need to make now. Hey, would you mind doing me one more favor? When you're sitting around the pool, celebrating your birthdays with your girlfriends, raise a toast to our mothers, would you? They helped show us what true friendship means."

"I'd be honored to do that, Georgia."

Chapter Twenty-Eight

ANNIE HAD ALREADY LOST sight of Jackie and Lynette. They couldn't be too far ahead, though the terrain of natural twists and turns along the desert hiking trail's incline would make it impossible for her to monitor their entire group unless they stayed close together.

She suddenly understood the sense of responsibility Kit had mentioned the previous summer during their trip to Maui. As the one who'd planned today's hike, she hoped she hadn't signed them all up for something they couldn't physically handle. The two main hiking trails up Camelback were a major draw for tourism in Phoenix, and Annie had hiked both in the past, but maybe this wasn't the best option for a bunch of women who were in town to celebrate their fiftieth birthdays.

Upon their arrival at the trail, they'd decided it wasn't necessary for their group to all stay together as long as they were at least paired up. Lynette mentioned she'd had lots of physical therapy and strength training on her ankle that had given her trouble in the past. Annie remembered how her friend had twisted her ankle while climbing down to the trio of waterfalls in Maui eight months earlier. She'd had to hobble around for the rest of that trip.

"I feel like putting my ankle to the test," Lynette had declared as they reached the trailhead. "Anyone up for a little more of a challenge? Like a timed hike to the summit?"

Jackie raised her hand. "Now that I'm not chained to a desk anymore, I've spent time at the gym near my new condo. There's this rock-climbing wall I've been working to master. I'd love to put my new skills to the test this morning."

"Wait," Kit said, a hand on Annie's arm. "We have to actually *climb* over rocks out here, like . . . for real? Annie, you practically killed me with your little ziplining adventure in Hawaii. I admit, I loved the ziplining once I got over my fear, but I still don't love heights. Besides, I've been a little busy with my new husband and our new teenager to get to the gym this winter. I'm afraid I might be in over my head here."

Renee stepped closer to Kit, gazing down the trail. "And this looks tougher than my regular morning walk through the woods back at Whispering Pines. Are you sure we can do this?"

Annie nodded. "We can do this, ladies. My seventy-five-year-old father still comes out here a few times each winter. If *he* can handle this, so can we. I picked Cholla Trail for today. The other one, Echo Canyon, is a little more difficult. I wanted you to experience the terrain of Arizona. And, trust me, the views from up top will take your breath away. We can take it slower if you like. This isn't a race, and if it gets too difficult, we can turn around and come back down. But I really don't think you'll want to, the closer you get to the top. It's a fun challenge, but not so hard you can't make it."

She hoped no one noticed the way she'd crossed her fingers behind her back.

That was fifteen minutes ago, and so far, so good.

She wasn't surprised that Lynette and Jackie were already out ahead. They were the more competitive ones in their group. Not that they were competing with anyone other than themselves, but they were always pushing, no matter what it was they were doing.

Kit, Renee, and Annie settled into a pace that still made visiting easy.

"Say, Kit, I've wanted to ask you how Isaac is settling in at school," Annie said. "It's never easy for a freshman in high school to start over in a new town, and he has lots more changes in his life besides school. Do you think things are working out for him?"

Kit laughed. "That boy is resilient. I suppose he's had to be for most of his life. I'd argue he does better with change than I do. Going from living alone to sharing my townhome with two males is taking more adjusting than I'd expected. I can't tell you how many times I've practically fallen into the toilet because one of them didn't put the seat back down and I'm not used to checking."

Annie laughed. "That is unacceptable. You need to break them of that nasty habit immediately."

"Working on it," Kit said as she shifted the straps on her small backpack.

Annie had ordered five inexpensive bags online, knowing easy access to bottled water and snacks during their hike would make the excursion more fun. They'd all appreciated her preparedness, but Lynette was particularly relieved to have an easy way to bring a small elastic brace along on the hike, just in case her ankle wasn't as strong as she hoped.

"But back to Isaac. His teachers tell me he's settled into his classwork without too much trouble. I wasn't sure how strong his academic background was and didn't know what to expect. There are all these things you don't think about when you make a spur-of-the-moment decision to foster a fifteen-year-old orphan."

Annie couldn't even imagine the things Kit and Dean hadn't thought about before they'd so generously welcomed the boy into their home, especially since they began fostering him at the same time as they took their five-plus-year relationship to a new level with their October wedding.

Renee pulled one of her two bottles of water out of her bag and took a sip. "You know, Kit, I actually moved with my kids from Minneapolis to Whispering Pines after our first summer out there, so my son, Robbie, had to change schools, too. It was the beginning of his sophomore year of high school, so I can relate a little to what you're saying. It's good to hear the schoolwork is going all right. How about friends? Does it seem like Isaac is having any luck there?"

The trio had just reached an area with a small rock overhang a few feet off the path where they could rest and take in some pretty views of the valley. The scene below them appeared to be shrinking as they'd climbed higher, but it seemed that each view was more spectacular than the last. Annie stepped off the main trail to give them all a brief reprieve. The other two followed.

"It doesn't seem like he's made any close friends. He hasn't brought anyone home from school yet. But there are a couple boys he's gone out to do things with. I think they sit together at lunch and have some classes together, too."

"Wait until that new friend is a girl. Then you might wish you hadn't been so eager for him to hang out with other kids."

Kit groaned. "Baby steps, Annie, baby steps."

Renee stashed her water bottle and turned to look at the sweeping scenery in front of them. "You were right, Annie. It *is* gorgeous up here."

"Just wait. It gets even better."

"Say, Kit, you're in Chanhassen, right?" Renee asked. "I think the family of one of my son's friends just bought a house in that suburb. His friend's name is Paul. They've been friends since grade school, played a lot of basketball together. They still try to stay in touch, even though they're both off at different colleges now. Anyway, the reason I mention it is that Paul has two younger brothers. One might even be Isaac's age. I know the family. If you'd like, I could put in a call to Paul's mom on the off chance that her boys go to the same school as Isaac. Or maybe they could connect outside of school, if not."

Kit shook her head, hands on her hips as she took in the view. "Look at us, arranging play dates. Did you ever think I'd be setting up a play date for a fifteen-year-old boy?"

It was Annie's turn to shake her head. "Nope. You always swore you'd never have kids. And look at you now. It just goes to show that we never know what direction our lives might suddenly take. I'm proud of you for taking on the challenge, Kit. This is a big deal. How are you keeping Isaac busy if he isn't hanging out with buddies all the time yet?"

Taking a step back toward the trail, Kit motioned to Annie and Renee to follow. "Come on. We don't want to lose Jackie and Lynette completely. I'm sorry I complained at the beginning. I'm actually doing okay."

The three women waited for another, faster-moving couple to pass, then stepped back onto the upward trail.

"Actually," Kit went on, "Dean is the one who's keeping Isaac busy, especially on the weekends. They have a new project they're working on.

The thing those two connected over right away was my old Mustang. Isaac's dad used to be a mechanic, and he loved old muscle cars. I don't know if I ever mentioned this, but a car accident killed Isaac's mother when he was three. He was in the car with her. In the backseat, I think. He lost an eye, but his prosthetic is so good, most people never notice."

Both Annie and Renee expressed their sympathies. Poor Isaac shouldn't have had to endure the death of both of his parents.

"Life just isn't fair, is it?" Annie said.

"So you always say," Kit replied. "Man, this is getting steep."

"Don't worry. There are plenty of more gradual incline areas up ahead."

She groaned before continuing about her foster son. "Isaac's dad became obsessed with making old cars safer. Sadly, he died in a work accident before he could make any genuine progress on it, but Isaac picked up his father's mantra."

"That's ironic," Renee interjected. "A man loses his life trying to make things safer."

"Right? Anyway, back when Isaac told Dean why he wanted to go to college to become an engineer—that was right around the time my Mustang was getting refurbished. It runs great now and is all redone, but it worries Dean a little when I drive it, because there aren't any airbags or other safety features we take for granted in newer cars. He did replace the old seatbelts, at least."

Renee nodded. "I saw your Mustang the day of your wedding. It looked great. Not much of a project there for Dean and Isaac."

"You're right, but that didn't stop the two of them. Shortly after we got Isaac settled in at home, they started looking for a different old car to work on."

Renee whistled. "And they bought one? Those things can't be cheap."

"Believe me, it wasn't. Dean bought a '67 Pontiac Firebird. It's in pretty tough shape, but even in that condition the damn thing cost about twenty grand. It was actually a Camaro Z28 that Isaac's mom died in, but they settled on this Pontiac. The cars are really similar."

Annie laughed. "I forget how you've always loved old cars, Kit."

Kit shrugged. "What can I say? My grandpa did, too, and when they gave me my mom's old Mustang, he spent time in the garage with me, showing me how to do some basic maintenance to take care of it. It's kind of fun that all three of us have the love of old cars in common. But I leave the tinkering on Dean's latest purchase to the two of them. They spend hours out there in the garage. I swear, we'll end up buying a different place just because we'll need a bigger garage. Dean has had to park outside all winter, and Isaac doesn't even have a vehicle of his own to drive yet."

"Funny you should say that," Annie said. "Henry and Relic were trying to fix the starter on Relic's car last weekend. Somehow, it was *my* car that ended up outside. Having to clear snow from a windshield and warm it up for ten minutes before leaving for work is a sure-fire way to never stop appreciating a garage in the future. Is Dean thinking he'll get the Pontiac fixed up so Isaac can drive that?"

"No. Realistically, getting the Pontiac back into pristine condition, along with testing out some possible new safety add-ons to the original model, is their goal. That will take a lot of money and probably a lot of time. We want to pick up an old beater for Isaac one of these days. At his age he'll need some autonomy, and he can get that with a vehicle of his own even if it isn't anything fancy."

"Not only do you get to worry about girls in Isaac's future, but also the sheer terror that comes with teen drivers," Renee said. "Welcome to the world of motherhood, Kit!"

CHAPTER TWENTY-NINE

THE ROCKY GROUND UNDERFOOT was looser in this section of the path, and their conversation trailed off as all three focused on their steps. At one point, Annie caught a bark of Lynette's laughter from somewhere ahead of them.

They could all reconvene once they reached the top. It would be a good place to sit and rest before starting back down. The temperature was comfortable, which meant there were other hikers on the trail they would need to coordinate with, since some stretches were only wide enough to allow one person through at a time. But they weren't in any hurry, and given it was February, the day shouldn't get too hot.

Many of the wildflowers in the scrubby, sparse vegetation were in bloom, adding shots of color to the arid landscape. The brilliant blue sky above added to the beautiful day and enjoyable hike, despite the sweat Annie could already feel trickling down her back.

She'd take this kind of hard work over sitting in her stuffy office back home or traversing icy roads any day. This vacation with the other Kaleidoscope Girls was exactly what she'd needed to get a break from winter and her empty house. She hoped Lemon was doing all right at Ava and Daniel's. They'd agreed to watch the dog since hers and Henry's trips overlapped and Relic's spring break wouldn't come until the middle of March.

"You know, I always felt left out when you guys would make comments about being a mother," Kit said, pulling Annie's attention back to the trail, which was once again easier to traverse as the looser gravel transitioned to hard-packed dirt. "It never seemed to bother Lynette, but I hated it."

This surprised Annie. "But, Kit . . . you always said you didn't want kids."

"I know. But now I'm thinking what I really didn't want was to be the kind of parent my mom and dad both turned out to be. Maybe it wasn't the kids that were the issue."

"Does this mean Isaac might be the first of many children in your future?" Renee asked. "There are plenty of kids in the foster care system."

Kit snorted. "No. I mean, who knows what the future holds, but right now I'm finding it fun to have Isaac around. I think we're really helping him find some stability that's been missing from his life for a long time. His grandfather, the man who's become such a good friend to my Grandma Hazel, had the best of intentions, but keeping a teenager out of trouble isn't an easy feat."

"You mean the guy whose underwear we found in your grandma's basement?" Annie asked with a laugh.

"What?" Renee cried. "I have to hear *that* story."

Kit grinned. "It isn't nearly as exciting as Annie makes it sound, though Hazel had me worried there for a bit. But I'm sick of talking about me. Renee, you mentioned moving your kids to Whispering Pines when they were still in high school. Was that before or after you got married again? I'd love to hear more of your story."

"As long as I don't get too winded talking, I'll tell you everything you want to know. But man, Annie, this is not an easy trail. I try to hike in the woods around Whispering Pines, but it's all pretty flat. And cool in the shade."

Annie skipped a little way ahead of them and then turned to face them, walking backward. "But doesn't it feel amazing to let the ice thaw from your veins?"

Before Renee could answer, Annie tripped on a loose rock and flailed, trying to keep her balance. Both Kit and Renee flung themselves forward to catch her, but they were only partially successful.

"That probably wasn't smart," Annie admitted, brushing the red dust and grit from the seat of her shorts. "I think I might have gotten a little rock stuck in the palm of this hand . . . but thanks for saving me from a worse fate."

"I suppose if a dirty butt and one scraped hand are the worst we leave with today, we'll all consider it a win," Kit said. "Now, Annie, if you'd please refrain from trying to scale a mountain backward, I'd like to hear about Renee moving her family to a lake resort in the middle of nowhere."

Once everyone was again heading up Camelback while facing forward, Renee began.

"Gosh, it's a long story. It would take significantly longer to tell it than it will for us to reach the summit. At least I hope we don't have that much farther to go. I'm not sure where to start . . ."

Kit fished out one of her water bottles. "Well, since this is only day two—if we count yesterday, even though it was a travel day—we still have plenty of time to catch up. Isn't that one of the main purposes of a girls' trip, after all? Just tell me how your kids fared, moving like that at such critical ages. A year ago you might not have held my interest with that part of your story, but lots can change in a year."

Renee nodded. "It sure can. And maybe that's my starting point for this story, too. You already know I inherited my lake resort from my great aunt."

Kit gave a mock shiver. "That sounds so bad-ass, Renee. How many women can say 'my lake resort' so nonchalantly, like it's no big deal?"

Before answering, Renee had to step around a large rock that must have tumbled onto the trail. "Trust me. I'm no bad-ass, and owning a lake resort is nowhere near as glamorous as it might sound. My Aunt Celia was the true bad-ass. Try to imagine your own mother taking over a lakeside property, all on her own, and figuring out a way to keep the lights on."

"My mother is the least self-reliant person I've ever met," Kit said. "No, I can't imagine her doing something like that."

"Celia took possession of Whispering Pines in 1966," Renee said. "She died in 2015 at ninety-two."

"That would put her in roughly the same generation as my Grandma Hazel," Kit said. "Maybe the toughness of that generation of women skipped our mothers. Mine, at least. I'd like to think we're pretty tough."

Annie thought Kit made a good point. Her own mother had become increasingly reliant on her father over the past decade, and it worried Annie. Relying too heavily on a man can be dangerous. She'd learned that the hard way in her first marriage.

"Hell, Annie, how much farther is it to the top?" Kit said, stepping to the side of the main trail to catch her breath. "My Grandma Hazel and Renee's bad-ass aunt probably wouldn't have been winded by now, but *I* am. Maybe their fortitude skipped two generations."

Renee and Annie both laughed.

"Kit, I think you've proven that you're pretty tough, too, over the past eight months," Renee said. "Adopting a teenage boy isn't for the weak."

"Fostering," Kit corrected.

"Actually, Kit's had to be tough her whole life. Renee, she practically raised her two younger brothers when her mother dumped the three kids on Hazel's front steps."

Kit dug a granola bar out of her bag. "Thanks for all these supplies, Annie. I may forgive you yet for dragging us out on another death-defying adventure. But like I said, enough about me. Let's hear it, Renee."

"You'll definitely forgive me for dragging you out here when you feel the adrenaline rush after you pull yourself up to the summit. You can't beat the three-hundred-and-sixty-degree view."

Kit quit chewing. "What exactly does 'pull yourself up' mean?" she asked around the food in her mouth. Then she shook her head and swallowed. "Never mind. Ignorance is bliss. It's too late to turn back now. We've come this far. Talk, Renee. It'll keep my mind off this torture."

They got back on the trail and Renee flipped her sunglasses up onto the top of her head. Shade from the close stone walls lining the trail blocked out much of the sun, making it hard to see the uneven ground.

"I didn't marry Matt until our second summer at Whispering Pines. I'd met him by the time we made our initial move out to the resort that first summer, but I didn't know, at that point, if I'd ever see him again. Anyway, you'd asked about the kids. Getting the resort open again took a ton of work. More than just Robbie and Julie and I could handle. My extended family helped a lot. Julie had finished most of her freshman year at college by that first summer and was an enormous help to me getting the business end of the resort up and running. You know, all the online stuff that kids are so good at these days."

"I know," Kit said. "At least with Isaac in the house, I have someone who can help me when I have a techy question at home. Dean put some of those speakers around the place—you know, the ones you can just ask to play a song or set a timer? One of them—the speakers, I mean—kept asking random questions in the middle of the night. Scared the crap out of me the first time it happened, and Dean was on a work trip. My cat didn't love it either. Isaac figured it out right away. So, yeah, I get it."

Annie listened without jumping in. It was just fun to be part of such a relatable conversation. She'd missed this kind of interaction with women her age.

"It didn't take me long to realize how hard it would be for me to keep our house up back in Minneapolis, which was a few hours from the Whispering Pines property. Where we technically called 'home' didn't matter as much to Julie, since she'd gone back to college in the fall, but Robbie was still heading into his sophomore year of high school. It was a tough decision, but I ultimately rented out our Minneapolis house, called Whispering Pines 'home' going forward, and switched Robbie's school. We're only about fifteen minutes away from a small town with a decent school system out there. Come to think of it, Julie almost dropped out of college at one point. She loved helping me run the resort, and she'd dated a guy who turned out to be a real creep during her freshman year, so she was a little leery. But I wouldn't allow it. Besides, our kids all inherit a decent chunk of change from Celia's estate if they graduate from college or a trade school. So that was another factor in her decision to stick things out."

The trail took another turn, and they were back in the bright sunlight. Renee settled her sunglasses back on her nose before continuing.

"I know you're curious about Robbie, since he made a change at almost the same age as Isaac. I'll be honest. He put up a fuss, and I allowed him to continue back at his old school and stay with the family of a friend I trusted. I was at Whispering Pines with my sister Jess, trying to get our retreats running for an additional source of income. But it was too hard to be apart from my son. I insisted he make the switch at the semester mark. I was prepared for him to hate it, but we got lucky. He's a good basketball player, and the school was so much smaller that the team had room for him. It didn't take him long to make some friends. I won't pretend it was a piece of cake. Kids are resilient though. I think Isaac will do just fine."

"I do, too," Annie finally added. She was so proud of Kit and Dean for opening their home to the boy.

Suddenly, the trail ahead took on a much steeper incline.

"Let's stop for one more quick break, and then we'll make this last push," Annie said, stepping into a natural gap between two large rocks to allow another group behind them to go ahead. "There's a section or two where you'll have to use both your arms and legs to keep moving. Don't let it intimidate you. Remember, you're a Kaleidoscope Girl, and we are invincible."

Kit eyed the path ahead with apprehension. "I don't recall the 'invincible' part being spelled out in our gang charter."

"I just added it," Annie said. "If we get separated at all, keep a close eye on the trail markers and don't veer off the designated path. Trust me—there are some wicked barbs on the short cacti within a few feet of where we climb up."

Renee glanced her way. "Sounds like you might be speaking from personal experience."

"What can I say? I'm not always great at following directions," Annie admitted.

Kit tightened the straps on her lightweight backpack. "Why do I feel like I might die today?"

Renee groaned, but Annie shook a stern finger at each of them. A sudden flashback of a demanding gymnastics coach flared into her brain, and she realized it was exactly the type of thing he used to do to her if she balked at the idea of executing a daring tumbling pass. Kit turned her nose up at her and Annie dropped her hand with a sigh. Was this how her old coach felt?

"Trust me. None of us are going to die," she said, hoping her faith in her two friends came through in her words and expression. "What kind of friend would I be if I let you get this close to the half-century mark just to kill you off before our big party tomorrow?"

"A shitty kind," Kit supplied. "Let's just get this over with."

"Do you want me to lead or bring up the rear?" Annie asked.

Kit thrust her thumb backward. "You bring up the rear. That way, if I fall to my death, I'll take you with me."

"What a lovely thought," Annie said, motioning for the other two to proceed.

Halfway up the steepest incline of the trail and just a short distance shy of the summit, Kit's foot slid, sending a shower of stones down on Annie's head. For a half second, the possibility of Kit's worries coming to fruition crossed Annie's mind, but she channeled her old coach again and did her best to banish the fear from her mind. With luck, no one would die on her watch.

Annie ignored the sharp sting shooting up her arm as she utilized a boulder to help hoist herself up the last few feet to the summit. If a scraped palm was the price she had to pay to have all of her friends reach this stunning vista, it was worth it.

Renee stood off to Annie's right, hands on hips. "We don't have views like this back home in Minnesota!" The breathless quality of her voice spoke to the level of exertion she'd drawn upon to reach the top of Camelback Mountain. "You were right, Annie. I can't believe how far you can see in every direction!"

Kit, two steps ahead of Annie, bent forward at her waist, as if she might be sick.

A pair of hikers came up behind them, waiting patiently for the two of them to move away from the point where the trail finally opened up onto the plateau at the summit.

"Doing alright?" Annie asked as she touched her friend's rounded back. She felt a shiver pass through Kit. "You made it, Kit! But we should probably move out of the way so others can pass. Once you catch your breath, we can find Jackie and Lynette."

Kit nodded and slowly straightened, as if she didn't quite trust her balance. "I need a minute."

Annie glanced apologetically over her shoulder at the other two hikers. Neither appeared even a little fazed by the challenging path they'd also just traversed.

"No problem," one of the younger women assured her. "I just hope we can still make it up this path when we're your age. There is no *way* my mom could hike all the way up here. Props to you ladies!"

Kit whipped her head around so hard that her sunglasses slipped down her nose as she squinted back at the hikers. "What did you say?"

Annie bit back a laugh, deciding to ignore the younger hiker's unintentional dig. At least she hoped it wasn't intentional. She placed both hands on Kit's shoulders and nudged her in Renee's direction and away from the top of the trailhead. "You did great, Kit! I don't know what you were so worried about. You scaled that last section like a mountain goat."

Her friend only put up a hint of resistance before moving out of the way. "What happened to women supporting women? First those two divas call me old and now you're calling me a goat."

Renee laughed. "They may be divas, but they aren't wrong. It *is* impressive that we made it all the way up here. I don't think I've ever felt this exhilarated! Thanks for pushing us to try this, Annie. And look. Jackie and Lynette are over there, taking pictures of the valley. Let's go."

"My legs feel so wobbly, I'm not sure I should walk anywhere right now," Kit said, looking between Renee and Annie. Then she glared at the two younger hikers as they finally passed by.

Annie leaned forward to whisper in her ear. "Don't let them see you sweat!"

Kit snorted. "It's a little late for that."

It was Annie's turn to laugh when Kit raised her arms to reveal the sweat staining her gray t-shirt from her armpits almost to her waist. "We made it up here. That's the important thing. When the going got tough, you didn't give up and turn around."

Kit shrugged as she watched Renee pick her way over to the rest of their friends. "Giving up has never been my style. Sometimes I just can't help but bitch on the way through the hard stuff. Grandma Hazel used to say my foul mouth helped me cope with the tough stuff."

Annie realized that Kit's grandmother was spot on with her observation. "Hazel always understood you best. Now, come on. Are you starting to feel steady enough to go see how Jackie and Lynette fared during their hike up?"

Kit pulled in a deep breath, then motioned for Annie to lead the way. "I'll be fine."

Jackie had already recruited a random hiker to take a group shot of them. "Any troubles with the climb, ladies?" she asked as they all primped for the camera. The five women lined up with arms around each other's backs and the valley behind them.

Annie noticed Kit stealing glances at the two young women who'd offered their backhanded compliment moments earlier. They were giggling and taking selfies as if they didn't have a care in the world.

"No troubles," Kit lied. "This isn't the first mountain I've conquered and it won't be the last. Figuratively speaking, of course."

"Why don't you girls turn and face the valley? I can get a couple shots of you from that angle, too," Jackie's impromptu photographer instructed, making a circular motion with her hand.

"Great idea," Jackie said, spinning around.

The other four followed her lead, linking their arms together again as they faced the far-off horizon.

"Does this mean we've reached the pinnacle in our own lives, too, Annie?" Lynette asked, hobbling as if she couldn't put much weight on her right foot.

Annie tightened up her arm to help support her friend. "Absolutely not. We're here in Arizona this week to celebrate turning fifty. In my mind, I'd say we should consider this more of a halfway point in life. With any luck, we have the young and dumb years behind us. We could all live another fifty years. Don't these upcoming years have to be easier, now that we are so much *wiser* than we used to be?"

"Unlike those pushy little blondes who implied that we're old enough to be their mothers?" Kit sniffed.

Renee clucked her tongue. "We probably *are* old enough, Kit. Just because you are a new mom to Isaac doesn't change the fact that those two are probably half our age. Let it go. Enjoy this view. Heck, enjoy reaching the half century mark. We've earned it. Those girls have no idea what life might have in store for them. We, on the other hand, have weathered so many things, and we're still here to celebrate together. All five of us. Does it get any better than that?"

Lynette dropped her head onto Annie's shoulder for a beat. "I don't know if things will be any easier, but I know I plan to make the rest of my years the best years."

Annie considered Renee's and Lynette's comments about the future, as well as all of their entangled pasts. None of them could have guessed, all those years ago when they first met at summer camp, that they'd be lucky enough to celebrate turning fifty together. They were all so lucky to have each other. "I can only think of one way it could get any better than this." She gave both Kit's and Lynette's arms an extra squeeze as they gazed out at the vast expanse of city and arid landscape before them. "And that would be if we did this again in another fifty years."

Everyone laughed.

"Why don't we stick with promising to try something like this again when we turn sixty?" Jackie suggested. "Every day I get to spend with you four is a blessing, but I'm pretty sure I don't want to scale this puppy when I'm a hundred. That might be too much to ask, even of the Kaleidoscope Girls! Let's take it a decade at a time."

"But just think about it. If we can make it to one hundred, that means we get fifty more of these annual girls' trips!" Renee pointed out with a wiggle of her hips.

The movement caused Kit to stiffen and inch her way back from the rock ledge at their feet.

Annie giggled as Kit glanced nervously at the valley floor below. "Don't worry. None of us would ever let you fall." As she uttered the assurance, the truth of her own words released a flood of peace throughout her body. Life would always present plenty of challenges, but together, the Kaleidoscope Girls could continue to adapt and thrive.

CHAPTER THIRTY

"Remind me again why we had to be out of the house by nine this morning," Lynette said, grabbing the front seat next to Annie before anyone else got to the minivan in the garage.

Annie punched the garage door opener, then glanced at her friend. "Because today is *birthday celebration* day, and I have a full schedule for us."

Lynette's head fell back against the headrest. "I kind of thought that meant we'd chill by the pool all day and then head to a nice restaurant so we didn't have to cook. Maybe we could even do a little bar-hopping after, like we did when we were in our twenties."

Thinking back to how early she and Henry had left Jackie's surprise party at Thanksgiving, she shook her head. "I don't know about you, but I'm usually ready for bed by ten. I didn't want to get started too late and run out of energy to celebrate."

Lynette rested one wrist on her forehead in mock dismay. "But nine in the morning? Girl, you're crazy."

She couldn't help but laugh at the drama in her friend's voice. "Come on, Lynette. I've known you for a long time. You didn't get ahead in life by sleeping in. Besides, your body is probably still on New York time, so for you, nine isn't even early."

"True," Lynette said. She sat up and dropped her hand to latch her seatbelt. "I was just giving you a hard time. This is great. Our trip is shorter this year, so we have to cram as much as we can into fewer days. We can sleep when we get home. Or when we're dead. Speaking of, I think you really had Kit nervous yesterday."

"She can be such a weenie," Annie said with a laugh. "I am stiff today though. How about you?"

"To be honest, my ankle is killing me this morning. Guess all that physical therapy and working out didn't help as much as I thought it would."

Annie backed out of the garage, curious what was holding up the other three. "You and Jackie practically flew up that mountain. What more could you ask out of your poor ankle? It isn't like we're in high school anymore. Much as I hate to admit it, some of my body parts feel a little achy this morning. I blame it on old gymnastics injuries."

"*Flew* up the mountain, huh?" Lynette grinned. "I like that. Sometimes I think I missed my calling. I should have been a witch."

"Tell me more," Annie prodded while they waited. There'd always been something about Lynette that made her think of a murkier, mystical way of being. Not that she believed in that kind of thing, but still . . .

"About wanting to be a witch? I'm mostly kidding when I say things like that. I know it keeps you four guessing."

The temperature inside the van was warming. She'd used up some of her luck yesterday in getting everyone up and down Camelback in one piece, but she hoped to still have enough left today to help ensure a sunny, hot day for the best pool experience. She switched on the air, then turned her body in the driver's seat enough that she was facing Lynette. "You said *mostly*."

Lynette shrugged. "What can I say? Sometimes I think I was once a beautiful, silver-haired witch living on the foggy moors of Ireland"—by now, she had adopted a thick Irish brogue—"selling love potions and casting spells for people who were a wee bit afraid of me."

Annie burst into laughter at the imagery Lynette had crafted with her words, made all the better by the fact that her accent was so on point that Annie had to wonder if maybe her friend really had lived a life like that, during a different wrinkle in time.

It felt so good to belly laugh again.

"What are you two giggling about?" Jackie asked, grinning as she climbed into the middle section of the van through one of its two sliding doors. "It sounds like summer camp all over again!"

Annie tossed a smile to Jackie, then turned her attention back to Lynette. "Actually, you aren't even that far off now. I love the way you're letting your silver come in naturally. I bet by our next trip your hair could be completely silver. Do you know that I've always been jealous of your amazing hair? And think about what you do for a living. It has a witchy vibe to it. You've built a crazy successful business, selling pretty clothes and jewelry to women online. They shop on a little electronic device—often from the comfort of their own homes—press a button or two, and *poof!* Items appear at their doorstep, like magic, practically out of thin air. Sometimes they buy your gorgeous things for their own enjoyment, but some will use those pretty outfits and bangles to enchant a love interest. Like a love potion. So, see, you are working your own magic, right here, right now!"

Lynette's eyebrows had shot up in surprise, and now she swirled her hands around in a graceful arc as if casting a spell.

"I'm not exactly sure what I just walked into, but you both sound a little nuts," Jackie said. "If you aren't careful, they'll lock you two old bats up in the looney bin."

"There are days when I already feel like I *work* in a looney bin," Annie said, making a circling motion beside her right ear.

The door behind Lynette slid open and Kit climbed in, followed by Renee.

"Sorry! Dean and Isaac called to wish me a happy birthday," Kit said. "Oh, and I'm supposed to tell you all that Isaac doesn't think it's fair that I have to share my actual birthday with all of you. But I told him that by the time you're fifty, you've learned how to share. And who's going to the looney bin?"

Annie glanced in the rearview mirror and saw Jackie point toward the front of the van.

"Those two are well on their way. Talking about magic again."

Renee slid her door shut. The electric button no longer worked. "Don't you believe in magic, Jackie? Even a little?"

"No, not even a little. Don't tell me *you* do."

Renee belted herself in. "Hey, Annie, at least you aren't stuck in the middle of the backseat on this trip. Sure, Jackie, I believe in magic. Don't be such a stick in the mud."

"Even *I* believe in a little woo-woo once in a while," Kit said.

Annie looked over her shoulder. "See, Jackie? And Kit's a scientist. By the way, since today is Kit's actual birthday, and the rest of us are just going to pretend, I don't think she should be stuck in the very back of the Grocery-Getter."

" 'Grocery-Getter'?" Lynette said, looking curious.

"That's what Ava used to call this van. She'd always go to the store with my mom when she was little. They had this vehicle up in Minnesota for many years. Once the mileage got a little high on it, Dad bought Mom something new and then drove this old thing down here so they'd always have a set of wheels when they came down to this house. They fly to and from Minnesota now."

"That's a cute memory. That Ava, she's such a delight," Lynette said. "I enjoyed visiting with her at Jackie's party. Remind me to tell you about what we discussed. She got me thinking about some things . . . but back to your earlier comment about our *real* birthday girl. Yes, I will crawl into the back after brunch, and she can sit up here. That way, I'll be in a perfect position to cast a spell on Jackie to teach her a lesson for doubting the old ways. I'm thinking maybe a wart on the tip of her nose before the next dawn might teach her a lesson."

The van's passengers all dissolved into another round of laughter as Lynette again slipped into her fake Irish brogue.

Annie wiped at her eyes, struggling to see her screen as she typed the address for the restaurant where she'd made brunch reservations while also backing out of the driveway. "Lynette, have you ever even been to Ireland?"

"Not in this lifetime," the woman next to her replied with a flip of her black and silver hair. "But I love watching *Outlander*. It makes me dream of someday finding a love like Jamie and Claire. So hot!"

Jackie slapped the back of Lynette's seat. "I'm sure you could just conjure up a Jamie of your own if you set your mind to it, witchy woman."

Lynette's hands were gesticulating again, but this time she was fanning herself. Annie continued to wipe away her happy tears, hoping she wouldn't crash the Grocery-Getter on the way to brunch.

"Annie, where did you say I'd find the sunscreen?" Kit said from the sliding patio door between the outer covered patio and the television room. "If I get any more sun on this skin of mine, I'll be one big, permanent freckle. Oh, with wrinkles thrown in, of course."

Annie gave the fifth reclining deck chair one last shove to get it into place. She'd arranged them so they'd be facing the sun while also positioned to make it easy to visit. Then she draped a gold-colored beach towel across each chair.

"Mom said to help ourselves to her supply. There are, like, four different SPFs in the master bathroom. Why don't you grab them all and bring them out, would you?"

Since they'd all likely slather themselves with sunscreen, facing the chairs in the most optimal way to catch the rays was more about the warmth of the sun than a search for a tan. Tanning days were well behind them.

Lynette and Renee came out with their hands full of tall, frosty cocktails. They'd impaled fresh lemon and lime slices onto the edges.

"Don't tell my dad I allowed glass out here by the pool," Annie said, thinking it might have been better if she'd hidden the glassware.

"Our lips are sealed," Lynette said with a wink. "It won't be the first time we pulled one over on your folks. Seriously, though, it was wonderful of them to let us use their place like this. It makes me think I might want to invest in a second home somewhere warm."

Annie accepted the spare drink in Lynette's hand and the three of them settled into the deck chairs.

"Kit will be out in a minute with some sunscreen if you need any. Where did Jackie disappear to?"

"She was on the phone," Renee said as she got comfortable in her chair. She pulled the back up so she could sit and enjoy her cocktail. "Well, ladies, this is certainly the life. I'm with you, Lynette. Having somewhere warm to escape to in the cold winter months would be ideal."

Lynette pulled the lemon slice off the edge of her glass and squeezed the juice out into her beverage. "Renee, I thought you and your husband had a place down in Fiji. Which sounds heavenly. If I were you, I'd be down there most of the winter."

Renee laughed. "If only that were possible. It would be fun, but we're both too busy to escape for long. Even this was a little tricky for me to arrange, just because it overlaps with one of our larger winter retreats."

This was the first Annie had heard of a conflict with the dates she'd suggested. "I'm sorry, Renee. You should have said something. We could have tried to find a different week."

Renee waved away her concern. "There would never be a *perfect* week. Besides, this gives Julie a chance to take more responsibility at the resort while I'm gone. Something she's been begging for since graduating from college."

"Back to this place of yours in Fiji," Lynette interrupted. "I remember last summer, when we were in Hawaii, you said you and your husband plan to go down there for a visit next summer. Why wouldn't you go in the winter?"

"Because he opens it up as a vacation rental, and it's always booked out during the winter months."

Lynette set her glass down on the concrete, taking extra care not to break it and bring on the potential wrath of Annie's father. "I suppose that makes sense. But how can he keep a place up from such a distance?"

"It's easy. He has some old friends down there he trusts. They used to work together. He pays them for their help and still has a little extra left over after expenses. It's worked all right for him to hang on to it, but he's considering selling it at some point. That's why I asked him to hold that week for us this summer. I'd love to go back there one last time before he sells. I mentioned to Annie and Kit, I actually kept my house in Minneapolis for a while after moving to Whispering Pines for the rental income, but I ended up selling it last year. It just got to be too much."

The patio door slid open again. Jackie and Kit joined them, bringing snacks, sunscreen, and drinks of their own.

"When are you going to tell us what we have in store for the rest of the day, Annie?" Kit asked. "Don't get me wrong—brunch was amazing, though it wouldn't surprise me if the video from the whole place singing 'Happy Birthday' to us five old ladies went viral on social. And an afternoon around a pool is never time wasted. But we will have to eat again at some point."

Annie shook her head. "Half the fun of birthdays are the surprises. You are just going to have to wait a little longer. In the meantime, Jackie has plenty of snacks in her arms. We won't starve."

"We sure won't," Jackie said, dumping her armful of chips, sweets, and a small bag of paper plates and napkins on the table behind them.

"Cute cover-up, Jackie," Lynette said, raising her glass in her direction.

Annie hadn't looked too closely at what their friend was wearing until now. "Wait. Twirl around once," she said, getting to her feet.

Jackie spun in a quick circle, and Annie clapped her hands together. She hurried to Jackie's side and fingered the breezy fabric.

"The pattern looks like the inside of a kaleidoscope! Lynette, did you make that?"

Lynette laughed. "If you want to get technical, I *designed* it, but I have people to do the actual sewing. Remember, we talked about maybe incorporating bright colors like that in a new line? This is a prototype. I brought one for each of you. I can go get you yours, or you can wear it tomorrow."

"Thank you! It's so pretty," Renee said. "With how generous both you and Annie are being, I feel like I should have brought something for everyone, too. I thought we said no presents!"

"We did. These aren't *presents*," Lynette said. "You are my guinea pigs. Wear these and decide how they make you feel. How does the fabric feel against your skin? Does wearing it feel cool and comfortable, or do you feel hot? A cover-up like this shouldn't make you too warm. When you go home, toss it in the wash. Let me know if it shrinks or loses any of its color. There's still time to fix any potential issues. This line is very important to me—I'm calling it *Kaleidoscope*—and I want to make sure they are perfect. There will be sundresses, shorts, tops, and maybe even swimsuits. I haven't decided on that yet."

Jackie wiggled her body as she sat in the last remaining lounge chair. "I'll gladly be your guinea pig, Lynette. Thank you."

Lynette wriggled a finger at her. "I've taught you well, haven't I?"

"Hey, Lynette, I ordered one of your bracelets that's inscribed with 'just say *thank you*' on the inside," Renee said. "I wear it all the time."

Annie remembered Renee mentioning that very bracelet during their trip last summer. Building these new traditions and connections was so fun.

"Take these towels home with you, too," Annie said, motioning to the one she was sitting on.

"That sounds like a gift to me," Kit said.

"Not really. It was more of a buffer against the actual possibility that all Mom's towels might be pretty threadbare. I think they packed that old van up with all the things they received for wedding gifts, *fifty-five years ago*, to stock this house, then bought new for the house in Minnesota."

Lynette whistled. "Fifty-five years . . . man, that's a long time to be with one man. Props to your mom. Now, if you'll excuse me, I need a refill. Anyone else?"

When she had no takers, she shrugged and slipped into the house.

"Annie, just promise to give us enough of a heads-up before we have to leave for our birthday dinner," Renee said, laying the back of her chair down so she could relax on her stomach. "And whatever other surprises you have in store for us. So we can get cleaned up."

Annie only grinned, then got off her chair, sauntered to the pool, and slipped over the edge into the deep end.

This was fun, keeping them all in suspense.

Chapter Thirty-One

BY 4:30 THAT AFTERNOON, they'd all enjoyed more than one cocktail, plenty of snacks, and enough sun that their conversation had died off to a companionable silence. Jackie was snoring softly on her back. Renee hadn't moved in a while and seemed to have fallen asleep on her stomach. Lynette didn't get into the pool, but she sat on the ledge where Annie had gotten in earlier, staring off into the distance and sipping on what might have been her fourth drink. Kit must have reached her daily quota of sunshine, because she'd slipped into the house an hour ago and hadn't come back out.

Annie checked the clock on her phone. She had time to read a few more pages, and then she'd need to go inside and get ready.

The girls still thought they'd have to get ready to go to the party she'd planned. No one seemed to suspect that Annie had actually arranged for the party to come to them.

The patio door opened, and Kit stuck her head out again. "Hey, Annie, some guy in a van is here asking for you?"

It had to be the caterers. And they were early.

Oh, well . . . they might as well get this party started.

"I still can't believe you did all of this, Annie," Lynette said from her spot in the middle of the swimming pool. The floating throne, made of a dark yellow plastic, had garnered plenty of laughs when Annie first brought it out of its hiding spot in the closet of her bedroom. "You made us all feel like queens!" Despite the wine she'd drank on top of her earlier refreshments, she seemed only slightly tipsy now. The food certainly helped. "Good thing I brought my white two-piece," she joked from her lofty, floating spot. "It has a royal vibe, don't you think? Especially with the sash."

Everyone still wore their black sashes emblazoned with gold glitter letters declaring them all *Fifty and Fabulous*. Aside from Lynette, they all also had their Kaleidoscope cover-ups on. The caterers had been gracious enough to snap some group shots of the five before the birthday girls sat down to dinner.

Annie laughed at Renee and Jackie as they rocked out with their air guitars to AC/DC's classic, "You Shook Me All Night Long," across the pool from her. She was so glad she'd thought to build a lengthy playlist of all their favorite songs from their high school days. Nothing beat music from the '80s. Her initial plan to pipe the music from her phone through the speakers strategically mounted around the pool area was foiled when she couldn't get the technology to connect, but a handsome young man who was part of the catering staff helped.

She hoped the neighbors wouldn't call in a noise complaint.

Her luck had held for a second day in a row. The weather turned out to be perfect for an afternoon of lounging around the pool, topped off with scrumptious food. She'd even gone to the trouble of contacting a family member of each of the other four women so she could have the caterers include at least one favorite appetizer for each of them, along with a flavor of cake they liked. Since everyone ended up liking a different kind of cake, she'd gone with an artfully displayed variety of cupcakes. They'd have to each eat dessert until they were sick, or she'd freeze some for her parents to eat when they got home.

"You did a great job on this, Annie," Kit said from the chair on her right. "I know this was a ton of work—not only because I planned last summer's trip, but because I saw what all went into planning the food for our wedding. Not that I did much of the planning for that, since Dean either did it or delegated to one of you. But the details can about kill a person. And the cost . . ."

"Just say 'thank you,' " Annie interrupted.

Kit smiled, and they both sat for a minute, watching the caterers clean up. The five women would soon have the patio and pool to themselves once again.

"I could handle being waited on like this every day," Annie said, nodding toward the workers.

Kit sighed. "I have a confession to make. Dean waits on me like this most nights. On both me and Isaac, in fact."

"Huh. That's because you guys are still in that newlywed phase. It probably won't last."

"Annie Pierce, that's not nice!" Kit said with a light slap on Annie's arm. "Don't burst my bubble."

They both laughed, then Annie cleared her throat. "You're right. This took some work to pull together, but I'm glad we didn't have to go out somewhere. This is so much more relaxing. And Dad actually suggested this part of the evening, and paid for the catering, as my fiftieth birthday gift. As *our* birthday gifts," she corrected.

"Seriously? Wow, that was very generous of him. I hope you know how lucky you are to have Lyle and Patsy as parents, Annie."

The woman in charge of the catering team approached just then. "Annie, we are all finished. I hope everything met your expectations."

Annie pushed out of her chair, pulling the cover-up away from her thighs where it had stuck. "Everything was perfect. Thank you so much. I want to run inside quick. I have something for each of you."

The woman reached out and touched Annie's hand. "No, but thank you. Your father insisted I wasn't even to allow you to give us a tip. He is taking care of that, too. Now, we'll get out of your hair and let you get back to your party. Your rock band over there looks a little light on members. You two might want to go join them."

"So lucky," Annie heard Kit whisper as the team showed themselves out.

Annie caught Kit up in a hug, wishing she could do more to erase the years of heartache her friend had suffered due to her less than mediocre parents. "Happy *actual* birthday, Kit. Thank you for letting us share it with you."

Kit squeezed her back. "Thank *you* for making this all feel so special."

"I need to go lock the door behind them. I'll be right back. Keep an eye on Lynette, will you? I'm not sure how drunk she is at this point."

Kit laughed. "Lynette could always handle her liquor."

Annie wasn't so sure about that, but she noticed Kit walk over to the pool and strike up a conversation with Lynette as she walked toward the house.

When she came back outside, Lynette was on the patio deck, pulling the throne floating chair out of the water. The other three had made their way to the hot tub.

Annie had to admit that sitting in warm, bubbly water sounded like a delightful way to cap off the day. It was dark, but still early, and no one seemed to be running out of steam yet.

Once everyone was relaxing along the ledge inside the hot tub, Lynette raised a hand to get their attention. Annie wondered what was coming, but smiled when the woman in white spoke. Her words were clear, her eyes bright. Maybe Kit was right and Lynette was a master at holding her liquor; she seemed perfectly fine despite her many cocktails throughout the day.

"Kit, since you are *officially* fifty years old today, I'd like to hear what this milestone means to you."

Kit shook her head. "Hell, I don't know what it means . . . Why don't you ask Jackie? She's been fifty a whole two months now. She should start."

"Because *you're* the birthday girl!"

Kit trailed her fingertips over the top of the water. "Fine. Give me a minute . . . but if I have to wax poetic about this momentous occasion, all of you have to, too. Deal?"

Everyone agreed.

"What does fifty mean to me?" Kit repeated slowly, as if giving herself more time to think. "Well, I guess I see it as the time when I can finally admit I was letting fear hold me back. I had a shitty family life growing up. I was terrified that I'd be just as bad at parenting and marriage as my parents were, given I never had a good role model. And it took me until recently to realize that I was wrong about that. Grandma and Grandpa took us in and helped us get through those tough years, and I'll always be grateful for that. My grandparents were great role models. So were your folks, Jackie, and yours, Annie. And your mom, Lynette. She worked so hard to build a good life for you. I finally figured out I'd witnessed plenty of genuine love in the family department, so I realized it was time to get off the pot and agree to marry the love of my life. I also felt like taking Isaac in wasn't just the right thing to do, it was my way to pay it forward, after my grandparents modeled what it means to be an actual family. I want to show Isaac that, too."

No one said a word for a minute, and Annie thought maybe there was a tear in Lynette's eye.

Then Jackie laughed and slapped a short spray of water at Kit. "How do you expect any of us to follow *that*? That was amazing, Kit!"

A water fight ensued, but no one wanted to get their hair soaked, so things died down quickly.

"Who's next?" Lynette asked. "Not me. I'm the last one who will turn fifty."

"Rub it in," Jackie said, sticking her bottom lip out in a pretend pout. "I'll go, since I'm the old lady of the bunch. For me, it's really pretty simple. It seems like it was just yesterday when we all went to prom together, and now, suddenly, we're fifty. I've learned we need to stop messing around, stop *settling*, and just go for whatever has been sitting on our hearts for too long. Because we just never know how much time we have left, and shame on us if we don't make the most of it."

Renee nodded her head emphatically. "Exactly, Jackie. I completely agree. That's why I turned down a new corporate job when I lost the one I'd already tolerated for twenty years. My dad challenged me to be creative, and when I took over my Aunt Celia's resort, I vacillated between wanting to do it and wondering what the hell I was thinking as a single mother to two teenagers. Then I remembered what all Celia accomplished in her lifetime, against all odds, and it was so much bigger than just buying Whispering Pines. I knew what she'd want me to do, even though she was no longer there to ask, so I just did the damn thing."

Lynette broke into a huge smile. "And now you're married to a hot sheriff, keeping your bad-ass aunt's legacy alive, and helping other women find the courage to chase their own dreams in your retreats during the off-season. Celia would be proud of you, Renee."

Tears definitely flowed from Renee's eyes at Lynette's words.

Kit reached across the water and squeezed one of Renee's hands. "See? Like I said. Bad-ass. All right, we still haven't heard from Lynette or Annie. Remember, tonight is about *all* of us."

The others all turned to Annie. She wasn't sure what to say.

Lynette saved her. She held both her hands up toward the inky black Arizona sky, where, far above, stars twinkled. "I believe time means nothing to our souls. We are here, in these bodies now, to either help our souls learn something important or teach other souls. We all play an important part in the complexities of the Universe, and our age is irrelevant."

She lowered her arms back into the water and waited. Everyone seemed shocked into silence.

"Or maybe it just means we're finally at the age when we've figured out just how powerful we really are," she added, "and we can tell anyone we don't like to just piss off."

Hoots of laughter, tangled with Poison singing about nothin' but a good time through the speakers, broke Lynette's spell.

Annie should turn the music down, or the neighbors really might call in a complaint. She made a move to get out of the water, but Jackie grabbed her hand. She yanked it free. "I just have to turn the music down," she explained.

But Jackie shook her head. "Not until you tell us what turning fifty means to you."

Knowing Jackie never gave up on something once she had her mind set, Annie sank back into the warm bubbles until they encircled her neck.

"Fine . . . I don't like it," she whispered.

Kit leaned forward, as if she hadn't quite heard her. "What?"

Annie closed her eyes and sank down even farther until the warm water covered her head. Things were so much quieter under the water.

Someone stuck a hand under her armpit and hauled her back up.

"Is turning fifty really bothering you that much, Annie?" Renee asked.

Annie flicked the water from her eyes. "Yes, all right? I admit it. I *hate* that I'm turning fifty. I used to be one of the youngest teachers at school. Now, aside from the handful of crotchety old ones who count down the days until retirement, I'm one of the oldest."

Kit shook her head. "Wendy teaches there. She's older, and *she's* not crotchety."

"She's leaving!" Annie cried. "And I can't imagine that place without her."

"You're literally in charge of the high school. It makes sense that you would be one of the mature ones on the staff. Is that all that's bothering you?"

She shrugged. "I suppose not. Sitting here, listening to you guys talk about all the big changes you've made in the last three years . . . I feel like a slug."

Jackie made a huffing sound. "I'd hardly call you a *slug*. You have a beautiful family, and you are about to become a grandma. Your kids adore you, as does your husband. I'd even venture to guess your ex-husband is still in love with you. I don't know anyone else with that much love in their life."

The "grandma" reminder brought a smile to Annie's heart and lips, but the reference to Michael reminded her of the flowers he'd sent on their "could have been" twenty-fifth wedding anniversary. Even things with Henry felt a little better lately, and they'd had a nice dinner to celebrate their *real* nineteenth wedding anniversary before she'd come here.

"You guys don't think I've lived a boring life, then?" she asked, searching their faces, surprising herself at the depths of her own lack of appreciation for her many blessings.

They met her question with an avalanche of supportive comments and hugs.

"I have an idea," Lynette said, once they'd all quieted down again. "Or maybe it's more of a suggestion. From this day forward, Annie, I want you to keep a gratitude journal. You need to appreciate how blessed you already are. Just because you didn't recently blow up your career, or finally say yes to a man you should have married a few years ago already, or inherit an amazing property from a distant relative, doesn't mean you have a boring life."

"I second that idea," Renee interrupted. "I got back into the habit of journaling after I got laid off. I swear it helped me through a confusing time."

Annie took a deep breath, realizing how right Lynette was, how right they all were. "Okay, then! To me, turning fifty with my very best girlfriends is one of the greatest blessings of all."

Shouts of agreement rang out, but Annie caught Lynette yawning.

"And you were the one who thought she could go all night tonight," she teased.

"I don't think I used those exact words," Lynette said with a big stretch. "I don't know, ladies, this has been amazing and all, but I'm tired. I might turn in."

Renee agreed.

"Wait," Kit cried. "We need a hot tub picture first!"

No one else looked thrilled with that idea, but since it was her actual birthday, they caved to her request.

"Dad keeps a tripod here that he uses to take pictures with his phone when they go birding," Annie said. "I'll grab that, we can get your picture, Kit, and then we can all wrap this spectacular day up however each of you chooses. Can you hold on another few minutes, Lynette?"

She yawned again, but nodded. "Sure thing. I never like to be the first one to leave a party, anyway."

Annie laughed as she got out of the hot tub and made a beeline for the house. She turned the music down a few decibels to a more reasonable level given the hour, then went inside. By the time she returned, Renee was also out of the tub.

"I thought we were getting a picture."

"We are," Renee assured her. "Kit just asked me to pull this chair over so the balloons can be in the background of the picture. I think they'll still show up."

Renee got back to moving the chair while Annie attached her phone to her dad's tripod and adjusted it so the angle was right. It took her a minute to remember how to use the timer, but then she started it and scurried back into the tub.

"Hurry, Renee, we only have ten seconds!"

Renee moved away from the chair, but her hand caught on the string of one balloon and accidentally ripped it loose. She cried out as the freed balloon quickly ascended out of her reach.

"Let it go!" Kit laughed. "There are plenty."

Renee jumped in with two seconds to spare, and the shot may or may not have captured them all gasping as water splashed everywhere.

"Should I try again?" Annie asked, wiping the salt water from her eyes. She'd started the day with tears of laughter, and it looked like she was ending it with more salty tears. The water stung.

"No, a candid is more fun anyhow," Kit said, wiping at her own eyes.

Renee glanced up. "I'm sorry about the balloon. Wow, look how high it is already!"

Annie searched the sky for the lost balloon, and it jarred something else in her mind. "Darn it! I forgot I was supposed to make a toast to an amazing woman today."

Kit waved both hands at her. "Enough already. I've had plenty of toasts already."

"Not *you*, dummy," she said, splashing her. "Just a minute. This is serious, ladies."

Lynette glanced up at the sky and then back at Annie. "Wait. Did someone die?"

"You *are* intuitive, aren't you?" Annie said, amazed. "And sadly, yes, someone did die. Betsy. She was one of my mom's best friends. I got a call from her daughter the first night I was here. She was expecting to get Mom, but honestly, I think she was relieved it was me. She hated to have to give Mom such sad news. Mom and Betsy were friends since they were young. Now I get to tell her the news when they get back from their cruise. I didn't want to ruin their trip."

"That's sad," Kit said. "I'm sorry you have to deliver that news. But I'm a little confused why you promised to toast Betsy tonight. None of us knew her."

Annie searched the sky again, but the gold balloon was gone. She brought her eyes down and scanned the faces of the other four women in the hot tub. "But Betsy is one of the reasons we are all here tonight."

They looked even more confused.

"I don't understand," Renee said, speaking for all of them.

Annie nodded. "Let me explain. Back when I was a kid, my mom used to take trips like this with her girlfriends."

Lynette was the first to catch on. "Your mom always came home, so excited about how much fun those trips were for her. I remember now! You suggested we all promise each other to take girls' trips when we were older, like they did, so we wouldn't lose touch. You wanted the same for us that your mom and her friends had."

Annie nodded. "And here we are."

"I'm so glad you included all of us Kaleidoscope Girls," Renee said. "Even though I didn't actually go to high school with the four of you, my memories from summer camp and prom are still some of my favorites from my early years. Did your mom and Betsy and their other friends keep taking their trips?"

Annie's mind jumped back to the conversation she'd had with her mother in the fall. She'd tried to convince Patsy to reach out to Betsy, to plan something, but it didn't seem like her mother had done that yet. She'd waited too long.

"Sadly, no. Life got in the way, and at some point they stopped. Mom talked about trying to get things started again, but Betsy was the only other one of their original group still well enough to travel. Look, I'm sorry, ladies. This feels like a bummer way to end an otherwise amazing day. Maybe I shouldn't have even brought it up."

"Nonsense," Jackie said, waving them all into the center of the hot tub. "I vow that poor Betsy's death serve as a reminder for all of us in the future that we can never *ever* let anything get in the way of us doing this at least once a year. I don't ever want to feel the pang of regret poor Patsy is bound to feel when she comes home to this sad news. Now, come on. Group hug and pinky swear. The Kaleidoscope Girls swear to never miss an annual girls' trip, no matter what!"

Annie thought Jackie's toast served as a fitting tribute to wrap up the perfect day. She hoped Betsy was up there, somewhere, smiling down at them all as their gold balloon floated ever higher. Maybe she could even help them keep their promises to each other, should the unforeseen put any of their future trips in jeopardy.

Chapter Thirty-Two

Annie's eyes popped open. She glanced around, disoriented. After her restless night of unsettling dreams, it was a relief to realize she was still in the spare bedroom at her parents' home in Arizona instead of her old apartment in Ruby Shores. Throwing the covers off, she swung her feet out of bed. She was curious what could have pulled those old memories out of her subconscious to dance through her dreams, raising havoc.

Was everyone else still asleep after their big birthday celebration?

The only sound was the hum of the air-conditioner, which had thankfully kept them comfortably cool ever since the repairman worked his magic a few days ago.

But then she thought she heard a shuffling outside her door, followed by the definite giggle of someone trying but failing to be quiet.

Curious, she padded across the cool tile and eased her door open, spying Kit and Renee slipping tennis shoes on by the front door. Neither glanced her way.

"Where you guys going?" she whispered.

Kit jumped and screeched.

"How about you guys shut up out there?" Lynette yelled from the opposite side of the house. She sounded either half-asleep or terribly hungover. Or both.

Renee shrugged. "Morning, Annie. We were trying not to wake anyone. Guess that didn't work out so well. I think Jackie is still sleeping. It's so beautiful outside. I already had a cup of coffee on the back patio, and when Kit joined me, we decided to wander around the neighborhood. Get a little exercise now, just in case it gets hot later or you had other plans for us today. As long as you're up, do you want to join us?"

Annie didn't need to be asked twice. She could see clear blue sky through the narrow windows that lined both sides of the front door. "I was going to make a big breakfast, but maybe that can wait. A walk sounds perfect. Give me two seconds to change." She turned to go but paused. "Wait for me out front so Miss Crabby Pants can get more sleep."

Five minutes later, she rejoined the other two, and they turned right at the end of the driveway.

"I don't think I could get lost in this neighborhood, but there's still lots of new construction happening, so I grabbed my phone in case we get turned around," Annie said. It felt good to stretch her legs. She was still a little stiff from their hike up Camelback, and they'd done too much sitting the day before.

Renee inhaled deeply. "Those flowering bushes in that yard smell yummy. Back home, all I've been smelling during my morning walks are pine trees and the crisp scent of new fallen snow. That's nice for a while, but by this time of year I'm ready for the smell of flowers."

"Unfortunately, we never get much of that until at least April," Kit said, her head swiveling as she took in all the unfamiliar sights and smells around them. "We better soak this up while we still can."

These views and the walking conditions were in stark contrast to their hike on their first full day. The ground was smooth asphalt with no uphill grade, and the well-manicured lawns contained plenty of green, even if some of it was artificial grass.

"This is always Mom's favorite time of year here. They used to make it a point to be back in Minneapolis by Easter when the kids were small, but they quit that because the weather is perfect here right now. Not so blasted hot. And things are in bloom," Annie said. Her legs were shorter than either Kit's or Renee's, making her step a little faster to keep up, but the pace was still comfortable enough to hold a conversation. "To be honest, I used to get a little irritated with them for missing so much back home by coming down here each winter. But I understand now. Winter is too long and harsh in Minnesota."

"Said every middle-aged Minnesotan on the cusp of becoming a snowbird," Kit said with a laugh.

"Tell me about your earlier life in Ruby Shores, Annie, after everyone else went away for college and careers," Renee said, glancing her way. "You girls have listened to me blather on about how the kids and I ended up at Whispering Pines, and I'm sure Kit knows your story, but I'm curious."

Annie squinted in the sunlight as she adjusted the baseball hat she'd thrown on to cover up her bedhead. She should have grabbed sunglasses. "It's not a terribly exciting story, Renee, but sure . . . What would you like to know?"

Kit, walking between the two women, snorted. "Annie, your story is hardly boring. Especially the part after college, before you went back to Ruby Shores. Renee, you wouldn't believe it. She shocked her parents with a surprise announcement, hours after her college graduation, that she'd made plans to fly to Peru and spend her summer on a mission trip. Then the spontaneity continued when she gave up her safe, secure teaching job she'd already lined up for that fall to work at a shelter in downtown Minneapolis. And you should have seen the two hotties this girl lived with while she did that."

Renee rubbed her hands together as if she couldn't wait to hear the details of that lead-in.

But Annie waved it off. "Oh, stop, Kit. I was just a young woman without much direction, and while your little synopsis there makes it all sound very adventurous and exciting, everything just culminated in heartache."

Kit shook her head. "Only if you look back at it with a 'glass half-empty' attitude."

At the sound of a car approaching behind them, Renee stepped closer to the curb and waved the other two women over, too. The sidewalk was too narrow for the three of them to walk side by side.

"Come on, Annie. I promise I won't judge," Renee said once the sedan had passed. "I know you've been married to Henry for a long time, but somewhere along the line I heard mention of an ex-husband, too. How do they fit into your story?"

"They were the two hotties," Kit said, clearly enjoying her role as narrator.

Renee angled her body, so she had to take a few awkward side steps before turning to face forward again.

"Careful," Annie warned. "When I tried to walk backward on the trail, I fell on my butt. Fine, I'll tell you all about my two *hotties*. To be honest, having both of them still in my life is a little like having a rock stuck in my shoe."

Renee looked slightly horrified, but Kit laughed.

"She exaggerates. Both Michael and Henry are great guys. At least now. They share kids, so still being part of each other's lives is part of the deal. There were several years there when I hated Michael for what he did to our girl, but he's matured."

Annie rolled her eyes. "Who's telling this story, me or you?"

"Fine, sorry," Kit said, raising both hands in surrender. "Take it away."

"Thank you," Annie said.

She told Renee about the initial mess she'd made of what could have been a perfectly satisfactory and platonic roommate arrangement. As she talked, the road angled right, taking them on the outer loop that surrounded the neighborhood.

"Hold up," Renee said. Annie knew she was referring to the storytelling and not their morning walk. "Let me make sure I've got this straight. Henry was interested in you romantically, but you wanted to keep him in the friend zone? And you planned to do the same with Michael, but in a weak moment, you two spent a romantic Christmas holiday together, and you ended up pregnant? How did you feel about Michael before Christmas? Did you only see *him* as a friend, too?"

Annie thought back to those long-ago days. She'd be lying if she claimed she hadn't been attracted to Michael in the months leading up to Christmas. Even in Peru she'd thought he was sexy as hell, but out of her league. She admitted as much to Renee.

"And sometimes I get the sense she'd still like to be with Michael," Kit said. "But he blew it, and Annie had no choice but to divorce him."

Hating the nugget of truth in Kit's words, Annie gave her arm a shove. She had no business ever thinking of Michael as anything more than the father of Ava and Colton. Anything more was disloyal to Henry. He'd been the one to step up and help her raise a family, not Michael. He'd deserted her and the kids. At least for a while.

Kit gave her a playful little shove back. "Come on. Admit it. I know you love Henry, and you feel you owe him a lot. I suppose you do. But you are one of those lucky women who has had more than one serious love in her lifetime."

"Honestly, Annie, if that is how you really feel, I understand," Renee said, cutting into the other two's playful banter.

"How so?" Annie asked, sensing a lifeline. And maybe a chance to change the subject from herself.

"You both know I was widowed when my kids were still young, right?"

Kit and Annie nodded.

"I'm not saying death and divorce are the same, but I think we all give a little piece of our heart away when we take part in a loving relationship with another person. I loved Jim—my first husband—and when he got sick and died, it took me a really long time to recover. I've never claimed to be 'over' him," she said, emphasizing her last words with air quotes. "I'm honest about that with Matt. I think he understands. I wasn't the first woman he ever loved, either. By the time we're forty or fifty, most of us have a deep pit or two in our hearts . . . and I don't think we ever feel completely whole again."

The three walked in silence for a minute or two, as if each of them was weighing Renee's words against their own life experiences.

"But Henry is so jealous of Michael," Annie went on eventually. "I hate to even say that out loud. It feels like a betrayal of my husband's confidence."

Kit brushed her bangs back from her forehead, looking deep in thought. "I think Henry has always known what Renee just tried to articulate to be true in your case, Annie. He's a smart guy. He knows he wasn't your first choice."

"And I've spent the last twenty years trying to make it up to him."

"Maybe that's where you're getting it wrong."

Renee put a hand up. "Wait. Do you feel like telling me the story of how you ended up married to Henry after you divorced Michael?"

"Sure. I was single for a few years after my divorce. Like I'd said, Kit and Lynette and Jackie helped move me and the kids back to Ruby Shores. If I had to raise Ava and Colton by myself, I at least wanted to be near my family. I worked at a daycare for a while so I could earn enough money for us to live on and not spend it all on childcare. The owner was kind enough to let them come with me, and in exchange I taught some preschool classes for her. I had my teaching degree, and wanted to get the job back that I'd originally given up when I stayed in Minneapolis after Peru, but I had to wait for something similar to open up again. Michael sent money periodically, but there were some lean years. Once I even had to take him to court for more support." She shivered despite the rising temperature.

"I'm sorry, Annie . . . that's rough," Renee said.

They were quiet, giving Annie a moment to collect her thoughts.

"Anyway, I honestly didn't think I'd ever see either man again," she said. "But in a twist of fate, Henry landed a job in Ruby Shores. He used to work at his father's business back in Tennessee, but he didn't see any opportunity for growth there. He'd also been engaged, but that fell apart before they ever married."

Kit snorted. "I think Henry dropped the fiancée when he heard Annie and Michael were having serious problems."

Annie shot her a frustrated look but didn't say anything. Henry had told her the whole truth, but she'd kept the details private. While her issues with Michael might have played into it a little, she wasn't the only woman to cause Henry pain.

"Henry and I stayed in loose communications those first few years," she went on. "But it surprised me when he picked Ruby Shores for a place to start his new career. I'm not dumb. I know I was a big part of his decision. But we took things slow at first. Henry's a good man. He was wonderful with Ava and Colton. I truly did fall in love with him. He made me feel safe. Henry and Michael were friends before the three of us met in Peru. I still regret playing such a big part in ruining the friendship between the two of them."

Annie thought back to those early days in Peru. How close Henry and Michael had seemed, despite their distinct personalities.

"You said you thought you might never see either man again," Renee said. "But Henry came to you. I'm following that part of your story. But what about Michael? By the way you and Kit talk about him, he mustn't have stayed away forever?"

Before Kit could comment, Annie pointed a finger at her to shush.

"Henry and I were married for about ten years before Michael became much of a factor in any of our lives again. One reason I divorced him was because he went into the Navy against my express wishes. He wanted to learn how to fly. After he completed his military commitments—during which he only saw his kids once or twice—he became a commercial pilot. That brought him to Minneapolis on a pretty frequent basis. When he could arrange it, he'd drive over to Ruby Shores to see the kids. They started building more of a relationship, the three of them, and I could tell it bothered Henry. He'd been the father figure to both Ava and

Colton, and suddenly Michael was back in their lives, muddying the waters. Henry and I also had a child together, Relic, and he was in grade school when Michael started coming around more. Over time, Henry's relationship with my older two began to suffer, and he shifted most of his attention to Relic."

The three women turned a corner and Annie's parents' house came back into view. They'd nearly completed the neighborhood loop.

"Family is always a complicated topic, isn't it?" Renee said as they walked toward the house. "Again, I know it isn't the same thing, but it hasn't always been easy for Matt to build a relationship with my Julie and Robbie, either. Jim is gone, and he's never coming back, but Julie remembers him well. Robbie remembers bits and pieces. In some ways, Robbie had become the man of the house before Matt came along."

As they approached the front door, Kit stopped them both. "All right, you two. You're making me worry about the viability of any kind of blended family. I have a kid back at my place who we've only known for less than a year, who has family we've never even met, and who we are actively trying to fold into our lives at the same time we are navigating a brand-new marriage. Are we crazy?"

Renee shook her head. "No. You aren't crazy. You are human. Love makes the world go round, and while sometimes the bonds we form make things difficult, those challenges are just the price we pay."

Annie opened the door and turned to face her. "The price for what?"

"To love and to be loved. Because that's all that really matters."

Chapter Thirty-Three

ANNIE PICKED A PLUMP red strawberry off the fruit tray she'd set out and settled back onto the outdoor loveseat with a sigh. After yesterday's early morning walk and a day lounging around the pool and house, she'd finally allowed herself to relax. Her idea of using her parents' vacation home for this year's trip had worked out perfectly.

Except she'd have loved another day or two in the sun.

"I wish I could stay right here until I know the snow is all gone back home," she said, nibbling off the tip of her strawberry.

"I'm not ready to go back to New York yet either," Lynette sighed, sipping her morning coffee as she relaxed next to Annie. "This is an ugly time of year in the Big Apple. Dirty snow and slush everywhere. It'll look better in a month, and April can be pretty as the trees bloom out again, but late February is always dreary as hell. Everyone's crabby, too, because we're all tired of winter."

Jackie set her coffee cup down and tucked her bare feet under her bottom on the chair across from them. "It's New York. Aren't people *always* crabby?"

"Of course not! I wouldn't have lasted there all these years if that was the case. It might appear that way to an outsider—things and people move fast—but when you live there, you become accustomed to the pace and the brusque nature of some folks. The city has been good to me, but I sometimes think I'm ready for a change."

This surprised Annie. She should probably head back inside, despite the beautiful morning, so she could get things cleaned up and leave enough time for a pleasant lunch out, maybe even do some shopping before taking everyone to the airport. But she wondered what Lynette might be contemplating.

"Are you thinking of moving, Lynette? Would your mom move with you?"

She shrugged. "We're toying with the idea. Remember all the trouble we had last summer with our board of directors? We put a new board in place, and it is much better, but I'm not sure I want to run a company of this size anymore."

"I could set up a franchise with my senior pet service and we could work together," Jackie suggested in a teasing tone. "Although I have plenty of things to figure out before expansion. Seriously, though . . . you've grown your business through lots of years of blood, sweat, and tears, my friend. You've made your fortune. Maybe turning fifty is the time for you to think about doing something different. I know I've never regretted leaving my corporate job, though if this thing doesn't start earning enough to pay the bills, my retirement savings are going to take a serious hit."

"You can always move back in with me, Jackie," Kit said from the side of the pool where she was relaxing with a red solo cup of orange juice and a bagel.

Jackie laughed. "No, I can't. You have a full house these days, Kit."

"Oh, that's right. I'm a married woman with a teenager in the house now. Funny how many things can change in a year."

"That's all right. Some months I do see a little profit. I have faith that it'll all work out."

Annie watched Jackie's face as she spoke. She didn't appear overly anxious about the state of her newish business venture, which was a relief. "I admire the entrepreneurial spirit you three have embraced. I wouldn't be brave enough to do something that didn't come with a guaranteed paycheck and benefits."

Renee let out a cackle at that. She'd just brought the pot of coffee out and was offering refills. "Trust me, Annie, there are no guarantees in working for someone else. Before I got the resort back up and running, I got laid off after more than *twenty years* at the company where I'd built my career. And they didn't even hold off until after the holidays to let me go. The bastards."

"You can just set that pot on the glass, Renee. It won't hurt anything. And I know what you mean. We can't assume anything in life comes with a guarantee. Other than death and taxes," Annie said, slapping her thigh at her lame joke. "But to start a business from scratch—and you've practically done that, too, with your Whispering Pines—that takes guts."

Exchanging the coffee pot for her refreshed mug, Renee wandered over and sat next to Kit by the pool.

"As yet another worker bee in someone else's cog," Kit said, "I get what you're saying, Annie. But, in my opinion, you are the bravest one of all. You run a high school filled with hormonal teenagers, and I bet you're constantly bombarded by helicopter parents. I'd give up my paycheck and clean dog shit from kennels with Jackie if it meant I didn't have to be responsible for a building full of kids for a living."

"Hey, I don't think I care for that comparison," Jackie laughed.

"Hear, hear!" Lynette said as she plucked a cube of cheese from the fruit plate. "Sometimes it *is* tempting to consider starting over. Building something new that hasn't morphed into an administrative nightmare. And to answer your question, Annie, yes, if I move, I'd bring Mom with me. We're a team. Always have been, always will be. I don't know how she'd do without me at this point. She's no spring chicken anymore."

"Not like us," Annie laughed.

Lynette nodded emphatically. "And speaking of spring chickens, I've been meaning to visit with you about that conversation I had with your daughter at Jackie's birthday party in November. She doesn't seem to have as strong of an attachment to a monthly paycheck as you do."

Annie didn't have to think long to realize what Ava might have discussed with Lynette. "You know, I thought it looked like you two were getting in cahoots about something that night when Henry and I said our goodnights. But she can't be serious about starting an online business right now. She'll be a mother of a newborn in less than a month. Plus, the big house they bought—against mine and Henry's advice, by the way—has an equally big mortgage that takes *both* of their paychecks to pay each month. Maybe if they wouldn't have gotten pregnant, she could have worked on a side gig. But I don't know how that's possible right now."

"I understand why the idea would scare you, Annie. I do. But therein lies the mystery of the entrepreneurial spark. Sometimes logic can't quite extinguish it. Don't worry. I didn't get the impression Ava was going to do anything rash. But she *is* thinking about it. And I'd love to help her think through things, if she ever wants to take it to the next step. Will you be sure she knows that?"

Annie thought about how much braver Lynette had always been with her career. She'd built something amazing that employed many people and provided unique products that her loyal customers loved. But she'd never made time to build a life with anyone else, other than her mother.

She smiled. "I'll make sure she knows that, Lynette. Thank you. If she ever pursues something, she'd be lucky to have you in her corner."

Jackie stood and stretched, turning slightly so the warm morning sunshine could caress her face. "Ladies, all this career talk has me excited to go home and keep rolling. I need to make a phone call right now regarding my new lease I'm taking over on the first of March. Then we need to pack, put this darling home back in order for Annie's parents, and get moving if we want to visit those shops we talked about and enjoy a leisurely lunch before our flights. I hate leaving you all, but having something fun to go home to is so satisfying."

Annie followed her lead, knowing this competent group of women could get the house whipped back into shape in no time. She wasn't thrilled about heading back to her school, but it wouldn't be long before she'd get to hold her first grandchild in her arms, and she was pretty sure nothing could beat that.

"This was a perfect little getaway, Annie," Kit said. She dropped her napkin on top of her luncheon plate and pushed it out of the way to lean her forearms on the tabletop. "We wouldn't be dining al fresco back in Minnesota or New York yet, but this might just tide me over until spring. I can't wait to show Isaac all the fun things we can do this summer in the city. The guys are already talking about which Twins baseball games they'll hit."

Annie smiled her thanks to the waiter when he refilled her water glass, then turned her attention back to Kit. "Will you spend some time in Ruby Shores this summer, too? I'm sure Isaac's grandfather would like to see him. And there's always fun to be had at the lake."

"Absolutely. Isaac still has a friend or two back there, too. He might want to see them."

"Just keep him away from Jason Carbo. I remember them hanging out once or twice."

Kit nodded. "I remember you saying that family was bad news. Go figure—I also found out the Carbos are part of some of Mia's worst nightmares, too. That's saying a lot where my mom is concerned."

Annie scooped up her purse and reached for her wallet, but Jackie put a hand on hers.

"You aren't paying. We already took care of lunch today. You did enough."

When she opened her mouth to protest, Lynette shook a finger at her.

Annie laughed. "Fine—don't even say it. Thank you. Anyway, the Carbo family has had even more trouble in recent months. I can't believe I didn't get around to telling you about the big drug bust back home."

She filled them in on everything, starting with the first day of school when Ferguson suffered the overdose at the lake. By the time she'd told them everything, her friends had all finished their meals, and the staff had cleared the table.

Renee tapped the table with a finger. "And you think your job isn't exciting? Wow, Annie. That's crazy. And hey . . . you mentioned a police officer named Ivory. That isn't the same Ivory who Kit threw into the stinky river water at summer camp, is it?"

This brought on a round of laughter.

"That's *exactly* who it is," Annie confirmed.

"They say prior criminals sometimes make the best cops," Kit said. "And I'm still convinced she was the mastermind behind Fran taking that money and setting me up to take the fall."

Lynette set her soft drink down with a shake of her head. "I almost took the fall for that, too."

"Yep. But I always had the feeling that wasn't their intent. Everyone liked you, Lynette. But I was a stranger," Kit said. "And they hated me."

Jackie snorted. "They didn't *hate* you. They just loved themselves. That hasn't really changed."

"I don't know," Annie said. "You might not think so poorly of Ivory if you got to know her now. She *is* good at her job, though I was furious at her for putting Ferguson in danger."

"It is cool that Henry played a part in figuring things out. And I bet his management appreciated it," Lynette said. "I can't imagine finding out my company was involved in illegal activities like that. It would kill me."

Annie nodded. "Oh, yeah. Guess where Henry is right now?"

"Don't tell me he's looking for a new job," Jackie said. "I hope they didn't make him the scapegoat!"

"No, no. At least, I don't think so. They insisted he fly in to their headquarters to meet with the owners. He said it was so he could help them put stronger controls in place so this never happens again."

"Where are their headquarters located?" Renee asked.

"London."

"Wait, good ol' Henry is in *London* right now?" Kit said. "And he didn't take you with him?"

Annie laughed and motioned around the table. "I had a prior commitment. Besides, I only had to take three days of vacation for this, since we spanned a weekend. But he thought he'd be gone for at least two weeks. He left after I did. Say, that reminds me. When I told Michael that Henry was going to Europe, he wasn't sure that was a good idea. Have you guys paid any attention to this talk of some nasty virus overseas? Michael seemed to think it could turn into kind of a big deal. Maybe even interrupt international travel."

Lynette shrugged. "One of our suppliers in China mentioned it when they missed a shipping deadline, but I'm sure they'll get it handled before it becomes a real problem."

Annie felt justified in her lack of concern by the other nods around the table. But then she realized Kit, their resident scientist, hadn't weighed in.

"Kit? Are *you* worried?"

Her friend took a deep breath. "I wouldn't say I'm *worried* . . . but I am paying attention to what's happening over in China and other parts of the world. Don't worry. Henry will be fine. With a little luck, this will all die down in a matter of weeks, and the world will go on as it always has. And speaking of *going on*, we haven't even talked about who is going to take over planning our next trip. Jackie, Lynette, or Renee, do any of you feel like volunteering?"

Annie saw Lynette glance between the other two women who also hadn't worked the job of girls' trip travel agent yet. Kit had handled the arrangements for Maui the previous summer, and now Annie would be off the hook for a few years. Lynette raised a hand, the silver bangles at her wrist making a tingling sound.

"I'll volunteer for next year. Jackie has her hands full with her new business. Maybe Renee could go next—after me, I mean."

"You planned that quick visit you all took to Whispering Pines for the retreat a while back, Lynette," Renee said, looking like maybe she should be the one to plan the trip for 2021.

But Lynette shook her head. "Planning that was nothing more than a quick phone call to you, Renee. No, I'm kind of in the mood for a new challenge. I'll do it. What are we thinking? Any ideas where we could go or when, just to get me started? Arizona was amazing, Annie, and it was great to escape the cold winter back home, but isn't it kind of hard for you to get away during the school year? I know you made it work this time because you wanted to be around to help this upcoming summer with your new grandbaby."

Annie hated to admit it, because escaping the brutal Minnesota winter felt amazing, but this wasn't something she could manage every year. "Summer is much easier for me."

"And I'll probably be in a better position to take another trip in a year and a half or so, too," Jackie said. "Getting this business off the ground is costing me more up front than I'd planned for. I'm doing all right, but these things take time. What about you, Renee? Summers are your busiest times, aren't they?"

"Yes, but if Julie is still available to help me next summer, she loves it when I turn the resort over to her and let her do her own thing once in a while. I should be able to make summer work."

"Great," Lynette said. "If no one objects, I'll start brainstorming on a trip we can take in the summer of 2021. And all of you should start socking away a little extra money each month, just in case I come up with something extravagant."

"You never were one to play small, Lynette," Annie said. It felt good to have her traveling responsibilities behind her. At least for now. She glanced at her phone. "And I hate to say it, ladies, but we need to head to the airport. Lynette's flight leaves an hour before ours, so it's time. But you know I'll be counting the days until we can do this again."

"You won't be the only one," Kit assured her. "I'll need a break from all the testosterone at my house! I'm not used to all this togetherness."

CHAPTER THIRTY-FOUR

HENRY WAS RIGHT: THE school did not implode during Annie's absence. But a stack of messages awaited her attention when she got back to her desk on Monday morning, as well as a time-sensitive report she'd need to complete on standardized test results.

At least they'd made it back home with only a two-hour delay, despite the winter weather advisory on Sunday. She'd be lucky if she got the report submitted on time. What she really needed was a nap, but that would have to wait. No more lounging next to a swimming pool under a balmy sun for her—at least for a few more months.

The school was still quiet. No one else was foolish enough to get there before seven on a snowy Monday morning. Her short but white-knuckled drive to work had her questioning her sanity. It felt awful to return to the terrible Minnesota weather after sunny Arizona.

But it wasn't like she'd had a choice.

Just as she was getting into the details behind the report, someone tapped on the doorframe to her office. She couldn't quite squelch the impatient sigh that escaped her lips at the first of likely many interruptions of the day.

"Welcome back, Annie," the woman standing there said. "I'm sorry to bother you. You probably came in extra early to catch up after vacation before the Monday crazies hit."

So why are *you bothering me?* Annie wanted to say.

Instead, she plastered on what she hoped was a passably pleasant expression and shook her head. "It's fine, Laura. I know you only rotate through here once a week, and you'll probably have your fair share of kids feeling under the weather on this wintery morning. Cold and flu season, right? What can I help you with?"

Laura motioned toward the chairs in front of Annie's desk. "Mind if I sit?"

Annie set her report off to the side. She knew the school nurse well enough to read the concern in her expression, so she gave the woman her full attention. "Of course. Sarah will be in before too long, so shut the door if this is confidential."

After closing the door to shut them off from the outside world, Laura sat. "I know you're just back from vacation. I hope you had a chance to recharge. You've already had a challenging year, and it isn't over yet. But, by any chance, have you heard about the coronavirus they are talking about more and more often in the news?"

The question gave Annie a start. Was there really a substantive health risk behind the virus Michael first mentioned before she left for Arizona? Things like this often got some press—particularly if there wasn't anything else newsworthy to report—but then fizzled from the news circuit just as quickly. When they'd discussed it at lunch yesterday, Kit seemed at least marginally concerned, but nothing too extreme.

Laura held her gaze, waiting.

"Oh, sorry . . . I guess I'm not as well rested after my trip as I'd hoped. Yes. Yes, a friend of mine mentioned something about it to me before I left on vacation. Why do you ask? There haven't been any cases reported in the United States, have there?"

The nurse raised her palms with a shrug. "There's lots of noise out there right now. It's hard to know what's true and what isn't. But information was forwarded to us over the weekend about possible symptoms we are being asked to watch for, and a hotline number to call if we happen across a student or staff member exhibiting more than one or two of them. I'm sure you have a copy of all this in your emails, too."

Alarm bells went off in Annie's head. "You haven't already come across someone who matched the criteria, have you?"

"No," Laura replied with a vigorous shake of her head. "And hopefully I never will. But my gut tells me we need to be at least marginally prepared should this virus spread to the States. How comfortable are you that we have a reliable contingency plan in this school district, if that were to happen? Some initial reports around fatality rates and such are pretty alarming. You and I both know that schools can be like petri dishes."

Annie pulled out a fresh notepad. "Now you have me worried, too. Do you really think it could get serious here, in the middle of the United States?"

"Truthfully? Yes. That's why I stopped by. But I'm not going to admit as much to anyone else. I had a professor in college who reveled in showing us how quickly a rogue virus can spread through the population. I tell you what, I lost sleep over the doom and gloom he preached. But the science behind what he showed us made sense. We don't live in a protective, isolated bubble. People are flying all over the world, all the time. I don't know if anyone can do much to stop a true viral pathogen without a known antigen."

Annie set her pen down on the notepad, still blank, and folded her hands together and waited for Laura to take a breath. When she did, Annie cleared her throat.

"All right, Laura. I can see that this really has you spooked. Maybe you're right to be. Maybe not. Let's *hope* not. But I appreciate you coming to me with this. I always want you to feel like I'm a safe space to come to with your concerns."

Laura took a second, deeper breath. "But . . . don't go starting rumors around here that could scare the shit out of people? Is that what you were about to say?"

Despite the seriousness of the topic, Annie couldn't help but smile. "Yes, that's pretty much exactly what I'm saying. I hear you. I really do. If this thing was to get legs in the United States, it could have far-reaching consequences, and we'd be smart to experiment with some what-ifs. We certainly run through enough fire, tornado, and active shooter drills around here. Preparedness is important. But, to be honest, I don't feel prepared at all for how to deal with the potential spread of a serious disease amongst our students and staff. Why don't we put our heads together and come up with a few questions I can take to the superintendent?"

Laura scooted her chair closer to Annie's desk. "I would feel better if we could do that. When I'd leave one of his terrifying lectures, I used to pray that my crazy old professor would never turn out to be not so crazy after all. He made me see that you just never know. I'd walk out thinking I better go straight home and get my affairs in order. And I was only twenty-three at the time! What affairs did I even have to worry about?"

Annie picked her pen back up and numbered the notebook paper.

Before they could start, her phone vibrated inside her suit jacket. She glanced at the screen, and her smile was instantaneous as she read Ava's text. The baby had her daughter convinced that she would birth a full-fledged gymnast in two weeks, given how active the little peanut had been last night.

Active was a good sign. It was when the babies settled down that Annie remembered panic setting in, and it had always happened to her right before she went into labor with each of her three babies. Her mind had started playing tricks on her, convinced something had happened to the baby in utero.

"Good news?" Laura asked. "A smile is always a good thing. I hate how worried I've been feeling lately."

Annie nodded. "My daughter just sent me a text. She's expecting a baby soon. We're all so excited. She'll be our first grandchild."

Then a scary thought occurred to her. "Oh wow, Laura . . . What if this virus really is something to worry about? That isn't an environment you want to bring a new baby into. I hope that possibility doesn't occur to Ava. She needs to keep her stress level as low as possible right now, for both her sake and the baby's."

Laura tapped the top sheet of Annie's notepad. "Don't even allow your mind to go there. I'm sure I'm overreacting. But let's at least get a few questions pulled together, and we'll feel better knowing we're prepared for any scenario."

Annie's worry was growing more and more that, if the threat was genuine, it wouldn't be as simple as Laura hoped.

Together, they got to work, preparing for something they both prayed with all their hearts, would never come to pass.

Chapter Thirty-Five

ORKING UP THE LIST of questions with Laura didn't actually make Annie feel any better. If anything, it revealed how uncharted this territory might prove to be. However, other duties called, and she'd done what she could for now by bringing her concerns to the district's superintendent.

Henry had flown out for his meeting in London while she was in Arizona, so only Lemon roamed the house with her when she returned home after work. Colton had kept the dog while both she and Henry were out of town, instead of Ava as originally planned, just in case the baby came early.

Before Relic had left for college, Annie hadn't yet appreciated how pervasive the quiet would be in an empty nest. She used to yearn for silence.

That was before she understood how lonely it could feel.

She should call Ava and check on her.

Ava was in full-fledged nesting mode every time she'd talked to her recently: cleaning out closets, organizing diapers and baby clothes, preparing freezer meals. The one thing that *still* wasn't completely pulled together was the nursery. The crib was up, the walls painted, but Annie didn't think it felt cozy enough yet. Maybe Ava and Daniel had worked on it while she was in Arizona.

She considered pouring herself a glass of wine before calling, but settled for ice water. Her body needed time to detox after the excesses of her girls' trip. With a full glass poured, she settled onto a stool at the kitchen island and called her daughter.

"How are you feeling, hon?" she asked when she picked up.

"Like a beached whale. I still haven't gotten the storage room in the basement organized yet. I know I have that box of my old toys you gave me down there somewhere, but just the thought of digging through the piles right now exhausts me."

Annie couldn't imagine their storage room could be very messy. The young couple hadn't even been in their new home for a year. Unless they had too many unpacked boxes still. "What about the nursery? Did you do anything more in there?"

Ava sighed. "Mom, it isn't that big a deal. I still can't decide exactly what theme I want to go with. I think I need to meet her first." She didn't seem moved by Annie's continuous nudges to get the project done while she still had the time. "Besides, if I go into labor early, you can just finish it for us. I trust you. Just don't go too crazy with butterflies and kaleidoscopes. I know you've always considered those things very symbolic in your life, but this is a newborn we are talking about. She won't be able to play with kaleidoscopes for a few years yet. I suppose butterflies could work . . ."

Annie laughed. If Ava didn't get things done and they ended up falling to her, she'd decorate that nursery in whatever fashion she darn well pleased. As she was admitting as much to Ava, her daughter cut her off with a moan.

"Wow, that one *hurt* . . . it felt like more than a kick. Mom, what do Braxton–Hicks contractions feel like?"

All thoughts of how to decorate the nursery flew right out of Annie's brain. "Well, honey, it's hard to distinguish between false labor and real contractions. When did you last feel what you *thought* was a kick? Or a roll?"

Ava didn't immediately respond.

"Honey, are you still there? Is Daniel home?"

"Yeah, I'm here. Sorry. I was just trying to remember when I last felt something more normal out of her. Oh, God. I can't remember. Mom! Do you think something is wrong with her?"

Annie almost laughed. It was like reliving her own impending birthing experiences again, all of which turned out to be blissfully routine. But Ava wouldn't appreciate that.

"No. Honey, I'm sure nothing is wrong. It's very common for babies to rest up before they make their way out into the world to meet us."

Ava snorted at that.

"All right, so maybe that isn't real medical jargon, but you know what I mean. Is Daniel home?" she asked again.

"He's home. He actually had another coach cover for him tonight. I wanted him here. I'm afraid of being alone right now. Is that dumb?"

"Absolutely not. Besides, you two are in this together. I'm glad he's there. Here's what I want you to do. If you aren't feeling strong, somewhat consistent, contractions, but the baby isn't moving either, drink a little orange juice and then go lie on your side."

"For what?" The skepticism was evident in her voice.

"I don't know why, but it just seems to work to get the baby moving again. It can reassure you she's doing just fine in there. You pulled this on me, by the way, right before I went into labor with you, too. I panicked, but Michael told me to do exactly what I just suggested to you. Don't ask me where he learned it, because I have no idea, but it worked. Not only with you, but with your brothers, too."

Annie heard Daniel speaking in the background. "Are you good, honey?"

"I think so . . ." Annie's sensitive ears picked up a wobble in her daughter's voice when she answered her husband. "Mom, I'll try the juice. Thanks."

"Don't be afraid to go in and get checked if you're worried or you think labor might be happening. What's the worst that can happen? They just send you home. It happens all the time."

"If you say so, Mom. And if baby Nora makes an early appearance, you'll be the first one we call."

Ava hung up, but Annie didn't think to lower the silent phone from her ear. Instead, she left it there as she slid onto the floor, coming eye to eye with Lemon.

"Did you hear that, girl? My granddaughter's name is Nora."

Annie hadn't expected so much anxiety as she waited for news from Ava. Baby Nora might take her own sweet time in arriving, it seemed, but at least the orange juice trick worked. There was still one more week until the actual due date, and Ava's pains earlier in the week had subsided.

Henry wasn't due back until next Friday. Annie ran errands and cleaned the house for part of Saturday. How should she fill the rest of her weekend? After working so hard to prepare for Arizona, having so much fun with her friends, and then digging out at work, she didn't even feel like leaving the house again.

She considered looking for a new series to watch. If it was a show that wouldn't interest Henry, she could binge through it before he got home and no one would even judge her for spending her weekend on the couch.

There were some advantages to being home alone.

She heated a plate of leftovers, then flipped on the television to see what she could find on one of the streaming services. The nightly news was on, and before she could change the channel, a breaking news segment snagged her attention. The first confirmed fatality in the United States related to the new coronavirus was confirmed.

The man who had died was reported to be in his fifties, with underlying health concerns.

"In his fifties," Annie repeated, her mind snapping back to the joy-filled poolside party with her dearest friends a week ago. If this thing spread, would they all be at higher risk because of their age?

Yet another segment on the coronavirus came on when they returned from a commercial break, but a different reporter was referencing a graphic of purported areas seeing significant levels of infection on a world map. The US government was issuing travel advisories, warning citizens not to travel to or from those areas.

Henry's meetings were in London. The reporter was tracing an area in Italy, much like an overzealous weatherman would warn of dangerous weather on a green screen.

Annie used to teach world geography. London was much closer to the danger zones that seemed to emanate from places like China, and it wasn't far enough from Italy for her comfort.

Maybe they should have listened to Michael after all.

Ignoring her fast-cooling food, she tried to call Henry. He didn't pick up, but then she remembered it would be the middle of the night there. She made an extra effort to keep the worry out of her voice as she left a message, asking him to call her back in the morning.

Her thumb moved to click on Michael's name, but she hesitated. Why did she feel compelled to call her ex? Henry wouldn't appreciate her reaching out to Michael without a valid reason.

She clicked on his name anyway.

Her ability to think straight was eroding as her mind bounced between Ava's impending labor and whether this new coronavirus could become a big deal in the States. How would she keep the kids at school safe from a dangerous virus? Now she was also worried about her husband. Was there a possibility that Henry could get stuck in a country on the other side of the world?

She knew the government could shut down air travel in and out of the country with little advanced warning. And not just government officials in the United States, but people in power around the world. Airlines were an interconnected maze of flight paths that passed through countless countries, their networks spanning the globe like intricate spiderwebs.

Anything could happen.

Henry shouldn't have left the country.

He needed to get back here. Her gut told her he shouldn't wait for his scheduled flight on Friday. That would be March sixth. Ava's due date was March fifth. She'd hated the idea that her husband might miss the baby's birth, but he'd felt pressured to go and had assured her that, assuming she was born on time, the baby wouldn't even be released from the hospital by the sixth.

He'd have a lifetime to get to know their first grandchild.

Deep down, Annie knew Henry still struggled to think of Ava's baby as *his* grandchild.

Why does blending families have to be so hard?

Her call eventually went to Michael's voicemail. She left what she was afraid was a rambling message. He'd call her back as soon as he could. He always did.

Lemon barked at her feet.

Annie set her plate of food on the floor. Her appetite had deserted her. "Have at it," she said.

If Relic or Henry had given the dog half a plate of food, she'd have yelled at them. But her mind was heavy with worry, and she knew a little turkey and rice wouldn't hurt the dog. If Lemon got sick from her treat, Annie would deal with it.

There was no one else here to do it.

Once Lemon licked the plate clean, Annie put it in the dishwasher, then took the dog out back. She didn't bother with a jacket, as the temperature had climbed above freezing earlier in the day. Lemon ran for her favorite patch of grass, her claws scrambling for grip on a patch of ice at the mouth of the downspout.

Annie pulled her sweater tighter around her arms as she sank onto the garden bench they hadn't bothered to stash in the shed when winter first arrived. She tucked her phone in the pocket of her sweatpants, just in case Ava or Daniel called with news. She doubted she'd hear from Henry until he woke up in what would be his morning. He'd probably wake *her* up instead of the other way around.

How soon would Michael return her call?

While she was no longer privy to his day-to-day activities—and hadn't been for over twenty years—she knew he'd never leave town with Ava's due date so close.

Lemon roamed the backyard, her nose taking the lead. The temperature was dipping now that the sun was setting, but Annie found the cold air refreshing after a long day indoors. Both she and the dog needed some time outdoors. Later sunsets and daytime thawing hinted at spring, but the weather in March would inevitably seesaw back and forth between the seasons. Winter never released her grip easily.

Annie checked her watch. Just after six. It was looking like baby Nora wouldn't have a Leap Day birthday. Ava and Daniel had joked that it might be fun if their baby was born on February 29, 2020, but Annie didn't want that for her grandchild. She might have felt like she only got to celebrate a real birthday once every four years.

At least that was one less thing for Annie to worry about.

She closed her eyes, wishing for insight into what the future would hold. She had an uneasy feeling, deep in her bones, that there was a storm on their horizon—and it had very little to do with the weather.

CHAPTER THIRTY-SIX

L EMON BOLTED TOWARD THE northeast corner of the house, barking at something. Annie sighed and allowed her eyes to drift open. The wooden slats of the garden bench creaked under her when she sat up straight to scan the backyard shadows. The fence would keep the dog from going far, and given the decent weather, someone was probably passing by out front, enjoying an evening stroll.

But the scrape of the side gate brought her to her feet. Someone was stopping by. Since Lemon was now yipping with excitement instead of barking, it wasn't a stranger. Maybe Daniel was swinging by tonight instead of waiting until Sunday. Ava had mentioned sending him over to pick up the spare rocking chair Annie had offered for the baby's room.

"Annie? You back here?"

Her heart gave a little leap, as it always did at the sound of Michael's voice. Would she ever be able to shut down that automatic response? It annoyed her.

"Sure am!" she yelled back. "I was just letting Lemon out."

Lemon pranced back into sight, with Michael close behind. This time the pup didn't escape the dangers of the refreezing water near the downspout. The little dog slipped, slid a few inches on her side, then scrambled back onto her feet and proceeded on, unscathed.

Michael wasn't so lucky. He had farther to fall.

He made a valiant effort, though, and Annie felt like she was watching the fall happen in slow motion. Arms flailed, first one foot then the other sailed into the sky, and Michael's tall frame reached a nearly perfect horizontal angle before thudding onto the frozen ground below. Even from where she stood, she heard the *whoosh* of air leaving his lungs on the still, chilled air.

She rushed to his side, having to prance around the little dog. Lemon had stopped and looked back at their guest as if to say, *Watch it. It's icy.*

She should have heeded Lemon's unspoken message, too, because the ice had spread into the grass farther than she'd realized. Her wide slippers offered zero grip, but at least they allowed her to stay upright for the moment, unlike Michael. She slid straight across the patch of ice until she rammed into his prone body, abruptly halting her momentum and flipping her off her feet. He broke her fall, and she rolled away and scrambled right back onto her feet, much as Lemon had a second earlier.

The beam of light coming from the back patio lit up his pained expression and his closed eyes. She stood over him, horrified.

"Michael! Are you all right? Did you break anything?"

He groaned in response.

"Should I call an ambulance?"

His hand reached toward her and grabbed at the fur of a slipper. "Annie. Shut the hell up, would you? Let me catch my breath."

Lemon approached, hesitant, apparently every bit as concerned as Annie. The yorkie skirted around Michael's body to his head, where she licked what she could reach of his face, much as a mother animal would soothe her injured young. He brushed the dog out of the way more gently than he'd grabbed for Annie, then used his left arm to prop himself up to a sitting position.

Annie got behind him, wedged her icy fingers under his armpits, and attempted to help him to his feet. Her fruitless efforts did nothing more than draw a laugh, then a moan, out of him.

"Annie . . . stop. For God's sake, give me a minute."

Although he'd let his head hang forward, he must have caught her movement when she pulled her phone out of her pocket.

"Put that thing away . . . I'll be fine."

Lemon barked, encouraging him to get up, too.

"I think you're both trying to kill me," he said.

He took a deep breath and rolled up onto his knees, stopped to catch his breath again, then reached for Annie's hand as he got his right foot positioned under his torso.

"I'll be fine. I twisted my left ankle, though. Help me up, would you?"

Her assistance proved more effective with his focused cooperation, and he was soon standing again, but his injured ankle refused to support him.

"Here—put your arm around my shoulders and keep your weight off your left side," she said, taking charge now that she thought he'd most likely be okay. "Do you want to get to the bench over there? Or go inside?"

He looked between the bench in the middle of the backyard and the back door. The house was closer. "Inside."

Together, they inched their way to the door and into the house. Lemon danced ahead of them. When Michael stopped to remove the work boots that had failed to help him stay upright, she insisted he not bother.

He eyed the distance between the back door and the sofa. "But the carpet—"

"Will be fine," she finished. "Sit over there, and I'll help you get your boots off."

A few minutes later, his boots were off, and they'd propped his injured ankle on an ottoman and draped it with a bag of ice.

"Are you sure you don't want to get that looked at? I can run you to the emergency room."

He readjusted his leg, grimacing at the effort, but shook his head. "On a Saturday night? They'll just tell me to stay off it and put some ice on it, which I'm already doing with your help. No. Besides, a hospital probably isn't a place any of us want to be hanging out at right now."

Nothing he'd said up to that last point surprised her. She'd nursed him through enough cuts, bumps, and bruises during their relatively short time together to know of his aversion to doctors. He usually chose to tough it out. But the last thing he said caught her attention.

"What do you mean by that?"

"What?" he said, bending to retrieve the ice bag that had slipped off and placing it back on top of his ankle. "The hospital?"

"Yeah. The hospital. You realize our daughter isn't going to have any choice *but* to go to the hospital any day now? Do you know something?" Her panic, first at the sight of him falling in the backyard, was now back in full force.

He dropped back against the cushions of the sofa and patted the space beside him. "Annie. You need to take a breath. Come. Sit down. I came over here because I was worried about you after listening to your message. And now you sound like something is really eating at you. What's going on?"

She checked her phone, just in case she'd missed a call from either Ava or Henry during the whole hubbub out back, but she hadn't. With a sigh, she sank into the spot next to him. She didn't even resist when he threw an arm across the back of the sofa and angled her so her head rested on his shoulder. There was nothing inappropriate about the movement. He was simply offering her comfort.

Comfort she desperately needed.

They just sat. He gave her the space to collect her thoughts. Michael used to push, but time had changed him. When they were young, she'd never considered him a patient man.

She supposed grandfathers should be patient.

A giggle snuck out at the thought. Before long, her shoulders shook with repressed laughter.

"If you are laughing at my lack of grace on ice, I swear I'll throw you out back into one of those shrinking piles of snow."

"Eww," she said, crinkling her nose and pushing away. "It's been a long winter. Lemon has sprinkled way too many little turds around on the snow out there. It's always been Relic's job to clean that up in the spring, but . . ."

Her eyes filled with unexpected tears. She flicked them away in frustration.

"I'm sorry, Michael. I don't know what the hell is the matter with me. I feel like my emotions are on a rollercoaster these days."

He patted her back as if to comfort her, but when it remained there a beat longer than necessary she inched away, and he let it fall to the sofa behind her.

"Sorry. Old habits."

She let it go. "I'm sorry I laughed at you, but that fall was like something straight out of *The Flintstones*. Yabba-dabba doo!"

He gave her back a playful shove, then crossed his hands behind his head, looking up at the ceiling. "I can already tell I won't be able to get out of bed in the morning."

She smirked. "Actually, I'm not sure you'll be able to get *to* a bed tonight."

She stood and checked his ankle. It was already turning purple with a tinge of green. "Oh, man . . . you really should get that looked at."

He leaned forward to have a look for himself. "Shit."

"Yeah," she agreed. But she already knew he wouldn't agree to a trip to the emergency room. "If you won't let me take you in, how about a beer? It might help with the pain."

"I wouldn't argue," he said. "But then we're going to talk about that message you left me. You sounded really worried about Henry. He's still in Europe, right? He needs to get his ass back here."

"Hold that thought."

She went out to the garage and grabbed one bottle out of Henry's beer fridge. She wasn't a beer fan, and if she ended up needing to drive Michael in to get his ankle looked at, she'd want to be completely sober. Besides, she still had detoxing to do.

When she returned to the family room, Michael's eyes were closed, his expression pained again. But his features smoothed when he heard her.

"You know, you don't have to pretend it doesn't hurt."

He accepted the bottle she offered and twisted the top off, helping himself to a big swig. "Annie, you'll see that by the time you're this age, everything hurts."

She snorted. He was only two years older. "Only when you're clumsy enough to fall on the ice."

"I blame her," he said, pointing at Lemon with his bottle. She was curled up on her doggy bed, looking innocent but keeping a close eye on them both. "Now, tell me about Henry. When is he supposed to fly home?"

Annie sat again, but this time she took the armchair that sat perpendicular to the couch. "Friday. But I wish it was sooner. Did you watch any of the news today? They're talking about travel advisories and stuff. Could they ever shut down air travel altogether if this virus thing gets worse?"

He nodded, his face grim. "They could. And they will if they deem it necessary."

"What can we do? I'd hate for him to get stuck over there . . ."

Michael set his beer on the side table. "I would hate that, too. Have you called him? Asked him to book an earlier flight?"

"I tried to call him a little while before you got here. He didn't pick up, but then I remembered they're six hours ahead of us. He was probably sleeping and didn't hear the phone."

"Henry always slept like the dead," Michael agreed.

The common saying, meant as a joke, felt all wrong.

He shook his head, as if he regretted his tasteless comment. "He'll call you back when he wakes up."

"Do you think there's anything we can do in the meantime?"

Michael considered this. "Yeah . . . we probably should be a little proactive right now. These don't feel like ordinary times. Besides, I talked to Ava a couple hours ago, and she thought she might be feeling labor pains."

"What?! She didn't tell me that!"

"Maybe I should just stop talking," Michael said, helping himself to another pull on his beer. "I seem to step into it every time I open my mouth."

"Not to mention what happened when you stepped *on* the ice outside."

"Cute."

His expression told her he wasn't amused, so she turned them back to the most important part of their erratic conversation.

"Ava is in labor?"

"I didn't say that. No. She's not officially in labor. And she didn't want to worry you. But, regardless, it won't be long before she *has* that baby. Henry shouldn't miss that. Couple that with this damn virus and all the uncertainties about how people might react if more get sick, and we need to get him back to the US as soon as possible."

She liked the way he said *we*. She used to think of the three of them like a team, before hearts and hormones muddied up their friendships.

She had an idea. "Maybe we should start looking for earlier flights he could grab to come home before Friday. It's easier to do that on a computer than it would be for him on his phone."

He nodded. "Good thought. Is there any chance someone at his work is already actively working to bring him home early?"

Annie considered it but shook her head. "They aren't usually that proactive. Maybe if he was a high-ranking manager or something, he'd be on someone's radar screen. But even if people at the plant are getting a little anxious about the situation, like we are at school, they already have their hands full with trying to come up with an overarching game plan for how to handle things."

"True. Why don't you grab your laptop and we'll look to see what's available. We can't be the only ones panicking just a little about getting someone home."

Two hours of searching through flight options didn't leave Annie and Michael feeling any better about the situation Henry was possibly facing.

"I don't care what it costs. We need to book something and get him back here," Annie said.

They'd sat next to each other on the couch, discussing various scenarios, but either the airlines were already cutting back on scheduled flights or people were snatching open seats at an alarming pace.

The laptop's low-battery warning notification popped up. The cord was probably in Henry's office, so she closed the computer and stood to go look for it. If she couldn't find it, she could always switch to her work laptop. This was an emergency.

"Check my ankle, would you? I hate to admit it, but it's throbbing like a mother again."

"I hate that saying." She'd find the cord after helping Michael. The swelling hadn't improved, and the bruise was spreading. "You probably need fresh ice. I don't like how this looks . . ."

He grimaced. "And I don't like the way it *feels*. Maybe I broke it. I'll head home in a bit, and if it isn't better in the morning, I'll go get it X-rayed."

"Like you can go anywhere on that thing by yourself."

For the first time since he'd limped his way over to the couch, he pulled his injured leg off the ottoman and made an attempt to stand. "I can't stay here. And if I don't use a bathroom pretty soon, we're both going to be embarrassed when you have to play nursemaid to me in a way neither of us would appreciate."

"Oh, for heaven's sake," Annie said. "You certainly *can* stay here. Henry would understand, given the circumstances. You can either sleep on the couch or in Colton's old room. That way you won't have to attempt the stairs tonight. Come on. I'll help you to the bathroom down here."

He opened his mouth to say something, but she recognized that gleam in his eye.

She held up a finger. "And no, I won't help you hold anything. You hurt your ankle. The rest of you is fine."

He shrugged, grinning. That grin made him look as young as he was when they'd first met. She couldn't believe that was half a lifetime ago. But he kept his mouth shut and, with her help getting to and from the bathroom, he took care of business before sinking back onto the couch.

"Oof . . . that took a lot out of me. I better park it here tonight."

Annie left him to go in search of the laptop cord. Henry used their home laptop more than she did. They shared it, but she spent so much time on her work laptop that she seldom used their personal one. As she entered his office, the mess struck her. Henry had lots of good qualities, but neatness wasn't one of them. It wasn't until she moved a third pile of papers on his desktop that she found the cord. If Ava didn't go into labor tonight or tomorrow, and Michael headed home after his ankle either improved or he saw a doctor, she'd spend her Sunday afternoon cleaning up Henry's office. She'd helped him out in the past with it, and he always appreciated the organization she brought to the chaos. It just never lasted very long.

"I've been thinking," Michael said when she returned. "Maybe this would be easier if we just tried to get Henry back as far as New York. There have to be more international flights into New York City than Minneapolis. Then I could fly over and pick him up from there. That way I could swing by and say hello to my old man."

While it was a generous offer, Annie didn't want to put Michael out like that. Besides, Henry would no doubt hate such a grand gesture on his old friend's part. "We couldn't let you do that."

He narrowed his eyes at her, as if considering her refusal. "Fine. But at least keep it in mind. It's been a while since I swung up there to see Dad—a fact he reminds me of every Sunday afternoon when I call. He can't remember what he ate for dinner, but he sure remembers my lengthy absences."

Annie had a tendency to forget Michael even maintained his pilot's license. He didn't own a plane, and she didn't think he flew often anymore, but surely enough that he could still rent a plane if he had to get somewhere in a hurry. She used to worry that he'd given up on his commercial flying career too soon to move to Ruby Shores to be closer to his kids, but he claimed otherwise.

Michael always did things his way. It was one of the things that splintered their marriage. Not the most serious of his offenses, but another weak link.

Annie heard her familiar ringtone, but her phone was no longer in her pocket.

"Maybe that's him now," she said, hurrying back to his office—she must have set it down after using it as a flashlight to check behind Henry's desk for the cord.

She took the stairs two at a time, thankful she wasn't the one laid up with a bum ankle. By the time she reached her phone, the ringing had stopped, but the push notification on the screen announced a missed call from Ava.

It was after nine. The kids didn't normally call this late at night. Annie and Henry had evolved into early-to-bed-early-to-rise people.

Is this it?

She returned Ava's call while heading back to the family room and Michael. If there was news, he should get to hear it along with her.

She'd almost given up on the fifth ring when Ava picked up.

"Hi, Annie. Ava tried to call you."

"Daniel? Why are you answering Ava's phone? Is she all right?"

"Just a sec," he replied—which told Annie nothing.

"Daniel? Is Ava okay?!"

Even Annie could hear the rising panic in her own voice. Michael rolled his eyes as she came into the room.

"You need to chill," he said. He eyed the phone in her hand. "What's up?"

She shook her head at him to be quiet. "Shh!"

He crossed his arms over his chest but shut his mouth.

"Sorry about that," Daniel finally said. "Ava couldn't get her seatbelt hooked."

"Her seatbelt? Why are you in the car? Are you heading to the hospital?!"

Daniel laughed. "Yes, Grandma Annie, we are going in. We think she's having contractions. They're strong but not consistent. The doctor wants to at least check her. Maybe it's another false alarm."

"Maybe not." Annie sat back down next to Michael and captured his hand in her own, squeezing so hard in her excitement that he winced. "All right. Thanks for letting me know. Do you promise to call me as soon as you know something? I want to be at the hospital when she goes in for delivery. Not in the room with you guys, but close by."

Daniel must have parlayed her message because she could hear muffled talking, as if he had his hand over his phone. He was only gone for a second. "Ava wants you to call Michael, too, to let him know. She's pretty sure this is it."

"He's right here, so I don't have to call him," Annie blurted out, not even thinking about how strange that might sound to anyone else.

"Umm, okay," Daniel said. "Maybe I won't tell Ava that part."

Then he groaned, as if Ava might have whacked him.

"Now is not the time to keep things from me!"

Annie couldn't help but grin at her daughter's terse tone. But then the genuine pain in her voice registered, and suddenly nothing else mattered but the safety of her daughter and granddaughter.

Our daughter and granddaughter, she thought as Michael gave her hand a reassuring squeeze.

"It sounds like she's in pain. I think we should head to the hospital, too," Annie said.

Daniel sighed. "I hate to have you waste a trip, but yeah, the pains seem to come every few minutes now. It's up to you."

She met Michael's gaze, and he nodded. He understood. He wanted to be there for Ava and Daniel, too.

"We're on our way," she said, then hung up so Daniel wouldn't have any further distractions—just a pregnant wife in the seat next to him, possibly about to give birth to his first child.

"I think this might be it. Nora might be born on Leap Day yet."

"Nora? Is that the baby's name? They didn't tell *me* her name."

And for the second time that night, Michael made Annie laugh.

"I think we're being a tad bit ridiculous here," she said, moving to help him up again. "Women have been giving birth to babies since the beginning of time. She'll be all right."

Michael hurried to his feet so quickly that he almost pulled them both down when he forgot about his injury and tried to put weight on the wrong ankle.

"We can take my truck," he offered, but Annie shook her head.

"It'll be easier for you to get into my car, and I'm driving. Maybe if little Nora takes her time joining us, we can have someone look at your ankle, too. Might as well kill two birds with one stone."

They were halfway to the garage when Michael pulled back, forcing Annie to stop.

"Go back and grab your laptop. We still need to figure out how to get Henry back here."

A surge of guilt coursed through her. She'd forgotten all about Henry in the excitement.

Michael was right. They needed to figure out a way to get Henry home to meet little Nora, too.

CHAPTER THIRTY-SEVEN

"**W**HAT TIME IS IT?"

Michael sighed. "Ten minutes later than the last time you asked, Annie. I didn't think you wanted the baby to be born on Leap Day. There's only an hour left, so whether or not you want it isn't going to matter."

Annie shook her head. "I don't care about that. It just seems like this is taking too long."

He kicked both footrests out of the way on the wheelchair he'd used to get from the hospital's main entrance to the family waiting room, and then again when he'd had to use the bathroom. "I hate this thing," he said, using his arms and one good leg to move from the wheelchair to a regular chair. "Annie, I know your labor with both Ava and Colton was under two hours, but I don't think that's normal. Hey, speaking of Colton, did you give him a call when I was down the hall? Or Relic?"

She shook her head. "Colton still lets me track him so I can always check to see if he's at work before I call. He's there now, which means they must have brought someone in rather late tonight. I'll check his location again in a little while. And you're right. Everyone's labor stories are different, even mothers and daughters. I need to be patient."

Michael nodded. "Yes, you do. I still can't believe our son works with dead people. I mean, we need people willing to do that, I suppose, but Colton?"

"I don't pretend to understand it either, other than he was always such an empathetic kid. And I don't want to call Relic until the baby is actually born. I'm not sure I want him driving back here from the dorm. There's snow in the forecast tomorrow morning. Honestly, Michael, I don't need one more thing to worry about."

Someone Annie didn't know stepped into the waiting area. The man had on a lanyard that pegged him as hospital staff. "Good evening. Are you both family members to a delivering mother?"

"We are. Our daughter is having a baby."

"Congratulations," he said with a smile. "Enjoy this special time. I need to inform you that the hospital is changing their visiting rules, effective tomorrow, so once you leave here, we ask that you refrain from coming back to the hospital. Wait until your family is home with the baby to visit."

Michael shifted in the uncomfortable chair, leaning forward slightly. "That doesn't sound like a change to the rules. That sounds like you're prohibiting visitors."

The man looked uncomfortable at Michael's accusatory tone, but he nodded. "I'm afraid that's correct. We've decided to err on the side of caution, given all the uncertainty right now."

"Do you mean related to the virus being covered in the news?"

"I'm hopeful these precautions turn out to be unnecessary, but yes. We're hearing word of a potential positive case in St. Paul, so hospitals are restricting visitors. We may allow up to two visitors per day in other sections of this hospital if the patient's situation is dire. But here on the maternity ward, we've decided to only allow delivering mothers and one support person. Does your daughter have someone else with her now?"

Annie nodded as she got to her feet. "Her husband. But can we at least stay until she's born? This is Ava's first child. It's possible that the delivery could take until tomorrow sometime."

The man glanced at a sheet of paper on his clipboard. "Technically, no. But things are evolving quickly, and it's possible that no one will make you leave before your daughter delivers. Don't tell anyone I said that, though. This is all so new . . . I'm not exactly sure how seriously they'll take all of this. I don't advise you leave this room. Someone could kick you out if you do."

"Even to go to the bathroom?" she asked, appalled.

He shrugged, then slipped away.

"Guess maybe we should have had someone look at my ankle already, too," Michael said. "Sounds like that window might be closing."

"I'm sure the ER is still open. I'll wheel you down there if it really hurts."

He reached over and captured her hand in his. "Thank you, Annie, but I'd never ask you to do that. You'd have to wait to meet Miss Nora for a few more days if we left now. I can always go in tomorrow if I have to."

Annie gave his fingers a quick squeeze, torn between being happy that Michael was there with her for their granddaughter's birth and missing Henry terribly.

As if her thoughts conjured him out of thin air, a rumpled Henry rushed into the family waiting room with a pink helium balloon in the shape of a huge pacifier in one hand and a white teddy bear in the other.

"Oh my God—Henry! What are you doing here?" she cried, springing from her chair and into his arms. "I was so worried you might get stuck over in Europe with all these warnings about this virus."

Henry hugged her back as well as he could with full hands, holding her there for an extra beat. "I couldn't very well miss our granddaughter's actual birthday, could I? Hey, Michael, good to see you, man. I know Ava will be glad you're here, too."

Annie stepped back but left one arm around Henry's waist. He sounded genuinely glad that Michael was at the hospital, too.

"It's a huge relief to see you back, Henry," Michael said, nodding from his seat. Ordinarily he was the type of guy who might have clapped Henry on the back over their mutual baby excitement, or even hugged him, despite the years of bad blood between them. He gestured down to his ankle apologetically. "Annie and I were plotting how we might get you back here before next Friday in case things go south in a hurry. Then Ava went into labor. It was killing us you were going to miss it."

Despite his earlier greeting, Henry's eyes narrowed slightly. He seemed to weigh Michael's sincerity. "You were worried about me, too?"

"I was," his old friend said.

The simple confirmation seemed more genuine than a lengthy explanation, at least to Annie. "Seriously, Henry, how are you back in Minnesota already? I tried to call you a few hours ago, but you didn't pick up. And how could you possibly know we were up here? I didn't call Colton to tell him yet because I could see he was at work. Relic doesn't know, and Lemon, while brilliant for a yorkie, isn't talking."

Henry looked around the room for somewhere to set the balloon and bear, then collapsed into a chair next to the one Annie had used, the front legs clanking down with his weight. He rested his head against the wall and closed his eyes. He looked utterly exhausted.

Annie spun to take her seat again but got tripped up on the wheelchair next to Michael. His hand shot out and caught her before she could fall.

"Easy there, girl, or you'll end up in worse shape than me. Sorry it's in the way in here," Michael said. He tried to move it back to minimize further tripping hazards.

"What the hell happened to you that you're using a wheelchair?" Henry asked. He must have been too tired to pull his head up straight, but he spared Michael a sideways glance.

"Ask your dog."

"You tripped over Lemon?"

"Not exactly," Annie jumped in. "It was the ice. He twisted his ankle. Come on, Henry, I'm dying here. Fill us in!"

Henry sat up straighter in his chair. "Fine. Our meetings were feeling productive, but then, things got a little strange. I think the CFO has family in another city where the government was requiring mandatory quarantines. People were getting a little spooked. They ended the meetings early, told me to catch the next flight home, and we'd reconvene in a month if things get back to normal."

Michael nodded. "What was it like at the airport? Did anything seem unusual when you were flying back here?"

Henry considered the question. "You know . . . yeah. I wouldn't say there was outright panic or anything, but there were definitely some sizeable crowds and short tempers. I was pretty relieved when we were wheels up leaving Heathrow. I'm not so sure I'd be comfortable making that trip again in a month."

Annie squeezed his knee, still so happy to see him back safe and sound. "Thank goodness. And now you won't miss the baby's birth. *And* you brought presents! That was sweet of you. I didn't think to do that. But that still doesn't explain how you knew Ava was in labor and to come up here."

Henry blew out a huge sigh. "I had the Uber driver bring me straight here from the airport, because when I landed in Minneapolis and turned my phone back on, I had that voicemail from you, Annie, but I also had one from Ava. She said they were on the way to the hospital, she was pretty sure this was it, and she'd call me back personally when she had more news. She said she wanted Grandpa Henry to hear it right from her, and not through you or anyone else."

Annie noticed a tear form in the corner of Henry's eye, but he dashed it away so quickly she doubted Michael noticed.

Aw, that's sweet . . .

Her heart felt like it might burst. She'd hated the growing distance between Henry and his two oldest, especially after Ava announced her pregnancy. When he hadn't acted excited about the baby, it almost killed her.

Based on his actions tonight, he'd had a change of heart. Maybe the precarious state of the world had helped him remember how much his family meant to him.

"I'm glad you're here, too, Michael," Henry said. "We both belong here."

She knew that couldn't be easy for him to admit. Maybe this co-grandparenting gig could work out after all.

Michael laughed. "I think we should both be here, too, but apparently the folks running your company over in London aren't the only ones getting nervous. Some messenger for the hospital administration popped his head in just before you got here and said they're taking extra precautions and limiting visitors."

"Oh, I know. I got the third degree when I hurried through the front door. I was afraid I might miss everything. If they were better organized down there, I might not have gotten in at all. Three staff members at the front desk started arguing amongst themselves over whether or not to let me in. They were caught up in their debate, so I nonchalantly ambled right past them and into the elevator. But I'm afraid once we leave we won't get back in."

"So we don't leave," Annie said, grabbing Michael's wrist to check the time on his watch again. She never wore hers during weekends.

He yanked his arm back. "Would you relax? You're making us nervous. That isn't going to make the baby come any quicker. Use your own damn phone to look at the time if you insist on checking it every five minutes."

"It's over there, charging," she said, motioning toward the kitchenette area.

Henry glanced that way. "Would you mind getting me a glass of water, Annie? I need to take something for this headache. And why don't you check to see if Colton is still at work? If he's off, we should call him, too. I don't think he should come up here, but just so he knows."

"Fine," she huffed. She stood and crossed the room.

"You always were better at dealing with her drama than me," she heard Michael say under his breath to Henry.

"I *heard* that!"

"Am I wrong?"

"No, Michael, you are not wrong," she said. She dug in the cupboard next to the sink and pulled out three plastic cups, each wrapped in more plastic. "That's because Henry never intentionally pushes my buttons."

Before they could fall deeper into the familiar argument, a doctor in a white lab coat and a nurse in pink scrubs entered. Both wore face masks.

The doctor looked from the kitchenette to the wheelchair. "Are you Ava Knight's family?"

"We are," Annie said. She dropped the cups and hurried to the doctor's side.

The woman took a step back, as if Annie had offended her by crowding her personal space. Maybe she had, but she knew she couldn't take a single deep breath until she knew her daughter and her granddaughter were safe and healthy. Screw the uptight doctor.

"Did she have the baby?"

The doctor nodded. "Yes, Ava delivered a healthy seven-pound, eleven-ounce baby girl a few minutes ago."

Annie clapped her hands with excitement. "Michael, for God's sake, what time is it?"

"Eleven fifty-eight, Annie. Looks like our granddaughter has a Leap Day birthday after all."

Annie decided she'd play up the uniqueness of Nora's birthday in the future instead of thinking of it like a bad thing.

The doctor didn't look at all interested in whether the baby was born on the twenty-ninth of February or the first of March. But she was eyeing each of them closely.

Is something wrong with Ava? The doctor said the baby was healthy . .

.

"Have any of you traveled internationally within the last two weeks?"

The question, seemingly random, threw Annie off for a moment. "Is Ava all right?"

"She's fine," the doctor said, looking back and forth between Henry and Michael.

"Why do you ask?" Michael said. Annie heard the challenge in his tone, but someone who didn't know him as well probably wouldn't pick up on it.

"Answer the question, please."

This chick isn't one to be messed with, Annie thought.

"Yes," Henry said, pushing out of his chair. He was looking even more tired than when he'd first arrived. Annie wondered how long it had been since he'd slept. He could never sleep on airplanes. "I just flew in from London tonight."

The doctor gave a no-nonsense nod, and the nurse slipped quietly away. "That's what I thought. Ava told me her mother and father were both out here waiting for news, but she felt bad that her other dad wasn't going to make it home from London on time. When I came in here and found three of you, I made an educated guess. I'm going to have to ask all of you to go home now. Baby and mother are doing fine. It's my job to keep it that way."

"But I just want to—"

The doctor held her hand up to stop Annie. "I know what you want. But I'm afraid I can't allow that. As of midnight, which has now officially come and gone, the hospital has new protocols in place. Ordinarily, I might bend the rules just a little. However, given you, sir, just deplaned from an international flight, I can't in good conscience do that. In fact, while I'm just the doctor on call tonight and not Ava or the baby's regular physician, I'm going to make a suggestion . . . and if you care about the health of your new granddaughter, you'll listen. Go home and stay home until you're sure you didn't catch anything in the airport or on that plane."

Henry's shoulders drooped. "For how long?"

The stern doctor's features softened. "Honestly, I have no idea. A few days, maybe? This is all so new—this virus that has everyone quite nervous. I'm sure they'll release more guidelines soon. Since you were the one who traveled, maybe you should bunk out in a more isolated corner of your home if you live with anyone else. Just as a precaution. You might be fine. But you look rather rundown."

"He lives with me," Annie said. "He's my husband."

"I'm sorry you won't be able to see your granddaughter tonight," the doctor said. "But I'm sure you are even more committed to keeping her healthy than I am. Ava and the baby are in excellent hands, and they should be able to go home in a couple days. Give them time to settle in before you go over. Be careful."

Annie thought she now understood the doctor's initial reaction when she'd gotten too close. "This virus has you scared, doesn't it?"

The woman studied her before responding. "I admit, I'm concerned. But if we are all careful, with luck this will all be behind us soon. Congratulations to you all. The baby is beautiful. I'll ask her father to text you pictures."

Message delivered, the woman turned and left as quickly as she'd entered.

"I don't think she wanted to breathe the same air as you, man," Michael teased.

Henry flipped him the bird.

Annie turned to them. "You guys, I have to see Nora. If that's even what they ended up naming her."

Michael stood, careful not to put weight on his ankle, and folded himself into the wheelchair. "Annie, I actually think the doctor has a good point. The health of Nora and Ava has to come before our personal feelings. Sure, Henry was just on an international flight, and maybe there's a tiny chance he was exposed to something, but any of us could have unknowingly picked something up in our day-to-day, too. I think we should follow the doctor's orders. Give the kids a little space, make sure all of us are healthy, and we'll be holding our granddaughter before you know it."

Henry moved behind the wheelchair and pushed Michael toward the door. "Come on, Annie. Michael's right. We have to be mature about this. It'll be fine. You'll see. And I liked her idea of giving you a little space, too. I'd feel terrible if I got you or anyone else sick."

"Just be sure not to breathe down my neck too much," Michael said, glancing over his shoulder.

Henry slapped him on the back of the head as they left the room.

Annie grabbed her phone and charger and followed them out to the elevator.

It wasn't until she'd showered and crawled into bed with Lemon—after they'd deposited Michael at home, and Henry grabbed his pillow and headed down to Colton's old room—that she remembered they'd left the balloon and teddy bear in the family waiting room. The thought of the balloon floating above the little toy bear in a lonely, darkened room tipped the scale and she dissolved into tears.

This wasn't how she'd planned to welcome baby Nora to the family.

Chapter Thirty-Eight

Annie woke to the smell of fresh coffee and sugar, but she allowed herself the luxury of leaving her eyes shut for a few extra minutes. Today she'd spoil her six-week-old granddaughter with her first Easter basket.

Her mind drifted back to that late-February evening when she'd sat alone in her chilly backyard, awaiting word from Ava and sensing a storm on their horizon. Henry's accelerated flight back from London and the hospital's initiation of emergency protocols on the very night of Nora's birth were the first definitive signs that none of them were immune to the upheaval to come, but they were finding ways to navigate the chaos, and today they'd celebrate Easter as best they could, given the circumstances.

She reached for Henry's side of the bed, disappointed to realize he wasn't there. Were the sheets still warm? She couldn't tell. She moved her foot slowly, checking for Lemon. No dog at the foot of the bed either. Maybe Henry was letting her out.

"Wake up, sleepyhead. The kids are ready to hunt for Easter eggs and baskets."

Annie smiled and stretched, still keeping her eyes shut for one more stolen moment of peace before beginning the day—a day that promised a break from the unique rhythm their days had evolved into since early March.

"Come on. Move your foot," Henry said, poking at it through their comforter. "I brought you breakfast."

She allowed her eyes to drift open and pushed herself to a seated position, her back against the carved headboard. "Breakfast? You put the rolls in! Thank you."

He nodded and set a fully laden tray across her lap. Her husband had done more than bake the sweet rolls she'd set out to rise the night before. Or had it been early morning when she'd gotten around to that last task?

"You're welcome," he said, helping himself to a piece of bacon.

"The house sounds awfully quiet. Nora must still be asleep?"

"More like *finally* asleep, but yes."

Annie sipped the hot coffee, appreciating the stillness while Henry sat by her feet and munched his bacon. "So you lied when you said the kids were ready to hunt for their baskets."

He laughed. "I was lonesome, and you were snoring."

She looked at him. Something had shifted in their relationship since he'd returned from London. It felt a little like the earlier days of their marriage, before things became mechanical. She liked it.

The faint cries of their granddaughter floated up the stairs and through their open bedroom door. They smiled at each other.

Annie loved having Nora with them around the clock, even if the newborn tended to mix up her days and nights, disrupting everyone's sleep. It was unfortunate that her parents couldn't quite cover their mortgage anymore without the extra income Daniel used to bring in through his coaching, but at least they'd figured out how to make the finances work by finding a renter for their house and moving into Ava's childhood home. The rent money gave them breathing space, and they wouldn't lose the house. Henry was right—they had taken on too big of a mortgage—but he'd respected them for being mature enough to ask for help.

"She didn't sleep long," Henry said.

When he reached for a triangle of toast, she slapped his hand away. "She never does. Hey, you brought me breakfast in bed. Are you actually hungry, or just eating my food because it's in front of you?"

He shrugged. "I may have sampled a roll or two already."

She wasn't worried. Two large pans would be more than enough for everyone, no matter how hungry the kids might be.

"Just think, Henry. Last Easter we were feeling sad that we'd soon be empty-nesters."

He laughed. "And now our house is even more full than before Ava left. We never could have guessed things would play out like this."

She noticed him eyeing her bacon and handed him another piece. There would be plenty of food all day. Since he'd been nice enough to bring her breakfast, she could share.

"Thanks," he said, accepting it with a wink. "We couldn't have guessed this, and neither could the kids. We're lucky we didn't downsize after Relic left and before the world went topsy-turvy. Don't tell Ava and Daniel, but I love having them in the basement."

Annie agreed, and she appreciated that Henry never said *I told you so* to anyone but her. When Ava and Daniel first approached them about possibly moving into their basement, the four of them sat down and discussed how it might work. The kids explained that they had, indeed, over-leveraged themselves and needed help. Ava was still on paid family leave with Nora. Daniel was teaching his classes remotely now, as were educators throughout Minnesota. There were no extracurricular activities, given the efforts to curb the ongoing spread of the virus, which meant he was bringing in less income.

Henry had refused to consider the kids' offer to pay them any rent. It was another stance Annie agreed with, because it meant the new parents could put some money away so that maybe they wouldn't find themselves in a similar predicament in the future. She knew all too well how hard it was to get ahead financially. If her family hadn't helped her out after she'd divorced Michael, life could have turned out differently for everyone. They'd never moved back in with her parents, but she did accept money from them until she was back on her feet.

Annie felt like they were paying things forward.

Colton didn't seem to mind crashing on the couch for their Easter weekend since his sister and family had taken over his old room.

"It's so quiet in here now that Lemon is back to sleeping with Relic," she said, glancing around. If the dog had been up on the bed, Annie never could have kept the energetic yorkie away from her breakfast tray.

Henry moved from his perch on the edge of the mattress, picking up her coffee cup so it wouldn't spill as he shifted his position, and sat next to her, against the headboard. "Has Jackie called back yet about that beagle she thought she'd be getting in? I still can't believe I let you talk me into another dog."

Annie took her cup back from him and took a sip. "Not yet. Maybe we're crazy to bring another living thing into this house right now. We already have Lemon, plus Ava and Daniel and Nora in the basement, plus Relic back in his room. But Relic told me he plans to get an apartment when he goes back to college in the fall, and when they eventually all leave us again, I won't be able to handle the loneliness."

"So, instead, let's bring in an old beagle that probably howls at the moon and needs to be lifted down the back step to go pee in the yard."

She laughed. "Older dogs are sweet! And it won't drive us crazy with too much pent-up energy. And, not to be too morbid, but it isn't as much of a time commitment as bringing home a puppy. By the time we retire . . . you know we've always dreamed of traveling, maybe even go on more mission trips . . . that will be harder to do if we have to board a dog all the time."

"Don't worry, you already sold me on the idea. If Jackie needs help to place an elderly beagle, we'll take it. I'm just going to eat this before it gets cold." He took the triangle of toast he'd tried for earlier. "I probably feel the worst for Relic. Ava and Daniel are here because they got a little too big for their britches, but I hate that Relic is missing out on the dorm experience."

" 'Big for their britches'!" Annie laughed. "I haven't heard that saying since I was a little kid. Are we getting old?"

He popped the remaining toast in his mouth and then used his free hand to tweak her breast through her nightgown. "Nope, we aren't old."

"I'll give you two minutes to stop that, Grandpa Henry."

His hand dropped. "That's a surefire mood-killer, *Grandma*."

But she knew from his expression that his good mood was still intact.

She sighed. "But I know what you mean. I hate that Relic was forced to move home and finish his freshman classes online. I hate that *all* kids are going through this. There's a place for online learning, but to have to switch to it one hundred percent of the time has been brutal. I'm worried about kids' mental health, and I don't just mean the college kids. Can you imagine trying to teach kindergarten and first grade kids via Zoom? But teachers everywhere are learning how to do it on the fly."

Henry swung his feet off the bed and came around, taking the tray from Annie. Nora's cries were escalating, and the baby would wake her uncles with that set of lungs.

"All right, *Mrs.* Pierce. I thought we agreed to avoid all conversations about everything that is wrong in the world. Today we pretend that life is still 'normal' and we're just enjoying another holiday with our kids."

He was right. These days, it was all too easy to slip into anxious thoughts and overthinking. Today she'd stay busy doing things like watching her adult children hunt for the baskets and plastic eggs she'd hidden the night before, and stuff them all with an Easter dinner of ham, cheesy potatoes, and all the fixings.

They'd leave the television and their phones off.

She was about to head for the shower before everything kicked into gear when she heard her youngest yell for her from down the hall. Apparently Relic didn't like Lemon's early morning kisses any more than she did. The dog made it impossible to sleep in.

The shower could wait. She had mothering to do, and it felt good.

Colton pulled the potato casserole out of the oven and set it on the side of the stovetop. "What else do you need help with, Mom?"

Annie checked her list. Patsy never seemed to need a list to serve a proper holiday dinner, but Annie wasn't as good as her mother at keeping all this straight.

"If you'd fill the goblets on the table with ice water, I'll warm the rolls, and then we can eat."

Colton dug her crystal pitcher out from the cupboard above the refrigerator—a feat she'd have had to pull out a stepstool to complete. Annie retrieved the package of dinner rolls from the pantry and turned the oven down.

"That'll just take a minute," she said, talking more to herself than anyone in particular. She thought back to the hustle and bustle in this room leading up to their Thanksgiving dinner. They'd hosted a larger crowd. So much had changed since November.

Her parents would spend the day at home. In fact, they rarely left their house these days.

They'd encountered travel troubles at the conclusion of their cruise. Instead of getting on yet another plane to fly home to Minnesota as people everywhere started shuttering themselves inside the relative safety of their homes, Patsy and Lyle decided to pack up the old Grocery-Getter and cross their fingers that the minivan could still make the long road trip. It did.

Annie hadn't even bothered to call her sister. As far as she knew, Millie and her husband were also staying home.

"Say, Mom," Colton said, returning from the dining room with an empty water pitcher. "I wanted to ask you about something before everybody else comes in here to eat."

Having decided the oven temperature would have to do, Annie shoved the cookie sheet full of dinner rolls in and shut the door. She set the timer before turning to her son. Otherwise, she was confident she'd forget all about the rolls and burn them.

"What's up, honey?" she asked, wiping loose flour from her palms onto her jeans. No one had wanted to bother dressing up for Easter dinner.

"My boss pulled me aside yesterday . . ."

Annie caught her bottom lip between her teeth. She thought she knew what was coming next. The funeral industry, like the world of education, was undergoing massive changes to their business model. "He did? What did he want?"

"He had to furlough me. I'm the newest hire, and now that funerals look so different, or aren't even being held at all, he doesn't have enough work to keep me busy. Frankly, I don't think he has the cash coming in to pay me."

The irony of her son losing his job at the funeral home, even if it turned out to be temporary, given all the misery and death right now, wasn't lost on Annie.

"Oh, Colton, I'm so sorry. I know how much your job means to you. Maybe he'll be able to take you back . . . later."

She stumbled over the word. They both knew neither had any idea what *later* meant.

"Mom, I can't afford my rent without a paycheck."

"Isn't there some type of mandate right now where landlords can't evict people? Lots of people are out of work."

He nodded. "I think so. But our lease is up on June first. Mom, I'm not comfortable living there with the roommates I have right now. They all have lots of contact with the public in their jobs. They can't really help that, but they aren't careful about it, either. I don't feel safe there anymore."

Annie jumped when the buzzer went off. The rolls only took a couple minutes to warm up, and she certainly would have burned them without the warning. Her mind raced, searching for a viable solution to Colton's dilemma while she pulled them out.

"I wish Michael wouldn't have given up his apartment. I could have stayed with him."

She also wished Michael hadn't made the decisions he had, but she could understand why he'd felt compelled to leave town to take care of his ailing father. He'd given up his job in Ruby Shores and sublet his apartment to move out by his dad. He'd considered bringing the ailing man back here to live, but there were medical resources in New York that were important to his treatment. Michael hadn't been comfortable leaving him in the facility where he'd lived for the past five years. His father had picked it based on cost, and Michael had always worried that the retirement home's lower cost also meant a lack of professionalism. When Henry had talked to him a week ago, Michael was still trying to get his father settled in the new apartment he'd rented for the two of them upstate.

She pulled her attention back to Colton's dilemma. "We'll make room for you here. It's really the only solution."

Colton shrugged. "You can't. You've already filled all the bed-rooms."

It was true; however, the room Henry had claimed for his office used to be Ava's bedroom. Her husband was still going out to the office building to work, though they were all practicing social dis-tancing and working with masks behind closed office doors. Henry wasn't using his home office much these days, but it *was* where Annie had set up her own shop, once the high school went fully remote.

They'd figure it out.

"We'll turn Henry's old office back into a bedroom for you. Hon-ey, we will make this work."

Colton probably didn't know she was currently using that room as her working space. If he did, he'd refuse, so she didn't mention it. He still looked extremely apprehensive.

"Is something else bothering you?" she asked.

"Won't Dad be mad to have me back in the house? Things haven't really been great between us for the past few years."

That Colton never stopped calling Henry "Dad" helped Annie maintain hope that someday her son and her husband would find their way back to the close relationship they'd enjoyed before Michael had moved to Ruby Shores. Henry and Michael seemed to have found their way back to a friendship of sorts, and she was confident that, with a little encouragement, Colton and Henry could as well.

"What will I be mad about?" Henry asked as he joined them in the kitchen.

Annie paused, looking between the two men who used to be so close. When Michael arrived, she'd acted as mediator between them all, almost killing herself to ensure peace within her blended family. Despite her best efforts, relationships had suffered.

Colton was an adult now, and ever since Thanksgiving, Henry had seemed more secure in his role of both husband and father. She'd fought so hard in the past to try to ensure everyone got a fair shake in life and no one's feelings were hurt. Her efforts hadn't always helped.

Maybe it was time she stayed off to the side and let them find their way back to each other on their own.

"I need to run downstairs and let Ava and Daniel know that dinner is about ready. I don't want to yell to them in case Nora is asleep," she said, fighting the urge to answer Henry directly. Instead, she offered Colton an encouraging nod and headed for the basement stairs.

Once out of sight, she paused. She wasn't above eavesdropping. She heard Colton clear his throat.

"What is it, Colton?" Henry said.

"I got some bad news, and I wanted to talk to you about it. My boss at the funeral home had to lay me off. I know they can't legally kick me out of my apartment right now because of all the rent relief in place at the moment, but I'm not really comfortable around my roommates anymore."

There was a beat of silence, as if Henry might be processing what Colton was actually asking. She chanced a quick peek into the kitchen to see how the two of them were navigating this without her. To her surprise, Henry strode to Colton's side and laid a hand on their son's shoulder.

"Our house may be getting full, Colton, but you need to know that you are always welcome here. We'll find a way to make it work."

Annie breathed a sigh of relief and turned toward the basement. Henry and Colton needed to figure things out between them. She couldn't do it anymore. This was a solid start.

What she needed right now was a baby snuggle to remind her that, despite her many failures as both a mother and a wife, life would go on, and there was plenty to look forward to in their future.

catching up with friends

FROM HOME

July 2020

EPILOGUE

THE DOORBELL RANG, SENDING both Lemon and Daisy into a frenzy. It sounded foreign, even to Annie. Visitors were rare.

She answered the door, surprised to see Michael on the top step.

Despite months of social distancing and limited interactions with people outside this house, she threw herself into his arms and squeezed him tight.

He laughed. "Hello to you, too, birthday girl."

She gave him one last squeeze, then stepped back to let him in. "What are you doing here?"

"Isn't there a party going on in the backyard?" he asked. He held up a plastic grocery bag that she hadn't noticed. "Henry invited me and told me to bring brats and buns."

"He did?" She still wasn't used to this new dynamic between her husband and her ex. "Sorry. That didn't sound very welcoming. Honestly, it's great to see you in person. I'm so sorry about your dad. I'm sure you did everything you could."

Michael's smile slipped and he rubbed the back of his neck. "I just wish it would have been enough. But I got lucky. The traveling nurse and his wife who rented my apartment got reassigned to Kentucky, so I moved back home. I thought I'd even check in with Colton. See if he might still want to bunk in my extra bedroom now that I'm back. You have to be pretty crowded around here."

Selfishly, Annie thought her life would be a little easier if she could move her office back out of the spare garage stall and into Ava's old room, but she'd let Colton decide. Relic was still planning to get that apartment in a month. It was sounding like some of his college classes were reverting to in-person for the fall semester. But time would tell. She'd become accustomed to the whipsaw of two steps forward and one step back that these unprecedented times seemed to bring.

Her nest would be empty again at some point. The quiet might be a little easier to tolerate this time, after a whole lot of togetherness.

"We've managed," she said. It was true. Juggling space for so many of them to work and study from home was trickier than sleeping arrangements, but they'd coped. "Check with Colton."

He nodded to the wineglass and bottle of chardonnay she'd set on the small table when she answered the doorbell. "Looks like the party might have started without me?"

"Oh, shoot," she said, checking her watch. "The birthday party *Henry* planned hasn't started yet. I think he's out back, cleaning the grill. I actually have a Zoom call at one, and if I don't hurry, I'll be late. Go on back."

"We both know this might be the first birthday party *Henry* has ever planned in his life, so I better go give him a hand."

He stopped and pointed at his shoes, but she waved him on.

"Don't worry about it. Leave them on. Is your ankle healed?"

"Completely. Believe it or not, I've even started running a little. I can't stand all this time inside."

Annie nodded. "I hear you. But now I really am going to be late. Go. I think Ava already has Nora back there, too. I know you haven't gotten nearly enough time with her. I'll come out as soon as I'm done with my call."

He started through the house toward the backyard when he noticed her cross over to the door to the garage. "I thought you said you had to take a call. From the garage?"

Annie raised her empty wine glass and full bottle of Chardonnay. "Part of the garage is now my office. I'm taking the call from there. Because a girl's gotta do what a girl's gotta do."

She could still hear his chuckles when the door closed behind her and she crossed to her makeshift desk. It sat behind a tarp Henry had hung to section off the third stall. The garage office was their solution to Colton's living dilemma. Her three kids were all living at home at the moment, but she'd relegated their cars to the street and driveway. It reminded her of the way first Dean and then Kit willingly gave up their garage stalls so he and Isaac could have room for their vintage car projects.

The portable air-conditioner had cooled the air nicely, and she flipped her laptop open. At least she shouldn't have any bandwidth issues today since it was a Saturday and the rest of her family should be off their computers.

When her connection went through and she popped into the scheduled call, the four smiling faces of her besties all started singing a heartfelt, slightly off-tune rendition of the "Happy Birthday" song with glasses of their own raised in a toast. As they reached the last stanza, their laughter replaced their words.

Except for Renee. It looked like she'd decided to sing another verse, but there was no sound, only her mouth moving.

"Renee, you're on mute!" Lynette yelled, doing her best to be heard over Kit's, Jackie's, and Annie's laughter.

Renee mustn't have heard her, because she went right on singing. At least that was what it looked like she was doing.

Annie found the chat feature and typed a warning to Renee that if she didn't stop, the birthday girl was going to wet her pants from laughing, and that wouldn't be a good look for the birthday party that was following their call.

Eventually, everyone settled down enough that they could hear what each other was saying.

"Good God, Renee. Haven't you done enough of these calls this year that you know how to use the mute button?" Lynette asked, wiping at her eyes.

Renee shrugged. "Sorry, ladies, I'm out of practice." She didn't look particularly fazed at having delivered a silent serenade. "This was a great idea, though. Thanks for setting it up, Lynette. And since you couldn't hear me earlier, happy birthday, Annie! You look damn good for a fifty-year-old."

"Thank you, Renee. And you look damn good for a fifty-year-plus-two-months-old. I'm sorry, we should have thought to do one of these calls on your birthday, too."

That started another full round of the "Happy Birthday" song, this time for Renee.

Kit's face fluttered on the screen and then she was gone.

"We lost Kit," Lynette said. "She'll probably get back on in a second. In the meantime, I can't wait to hear what everyone's been up to. And I hope it's all good news! I'm so sick of all the doom and gloom. I don't mean to sound insensitive. I know these are really tough times for so many people, but I've always been able to turn to you four when I need a pick-me-up."

Jackie nodded. "I vote we go around and get an update from each of us. I know we've done some texting over the last few months, but I really needed to see your faces, too. Annie, since you're the birthday girl, you go first."

Annie unmuted the microphone on her laptop but took a second to pour wine from the bottle she'd uncorked during the second song rendition. "Sure, I'll go. It's crazy around here, just like I'm sure it's been for all of you, too. But first—did you guys realize that exactly one year ago today we were wrapping up our Maui trip?! Doesn't that feel like practically a lifetime ago?"

Kit popped back onto the screen. "Sorry. I had to go send both Isaac and Dean out to the garage to work on that old car in order to get them off the Wi-Fi."

"I can relate," Annie said. "Kit, we're taking turns giving updates. And since I'm the birthday girl, I get to go first."

"Sounds good. I was tired of being the center of attention in Arizona. Now it's your turn."

The barking of a dog cut in.

"Everybody mute when you aren't talking," Lynette said. "Catching up at the beach in Hawaii and around the pool in Arizona was more effective than this is going to be, but hey, a girl's gotta do what a girl's gotta do!"

Annie clapped her hands at that. "Oh, wow! I just said the same thing to Michael when he asked why I was going out to my garage to take this call."

"I was kind of wondering why you had bikes hanging upside down behind your head," Renee said.

"Welcome to my office," Annie said, motioning around her with her wineglass. "All right, ladies. If we don't focus, I'll be late for my birthday party Henry set up in the backyard. First, my little Nora is amazing, and she's been living in my basement with her parents since she was three weeks old."

All four of her friends clapped and looked like they were whooping it up in their little squares on her screen. She explained how all three of her children—plus one spouse, one newborn, and a second dog—had come to live in her once-empty nest.

"How is Daisy doing? I know she was awfully timid at first, but I'm hoping she's acclimated to your household by now," Jackie said. "I was so excited when I could match the two of you up."

Lynette seemed to struggle to unmute herself, but her arms were clearly communicating her surprise. "Wait!" she eventually said, cutting Annie and Jackie off. "We aren't too young to be considered as a customer for you, Jackie?"

Jackie shrugged. "Technically, I advertise for over fifty-five, but I'd make an exception for any of you."

"Good to know," Lynette said. "I've been thinking about getting a cat."

"Sorry, Lynette," Kit broke in. "Jackie isn't really a cat person like us. She only places dogs."

Annie did what she could to take back control of the conversation, explaining how all three kids had ended up back under their roof. All were happy to hear that Henry and Michael seemed to be working on repairing their friendship, too, as well as Henry on his relationships with Ava and Colton.

"That's amazing, Annie," Kit chimed in. "I could tell that something was bothering you the few times we've been together, and based on our talks in Arizona, I was pretty sure the turmoil within your family was at the root of your troubles. I'm glad to hear things are looking up, despite the unusually tight quarters. I am sad to hear Michael's father passed away, though."

Annie appreciated Kit's empathy. "And I suppose that's about it for my updates, other than work, which has been a slog, of course. But isn't that the case for everyone these days? We spent most of our time remote, and it's been one headache after another, but we made it through. I think we'll be back in school come September this year."

She took a sip of wine, then held up a finger. "Sorry, before I turn it over to whoever wants to go next, I thought of two more things. First, I celebrated completing my twentieth year with the school district in May. It wasn't terribly exciting, having a party over Zoom—kind of like this—but at least Sarah, my assistant, had a cake delivered to the house."

More cheers from her forever friends erupted from her laptop, and she felt her eyes well with tears. "Honestly, ladies, that right there gave me more of a thrill than the party with the staff and superintendent. The second thing was I thought maybe you might like an update as to what Wendy is up to."

"Camp-counselor-turned-art-teacher, Wendy?" Kit asked.

Jackie held up a hand and unmuted herself. "Kit, Wendy surprised me at my fiftieth at Thanksgiving. Actually, the entire party was a surprise, but you know what I mean. Anyhow, she looked fabulous, and told me she was looking forward to the end of the school year and her retirement.

She alluded to some fun plans, and I got the impression they might include a new man, but she wasn't willing to talk details. She's a widow, right, Annie?"

"Right. I was dreading her retirement, and did everything I could to talk her out of it, since she's only fifty-six, but she had her mind made up. Then, with how things started going sideways in March, by the time the end of the school year rolled around, I couldn't blame her for wanting to try something new."

"Thanks for catching me up," Kit said. "She was such a great person when we were kids. What plans does she have now?"

Annie pounded on her desk, her excitement over Wendy's latest news still fresh since the woman had called to wish her a happy birthday that very morning. "Well, she made travel plans, including traveling around Europe to visit artwork by the great masters, which sounds like a dream to me. Of course, the trip is on hold for the time being, but guess who her travel companion will be? In fact, they even moved in together when things shut down."

Lynette was shaking her head. "How could we possibly know, Annie? Aside from Jackie's party, I hadn't talked to Wendy since high school."

"Oh, you've met him. In fact, we all have, if I remember right. Think *summer camp.*"

Kit gasped. "Not Pratt? I never thought Wendy liked him much, even though she was too nice to admit it. Ick, he was old back then!"

"Pratt? God, no!" Annie cried. "No. Remember the guy who showed up on our last day the year Kit first came? The counselor who saw Fran drop the money box back at the office and helped clear yours and Lynette's names? We could tell right away that Wendy had a crush on him. His name is Scott."

Jackie did a little shimmy, knocking whatever device she was using to take the call crooked. "I remember him! He was sexy!"

"And he's *still* sexy. In fact, I can confirm he's sexy *everywhere*. I even saw him nude," Annie teased, then sipped her wine as all four of the other Kaleidoscope Girls sat staring at her, mouths agape.

Kit was the first to recover. "Thank God you didn't have to see *Pratt* nude. Don't keep us in suspense. There's obviously more to this story."

"There is," Annie admitted. "Back in September, on the first day of school, Wendy was walking into the building next to me with her trusty old art portfolio. The black leather was so beat up, I'm guessing she used the same one for her entire career. She was probably hoping to get one more year out of it, but the strap broke and, when it hit the ground, it split open and some sketches fell out. She snatched them up, but not before I grabbed the one closest to me. It fell face down, but when I flipped it over . . . mercy!" Annie fanned herself.

"Was it a picture of Scott?!" Jackie asked. "Like . . . Scott in his late fifties, or Scott at twenty or whatever he was that summer?"

"It was a charcoal drawing of *young* Scott. Maybe that's what threw me. When I saw it I thought the guy looked familiar, but I couldn't place him."

"Which part of him did you think you recognized?" Lynette asked. She might have winked, but Annie couldn't be sure.

"Sadly, I only ever saw his face in person. Anyway, it wasn't until Wendy called this morning and told me about her upcoming travels with her old friend Scott that something clicked. She didn't deny it, but she claims she used her imagination on the parts she didn't see on him when they were teenagers."

Everyone laughed.

"But I bet she's seen plenty of him now," Kit choked out around her giggles. "You know, just to make sure her sketch was *anatomically* correct."

Once the laughter died down, Annie held up both hands. "That's enough of my story. We are all healthy here at the house. We've been lucky. Fingers crossed it stays that way. Who's going next?"

Jackie volunteered. "My story isn't too terribly different from Annie's as far as family goes. The girls weren't going to come home at first, but I think they eventually got a little freaked out, a little scared, so they packed some bags and came home. They're still paying for their apartment and hope to go back when classes start up again. Nikki loves having them home. The apartment feels a little tight some days, but I'd rather have the girls under my watchful eye."

"I'm glad to hear that," Lynette said. "It was fun to visit with them at your party in November. They seemed like smart girls, but it's best to have them close right now."

"It is," Jackie agreed. "Things in my business are a little crazy. Many elderly people are shut up at home and are terribly lonesome. I feel like I'm making a positive impact right now. They always light up when they get their new pets."

"Where do most of the dogs you place come from?" Annie asked.

"Most come from the various shelters around town. More people are adopting right now, but there are also plenty who are making the tough decision to give up their pets. Some have less income coming in, houses that are too full, or any other number of reasons. It can make things a little easier for them when they learn someone like me is actively working to match the older dogs with seniors. They feel a little less guilty. There's also the occasional stray that gets picked up. Regardless, they all go through a thorough medical exam before going out to homes. I set my location up with a small area where I can house some dogs that are at various points in the placement process, and I've contracted with others for overflow. I've made a few mistakes along the way, but I'm learning as I go."

"Daisy really is a joy. Thanks again for finding her for me, Jackie."

"You are welcome, Annie. She's a lucky beagle. Who wants to go next?"

"I can go," Kit said. "But first, are your folks doing all right, Jackie? Your dad is in a memory care facility in Ruby Shores, right?"

Jackie took a deep breath. "Right. It's scary having him in there, but we don't have any better alternatives. He needs around-the-clock care now. Mom misses him, and I know she's terribly lonely. At least she has Hoover to keep her company. I still can't believe Dad took that dog when his buddy died a couple years back, but she's been such a blessing. We're all getting through this."

Kit nodded. "Good. Well, let's see . . . I updated all of you on Isaac and Dean when we were in Arizona. I guess not much has changed there, other than all of us trying to work and do school out of the townhouse."

Annie held up a finger. "Kit, I'm sorry to cut you off, and I'll make this quick, but I'll forget if I don't tell you right now. Speaking of Arizona, you'll never guess what Dad told me. They had to close down the hiking path that we climbed when we were there in February. The one on Camelback, I think it was called the Cholla Trail. A big boulder fell on some poor guy's legs. Dad said they didn't know how long the trail would have to be closed. Isn't that wild?"

"One of these times your little adventures are going to get us killed, Annie," Kit said with a shake of her head. "Okay, where was I? Back in

February, remember when I said we might have to move to a place with more garage space? Well, now I'd like a little more space *everywhere*. My quiet days of living alone are well back in the rearview mirror."

"But would you change anything?" Annie asked.

"Absolutely not. Say, Renee, I reached out to that mother of your son's friend. Turns out the boys don't go to the same school, but we'd planned to get them together at some point. But that was before all this madness, so we'll have to try again when things get back to normal. Let's see," she said, tapping a finger against her cheek. "Work is all happening from home these days, and I feel lucky that I can do that. I'm sick to death of calls like this—not with you four, but for work. My extended family is doing all right. We heard through the grapevine that my dad got sick and was in the hospital on a vent, but he eventually recovered. I don't know any more than that. And, honestly, I don't care. He's dead to me."

Annie thought of her own sweet father. She'd been so lucky to be raised by a man like that. Kit hadn't been so lucky.

"Grandma Hazel is fine, and so are Mia and Marge. Oh, get this. Marge got so bored at home by herself, and the Crystal Café's been closed for months now, so she finally agreed to move in with Hazel. Mia told me it's going fine, but when I talked to Grandma, I got a different story. There's been some fireworks, but I could have told them that. Whatever. Sisters are always going to have their disagreements. At least none of them are alone right now."

The tarp behind Annie rustled, and Relic appeared. He froze when he noticed himself on Annie's screen. "Um, hi, ladies. Sorry, I forgot what Mom was doing in here. I didn't mean to interrupt this little . . . whatever it is."

"It's a party for your mother, Relic. Hello!" Kit said, waving at him from the screen.

He grinned, and Annie thought he might be blushing. "Mom, Dad sent me in here to tell you we'll eat in thirty minutes. Will that work, or should I tell him to wait?"

Annie checked the time. "He doesn't have to wait. The baby is going to be getting close to her naptime, and I don't want her cranky at my other party. If we aren't finished talking, we'll do this again."

Once he'd slipped away, Kit said, "Well, I'm done. Renee? Lynette? What have you ladies been up to?"

Lynette pointed toward her screen. "Go ahead, Renee, and then I'll wrap us up."

Renee unmuted herself this time. "I guess we're pretty lucky, being able to hole up at Whispering Pines. Both of my kids are here with us. Robbie is doing college courses online. Julie graduated, but she's taken a few extra classes to keep busy. We're considering opening back up to guests again, but I'm nervous about cleaning the cabins between groups. Matt insists we'll be all right with one summer of missed revenue from the place, and my Aunt Celia left me a little in reserves for emergencies. I'm leaning toward remaining closed for the rest of this season, since it's already mid-July. Unless things change pretty drastically, we won't do any fall or winter retreats. Honestly, I'm worried about taking the financial hit, but at least none of us have gotten sick. Well, I take that back. We think Robbie might have had it, but he only ever had mild symptoms, and we couldn't get our hands on an at-home test at the time. It's actually been really nice to have this place to ourselves this summer, but we couldn't afford to shut down the resort for more than a year."

Lynette nodded. "Are you open to taking reservations for next summer yet?"

"I really haven't thought that far ahead. I'd hate to get anyone's hopes up, but if things don't turn around, I don't even want to think about what might happen. We'd have to make some difficult decisions."

Lynette nodded. "I've been tossing around an idea, and I wanted to save these last few minutes at the end of our call today to see what you guys think. Maybe I should have called you beforehand, Renee, but I'm not that organized."

Annie had an inkling of where Lynette was going with this.

Lynette adjusted her camera and scooted closer to her device. "I know we promised each other to never miss a single annual girls' trip," she began.

"Yes, but no one took the possibility of a worldwide pandemic into account!"

"I know, Kit, but maybe we can still get together in 2021, even if, God forbid, the world doesn't open back up by then. What if we penciled our names into Renee's reservation calendar at Whispering Pines for a full two weeks in July? Renee, how many cabins do you rent out?"

"We have six cabins, plus two separate units in a duplex."

"How much would it cost to reserve the whole place for that long?"

Renee looked confused. "But we don't need eight separate units for five people—make that *four* people. I can stay at my house on the grounds. Or we could kick my husband and kids out, if the kids are there next summer, and all stay in my new house."

But Lynette shook her head. "I don't care if there are empty cabins. I could pay for those. My point is, we might feel relatively safe, even if the world hasn't righted itself yet, if we can each have our own separate sleeping quarters, spend most of our time outside, and still keep our promise to each other. I'd imagine that would help you sleep a little better at night, too, Renee, if you knew you had the promise of at least some income coming in next summer."

Renee sighed. "I'd never expect you to pay if it didn't end up working."

"Nonsense," Lynette said. "I can see I need to teach you a few things about protecting yourself in business, Renee. I'll pay regardless, and if it works for us to gather together, Jackie and Kit and Annie can pay for their own little cabins. What does everyone think of that idea?"

Annie loved it, and it looked like everyone else liked the idea, too.

"If you're sure, Lynette, I can pull some numbers together and get back to you before I'd consider accepting anyone else's reservations next summer."

"Perfect," Lynette said. She checked the clunky silver watch on her wrist. "And it looks like Annie has exactly three minutes before her next party starts. So I'll wrap us up with that and wait to hear from you, Renee. I love you girls!"

"Wait!" Annie cried. "My family can wait a few more minutes. We still haven't heard any updates from *you*, Lynette."

"Trust me, Annie, you don't have time to hear about everything that's been going on in my life since we last saw each other. I'd barely have time to hit the high points of how I sold my business, broke the lease on my apartment in Manhattan, and bought one of those old homes on Breconwood Road. Mom and I will move in next week. We're both looking forward to being back in Ruby Shores. By the way, we won't be far from Owen, Jackie. But it's my birthday in August, and we'll have to do this again. I'll get it scheduled. And I promise to give you all the details then. Tootles!"

Lynette's square disappeared.

The remaining four sat in stunned silence for a minute, then erupted into one last round of laughter.

"Only Lynette," Annie said with a shake of her head. "I can't wait to hear what is behind all that! Since this is the first birthday party Henry has ever actually thrown for me, I better get out there. But promise me you'll stay safe, my friends, and we'll talk again in a month!"

She sat back and closed her eyes once the last of the four squares that held the laughing faces of her friends had disappeared from her computer screen. She would join her family out back to continue her birthday celebration, but she wanted a moment to herself first. Long before any of the people that were waiting for her in the backyard had become so integral to her life, there were her very best friends, the Kaleidoscope Girls. Jackie, Kit, Annie, and Renee had all helped her navigate many of the highest and the lowest points of her life.

She was so lucky to have their unwavering friendship.

Her mind drifted back to that warm February afternoon when the five of them celebrated reaching the summit of Camelback Mountain together. As they'd posed for that group shot, trying to guess what their futures might hold, none of them could have predicted the magnitude of the challenges that people everywhere would face in the months ahead.

Regardless, based on Lynette's parting comments, her old friend wasn't letting anything hold her back from making big changes in her life. Was this what she'd meant when she vowed on the mountaintop in Arizona to make her rest the best?

Leave it to Lynette to keep them all in suspense.

Annie loved her husband and kids. Her heart had doubled in size with the addition of little Nora. Michael would always hold a special place in her heart, too. Despite the many challenges of the last year of her forties, the progress they'd all made in finding their way back to each other gave her hope.

She heard the door open between the garage and the backyard. Someone was coming for her and she should probably go give Henry a hand with the party logistics. He'd come a long way, but she didn't want to push her luck.

After all, a girl only turns fifty once. Unless she'd turn out to be lucky enough to reach the century mark with her besties beside her.

Author's Note

I hope you enjoyed this third book in *The Kaleidoscope Girls* series! It was so fun to travel back to Arizona in my mind as I wrote the girls' trip portion of **Five Golden Friends**. I'm glad I could help these fabulous women to slide in their annual girls' trip in early 2020, before the world went topsy-turvy.

Having always lived in North Dakota and Minnesota, I deeply appreciate the appeal of escaping this climate during the harshest months of winter. My memories from a variety of trips to Arizona helped my write this book. Back in 2014, we took a mother-daughter trip with friends that included a hike up Camelback, and I was every bit as fearful as Kit when we started out, sure I wouldn't be up for the challenge. But we did it together, and reaching the beautiful views at the summit with our group of moms and high schoolers felt like an amazing accomplishment. Thank you, Terri Young, for having more faith in me than I had in myself!

We are always capable of more.

I debated over how to address the incredibly difficult days we all experienced in 2020. While we faced many universal struggles, everyone's situation was also unique. In many ways, the scars are still too fresh, and

"""

I was reluctant to go too deep into things experienced during that challenging point in our history. I didn't want to pretend it didn't happen, but I also didn't want to dwell there for long. Like many of you, I jumped on Zoom calls to stay in touch with friends and family, and I thought it was the perfect way for Annie, Jackie, Kit, Lynette, and Renee to do the same.

Good news—summer 2021 will find these fun friends together again!

Next up in *The Kaleidoscope Girls* series will be Lynette's story in **Gift of Friends** (Book 4). I hate to play favorites, but I couldn't wait to craft this one! Based on the bombshells Lynette dropped during that group call at the end of Book 3, she is facing exciting, life-altering changes. She'll need plenty of help from her friends to figure everything out!

Not only am I excited about following Lynette on her journey, but I'm also thrilled about *where* these friends will spend their 2021 girls' trip: we are heading back to Renee's very special Minnesota lake resort, Whispering Pines! If you've read my *Celia's Gifts* series, you've already spent lots of time at Whispering Pines, and I hope you grew to love it as much as I do! Let the fun begin!

But these stories are about so much more than a few special days spent together each year. All the books in this series also explore the other relationships that mean so much to our Kaleidoscope Girls. For Jackie, this included her young adult twins and her aging parents, especially the complicated relationship with her father. For Kit, it was her fractured family, her life partner, and a teenage boy who reminded her of her own painful childhood. Annie's blended family is a source of both deep love and endless frustrations.

Lynette's circle is smaller, despite her success in the business world. Aside from her four besties, the relationship with her mother is the one stable thing she has always relied on throughout her lifetime. Mother-daughter relationships may be one of the most complicated relationships of all, and we'll explore this in **Gift of Friends**.

I lost my mother at the beginning of my writing journey, only three months after publishing my first book, and it's taken me six years to be willing to delve into this theme in more detail. Writing about the dysfunctional relationship between Kit and her mother, Mia, was easier than this will be. But I'm up for the challenge! I hope you are, too.

You'll find more information on all my books and links to them on various storefronts on my website. While you're there, be sure to sign up for my newsletter so you never miss the latest news, including release dates, glimpses into what goes into creating my books, and more.

Thank you for coming on this writing journey with me. I love reading and writing alongside you!

www.kimberlydiedeauthor.com

THANK YOU!

Dear Reader,

I would like to thank you for taking the time to read **Five Golden Friends**. I am so grateful you selected it and I hope you enjoyed this third book in my *Kaleidoscope Girls* series.

If you don't mind taking a few more minutes with this book, I'd appreciate it if you would leave a review. Reviews are extremely helpful and much appreciated.

Next up in this fun series is **Gift of Friends (Book 4)**. This time the girls are going back to Whispering Pines for their annual trip! If you've read my *Celia's Gifts* women's fiction series, you know what a special place Whispering Pines is. Will Lynette find answers while vacationing at Renee's resort, or will she be left with even more questions? Either way, it is sure to be a trip none of them will forget!

Pack your bags and come join the party!

For links to all of my books and to sign up for my newsletter, please visit my website at www.kimberlydiedeauthor.com.

Wishing you my very best,
Kimberly

There is no greater gift than friendship.

For the first time in fifty years, Lynette Howe's financial struggles are behind her. Her wildly prosperous online boutique is now someone else's headache. It wasn't hard to bid farewell to the fast-paced lifestyle of New York City, but designing her new life in the quiet town she left decades ago isn't working.

Men used to find her intriguing—mysterious, even—when her role as a stylish CEO demanded most of her time. Women's desire to emulate her only helped fuel her success. But now? Now she spends her days poking around the small town of Ruby Shores, talking to a cat.

She isn't the only one struggling. Her mother, Donna, remains by her side, but sometimes it feels like their roles have reversed. Even though they've accomplished great things together, both women harbor unspoken dreams. Will their codependency lead to regrets?

Lynette welcomes the distraction of her annual girls' trip with her four best friends. This year's destination isn't a plane ride away. Instead, they'll go back to the peaceful solitude of Whispering Pines. It'll feel like summer camp all over again . . . except for adults. She could use some girlish giggles, along with coffee on the dock at sunrise or wine around a sunset campfire.

But unexpected guests bring turmoil to the resort. When long-hidden secrets come to light and unsettling news arrives from New York, not even the tranquility of Whispering Pines or the reassuring presence of her girlfriends can stop Lynette from questioning every decision she's made during the past two years.

Slip away with this uplifting group to the restful Minnesota lake resort of Whispering Pines in **Gift of Friends** by Kimberly Diede. You're sure to catch their laughter floating on a warm lakeside breeze in this fourth book of the Kaleidoscope Girls women's fiction series.

Hopeful expectations, mixed with delicious surprises and shocking truths, will have you cheering on both daughter and mother in this colorful celebration of female friendships.

You'll find information on where to purchase books on my website at https://www.kimberlydiedeauthor.com

ALSO BY KIMBERLY DIEDE

THE KALEIDOSCOPE GIRLS SERIES
BETTER WITH FRIENDS (BOOK 1)
SUNSHINE AND FRIENDS (BOOK 2)
FIVE GOLDEN FRIENDS (BOOK 3)
GIFT OF FRIENDS (BOOK 4)
with additional books to come...

CELIA'S GIFTS SERIES
WHISPERING PINES (BOOK 1)
TANGLED BEGINNINGS (BOOK 2)
REBUILDING HOME (BOOK 3)
CHOOSING AGAIN (BOOK 4)
CELIA'S GIFTS (BOOK 5)
CELIA'S LEGACY (BOOK 6)

WHISPERING PINES CHRISTMAS NOVEL
CAPTURING WISHES (BOOK 3.5 OF CELIA'S GIFTS)

FIRST SUMMERS NOVELLA
FIRST SUMMERS AT WHISPERING PINES 1980

ABOUT THE AUTHOR

Kimberly Diede writes contemporary novels that weave together family, friends, hope, and romance. She writes family sagas, suspense, and women's fiction that you'll find hard to put down. She truly believes we are never too old for second chances in life.

Kimberly enjoys spending the short months of her Midwest summers on the lakeshores of Minnesota and North Dakota. Nothing beats writing and hanging out with family and friends at their cabin. Her love of tradition and all things vintage comes through in her decorating and her stories.

Be sure to follow Kimberly on social media to catch glimpses of the junk she drags home to repurpose and to get updates on her latest books.

Website: https://www.kimberlydiedeauthor.com/
Facebook: https://www.bacebook.com/KimberlyDiedeAuthor/
Instagram: https://www.instagram.com/kimberlydiedeauthor/
BookBub: https://www.bookbub.com/authors/kimberly-diede